PATRIOT AT THE RIVER

FOR LIBERTY & CONSCIENCE
Promise of Refuge (short story prequel)
Preacher on the Run
Patriot at the River

FOR LIBERTY & CONSCIENCE ✗ 2

JAYNA BAAS

Patriot at the River

A Novel of the American Revolution

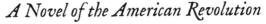

THE TRUTH WILL MAKE YOU FREE.

This is a work of fiction. While historical accuracy has been maintained as far
as possible, this work is not intended as an authority on any historical subject.

All Scripture references are from the King James Bible.

Cover design by Jayna Baas with images by Jayna Baas and Depositphotos.com.
Part I/Part II title page design and NC Piedmont map by Jayna Baas
(accents from German map of Bethabara, NC, 1766).
Author photo by Bethany Baas.

Typeset in IM Fell English, Imprint MT Shadow, and Book Antiqua.

booksbyjayna.com
PO Box 173
McBain, MI 49657

Publisher's Summary
(provided by Jayna Baas)

Baas, Jayna (1999–)
Patriot at the river: a novel of the American Revolution
ISBN 978-1-7347175-4-9 (paperback)
ISBN 978-1-7347175-3-2 (ebook) | ASIN B0DGDL62QM (ebook)

Summary: A young Patriot militiaman must save his family and settlement
from the man who had a hand in his father's death.

For Pastor Keith.
So much history, so little time,
and you're always so willing to share either one.

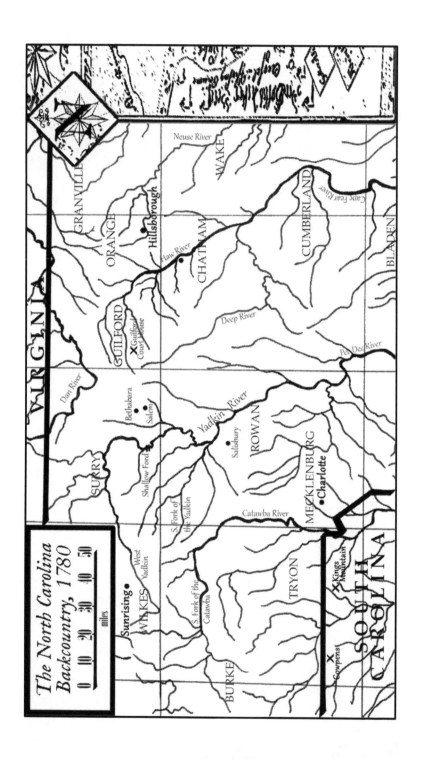

The North Carolina
Backcountry, 1780

miles
0 10 20 30 40 50

VIRGINIA

GRANVILLE

ORANGE

Hillsborough

Haw River

Neuse River

WAKE

CHATHAM

CUMBERLAND

Cape Fear River

BLADEN

GUILFORD

✕ Guilford
Court House

Deep River

Pee Dee River

Dan River

Bethabara
Salem

Yadkin River

ROWAN

Salisbury

MECKLENBURG
● Charlotte

SURRY

Shallow Ford

S. Fork of
the Yadkin

Catawba River

Sunrising ●
West
Yadkin

WILKES

S. Fork of the
Catawba

TRYON

✕ Kings
Mountain

SOUTH
CAROLINA

BURKE

✕
Cowpens

The Historical Backdrop of
Patriot at the River

It is the eighteenth century in North Carolina.

Two factions have been at war for a very long time. One consists of men called Loyalists, Tories, and king's men. The other consists of men called Patriots, Whigs, and rebels.

They are often divided in more than politics.

For centuries the Church of England has held sway with a hierarchy that reflects Britain's political structure—laity must rely on clergy for proper interpretation of Scripture, just as the masses must rely on the elite for proper interpretation of the law.

But there is another way of thinking, a dangerous idea that has spread like wildfire through the Colonies. It is called soul liberty, and it holds that each man is responsible for himself before God, fully capable of understanding both Scripture and law.

Some believe in the king's right to rule in matters of conscience. Some believe civil government has no authority over a man's dealings with his God. Some believe only in their own welfare. And some believe in nothing at all.

Declare war between England and her defiant children. Set neighbor against neighbor in a wild and untamed mountain country where courage is as vital as breathing, where each day is a fight for survival.

And let the story begin.

PART I

VENGEANCE
October 6–December 31, 1780

O wretched man that I am! who shall deliver me from the body of this death?
Romans 7:24

One

ONE MORE DAY.

A shiver of wind rattled the wet hickory leaves above Benjamin Woodbridge's head. Resting the butt of his rifle on the ground, he brushed the tail of his neckerchief over the dampness on his face and tucked the red silk back inside his beech-dyed hunting shirt. The westering sun burned crimson between ribbons of lowering rain clouds.

One more day, and he would have the fight he was waiting for.

The scent of beef and corn, claimed from a nearby farm as spoils of war, drifted from the meadow where his fellow volunteers rested before another long night of hunting enemy troops. Benjamin's stomach growled, though he'd already eaten his share.

He fished in his leather scrip and found a last piece of jerked venison under his New Testament. Better to save that for tomorrow, in case there was no time to stop at all.

A heron croaked in the swampy reaches along Thicketty Creek. A chorus of crickets answered. Brush snapped in the distance, so softly Benjamin thought he'd fancied it.

The crickets went silent. The heron flapped out of the

trees along the creek, too sudden.

Brush snapped again, closer. Benjamin cradled Old Sandy, the long-barreled Deckard that had seen his father's fights before his own, and scanned the thick brushwood along the creek.

Back home in the Blue Ridge, he'd figure Indians were nearby, though he had friends among them. But he wasn't back home in the Blue Ridge. He was standing watch for a camp of Patriot volunteers. And Major Patrick Ferguson and his British militia were out there somewhere, threatening to march across the mountains and ravage Patriot settlements.

A dark horse picked its way out of the trees on the near side of the creek, bearing a lone rider. The man dismounted with the easy grace of a man accustomed to riding. He glanced behind him and led the horse to the water's edge, not twenty yards from Benjamin's post.

Benjamin eased behind the hickory. Ferguson was not the only man on his mind. He'd heard rumors of another officer, one who had left the Carolinas as a civilian and come back with the king's commission and a hatred of the back-country rebels who had outdone him nine years ago.

If the rumors were true and Major Malcolm Harrod was in Charlotte Town, tomorrow's fight with Ferguson would be just the beginning.

But this stranger was not a British officer. He was young, same as Benjamin, and wore a fringed linen hunting shirt, also same as Benjamin. Yet the shirt fit him poorly, and a cloak of broadcloth hung open over it.

The man was not a frontiersman either, standing as he did with his face to the sunset. Looking into the sun would blind him to danger in the shadows. His white cravat showed plainly in the golden light, his riding boots a far cry from the moccasins favored by Benjamin's fellow scouts. No leggings protected his well-fitted knee breeches from thorns or brushwood.

Whatever he might be, he was not near enough to camp to be a threat. Not yet.

Farther upriver, the night heron croaked again. The horse pricked its ears. The stranger turned, suddenly alert, one gloved hand moving under the cloak.

His hat, cocked on all three sides instead of only on the left like Benjamin's, shaded finely cut features and a tidy queue of curling black hair. But it did not hide the pale scar that reached from his hairline to his right cheekbone.

There was nothing about the man that matched such a scar. Or the way he kept looking over his shoulder.

The heron stopped croaking. The stranger relaxed. Benjamin did not.

The wind freshened, brushing his neck with the leather thong that held his own wheat-brown hair in a short tail. A new sound came on the wind.

Horses, running hard.

The stranger lifted his head again, alarm clear on his face.

Benjamin stepped from behind the hickory and whistled sharply. "Over here."

It took the stranger a moment to see him, as Benjamin had expected. "Who are you?"

"Not one of the men who are after you." Benjamin beckoned the stranger into the woods.

"They're the king's men. I thought I had evaded them." His voice held a hint of British or Irish or both. "How do I know I can trust you?"

"You don't. Nor I you." Benjamin nodded toward the creek. "But it looks like you don't have much choice."

The woods on the far side of the creek seemed to erupt. Six mounted men charged out of the snapping branches and splashed through the stream. They spread out along the creek. One shouted, "We know you're here, Armistead!"

Benjamin looked at the man beside him and mouthed, "Armistead?"

The man hesitated. "Yes. Rane Armistead."

"Have you a weapon?"

Rane Armistead pulled back his cloak, revealing a brass-fitted pistol with a belt hook and shortened steel barrel.

"Get behind that stand of pines. I'll follow."

Rane led his black gelding toward the pines where Benjamin's mare was picketed. The half dozen horses were coming closer. Benjamin slipped into the cluster of loblolly pines behind Rane, took a knee behind a thick branch, and rested Old Sandy across his thigh. Rane muffled a cough.

A muzzle flash burst bright in the dying light. A chip of bark sliced Benjamin's cheek, pine sap spattering his skin. Rane tensed, and Benjamin put out a hand to keep him still.

"I'm the one they want," Rane whispered.

"Aye, but I'm the one they shot at. Whether or not they know it." He swiped his face with his wrist. "Stay down."

The riders forged into the edge of the woods. Benjamin wished for his bow, as deadly as a rifle but with no telltale muzzle flash to betray their hiding place. He leaned over and whispered, "Back yonder of us is a camp of seven hundred Patriots. I'm a picket tonight. If those men get much closer, I'll have to show myself."

Rane nodded. The horsemen spread out again, quiet now. A prickle of unease crept beneath Benjamin's kerchief.

These men knew their work, if he could judge by the way they studied branches and stones and kept the thickest trees between them and anyone who might lurk in the shadows. Like Benjamin.

One pointed to the ground and called to the others. He had found a trail.

Time to play sentry.

Benjamin motioned Rane to stay where he was and came silently to his feet. He slipped away from the pines, toward an open space flanked by lofty tulip poplars. The damp pine needles and leaf litter gave no sound beneath his moccasins.

If these men were at home in the forest, so was he.

He pivoted so he could still see Rane's position, then stepped into the open with rifle lifted. "Declare yourself!"

The men reined up. He could see their confusion, knew they were wondering if they'd wasted time on the trail of a backcountry picket.

"We mean you no trouble," the leader finally said. "We were seeking a friend of ours."

"A friend of yours and the king's?"

"You could say that."

"Then keep looking," Benjamin said. "Somewhere else. Before I sound the alarm."

"There's no need for that," the man said hastily.

"Oh, but there might be." Benjamin gave him a taut grin. "You're mighty close to a whole lot of backwater lads who don't take kindly to king's friends."

The men exchanged glances. The leader said, "Come on, we'll look upriver."

They turned their horses toward the creek. At the edge of the forest, they paused, evidently discussing the situation.

Benjamin watched them until he was certain they would not return to challenge him. Then he left the clearing and weaved silently through the woods toward the pines.

Rane rose, pistol in hand. "They've gone?"

"Back toward the creek. Still there, but off your scent. Where are you bound?"

"I was looking for your camp, I think." Rane slid the pistol's belt hook over the strip of linen that secured his ill-fitting hunting shirt. "I was told I would find a band of Patriots west of the Broad River."

Who had told him? But questions would have to wait. "Come on, then."

Benjamin untied Sassafras and led her away from the pines. Near the creek, Rane's pursuers argued loudly enough that the wind carried their voices, though not their words.

The earth turned soft near the spring at the edge of camp. Benjamin stepped over a clump of tangled possum haw vines. Rane snagged the toe of his boot and stumbled. He caught himself on one knee, his horse's reins still coiled in his hand.

The black gelding whinnied long and loud at the sudden jerk on his lead. Benjamin swung around. The six horsemen wheeled their mounts.

"There are two of them!" one man shouted.

Rane was already back on his feet. The riders plunged into the woods after them.

Benjamin planted a foot in Sassafras's near stirrup and swung himself up. "Mount up and follow!"

Rane sprang astride the gelding. Benjamin spurred Sassafras as soon as Rane came abreast of him.

"You'll be safe enough in the camp," he said over the rumble of hooves. "For now, leastways."

The flicker of firelight glimmered between the trees. Broad, rolling pastureland opened before them, dotted with campfires.

One of the pursuers shouted a warning to his mates. The horsemen stopped short and swung their horses back toward the creek.

Rane let out a long breath and coughed. Benjamin pulled Sassafras to a walk, releasing a breath of his own.

A familiar shadow separated from a gnarled tree. "Who goes there?"

"Let us pass. It's me, Woodbridge."

Alec Perry lowered his rifle just enough that a hair trigger wouldn't blow Benjamin back to the Blue Ridge. "That much I can see. Who's with you?"

"Name of Armistead. Those riders were after him."

"Captain Boothe's just over yonder. He'll know what to do." Alec turned and whistled. Robert Boothe's shout answered him.

Benjamin dropped lightly from the saddle, motioning

Rane to do the same. "We riding out soon?"

"Soon." Alec had a fighter's build, all rangy lines and hard edges, canted slightly to the left by an old wound. His russet hair, coppery in the firelight, was still without a trace of gray. "Making a habit of bringing stragglers into camp?"

"Does he look like a straggler to you?"

Alec ignored him and said to Rane, "Last time it was a refugee woman he found hiding in the woods."

"She knew which way Ferguson had marched." Benjamin only hoped Rane could sense friendliness in Alec's banter.

"You'd have helped her even if she didn't," Alec said.

"But so would I. The Christian thing to do."

"What's the trouble here?"

Captain Robert Boothe stepped out of the shadows, his voice as calm as if he were speaking to his congregation at Sunday meeting back in the Blue Ridge. A broad-shouldered man, rugged with the strength of the mountains, he was bronzed and brownheaded in a manner that made some folks think he and Benjamin were father and son. Which they were, in a way.

"I was at my post and saw this man stop to water his horse." Benjamin gestured to Rane. "Next thing I knew, we had six men after us. His name is Rane Armistead."

Robert turned to the stranger. "Care to add to that?"

"There's little to tell," Rane answered. "I lived in Charlotte Town with my uncle. He went to the British for protection four days ago."

"Nephew of a Tory," Alec said. "That's a fine beginning you've got there."

Robert held up a hand. "And then?"

"He was aware that I disagreed. Strongly. We parted ways. The British Legion—" Rane hesitated. "They knew where my loyalties lay. I fled Charlotte and went to Colonel Davie's militia for asylum, but he was too near Charlotte to be safe. He told me I would find a larger band of Patriots to the west."

"And here we are."

"Yes, sir. Here you are."

"I ought to take you to one of the colonels," Captain Boothe said. "But there's no time. We ride out in a quarter hour. Shelby and Campbell have all they can do to form up the column, what with the new recruits just come in."

"He can ride with me, Captain," Benjamin said. "I'll keep a watch on him." Armistead had handled himself well in the last hour's danger. A man like that deserved a chance.

Robert deliberated a moment, then nodded. "Fair enough. Welcome to Hannah's Cowpens, Armistead."

Benjamin beckoned Rane to follow. Rane matched his pace and asked, "Hannah's Cowpens?"

"Folks used to gather cattle here to drive them to market. Most of the fences are down now, used for campfires. It's a good meeting place."

Rane guided the black gelding past a cluster of volunteers. "Your name is Woodbridge, or so you told the sentry."

"Aye. Benjamin Woodbridge. Wish I could say it's a pleasure." Benjamin nodded to the horse. "Fine animal. What's he called?"

"Macy. Named for a settler in Massachusetts, I think; his last owner hailed from there." Rane touched his pistol as if assuring himself it was still there, then fingered the front of the hunting shirt, likely a parting gift from Davie's militia. "I'm obliged to you."

"Don't mention it. Did Colonel Davie tell you what we're after?"

"Loyalists, he told me. I heard something about a British officer named Ferguson and his band of Tory militia."

"Loyalist, Tory, king's man—they're all the same." Benjamin paused by a fire of split fence rails. "Three names for folks who will turn on their neighbors if the king tells them to."

"Rather the same way Patriot, Whig, and rebel are three

names for folks who will do precisely what the king tells them not to."

Benjamin shared a half smile with this man he had just claimed as his responsibility. "Right. Major Ferguson threatened to hang our leaders and lay the land waste with fire and sword. All the Patriot militia in this part of the country turned out to stop him."

"Colonel Davie said you were a hardy lot."

"We have to be. We've been trailing Ferguson for days, and he's only a little ahead of us now. Ever done any fighting?"

Rane's silver-gray eyes went steely in the firelight. "That rests on your definition of fighting."

That stub-barreled pistol, with its belt hook and brass fittings—Benjamin had seen none like it in the backcountry. Mayhap Rane was the sort to fight his battles with words. Benjamin had done it a time or two himself. Words and a crooked grin. Aunt Kate said that grin had gotten him into and out of more trouble than one lad was worth.

But there was no grin on Rane's face. What had he done to draw the notice of the British Legion?

"You're not bound to stay," Benjamin said. "You came looking for asylum, not a fight."

"Sometimes a fight is the only way to find asylum." Rane motioned to Benjamin's face. "Your cheek is still bleeding. Your kerchief might—"

"Not the kerchief." Benjamin swiped the blood away with the back of his hand. "I'll find you something to eat. The officers are ready to move."

The camp was alive with men running hither and yon, packing saddlebags and dousing fires. Some were of Benjamin's own settlement, men who had come west with his family and who sat in the meetinghouse while Captain Boothe preached. Others had come from settlements as far north as Virginia.

They were a motley band. Buckskin, homespun, the

occasional militia uniform. Nothing like Patrick Ferguson's well-trained King's American Regiment. Even less like Banastre Tarleton's hated British Legion, a county's width away in Charlotte Town.

The British Legion . . .

Rane had said the British Legion had been his cause for fleeing Charlotte. But the men who had burst out of the woods had not been legionnaires. No green jackets, no sabers, no bearskin-crested helmets.

Benjamin begged a piece of beef and a roasting ear from a fellow scout and went back to his new charge. "Armistead."

"Yes?"

"Who was after you tonight?"

Rane hesitated. Then he said again, "The king's men."

"But not the British Legion."

"No." Rane tugged off his riding gloves and took the victuals. "Though they did know my loyalties, as I said."

"I've heard rumors," Benjamin said.

"What manner of rumors?"

"About an officer named Malcolm Harrod, lately come to Charlotte. No relation to the James Harrod who explored Kentucke. This Malcolm Harrod—going by the rumors I've heard, he got to Charlotte around the same time you left. I wonder if you saw him."

Rane did not answer. But Benjamin saw the tightening of his face.

"Or maybe," he added quietly, "if he saw you."

Rane still did not answer. But he did not look away.

Benjamin gave a single nod. "Eat and saddle up. Then we ride."

Two

ON THE NARROW CREST OF LITTLE KINGS Mountain, Jem Flannery gripped his reins and prayed to a forgotten God that his horse did not sense his own fear.

There was no room for fear in this band of men. The King's American Regiment was the best of the best, Loyalist militiamen who wore the scarlet of the king's troops and boasted of their training and discipline. Under a man like Patrick Ferguson, such things mattered a great deal. Jem barely remembered a time when other things mattered.

Most days, it was forgetting he was after.

He cast a glance down the long line of men beside him, some mounted, some on foot. Only a handful of them were of the American Volunteers, come from New York for this beastly war of brothers. It was different here in the South, it was. A man could not keep his distance from the enemy.

Jem tried to be thinking of the rebel volunteers with their long, matted hair and fringed buckskins. But it was the other kind of enemy he saw instead. The civilians, the families, the women and children whose homes had gone up in flames . . .

He was tired, that was all. Tired of marching and bivouacking and long wet nights. The rebel volunteers, if they were on the march as Ferguson's scouts said, had no doubt been well and truly drenched last night.

A distant popping interrupted his runaway thoughts. The noise gathered and strengthened. Shrieks like the war cries of Indians shrilled above the gunfire.

Aye, the rebel volunteers were on the march.

Shadows took on human form. Jem's blood ran cold. He reached for his saddle holsters, fighting the trembling of his hands, and muttered, "How many of them are there?"

Beside him, Lieutenant Anthony Allaire gave him a soldier's smile and shifted with the movement of his elegant mount. "Twenty men such as our Volunteers could defy all of Washington's army."

But this wasn't Washington's army. These were the backwater lads. Jem had heard the tales.

Men packed the narrow space on either side of him. It was the high ground, sure, scattered with rocks and hemmed by trees. But there were no defenses, no retreat.

And why should there be? Major Ferguson's words rang loud in Jem's mind through the pounding of the blood in his ears. *I am on Kings Mountain, I am king of this mountain, and God Almighty could not drive me from it.*

The first war cries raised the hair on Benjamin's neck. On the other side of a pair of knobby outcroppings, Little Kings Mountain came into full view. The red and gold of autumn leaves half hid the tents atop the hill.

They had found Patrick Ferguson.

Yesterday that would have been enough. Catch Ferguson, fight the good fight, go home to Aunt Kate and his sister. Now, with Rane Armistead beside him and the certainty that one of the king's right-hand men was back in North Carolina, Benjamin was not so sure.

"Don't fire until they come in past rifle range," he said. This was no place for a man armed with a pistol like Rane's, but every man here would do the best he could with what he had. "And stay in tight behind me."

Rane fell into step without a word. Benjamin tossed a handful of rifle balls into his mouth to ward off thirst and started for the hill behind Captain Boothe, praying Rane hadn't escaped Charlotte just to die on Kings Mountain.

His sleeves stuck to his skin under his outer hunting shirt. Three o'clock in the afternoon, and he still had not dried out. A torrent of rain had lashed them most of the night, and he'd wrapped the hunting shirt around Old Sandy to keep the firing lock dry. Rane had handed him his cloak. Benjamin had heard Rane's ragged cough and handed it back.

"Can you scream like an Indian?" Benjamin asked now, the words garbled by the balls in his mouth.

"I can try." Rane already sounded breathless.

"Never mind." Benjamin was certain Rane had never screamed like an Indian in his life. "I'll do it for both of us."

Atop the hill, British troops formed ranks. A musket ball slammed into a tree behind Benjamin, showering his hat with chips. He fired back, spat out a rifle ball, loaded, and fired again.

"Shooting downhill, they're firing over our heads," Captain Boothe shouted.

"They shoot like Tories is all." Benjamin spat out another ball and screamed like an Indian. The report of Rane's pistol boomed in his ear. Smoke burgeoned over the forest floor, turning the old hardwoods to ghostly shadows.

Pa had died in a battle like this one, fighting men like Ferguson. Men like Malcolm Harrod, like the men who had hunted Rane.

Ferguson's line of Tories charged down the hill, muskets held low.

"Stay down," Benjamin shouted at Rane. "Bayonets."

"Staying down won't stop a bayonet," Rane shouted back.

The narrow blades flashed amid the smoke. The pistol bellowed again.

Benjamin gestured for Rane to join him and started up a steep incline behind a major from the South Fork of the Catawba. William Chronicle, still Billy to most of the men around him, was only a few years older than Benjamin. Ten paces ahead of Benjamin, he stood on a sharp upward slope and waved his hat. "Face to the hill!"

Then he stopped short, his hat still off, and staggered and sprawled headlong. Benjamin halted to keep from trampling him.

The young officer's eyes were still open, blood spreading across his chest, and then he was gone.

War cries and rifle fire rang in Benjamin's ears. So it would not be an easy fight after all. Some of them were going to die. Same as Pa had.

The knowing of it was hard and raw and sudden. Benjamin screamed his own war cry into the smoke, the thrill of it gone, replaced by a familiar burning hatred.

He had often hidden that hatred behind an easy grin or flippant word. But here there was no need to hide it.

The smoke atop the hill drifted upward, showing a rider on a white charger, blowing a silver whistle.

"Is that—" Rane said.

"Ferguson," Benjamin answered. The name felt like a curse. He raised his rifle.

The Tory lines closed. Ferguson disappeared.

Benjamin shoved through a clump of drooping mountain laurel. Almost to the top now. The Virginia militia crested the opposite side of the ridge.

Captain Boothe waved his rifle. "Come on, boys! The battle is the Lord's!"

Benjamin took a hard breath of the foul, choking smoke and dashed forward, up and over the rim.

The hill was longer and narrower than he had expected, crowded with tents and baggage. Lines of Tories gave way, only to be trapped by the Virginians on the other side.

He glanced back. Rane was still behind him. Benjamin waved him behind a boulder. The hill was madness now, a riot of sound and anger and fear.

A white flag appeared. Then a second. And a third. Ferguson's whistle shrilled. The major himself rode through the huddle, sword in hand, slashing down one white flag after another.

"Someone shoot Ferguson or they're all going to die," Captain Boothe said in disbelief.

Give me a straight shot and I'll do it, Benjamin thought. He fumbled more balls out of his shot pouch, hating that his hands shook.

Rane shouted. Benjamin saw movement at the edge of his vision, started to turn. Stars burst amid the smoke.

The ground was hard, shaking with pounding feet. A dim and distant thunder rolled through Benjamin's head.

Not thunder. Hooves.

Hands caught his hunting shirt, dragged him behind the rock. The pistol gave forth a thunder of its own.

He opened his eyes, saw damp leaves and red clay and Rane Armistead's riding boots. Rolling over, he lifted his head. A riderless gray galloped away from a red-coated man who lay clutching his bloodstained shoulder, saber shining against the leaves.

"All right?" Rane shouted, his voice hoarse.

"Right enough." Benjamin pulled himself to his knees. The back of his head throbbed, but better the flat of the blade than its edge. He had Rane to thank for that.

The Tories crowded back against bullet-riddled tents. Then a shout went up, louder than the din of battle. Benjamin jammed his hat over the bruise and got to his feet.

Patrick Ferguson and the white charger plunged through the Patriot lines, a handful of officers in their wake.

Benjamin primed his rifle faster than he ever had before. But the crack of his shot was lost in the roar of fifty rifles firing as one.

When the smoke lifted, Patrick Ferguson and the charger were gone. In the midst of the Tory camp, a white flag went up.

Was that surrender at last? Or only another vain attempt at it?

A burst of rifle fire exploded on the far side of the tents. Benjamin reloaded and cocked Old Sandy.

"Woodbridge!"

Robert Boothe dashed out of the smoke and knocked Benjamin's aim away. "Hold your fire! It's murder now that the flag's been raised."

The world seemed vaguely unsteady, pulsing in time with the throb of his head. "But Captain, there's still—"

"Not everybody's seen it. And some don't want to."

For the briefest moment, Benjamin did not blame the men who wanted to ignore the white flag. He hated himself for the thought as soon as it came to him. "Yessir."

Robert wheeled away, shouting at another volunteer Benjamin could not see. Rane coughed, hard and long.

"Obliged for the warning," Benjamin said. "You saved me—from the sword and from the horse too."

Rane straightened and cleared his throat. "There's no kind of glory in being trampled by a horse."

"Aye, that's not the legend that goes down to posterity." Benjamin surveyed the wreck of the mountain, the clusters of Tory officers grounding their arms, the dead and wounded where they had fallen.

Was there glory in any of this? Satisfaction, mayhap, of protecting hearth and home. But glory?

He breathed hard, waiting for the rush of danger to ebb away. He had gotten the fight he'd been waiting for. But the fight was still with him.

Three

THE DAYS AFTER THE BATTLE FORMED A BLUR
of grueling marches and rainy nights. After the worst march
of all, twenty-four hours and thirty-two miles through pouring rain and swollen fords, Benjamin rolled himself in his
blanket beside the fire and stared into the dusk.

He should sleep while he had the chance. But sleep had
come fitful ever since the battle. Slim rations, troublemakers
in the ranks, swift retribution for prisoners who tried to
escape and even for those who didn't. Only yesterday—or
was it the day before that?—a court of Patriot officers had
tried three dozen Tory prisoners for looting and burning and
most of all for treason. Nine of them swung for it. The rest
were pardoned only when Colonel Shelby, his face set like
flint, turned from a taut conversation with Colonel Campbell and said simply, "There has been enough of it."

Not everyone agreed. Captain Patrick Carr of the Georgia
militia had said the wilderness ought to bear more fruit like
that of the gallows.

Benjamin got up and gathered an armful of chopped-
up fence rails from the pile nearby. When the fire was roaring,
he sat with his back against his saddle and pulled his New

Testament from his scrip. He opened the book and leaned closer to the firelight.

"What are you reading?"

He looked sideways. Rane Armistead was sitting up on the blanket next to Benjamin's.

"The epistle of James," Benjamin said. "Still awake?"

"After all that's happened . . . 'In my heart there was a kind of fighting that would not let me sleep.'"

"Who said that?"

"Shakespeare. *Hamlet, Prince of Denmark.*"

"Sounds like he knew what he was talking about."

Rane nodded toward the book Benjamin held. "You have a Bible so small?"

"Just a New Testament. Some fellow in Philadelphia printed it. A traveler left it at Aunt Kate's ordinary. No way to find him again, so Aunt Kate and my sister gave it to me."

Rane fell silent. Benjamin returned his focus to the small print, ignoring the pinch of hunger. Everyone was hungry. Yesterday's scavenged corn and pumpkin had seemed the sweetest thing he had ever tasted.

From the tail of his eye, he saw Rane draw a small book of his own from under his hunting shirt. A . . . prayer book?

Well, he would not begrudge Rane his comfort, even if the Church of England stirred up too many hard memories.

But after a few minutes, Rane stopped with an inscrutable look on his face. Benjamin glimpsed only the title at the head of the page as Rane closed the book. *A Prayer for the King's Majesty.*

"Woodbridge," Rane said quietly.

"Aye."

"How did you know about Malcolm Harrod?"

It was the first time Rane had spoken the name since Benjamin had mentioned it in the camp at Cowpens.

"He was one of Governor Tryon's henchmen, nigh on to ten years ago. Helped him crush the folks who wanted fair taxes and freedom to worship. One of them was my pa."

Rane slid the prayer book into his hunting shirt and stared at the fire. Benjamin said, "I'd not do that if I were you. Blinds you to what's in the dark."

Rane jerked his gaze away. "Crushing those who desire freedom is Harrod's way."

Benjamin returned his New Testament to his scrip. His fingers met the rounded wood of a half-finished spoon he'd been carving for his sister. He pulled it out and slid his hunting knife out of its sheath. "Armistead, I don't aim to pry, but what does Harrod want with you? It's clear enough that he had something to do with your leaving Charlotte."

"He thinks I know too much of his strategy."

"And do you?"

The firelight danced across Rane's scar. "Sometimes a man is simply in the wrong place at the wrong time."

A damp leaf landed on the bowl of the spoon. Benjamin tossed the leaf into the fire, sparks bursting on the rising smoke. *Man is born unto trouble, as the sparks fly upward.* "If Harrod's of a mind to cause more trouble, you can wager I'll be the first to hunt him down. Somebody ought to pay him double for what he's done to decent folks."

"Vengeance is the Almighty's domain."

"Aye, in the end. But when it comes to folks like Harrod, I've no time to wait for judgment day."

Rane nodded toward the carving. "What is it?"

"A spoon. Mouse—my sister—is fond of cooking."

"Your sister's name is *Mouse*?"

"No, it's Elizabeth. But I've always called her that, on account of how shy she is when new lodgers come to stay at Aunt Kate's ordinary." Elizabeth had always been shy, but more so since the fever had taken Ma.

"Have you many new lodgers?"

Benjamin turned the spoon over. "Not since the war."

"Yet another reason for you to hate the king's men."

"There's a Tory on the ridge where I come from. Name

of Taggart. The last time we crossed paths, I'd have killed him if I could have. He'd have killed me back. And you might say that goes for near about every Tory I ever met."

"Is that why you intervened for me as you did?"

"Maybe." Benjamin twisted his knife, rounding out the inside of the spoon. "Mostly I just can't stand by and watch while other folks are in trouble."

He still remembered the shock on his sister's face after his brawl with Nolan Taggart in the eating room of the ordinary. Taggart was a full twenty years older than Benjamin, though hard muscled and wily as an old coon. Elizabeth had likely never known her brother carried such seething rage. But Aunt Kate had probably always suspected.

That was the day Susanna Boothe had drawn away from him. He regretted that. But he could not quite regret what he had done to Taggart.

The fire crackled. Benjamin put the spoon back in his scrip and sheathed his knife. There would be other long nights in camp. "What plans did you have before the war?"

"I intended to study for the bar."

"Not enough lawyers in the world to suit you?"

"Not enough who defend the defenseless." Rane started to say something else, then shook his head. He fell silent, staring up at the night sky.

Benjamin wondered what Rane had thought of the swift backcountry trial the Tories had gotten. He followed Rane's gaze, deciding not to ask. Stars winked between blowing wisps of cloud. "A fine sight," he said quietly.

"It is that."

"What is it Milton said? 'And all the spangled host keep watch in squadrons bright.'"

Rane looked at him quickly. "Milton?"

"'On the Morning of Christ's Nativity.' Though it's a bit early for that, I grant."

"I'd not have expected . . ."

"A backwater man to be quoting Milton? Maybe I haven't read Shakespeare or studied law, but Milton's not too far behind. Aunt Kate has some of his writings that her husband brought upmountain. I read to her of an evening. When a man has few books, he learns them by heart."

"Have you read his *Areopagitica*?"

"Aye." John Milton's arguments against censorship had spread far among lovers of freedom. "'Give me the liberty to know, to utter, and to argue freely according to conscience, above all liberties.' One of my favorites, though he took it for granted that government should interfere with outright blasphemy. Most folks in his time thought the same."

"Surely you don't support the spreading of heresy."

"Who decides what's heresy?" Benjamin pulled his rifle to him and took an oiled rag from his shot pouch. "Take a man like Malcolm Harrod. Should he decide such a thing?"

A footstep shifted the damp leaves. Benjamin looked up. Captain Boothe was back from checking the evening patrols.

Robert motioned for both men to stay seated. "What's this about Harrod?"

"His men were the ones who followed me from Charlotte Town," Rane said.

"God help us." Robert rubbed his neck where brown hair brushed his collar. "Harrod knew more about our settlement in the Blue Ridge than any other king's man but Colonel Drake. Drake's no threat now, but Harrod . . ."

"I never heard him mention Drake," Rane said.

"You wouldn't." Benjamin worked the rag into the corners of the firing lock. "It was ten years back yonder. Governor Tryon's cronies locked up Captain Boothe for preaching and taxed folks' land away and gave our hard-earned money to their own blaspheming clergy."

He saw Rane wince and knew he'd gone a step too far. Even if it was true. "Beggin' your pardon, Armistead."

"Because I carry the Book of Common Prayer?" Rane

shook his head. "That is a subject for another night. Harrod is enough to consider for now."

"He was Tryon's man," Benjamin said. "Like Edmund Fanning. Drake did his work for him—chased us clear to the mountains and tried to take Captain Boothe for treason."

"Drake is dead," Robert said. "Leave it at that."

Benjamin jammed the rag back into his shot pouch. "Harrod won't."

"Would you know him again if you saw him?" Robert asked Rane.

"Brownheaded, lean and tall, with a thin face." Rane spoke as if the features were graven in his memory. "His jaw is misshapen on one side, as if broken and poorly healed."

Benjamin looked at Captain Boothe. "Is that—"

"Where I struck him? It's likely."

"But not likely Harrod has forgotten."

A spate of angry shouts erupted across camp, then went silent. Benjamin glanced around at the flickering campfires.

A hundred men had escaped on yesterday's march. How many of them had found another leader to follow?

He ran a hand over Old Sandy's smooth curly ash stock. "Seems to me somebody in this lot of Tories ought to know what Harrod's about."

"I doubt you'll convince them to tell you," Rane said.

Benjamin gave him a half grin. "Your lawyering ways might get it out of them."

The shouts came again, nearer this time. Robert lifted his head, listening.

"What is it?" Benjamin asked.

"Same thing as always," Robert said. "A Tory crossed a Whig or a Whig crossed a Tory. We just hope and pray it doesn't end with more hangings."

Another angry shout brought Benjamin to his feet. Robert beckoned him to follow and headed for the neighboring fire.

Four

JEM FLANNERY HAD FELT NUMB AS HE WATCHED Major Ferguson's charger bolt down the hill, dragging the fallen officer a full hundred yards. He had felt numb as the rebel officers knocked up rifles and shouted at their men to stop firing. He had felt numb all the way down the mountain, all through the slow march northward, all during the trial and hangings. Justice, revenge, what did it matter?

Now here he stood by a campfire in the rebel camp, nose to nose with the meanest rebel officer he'd seen yet. Captain Patrick Carr, a fellow Irishman and the worst Tory-hater in the camp. The men who had shared Jem's campfire had scattered when Carr's cronies started shouting.

Maybe Major Ferguson was the lucky one after all.

"I'll give you one chance to make up for the misery your traitorous kind have caused." Carr's voice was calm and easy. From what Jem had heard, the calm wouldn't last long. "Your freedom if you'll train my men as you trained yours."

Jem hadn't trained the American Volunteers. But to be bargained with by the Tory-hating officer left him with a taste so bitter he wanted to spit his answer. "No."

He saw murder in Carr's eyes and did not care. The captain whipped his sword from its sheath, only a flash in the firelight before the flat of it sent stars through Jem's vision.

Jem stumbled and fell, groping for his hilt, remembering it was not there. The rebels had not abided by the convention of allowing captured officers to retain their sidearms. He dug his fingers into the rain-sodden earth and wished he had strength enough to be shoving Carr's face into that very ground.

The next blow did not come. "Enough, Captain."

Jem raised his head. Two men stood between him and Carr. One, a young man with wheat-brown hair, was a rebel militiaman whose name Jem did not know. The older man, the one who had spoken, wore quiet authority with the same ease as his worn buckskins. He had been at the hangings, had argued for a fair trial and seemed as torn as Colonel Shelby at the end of it.

Why couldn't these have been the men to offer Jem his freedom? Jem might have been inclined to agree.

Carr eyed the older man. "You hold with Tories, Boothe?"

"There's been killing enough."

For a moment Jem thought the two men meant each other harm. Then Carr sheathed the sword, wheeled, and strode away. His henchmen followed him.

"All right?" the younger man asked.

"Aye, more or less." Jem got gingerly to his feet. "I wish you'd be shooting me and have it done with," he added, hating how the bitterness brought out the Irish in his voice. He'd worked hard to hide that, he had.

"You don't mean that and you know it." Boothe motioned Jem away from the light and the staring eyes.

The younger man propped his rifle against a tree and took a rag from his leather scrip. "Captain, you have your flask?"

Boothe took a leather flask from beside his canteen and handed it to the younger man, who dampened the scrap of homespun with a splash of rum and added a bit of a dried plant he took from his scrip.

"Aunt Kate comes through," he said, and passed the cloth to Jem. "Hold that on your face awhile."

"Obliged for the help," Jem said reluctantly, offering his free hand. The cloth stung against the cut at his hairline.

"I'm Benjamin Woodbridge. This here is my captain, Robert Boothe."

"James Arnold Gregory." The lie came easy. Telling the same lie for four years would do that.

"Looks like you riled Paddy Carr up some," Woodbridge said.

"He wished me to train his men."

Robert Boothe leaned against a tree, blocking out the rest of camp. "I regret how some of our lads have treated yours. If it means anything, we've naught to eat, either."

"Not all Tories are like Ferguson," Jem said abruptly.

"Not all Whigs are like Carr," Woodbridge said.

"No. No, I . . ." Jem trailed off to keep from wincing at the pressure on his wound. "I'd repay you if I could."

Boothe waved that away. "We all have debts we can't pay. To the Almighty most of all. It's why we need a Savior."

Jem let out a laugh. His head throbbed. "The Almighty does not trifle with the likes of me, I assure you."

"You'd be surprised."

"I've had surprises enough for today." Jem eased the cloth away from his face. "But I thank you all the same."

He started to turn away. Woodbridge said, "There's one thing you could do for us, James Arnold Gregory."

For an instant Jem thought he heard mockery, as if Woodbridge knew he was not James Arnold Gregory but Jem Flannery, Cork Harbor wharf rat. But when he turned around, Woodbridge's face held no trace of sarcasm.

"What?" Jem said.

Woodbridge stepped closer. "Do you know a man by the name of Malcolm Harrod?"

Captain Boothe opened his mouth, then closed it again.

"I know the name," Jem said. "A subordinate of Lord Cornwallis, much as Major Ferguson is—was."

"Where is Harrod now? Was he with Ferguson?"

"No." Lucky for him, Jem added silently. "When this campaign was over, we were to join Harrod and Cornwallis at Charlotte. But I've heard rumors that Harrod is gathering a band of his own somewhere in the hills."

Woodbridge exchanged glances with Boothe. Then he said, "Was it Carr or his bargain that riled you?"

Jem studied Woodbridge. The man was a little younger than Jem, handsome in a rugged, roguish manner with broad shoulders and fringed hunting shirt and a hint of swagger to match the flaming red silk at his throat. But his face was open and honest.

"The thought of freedom never riles me," Jem said.

"I do believe I know that feeling." Woodbridge offered a crooked grin. "So you're not against helping a rebel if the rebel takes the right tack."

"No, I don't—I don't understand you."

"Nor do I," Boothe said. "But I'm beginning to."

"I figure if Paddy Carr could make him a trade, so could we. Say, if he could find out where Harrod is and what he's about. Maybe do some investigating in those hills where Harrod's said to be."

Woodbridge was watching him closely. Jem could feel the intensity of it.

"Seems fair enough," Boothe said.

"It's madness," Jem said.

Woodbridge shrugged. "Have it your way."

He picked up his rifle and turned toward the glow of the fires. Boothe pushed away from the tree he'd been leaning on.

Jem balled the strip of damp homespun in his hand. "Woodbridge, wait."

Five

BENJAMIN THUMPED HIS HAVERSACK DOWN beside the fire and leaned Old Sandy against a stump. "You ever eaten groundnuts before?"

Rane Armistead peered into the mouth of the sack. "I may have and didn't know it. What are they?"

"Wild bean roots. Some call 'em Indian potatoes. I found some this forenoon when I was on patrol with Saul McBraden. They'll be good eating, roasted in the coals."

"Have I met Saul McBraden?"

"Seen him, most likely. He scouts with Alec Perry most times. We've been friends a good while, he and Alec and I."

Benjamin propped one foot on the pile of firewood and tightened the straps that secured his leggings over his canvas breeches. As he did so, Captain Boothe passed on the far side of the campfire. He paused behind Rane's back and gave Benjamin a tight nod.

Benjamin nodded back. Captain Boothe walked on.

"Time for patrol," Benjamin said, reaching for his rifle.

Rane paused in the midst of cutting a groundnut open with a clasp knife. "You said you were on patrol this forenoon."

"Aye, well, I can't help that." Benjamin was not about

to explain that he had a Tory prisoner to sneak out of camp and Captain Boothe had just signaled him. It was a risky business, even if the commanding officers had approved it. Captain Boothe and Alec Perry were the only other men in camp who knew.

"Save me some supper," Benjamin said, and sauntered away.

Three campsites to the west, James Arnold Gregory was waiting, as expressionless as he'd been when Paddy Carr assaulted him. His men were arguing about the pitiful foraging. The young officer slipped away and joined Benjamin behind the shelter of a thicket at the edge of camp.

"Ready?" Benjamin asked in a low voice.

"Yes."

Gregory sounded nervous. Benjamin didn't blame him. He would have preferred to get their tame Tory out of camp as soon as the commanding officers agreed to look the other way, but too many prisoners had escaped in earnest, and the pickets were edgy. The last thing Gregory needed was to be shot before he got a hundred yards from camp. They had waited days for an opportunity, and another was not likely to come. Tomorrow they would be in the Moravian towns, a far harder place to arrange an escape.

"Captain Boothe has two couriers out yonder somewhere," Benjamin said as he led Gregory deeper into the woods. "Hank Jonas and Gunning."

"Gunning who?"

"Just Gunning. He used to be Captain Boothe's manservant, but he's a free man now." Benjamin could envision both men—Hank Jonas, with his buckskins and bushy beard and game ankle, and Gunning, all but invisible in the shadows. They'd latch on to the Tory officer's trail and not let go unless he walked straight into the British army, and even then it was doubtful. "I don't know where they are, and you won't either unless they want you to. But one or the other will have an eye on you, be sure of that."

"And they'll carry any word to Captain Boothe?"

"Aye. Your horse is waiting by the creek. We'll signal you when the last picket is past. Ride upstream along the creek bed where you won't leave a mark. And be careful. Word in camp is that Harrod is looking for officers."

"Surely he won't trouble me if I'm merely riding cross country."

"Let's hope so."

They came in sight of another small clearing. Robert Boothe and Alec Perry waited there. Flame-colored light slanted through the trees, blurring whatever lay beyond.

It hit Benjamin then. He was helping a Tory escape. A man like the men he had always hated for what they had done to his father.

He knew it was only so they could stop a worse man. But tonight that hardly seemed enough.

"Woodbridge," Robert said sharply.

Benjamin snapped to attention. "Yessir."

"Watch for that last picket."

"Yessir."

"Hard to see much of anything this time of night," Alec said. "But I reckon that's the general notion. I hope this is a good idea."

So did Benjamin. "If it weren't, Captain Boothe would have stopped us by now."

"I'm still not sure I shouldn't do just that," Robert said. "But I'll own a mortal craving to know where Harrod is and what he's doing."

"You and me both." Benjamin glimpsed movement beyond Robert's shoulder. "Picket coming."

"Get behind cover," Robert said to Gregory.

The Tory ducked behind a stout hickory. Benjamin rested the butt of his rifle on the ground and turned to Robert, grasping for a thread of conversation. "You said something this morning about what we'll do after we get to the Moravian towns. Something about riding with Colonel Shelby."

"Aye. He needs more men who will be fair toward the prisoners, and he wants me to join his command to escort them to Virginia. Colonel Campbell's neck of the woods."

The sentry was coming closer. Benjamin forced himself not to look at Gregory's hiding place. "Will you do it?"

"For Shelby, I will. But it's not only Virginia. Shelby's thinking of going on to Hillsborough to tell General Gates what's gone on in this part of the country."

The sentry saluted Robert. Benjamin lifted his rifle in easy greeting. Alec did the same. Just three bored men, enjoying the sunset and talking about the war.

"I heard Gates got thrashed at Camden," Benjamin said.

"Thrashed ain't the word for it," Alec said. "He didn't stop running till he hit Hillsborough. Left good men to die in his dust. I thank the Lord I wasn't there, or I'd have been court-martialed sure for what I would have said to Gates."

The sentry passed from sight. Robert nodded to Benjamin.

"Run for it," Benjamin said to the hickory.

Footsteps rustled through the woods toward the creek where Gregory's horse was hidden.

"Linger awhile," Robert said in a low voice. "Keep folks from wondering."

Benjamin forced himself to relax again. His stomach growled. Rane Armistead would be roasting those groundnuts right about now. "Captain, does Shelby want all of us?"

"He'll need as many of us as he can get," Robert said. "Why do you ask?"

"Thinking of Rane Armistead. He's a good sort, but he's no scout."

"True enough," Robert said. "And if Harrod is still after him, it might be just as well if Armistead weren't in the wide-open country much longer."

"You mean take him home to Sunrising."

"The place was made for folks on the run. Does he have anywhere else to go?"

"I'll ask him, but I doubt it." Benjamin paused. "Can we get leave? I heard about Colonel Campbell asking the officers not to discharge their men yet."

"He's worried about Indians on the frontier. Everyone's fretting about that. If you head for the Blue Ridge and send word of any Indian trouble, Campbell would be as grateful as the rest of us. I'll talk to him tomorrow."

Alec grunted. "If you're bound to bring stragglers into camp, at least you found one worth keeping."

Benjamin shrugged. "I couldn't see leaving Armistead to fend for himself."

That was why he'd helped Rane, true enough. But was it also why he'd intervened for James Arnold Gregory? Or was that out of guilt that some part of him, deep down, had been glad to see Ferguson's men get their reward?

He thought of what he'd told Rane about Nolan Taggart, the worst Tory within sixty miles of home and the man who had goaded Benjamin to lose his temper in front of an innful of lodgers. Whatever guilt he felt for Ferguson's men didn't change his feelings toward Taggart one lick.

His stomach growled again, and he ripped off a strip of hickory bark to chew. In the mountains, the nuts would drop soon and Aunt Kate would go a-gathering. There had been quiet jokes that this was the year Susanna Boothe would bake a hickory nut cake for Benjamin . . .

But it was little use thinking of Susanna. The hard work of making a hickory nut cake was what made it a token of regard in Sunrising. And a woman who barely looked at him anymore would hardly go to such trouble.

A shout broke into his thoughts. Benjamin wheeled.

"We've got trouble," Alec muttered.

A private hurried out of the strip of trees that hid the camp. "Captain Boothe, sir, I can't find one of the prisoners.

An officer, that Gregory fellow."

"Look again," Robert said. "Mayhap you missed him."

"I've checked three times, sir. Nowhere to be seen. His men don't know where he went. Did anyone pass this way?" Benjamin caught Robert's gaze. "I'll look out yonder in the woods."

Robert nodded. Benjamin pivoted away and broke into a light sprint.

Once he was deep in the woods, he paused to listen. More shouts erupted in the distance. The camp was waking to the alarm. But no sound came from the direction of the creek. Gregory should be well on his way by now.

Benjamin still didn't like the notion of turning a Tory loose. But he could hide his vexation. He had done it often enough. Turning eastward, he headed downriver.

A hundred paces downstream, around a sharp bend in the creek, he fired into a tree and unleashed his best sentry shout. "You there! Come back, Tory!"

As he'd hoped, the shouts at the edge of camp changed directions. He ducked a branch, weaved around a spinney of loblolly pines, and spotted the dark length of a fallen tree. He stepped onto the end and ran the length of it, then jumped to a boulder and from the boulder to a stump.

"Downriver," someone shouted in the distance. "I hear somebody downriver."

Benjamin stepped from the stump and waded into the creek. He skirted a rock midstream and waded farther downriver, giving another shout for good measure. Then he stepped out and headed back toward camp, circling wide. When he passed Robert and Alec on his way, the captain gave him a nod of approval.

Had they done the right thing? He hoped so.

MALCOLM HARROD SAT AT A MAKESHIFT TABLE
in a makeshift hut deep in the hills along the Yadkin River,
reading Lord Cornwallis's finely slanting script in the waver-
ing light of a tallow candle. Negotiations with the Cherokee
agents had been successful; Cornwallis was pleased. But not
pleased enough to give Harrod the reinforcements he wanted.

A rap at the door raised his head. "Enter."

Sergeant Nolan Taggart opened the door and escorted
a man inside. "Another one, sir. American Volunteers."

Harrod laid the letter aside and scrutinized the new
arrival. Tall, square of shoulder, the powder gone from
auburn hair, he might be twenty-five or thirty. The epaulet
of a lieutenant adorned his right shoulder, though his gorget
was missing from his neck. Perhaps the brass crescent had
been stolen by an enterprising rebel. Gorget or none, this was
an officer, and one who had served under Patrick Ferguson.
Precious few officers had sought out their camp in the hills.

"Dismissed, Sergeant," Harrod said to Taggart.

The sergeant stepped out and shut the door. The new
arrival turned to face Harrod, seeming reluctant to do so.

"Your name?" Harrod asked.

"James Arnold Gregory, sir."

The touch of accent in his voice surprised Harrod. "A Londoner?"

"Yes, sir." Gregory fixed his eyes on the wall behind Harrod's head.

"I had been given to understand that most of the King's American Regiment are of colonial extraction."

"Most of us were, sir."

"Were? Not are?"

The faintest change came to Gregory's countenance, as if he were steeling himself. "You've not heard, sir?"

"Heard what, Gregory?"

"The Volunteers were ruined at Kings Mountain, sir."

Harrod came to his feet. "And Major Ferguson?"

"Dead, sir."

No emotion in the man's voice. Harrod schooled himself to speak likewise. "How?"

"How, sir?"

"How did he die?"

"He—" Gregory hesitated. "He was with his officers, sir, trying to find a path down the mountain. The rebels saw him—they all fired at once. His horse dragged him . . ."

Harrod swore silently. Fiery-headed Ferguson, a man marked for great things even in military academy. They had been an odd pair, perhaps—dashing marksman and taciturn strategist, boys becoming men. They had studied together, argued together, laughed and cursed together. Then they had gone their separate ways, Harrod to Ireland and Ferguson to Germany. The American rebellion had reunited them.

He cleared his throat. "You're wise to join us."

"Sir, there's been some mistake. I was merely riding through the countryside, and your sentries accosted me."

"No one merely rides through the countryside in these times unless he has a reason. If your reason was not to join us, I suggest you explain to me what it may have been."

The officer hesitated, no doubt realizing he could be charged with desertion if he did not join the nearest regiment.

"Well, I was looking for you, after a manner of speaking."

"As I thought." This man might not be Harrod's most trustworthy ally. But what backwater volunteer ever was? "I am confident you will serve under me as you served under Ferguson."

"Yes, sir."

"Sergeant Taggart is waiting outside. He will show you to your quarters."

"Yes, sir."

Gregory saluted and went out. Harrod cursed savagely, fighting the rising of his temper. Malcolm Harrod never lost his temper. Not since Ireland, when he had seen what it could do.

If only Ferguson had listened to Harrod's warnings that it was folly to rely on the fickle courage of backwater commoners. That such men were useful only to shield the regular troops.

But Ferguson had not listened. And now he was dead. Betrayed by the men he had trained, killed by rebels of a lower class yet.

Harrod glanced at the orders he had received from Cornwallis. Ferguson had once written that the Colonies could be subdued only by fire and sword.

Cornwallis would never countenance such total destruction. He had been a Whig in Parliament before the war, opposing coercive measures in the Colonies, though George III had counted him a friend.

But Cornwallis was not here. Harrod trimmed the guttering candle and reached for pen and paper.

SOMEWHERE IN THE
BLUE RIDGE MOUNTAINS

Seven

THE TRAIL HOME TO SUNRISING WAS LONG,
though not nearly as long as it had seemed when the men
were bound the other way, hunting Ferguson. Benjamin
kept a sharp eye on their back trail as the horses climbed the
ever-steepening path. If anybody was following them, he
was mighty sly about it.

The quiet of early morning hung heavy over the ridge
as he guided Sassafras forward. Wet snow crusted the tops
of his moccasins. "Not much farther now."

Rane stifled a cough with the back of his riding glove.
"It seems fantastic that there should be a settlement in such
wild country."

"When Captain Boothe first came, it was a pretty well-
kept secret. But the more folks head west, the more they hear
about a stopping place in these hills. Aunt Kate's ordinary
has made a name for itself. Or did, before the war."

"It was her husband who brought Milton's writings
with him?"

"Aye, though he died before my family came."

"I've been considering what you said about Milton's
arguments in *Areopagitica*."

"Most of what he said was gospel truth. But there've been folks all down through history who believed the truth and were called heretics for it. Milton himself spoke of that."

"His eighteenth sonnet." Rane nodded. "I know it well."

Benjamin quoted it thoughtfully.

> "'Avenge, O Lord, thy slaughter'd saints, whose bones
> Lie scatter'd on the Alpine mountains cold,
> Ev'n them who kept thy truth so pure of old,
> When all our fathers worshipp'd stocks and stones.'

"It's true, you know," he added. "The early believers in Europe were butchered by the Romish church."

"'Tis a far cry from declaring a book to be heresy."

"Is it?"

"Government must have some defense against error."

"Truth is the best way to fight lies. Milton makes that point well."

Rane was silent. Benjamin said, "Reckon I've shocked you a mite. Same as when I called the clergy 'blaspheming.'"

"Do you hold to freedom of conscience even for those who disagree with you?" Rane's voice held a trace of a smile.

"Spoken like a lawyer."

"Sir William Blackstone did say in his *Commentaries on the Laws of England* that dissenters ought not deny members of the established church their own 'indulgence and liberty of conscience.'"

"That's fair enough. Where do you stand on matters of conscience, Armistead?"

Rane sobered. For a moment Benjamin thought he was not going to answer.

At last Rane said, "I have no hope but the merit of Christ. That much I know. But to speak of where I stand seems too strong when I feel cut adrift."

"A man with no hope but the merit of Christ doesn't

sound adrift."

"I stand with the Church of England. But I've come to fear the Church of England does not stand with me."

"If you stand with the Church of England, maybe I'd best warn you about Sunrising."

"What about—"

Something rattled over the side of the trail far ahead. A rock had been knocked loose of the snow.

Benjamin halted Sassafras and held out a hand. Rane stopped Macy abreast of him.

Another sprinkle of rock clicked down over the ledges. No doubt about it. There was a varmint on this trail. Of the two-footed variety.

Benjamin dismounted, Old Sandy in hand. "Take the horses back thataway," he said from the side of his mouth, motioning back down the trail. "Get off the trail if you can, but don't get lost. I'll see what's up ahead and come back."

Rane gave a single nod and took Sassafras's lead in the hand that held Macy's reins. His free hand moved under his cloak as he rode back down the trail. Benjamin waited, listened, and walked on, heel before toe, silent as the Cherokee hunters who had taught him their trade.

The trail was clear as far as the next corner, where it turned sharply around a mass of trees and looming boulders. Sound ran a long way in these hills, more so in the shadowy mist of daybreak. Benjamin paused to listen again, then rounded the jink in the trail.

The crack of a fowling piece blasted off the rocks. Fire stung Benjamin's right arm. He ducked behind a boulder and cocked the rifle.

Lanternlight flashed out, harsh against the gray dawn. A brusque British voice said, "State your business."

"Next time ask that before you shoot at a man," Benjamin said.

The lanternlight danced over snowy granite and towering

pines on one side of the narrow trail, gaping emptiness on the other. A man in a military cloak and cocked hat held the reins of a dark charger. Beside him stood a wiry, chestnut-haired man Benjamin knew all too well.

Nolan Taggart, the ridge's worst Tory and the bane of Benjamin's existence.

Taggart swore. Benjamin said, "What? Not the easy pickings you were after?"

He turned his attention to the man beside Taggart. Brownheaded. Tall of frame and narrow of face, with a bony ridge on the angle of his jaw.

Benjamin's hands tightened on Old Sandy. "You're Malcolm Harrod."

Malcolm Harrod stood half in shadow, one gloved hand resting on the sword in his officer's sash. "It would appear my fame precedes me."

"Your men shot at me, down at Hannah's Cowpens. I don't like to be shot at." If only he could see Harrod's eyes, see if he knew or cared that his kind had brought good men to their deaths and were doing it again.

"As I recall," Harrod said, "they intended to shoot at the man who sought asylum with you. Where is he?"

"Not here. As you can see. Did you come clear out here just to ask a thing like that?"

"My business here is none of yours."

"And that's another thing." Benjamin held the rifle lightly, easily, but leveled suggestively in Harrod's direction. He wanted nothing more than to shove Harrod off the side of the mountain, but that wouldn't give him the answers he needed. "How'd you come to be here when you're supposed to be rallying Tories along the Yadkin?"

Harrod motioned with his head. The nape of Benjamin's neck prickled.

He swung half around as shadows closed from behind him. Two men slammed him against the boulder, knocked the rifle up, ripped it away.

Pa's rifle. No.

Benjamin wrenched free of the first man and laid him in the snow with an elbow to his throat, spun and kicked the second man in the knee. The man dropped, flinging his arms out to catch himself. The rifle flipped over the side of the trail and discharged, its report ringing off the rocks. The clatter of its fall stopped abruptly.

Taggart wore the same smirk he'd worn when he stood up in the great room of the Dove & Olive Inn and said John Woodbridge was a rebel who deserved what he'd gotten from the governor's men. Benjamin had pummeled the smirk right off Taggart's face that time.

But today Taggart had help. Benjamin reached for his hunting knife.

Hands seized his wrist, jerked his arms back, dragged him against the boulder. He wrestled with the grip, but the two men had him fast. Blood oozed through his sleeve.

His rifle hadn't fallen far. There must be a ledge down there somewhere, below the edge of the trail. Surely he could climb down and find it . . .

"Aye," one of the men said. "It's him, sir. The sentry we told you of, sir."

The sword sang from Harrod's scabbard, catching the rising sun. "Tell me again. Where is Armistead?"

He knew Rane's name. That wasn't good. "Far away from you and your kind, if I have aught to say about it."

"You insist on protecting him?"

"I'm answering your question, that's all."

"It may serve you well to know that the man whom you shelter is a member of His Majesty's Royal Navy."

His Majesty's Royal Navy.

The eerie stillness of the mountains filled the span of a heartbeat. Then Benjamin offered as much of a smirk as Taggart had ever given him. "Armistead a Navy man? You're a sorry excuse for a liar, Harrod."

"'Tis no lie. You've seen the sea service pistol he carries."

"Aye." That explained the belt hook and brass hardware. It also explained the chopped-off barrel; a twenty-inch pistol would have been hard to hide. "Sure, he might have been a Navy man once. But you're a sorry excuse for a liar if you say he still is."

"He had no leave to end his service."

"We had no leave to be independent either, and here we are." He squared his shoulders, ignoring the burning of his grazed arm. "I'd light a shuck if I were you. The men who licked Ferguson will be coming for you next."

Taggart looked to Harrod. Harrod nodded, sheathing the sword. Taggart handed him the lantern and moved forward. The grip on Benjamin's arms tightened.

"You no-account turncoat," Benjamin said.

"You son of a no-account turncoat." Taggart's smirk deepened. "This time your rebel cronies aren't here to help you."

Eight

KATHERINE LENNOX McGUINESS STEPPED INTO the dogtrot that divided the Dove & Olive Inn neatly into halves. In the light of the autumn sun, snow sparkled on the path in front of the double cabins. Smoke drifted from the chimney of the kitchen house a dozen paces past the north cabin, staining the misty air and blurring the stable beyond.

Thirty-nine days since Benjamin had left Sunrising and gone to hunt Major Ferguson with Captain Boothe.

Kate tugged her shawl closer, adjusted her grip on the pair of baskets she held, and started down the steps.

Elizabeth Woodbridge hurried around the corner from the kitchen, smudges of flour on the pinner apron that covered her green shortgown and striped petticoat. Another smudge adorned her tucked-up hair, a darker brown than her brother Benjamin's. "I told you to bide till I could come, Aunt Kate."

"Aye, lass, but you've enough to be doing." Kate handed her one of the baskets. Cooking, cleaning, washing, mending, looking after her lodgers and the stable and all the herbs the neighbors would want from Kate when their menfolk came home. And it would be hog-killing time soon; Kate dreaded the notion of such work without the strength of the men.

But it was the same for everyone, though not every woman in Sunrising owned an inn as Kate did. Kate straightened her spine and tucked a runaway silvery wisp under her linen cap. *Lord, forgive my complaining heart.*

The woods north of Sunrising stretched bare branches to the sky. Clusters of crimson and yellow still clung here and there, showing their double in the tossed-up surface of Button Creek. Kate paused to wave a greeting to Deacon Ashe's maiden sister, bound for the trading post across the settlement, then followed Elizabeth gingerly over the makeshift bridge upstream of Captain Boothe's cabin.

"Here." Elizabeth pointed to the spreading branches of a massive chestnut tree.

Kate kicked a clump of snow aside. Sure enough, a hint of prickly brown husk peeped from under a wet leaf. She picked up the nut and dropped it into her basket. The chestnuts might be larger than the chinquapins she had gathered back in September, but their prickles were just as sharp.

"Was that Judge Pembrook in the stable today?" Elizabeth asked suddenly.

"I reckon it was. I heard he's leaving for another Indian council." Kate raked aside a patch of fallen leaves. Somewhere far above, a tree squirrel scolded.

"Does he think there will be Cherokee trouble again?"

"He always thinks that, lass. 'Tis his duty, it is."

"But what if he's right?"

"Well, what if he is? Or what if he's not? You can't be taking that burden on your shoulders. Look your fear in the eye and go on with living."

"I know." Elizabeth sighed. A nut thumped into her basket.

Kate skirted the thick trunk of the tree and spied the shriveled leaflets of a snow-dusted ginseng plant. A patch of goldenseal, spotted with red berries, stood guard near the spot. 'Seng-sign, some called it, for the way it marked where ginseng roots grew. Kate would have to come back and dig the roots before the ground froze for good.

"Have you need of another pair of hands?"

Kate peered around the tree. Magdalen Boothe, the captain's wife, held a basket of her own.

"I thank you kindly, Maggie, but we're getting on all right," Kate said. "It's fierce cold today."

"Then let me help." Magdalen plucked a half-opened burr from the ground and flipped it into Elizabeth's basket. "Run along, Betty. Susanna was on her way to speak to you about the weaving she's had in mind."

Elizabeth gathered up her skirts in her free hand and made for the footbridge. It did Kate good to see her run so. Elizabeth was only sixteen, lissome and bonny as the day, but she'd been too quiet with Benjamin gone. 'Twas a thing not to be healed with bloodroot and yarrow.

"I never was meaning for the season to get so far by me," Kate said. "'Twould be a good deal easier with no snow."

"You've been busy, with Benjamin away."

"Does your sweet lass ever speak of him?"

"Not often. She hates that she's hurt him, I think."

"It's a hard thing to care so much. And when caring means not showing it . . ."

"So we'll pray. It's all either of them would want." Magdalen knelt at the base of the tree, her blue petticoat and bronze chignon a striking contrast to the white snow and golden leaves. A handsome, goodhearted woman, and her daughter was the spitting image of her in both ways. Kate didn't wonder Susanna Boothe had caught Benjamin's eye.

"I daresay it's what the Lord would want too," Kate conceded. "You're a dear to help me with the gathering, Maggie. You've enough to be doing."

"Not enough to keep me from thinking of Rob," Magdalen said with a little laugh.

Kate felt a pang. All these years her Arthur had been gone,

and still she knew what it was to long fiercely for the home-coming of a good man. "Rob's brother will be here soon, aye?"

"Tomorrow. Rob told me before he left that Mitch will try to be here as often as he can."

"'Twill be good to see him again."

"Now, Kate. And you a good Covenanter."

"A mite of preaching does a body good, and it's precious little we've had of any kind." Kate brushed snow from her deerskin gloves. "Has Judge Pembrook left for the council?"

The captain's wife nodded past Kate's shoulder. "You might ask the judge himself."

Kate turned. Simon Pembrook stepped between a pair of oaks, his tall form nearly as sturdy as the chestnut tree. "I do wonder what he could be wanting, now."

The former magistrate doffed his hat when he reached her. His head nearly brushed the branch he stood beneath. "Kate. I've a need to speak to you."

Had everyone in Sunrising seen her come a-gathering? "I hear you're off to the council again."

"Leaving at noon, with a stop at the fort tomorrow before I go on." Pembrook Station bore his name, and Kate could well imagine he felt some duty to the stockade there. "I need that good salve you compounded for my knee."

"Let me see what I can do." Kate sighed inwardly. The gathering would have to wait yet again.

"I'm much obliged, Kate."

She felt wee as a mouse beside him, even when he bent his head to her. "It's no trouble, Mr. Pembrook."

"You might call me Simon, you know."

"I know." She'd not told him to use her Christian name. But then, most of the settlement did. And Pembrook was a good man, no longer an acting magistrate but still the nearest thing to it in Sunrising. "Come to the kitchen when you fetch your horse, and I'll have the salve waiting."

He nodded and strode toward the creek, making scarce

a sound on the damp leaf litter. Kate tossed a final nut into her basket. "I'd best get to the kitchen and make that salve."

"I'll finish here," Magdalen said. "Go on."

"I hate to be beholden."

"There's no shame in taking a helping hand. You can make Rob a chestnut pie when he gets home, if your conscience troubles you." Magdalen shooed her with one hand. "Folks aren't going to stop asking for your help."

"Lord love you, Maggie," Kate said, and meant it. "You're as stubborn as I am."

"Not by half. But I can learn if it means helping you. Now go on."

Leaving Magdalen beneath the chestnut tree, Kate hurried toward the footbridge, basket in hand. As she reached the fork in the path, where one trail led to the ordinary and the other led down the mountain, the thump of hooves met her ears.

She squinted at the place where trail met forest. A man was riding across the McGuiness Creek bridge into the settlement, leading a packhorse.

Kate quickened her pace. A traveler would need lodging, and the Dove & Olive would be the first place he'd look. What was a lone rider doing here with naught but a bedroll strapped to his packhorse?

She stopped as he drew closer. Mercy. That wasn't a bedroll, that was . . . a man?

A man in a bloodied hunting shirt, with a trailing edge of red silk hanging from his collar.

Sweet Jesus, help us, Kate prayed silently. Chestnut burrs rolled across the path. When had she dropped the basket?

The rider dismounted. "Are you Aunt Kate?"

"Yes," she said. "Yes. Is he—"

"He's alive, madam." Up close, the stranger was young, and might have been quite a bonny lad if he did not have such a scar and did not look so unspeakably weary. "The rest is up to us and the Almighty."

Nine

BENJAMIN WAS FALLING. A DEEP, ROCKY WELL, no light in it. Throbbing pain pulsed in his shoulder, down his arm. He jerked against it, but a weight pressed him to the hardness beneath him. Fire blazed through his shoulder. He groaned.

"There, now. Easy, lad."

A cold draft blew past him. A door closed. He opened his eyes, or tried to. One eye would not obey. Firelight leaped in the hearth, then disappeared behind the sweep of a dark skirt.

"He's awake. Praise be."

Aunt Kate's voice. A soothing warmth settled over his shoulder and arm. What was wrong with his arm?

"Harrod," he said.

"Mr. Armistead already told us," Kate said. "Keep still, lad. You're all right."

Voices drifted and swirled around him. Rane Armistead and Kate, both calm and measured. Elizabeth, timid and trying not to show it. Then another woman's voice. This one hurt somehow, though he didn't know why.

"I've brought enough stonecrop leaves for a fresh

poultice. And more boneset if you have need of it."

Susanna Boothe? The captain's daughter was here, seeing him like this? He tried valiantly to open his eyes again, glimpsed blue linsey and bronze-colored hair.

"Thank you kindly, lass," Kate said. "'Tis all I needed."

"I'll be going, then." Susanna spoke barely above a whisper.

"Bide awhile," Elizabeth said, pleading.

"He's got you and Aunt Kate to look after him. And I'm not—the two of us—things aren't the way they used to be, and I don't want . . ."

Susanna trailed off into silence. Didn't that just figure. Silence was about all she'd given him these last six months.

"Stay," he tried to say, but the word stuck to the roof of his mouth. The door shut, softly but firmly.

Lifting his head shot pain through his ribs. Heavy wrapping swaddled his right arm.

He was not falling. But he *had* fallen, he knew that for certain sure. Every bone in his body knew it.

"Don't try to move, lad," Kate said. "You're mighty banged up."

He clenched his teeth over another groan and settled back onto hard wood. Not a bed. A table. "Where—"

"You're in the great room," Elizabeth said. "At the ordinary. The last lodgers left at dawn."

"Old Sandy?" Benjamin managed.

Rane said, "Who is—"

"His rifle." Kate spoke to Benjamin again. "No sign of it yet, lad." Her fingers brushed a lock of his hair off his forehead. "Likely landed on a ledge, same as you."

The bruise near his eye throbbed. "I landed on a ledge?"

"Somebody pushed you over. Thank the Lord the ledge was there and Mr. Armistead went looking for you." Kate bent closer, her face blurring. "It's not just the way we'd like it, mayhap, but I'm that glad you're finally home."

Home. The world was slipping away again, taking the words with it. But that one stayed with him. For better or for worse, he was home.

Rane took the linen toweling Kate held out and wiped his hands, sweating as if he'd run a hard race. He passed the towel to Elizabeth, who twisted it into a hard knot and asked quietly, "Will he be all right?"

"Aye, in time." Rane ran his eye down Benjamin's still frame. Dislocated shoulder, fractured forearm, wrenched ankle, bruises everywhere. Not to mention cracked ribs and the crease wound above the elbow. "Your brother appears to take a good deal of killing, Miss Woodbridge."

"He's always been that way." A tired smile hovered at the edges of Elizabeth's mouth. She had a face made for smiling, if Rane was any judge, though she hadn't done much of it tonight.

"Let's move him real careful-like to a bed." Kate gathered up Benjamin's hunting shirt and scrip and the battered hat Rane had found lying on the trail, its cocked left side bent out of shape. "Then it's a hearty meal for you, Mr. Armistead. You look near to fall over."

Together Rane and Elizabeth carried Benjamin to Kate's bed in a curtained corner of the great room below the sleeping loft. Rane felt exhausted in every nerve, though the women had done most of the work.

He was no physician. His medical knowledge had been gleaned in snatches from the kindhearted Surgeon North of HMS *Solebay*. But Benjamin would pull through. That was all that mattered.

No. Not all that mattered. Harrod was on the ridge, and that was not a thing easily forgotten.

He followed Kate to the kitchen and ate a meal he did not taste. Harrod was on the ridge, and Rane was a stranger in a strange settlement, no place to go, nothing but his

saddlebags and the horse he had left at the rail—
Macy.

He sprang to his feet. He had never forgotten his horse.
Never. If Macy had stayed at the hitching rail all this time—

"Pardon me," he said to Kate's astonished look, and
dashed out of the kitchen.

Macy was not at the rail. Rane turned the other way and
stepped into the stable.

The gelding was in a stall near the door. He snorted a
greeting as Rane crossed to the stall.

"Hullo," a youthful voice said behind Rane. "You must
be Mr. Armistead."

Rane wheeled. A lanky boy of nine or ten stood in front
of the opposite bank of stalls, bits of straw in his tousled
shock of dark brown hair. The boy nodded toward the black
gelding and added, "'Tis a fine horse you've got, sir."

Rane leaned on the gate of the stall, willing his heart to
slow. Only a boy. Nothing to fear. "His name is Macy. And
what might yours be?"

"I'm Ayen. Ayen Boothe." The boy tossed a wayward
curl out of startlingly blue eyes. "I'm called after Ayen Ford,
the town where Ma and Pa used to live. Only I'm Ayen John,
not Ayen Ford." He came over and eyed Macy admiringly.
"Where'd you get him?"

"From a woman near the Waccamaw River."

"Where's that?"

"Bladen County. A long way from here." Rane laced his
fingers into Macy's mane. "The finest horse I ever had."

A Carolina marsh tacky, finer than the thoroughbreds
of his father's estate. Smaller, to be sure, but much more
surefooted. How things did change.

"And she just up and gave him to you?" Ayen regarded
him with a mix of skepticism and awe.

"Her husband won him at a game of cards." Rane slid
his fingers deeper, feeling the solid strength of the gelding's

muscled neck. "He named him for the founder of his hometown in New England, as I recall, a man of courage and independence. But Macy had been mistreated. His new owner died before Macy could be gentled, and the widow was glad to be rid of an animal for which she had no use."

"But he's such a beauty."

"He is now." The winning of Macy's trust had healed them both, had given Rane hope that someday he, too, might be strong again. "I'm indebted to you for your care of him."

Ayen shrugged. "I always look after the horses for folks when they stop at the ordinary. But Aunt Kate lets me keep my pony here too." He nodded toward the stall opposite Macy's. "A blue roan, see?"

"Widow McGuiness is your aunt? I thought she was Benjamin Woodbridge's aunt."

"She ain't anybody's aunt," Ayen said. "But everybody calls her that. She took on Benjamin's ma when they came here after his pa died, and then when Miz Woodbridge died, Benjamin and Elizabeth just naturally stayed on."

"I see." Rane turned Ayen's name over in his mind. "Ayen Boothe. Your father is the captain, then."

"When he ain't being a preacher, he is."

Benjamin had said something about Captain Boothe being jailed for preaching. "How long has he been a preacher?"

"Since forever," Ayen said. "Him and Uncle Mitchell both. Someday I'm gonna be a circuit rider same as them. Pa ain't a circuit rider n'more, but Uncle Mitchell is. He preaches now and again when Pa's gone."

"I see," Rane said again. His own uncle had once been an Anglican itinerant, but Rane could not conceive of the Reverend Doctor Ezekiel Warwick leading any sort of militia, let alone Patriot militia.

"You come with Benjamin, right?" Ayen said. "What happened to him? Susanna wouldn't tell me."

"Susanna?"

"My sister."

"If she wouldn't tell you, perhaps I ought not."

"Oh, it ain't that she don't want me to know," Ayen said. "It's just that she don't talk much about Benjamin. They used to be—" He made a face. "Well, you know. Anyhow. I guess he's banged up some."

"He'll recover. Widow McGuiness tended him well."

"You going to stay here long?"

"I don't know, Master Ayen."

"Well, if'n you do stay, you might should start calling her Aunt Kate." Ayen pointed to the corner near the door. "Your saddlebags are over yonder. Go ahead on in. I'll look after Macy."

Rane pushed away from the stall and hefted the saddlebags that held his prayer book and riding gloves, a change of linen, and the coat and waistcoat he'd shed when Davie's militia gave him a hunting shirt outside Charlotte. "Goodnight, then."

"'Night." Ayen flipped up a hand in a quick wave. Rane walked slowly out of the stable and gathered his hat and cloak from the great room. He checked the pistol at his hip and the letter tucked against his skin, ready to be rid of the ill-fitting hunting shirt with its rips and bloodstains.

Kate came out from behind the curtain around the bed, the red silk kerchief in her hand.

"How is he?" Rane said.

"Some better," Kate said with a weary smile. "Mighty fed up when he's awake enough to know what's happened." She lifted the kerchief. "Thought I'd wash this while he's sleeping."

"It seems important to him."

"'Twas his father's. A wedding gift. Benjamin found it in his ma's things after she went on to glory these three years past. Worn it ever since."

"He said his father was one of the men who opposed Governor Tryon."

"Aye. Killed in the fight at Alamance. But that's a long story." She studied him. "What of your own family, lad? You came alone."

"I lived with my uncle in Charlotte."

"No other kinfolk, then?"

"My father holds lands in Ireland. I was the youngest."

"A second son," Kate said knowingly.

Many a man had come to the Colonies in search of a fortune he could not expect as less than firstborn heir. Rane had not, though his sisters were both married to good advantage and his older brother would inherit the estate. But he said merely, "Yes."

Kate nodded. "You'd best get some sleep. You're plumb give out."

"Widow McGuiness, I've not come prepared to offer remuneration."

"Whisht, lad," Kate said. "You so much as mention money to me, and I'll give you a proper talking-to, I will." Her eyes welled with sudden tears. "You've more than paid me already as it is. And no more of this Widow McGuiness business. I'm Aunt Kate to all the settlement, and I reckon anybody who hauls another man clear up the mountain is sure enough one of our own."

One of our own. The vise constricting his lungs loosened a notch. "Aunt Kate, then."

"That's more like it. Now go on and lie down before you fall down." She ushered him out into the dogtrot, waved him through the door of the sleeping cabin, and walked back into the great room.

Ten

IT TOOK A FORTNIGHT FOR BENJAMIN TO GET back on his feet, getting about as best he could with a sling and a bad limp and bandaged ribs. It was far longer before he felt almost back to his old strength, annoyed with the sling's constant presence and the ache that lingered in his ankle and arm.

By the time Mitchell Boothe, the captain's circuit-riding brother, came to the settlement to preach Sunday meeting, Benjamin was hungry for something to take his mind off the slow healing.

He went out into the dogtrot, missing the familiar heft of Old Sandy. Not that he could fire his rifle even if he had it. He could not draw his bow, could not paddle his trapping canoe, could not even split firewood for Kate. He had done what he could to help with last week's butchering of the hogs that ranged in the forest, but it had been hard going with only his left hand.

Still, they had meat for the winter now. And all seemed peaceful in the settlement; no sign of the trouble he'd feared after meeting Harrod on the trail. If he could do nothing else, he should at least be grateful for that.

Rane Armistead came up the porch steps, a stray piece of straw on his cloak suggesting he'd been in the stable with Ayen. The oversized hunting shirt had disappeared weeks ago, replaced by a well-cut coat and waistcoat that must have been stored in his saddlebags. "Shall we go?"

"Where's Aunt Kate?"

"Coming later. She and your sister had food to prepare."

The settlement was quiet as they crossed it, more than the usual Sunday morning hush. The wives of Captain Boothe's scouts managed their husbands' duties well, but a few buildings had the blank-eyed look of being too long deserted. No hammering had sounded from the smithy in Benjamin's weeks at home. Few travelers passed to visit the trading post.

Even the meetinghouse was still mostly empty, though Mitchell Boothe was already at the front. Benjamin led the way to a bench at the back near the wall, the ache in his ankle more piercing than he'd hoped.

Mitchell set his Bible down and came over, a lock of dark hair flipping over his forehead much as Ayen's did. "Woodbridge. Good to see you're up and kicking." He offered his hand to Rane. "And you must be Armistead. Mitchell Boothe. Glad to have you."

A flicker of discomfort crossed Rane's face, like the fleet shadow of a low-flying hawk. "I'm merely here for Woodbridge's sake."

"Sure. Glad to have you anyway." Mitchell turned as Alec Perry's wife and children filed into the meetinghouse. "Be speaking with you later, I reckon."

Benjamin gave him a nod. Mitchell crossed the space to the front with long, lanky strides and took up his Bible.

"Merely here for my sake?" Benjamin repeated. He'd meant to warn Rane of how strongly dissenter Sunrising was, but Harrod and Taggart had put a stop to that.

"Kate said you wished to see Mitchell Boothe. I offered my assistance."

"You didn't know it was a preaching meeting?"

"Not of this variety. My uncle in Charlotte was a minister of the Church. An itinerant under the Society for the Propagation of the Gospel."

An uncomfortable suspicion rankled Benjamin's mind. "Did he ride the frontier?"

"Throughout both Carolinas."

"Your uncle was *Ezekiel Warwick*?"

That drew Rane's head around. "He came here?"

"No, but close enough. The things he said—beggin' your pardon, Armistead, you're a guest. But he was everything I hate about Anglicans." And a Tory, but that was part and parcel with the rest.

"Then it's true that the dissenters ill-used him."

"I'm a dissenter, and I never did aught to harm him."

"I'm a churchman, and I never did aught to harm you."

That lingered between them. Then Benjamin shook his head. "No, I'm beholden to you for a lot of things. Not least of which is hauling me up the ridge."

"You'd have done the same for me." Rane turned toward the front of the meetinghouse. "And, to be quite fair, you attempted to warn me of the feeling in Sunrising."

Mitchell laid his Bible on the hand-carved pulpit. The benches had filled with settlement folk and a few settlers from farther afield.

"You're not obliged to stay," Benjamin said quietly.

Rane did not answer.

"I see. You told Aunt Kate you would."

Still no answer, which was answer enough. Benjamin rested his shoulder against the wall. Did he know this man at all, really? This quiet outsider who had studied law and was the nephew of a Tory clergyman and, if Harrod was to be believed, had served in the Royal Navy?

But they had been under fire together. That was not a thing to be forgotten.

"Well, you're here now," he said. "Mayhap you'll find we're a different lot than you expected."

Mitchell prayed, and Benjamin stood for the singing. The swell of voices around him, ringing off the wood of the rafters and walls, salved something inside of him.

> Shall we go on to sin
> Because thy grace abounds,
> Or crucify the Lord again
> And open all his wounds?

It was one of his favorites by Isaac Watts; he had it written on the flyleaf of his New Testament. The book was likely still in his scrip or in a saddlebag somewhere. Kate's family Bible had served in its stead while he recovered, but he'd not felt much like reading. He regretted that now.

> Forbid it, mighty God,
> Nor let it e'er be said
> That we whose sins are crucified
> Should raise them from the dead.

His strength and his ankle both failed him at the same time. He lowered himself to the bench as the singing went on around him. When it ended, Mitchell didn't so much as glance at the worn Bible in his hand. "'For in him dwelleth all the fulness of the Godhead bodily. And ye are complete in him, which is the head of all principality and power.'"

He thumped the Bible with an open hand. "Anybody want to tell me what *complete* means?"

Ayen's hand shot up. "Done."

"That's right. It's done. Nothing more for God's children to do. Christ did it all, amen?"

Benjamin glanced at Rane. The man's face was unreadable, eyes fixed forward. Benjamin wondered what tales he'd heard from his uncle.

The door creaked. Benjamin turned to look, expecting Kate and Elizabeth.

Two Cherokee men stood in the doorway, scanning the gathering. The younger man beckoned to Benjamin.

Rane tensed. Benjamin leaned toward him. "They're friends. Selagisqua and Walks-in-Winter." They'd agreed long ago that Benjamin should stop attempting the Cherokee pronunciation of the older man's name.

He could tell Rane was trying to avoid gaping at the braves' intricate gunpowder tattoos and the silver wire wound around the split outer edges of Selagisqua's ears. Benjamin rose and slipped outside with the two men, hating how the shuffle of his limp was loud in the meetinghouse.

"*Osiyo*," he said when Selagisqua had closed the door. "Is there trouble?"

"Not yet, but soon." Walks-in-Winter lifted two pieces of a broken rifle. "This is yours, *oginalii*. We found it down on the rocks. You were not with it."

"I was at first. But a friend found me." Benjamin took both pieces awkwardly with his left hand. The stock had been cracked clean through at the wrist, the narrow place where it met the barrel. That would take mending.

"You fell from the trail?" Selagisqua asked.

"I was pushed. Some king's men."

"We've seen more on the mountain. Many more." Selagisqua paused. "Come to the water. We must speak."

Something was gravely wrong if Selagisqua feared to be overheard. Benjamin set the broken rifle beside the door and fell into step between the two Cherokees, men who might have been his enemies if they had not shown themselves friends long ago.

Button Creek sparkled in the sun, ice rimming its banks. Walks-in-Winter moved a few paces away as if to keep watch. Selagisqua stopped in the meager shelter of bare willows and alders, the silver and copper ornaments at his neck and arms and ears sparkling like the water. "We have been cast out from the council."

A coldness hardened in Benjamin's gut, as if the ice of the river had congealed there. "Who's the British agent this time? Alexander Cameron from down south?"

"I do not know. We are not told."

Once, they would not have had to be told. "You're not even allowed in your town anymore."

"Others are with us."

There was no emotion in Selagisqua's voice. But this loss of honor must trouble him. How riled must the Indians be to cast out two of their own? And Walks-in-Winter was an old man, deserving of honor at the council fires.

"You're welcome here as long as I have any say in it."

"I know, and I thank you, oginalii. But we would bring danger. More than comes already."

Walks-in-Winter stilled, as he so often had on the hunt. "Someone comes."

Benjamin heard nothing. But he knew better than to doubt Walks-in-Winter, the old hunter's senses honed far keener than Benjamin's own.

"I go see." Walks-in-Winter turned, his braided scalp lock brushing the tips of the arrows in his quiver. He still moved like a young man, silent as when he'd taught Benjamin to track.

"My uncle will go back to the village," Selagisqua said when Walks-in-Winter had moved beyond hearing. "He wants to see who stirred up the People against those who were our friends. But the Beloved Men are angry with him. He does not come to the dances. He does not go to water to wash away his sins. You have said too much to him."

"I've said the same to you. Jesus is the only one who can wash away sins. Walks-in-Winter knows that now. If everybody did, there'd be a lot less war."

Walks-in-Winter reappeared as if hearing his name. "Men

come. Many men, up the mountain. Some with red coats."

"I'll warn folks at the meetinghouse," Benjamin said. "You'd best go before you're seen here. You've trouble enough already."

Selagisqua sprinted down the bank and across the creek, lithe as the muskrat for which he was named. Walks-in-Winter followed. Benjamin wheeled as quickly as his ankle would allow and started toward the meetinghouse.

Then he smelled the smoke.

Not the good honest smoke of the settlement's chimneys. The tarry, acrid stench of burning pitch.

Nolan Taggart and two other men rounded the corner of the meetinghouse, carrying torches.

And leading them, Malcolm Harrod.

Nolan Taggart stopped beside Harrod, his features pinching in surprise before he could hide it. "Woodbridge."

"Aye. Next time pick a higher cliff."

Taggart's gaze drifted to Benjamin's sling. He didn't need a higher cliff. Benjamin was helpless enough already, and Taggart knew it.

"This is the rebel we met on the trail?" Harrod said.

"Aye. Want I should finish things proper this time?"

"You'll only raise the alarm." Harrod's sword was suddenly out of its sheath. "Dare I assume Rane Armistead is in the settlement as well?"

"Don't you wish you knew."

"Mind your tongue, rebel. I'd as soon run you through as look at you."

"I can say the same for you."

The flame of Taggart's torch flickered in the breeze. Benjamin measured the distance from the corner of his eye, still keeping his focus on Harrod. The British burned churches; Benjamin had heard tell of such things. And Harrod would not care how many women and children were inside.

Harrod studied him a long moment. "Never you mind.

If Armistead is here, I'll know it soon enough." He motioned to Taggart. "Proceed."

Benjamin lunged for the torch. Harrod backhanded him with the hilt of the sword. Benjamin staggered and landed on his injured arm. The bright burst of pain blended with the bright flash of the torch.

When the world cleared, flames flared along broad smears of pitch on the logs of the meetinghouse. Harrod and his men were gone.

Benjamin got to his feet, caught up the broken rifle, and opened the meetinghouse door. He had to force himself to speak calmly. "Everybody. Go out the back door, quick and quiet as you can."

Mitchell shut his Bible. Mothers gathered their children and streamed toward the far end of the room. They had all lived through such interruptions many a time.

But they did not know who was behind this one.

On either side of the front door, the oiled paper that served for windows flared up and fell away. Flames shot upward past the empty casements. A child screamed.

"Young 'uns out first," Mitchell said swiftly. "Able-bodied folks meet by the creek."

Outside, a sharp drumbeat of hoofbeats rattled the bridge over McGuiness Creek. Those were likely the king's men Walks-in-Winter had seen coming up the mountain.

Benjamin motioned Rane toward the back door. "Keep your face hidden," he shouted over the roar of the flames. "Harrod's out there."

Rane flipped up the collar of his cloak and caught up his hat from the bench. Smoke rolled through the building as the front door fell with a crash. Mitchell slid his Bible into his coat and waved Benjamin and Rane out ahead of him.

"Elizabeth and Aunt Kate are still at the ordinary," Benjamin said to Rane. "Help Ayen hide the horses if you can. And stay out of sight."

Rane choked back a racking cough. "Woodbridge, you can't possibly—"

Benjamin ducked around the corner of the burning meetinghouse, the heat sticking his shirt to his back. His ankle slowed him, but he paid it no mind.

The path along the creek was bedlam. Kate and Elizabeth couldn't fail to hear the commotion even at the ordinary. Settlers with buckets dodged clusters of mounted men and Tory foot militia. Men in red wool or faded homespun dotted the straightest path to the inn, a back-alley route past Alec Perry's house.

If only Alec were here—Alec and a few dozen more of Captain Boothe's best men.

Across from the meetinghouse, the door of Captain Boothe's cabin hung crooked on its wooden pegs. Benjamin hesitated. If Susanna needed help . . .

But he had seen Susanna and her mother in the mass of meeting-goers. Kate and Elizabeth had no one near at hand. They had been alone in the great room, using its wide hearth to cook what they could not fit over the kitchen fire.

Benjamin crossed the path and limped behind the stable, took the back steps into the dogtrot and burst into the great room of the inn. The click of a gun's hammer greeted him.

"Hold your fire, Aunt Kate." He shut the door. "I've had enough close calls as it is."

"Mercy, lad, you gave us a start." Kate lowered the ancient fowling piece she held, a relic of her husband's that she usually kept in the kitchen. "Where's Mr. Armistead?"

"Helping Ayen hide the horses, if he's doing as I said."

"Can we make it to the fort?"

"We're cut off." The fort at Pembrook Station was easily a day's ride away, and the Tories would not leave the route unguarded. And Elizabeth had dreaded the fort ever since the Cherokee War, when fever had taken Ma from among the crowded settlers. "Best thing we can do now is fort up right here. Help me with this bench, Mouse."

Elizabeth helped him flip one of the long benches onto its side across the door to the dogtrot. Another bench went across the back door, the one that led to the kitchen yard.

"It won't slow them much, but it might give us a little warning," Benjamin said. "Is that thing loaded, Aunt Kate?"

"Aye, that it is. But—"

"Give it to me." Benjamin dropped to a knee and ran the fowling piece through one of the rifle slits that lined the great room. He braced the stock as best he could against his right shoulder and reached for the trigger with his left hand. It would be a miracle if he felled any Tory in such a state, but he had to try.

"Benjamin—"

He thumbed the hammer and squeezed the trigger.

The kick of the gun blasted through his shoulder and knocked him backward. His eyes watered. He breathed hard to keep from crying out.

Kate bent over him. "I thought you'd put that shoulder right back out of joint."

"Did I?" he said through clenched teeth.

She felt of it, quick and gentle. "No. Just thumped it again but good."

"You'll have to load for me." He pulled the fowler free of the rifle slit.

Boots thumped in the dogtrot. The bench against the door tumbled over with a thud as the door crashed open.

Benjamin could not get to his feet as fast as he wanted to. Not that it mattered. Men filled the great room, more than he could fight off if he'd had two good arms and a dozen loaded weapons.

Malcolm Harrod led them, sword in hand, a smear of pitch on one cuff the only sign that he had just set fire to a dissenter meetinghouse. "You again," he said. "For a man with your injuries, you certainly made good time."

Benjamin stepped in front of Elizabeth. "These women are under my protection."

"They are under little threat. 'Tis the building I require."

"The building is under my protection too."

"Not any longer." Harrod motioned with the sword. "Gregory. Secure this man and escort the women out whilst I oversee our preparations."

A ginger-haired man in a scarlet uniform, epaulet on his right shoulder, stepped out of the mass of men. Benjamin felt as if he'd been kneed in the gut.

The first time he'd seen this Tory officer, the man had been facing an angry Patriot captain. The last time Benjamin had seen this Tory officer, the man had been hiding behind a hickory, about to go in search of Harrod. A search that had been Benjamin's idea.

Harrod sheathed the sword and turned away. Benjamin started to lift the fowler, unloaded though it was.

James Arnold Gregory grabbed him by his sling and pushed him against the wall. "They'll kill us both, and your women will have no one."

His voice was nearly too low to be heard over the racket of boots and voices. But it held a trace of something that was not British, something almost a brogue.

Kate tapped his arm. She had no idea this man was supposed to be on their side. "And who might you be, sir?"

"Lieutenant James Arnold Gregory, of His Majesty's Second Associated Regiment." He said it *leftenant*, his London accent clipping the word to bits. The trace of brogue was gone.

Benjamin eyed his uniform with its red coat and olive facings, the same colors Ferguson's American Volunteers had worn at Kings Mountain. Whatever the Second Associated might be, at least it was not the British army proper.

"Take what you can and go to the kitchen," Gregory said to Kate. "I'll see the men do not trouble you."

Anger frissoned through Benjamin, hot and quick like

the sparks of a priming pan. He had thought he'd laid that anger to rest when Patrick Ferguson fell on Kings Mountain. He had been wrong. "Gregory, this is—"

"This is *war*." Gregory cut him a warning glare. Eyes the color of moss and the hardness of iron. More men filed into the great room. "Get out while you've the chance."

The injustice stung as deep as the nagging pain in his arm and ankle. The Tories were taking over his settlement, his very home, and nary a thing could he do. Even with an ally on the other side.

All this time he'd been looking for a fight . . .

He held the door open with his elbow and escorted a thin-lipped Kate and a pale Elizabeth across the open space to the kitchen.

The fight had found him. And he could not fight back.

Eleven

THE FIRE WAS STILL RAGING WHEN MOUNTED men rode through, scattering the settlers. Rane kept his face turned away, though he longed to speak out. Would the king's men never tire of taking what did not belong to them?

The thought made him angry, angry enough to ignore the searing in his lungs and the ache seizing his back. He stubbornly emptied his last bucket before he let Mitchell Boothe push him to safety against the nearby smithy.

He tried to speak, choked on the smoke, tasted sweat. "Isn't there anything—"

Mitchell Boothe shook his head. "Unless God sends rain, it's all over."

His voice was hoarse, whether from the smoke or his sermon, Rane didn't know. Or perhaps it was emotion. Ayen Boothe stood beside his uncle, his young face reddened by the fire's glow. Rane gripped the empty bucket and felt the answering fire of grief and anger for people who were still strangers.

But there could be no strangers at a time like this. He thought of what Uncle Warwick would say if he knew Rane had tried to save a Baptist meetinghouse, and Rane decided he did not care. Not today.

"Obliged for the help," Mitchell said, offering his hand.

"'Twas only right." Rane didn't realize they both had blisters until Mitchell gripped his hand.

"Sorry." Mitchell gave a quick, tired smile. "I've got to look after Maggie and Susanna. You'd best help Ayen hide the horses. Hide Benjamin's canoe while you're at it."

Ayen cast a final wide-eyed glance at the fire, then waved for Rane to follow. They slipped behind the smithy and between cabins until they neared the inn.

Loyalist mounts still waited in the path outside the ordinary, a sign that the stable had not yet been disturbed. Rane held back a cough as he stepped inside the long, low building. Smoke tinged the air even here.

"There are caves all over these mountains," Ayen said. "Grab Macy and Sassafras. I'll get the others. The Tories won't bother with my pony, and Judge Pembrook's overmountain with his horse."

Rane swiftly saddled and bridled Macy and Sassafras. Ayen did the same with Kate's mare and Mitchell's gelding. The yard outside was still empty. Rane followed Ayen to the edge of the woods, past the springhouse, and across Mc-Guiness Creek. A birchbark canoe was drawn up high on the bank near the springhouse.

Ayen stopped at a hollow formed by an overhanging ledge and vine-covered rocks on each side. "Don't fret none about Macy. I'll check on him every day."

Benjamin's mare didn't seem to mind the cave. Perhaps she had been hidden here before. Macy balked a bit before evidently deciding that if the hollow was safe for the others, it was safe for him. Rane helped Ayen pull the tack from all four horses and pile it at the back of the space. A sack of oats already lay in a dry corner.

"We hide horses here when there's Indian trouble," Ayen said. "Ain't had much of that here lately. A good thing—

it's a far piece to the fort, halfway between here and the next sizable settlement. Pembrook Station, it's called, on account of Judge Pembrook's peace talks with the Indians. We forted up there during the Cherokee War, when Benjamin's friends warned us there was trouble coming."

"Were those the Indians who came to the meetinghouse today?"

"Aye. Walks-in-Winter and Selagisqua."

"They looked to be father and son."

"Uncle and nephew. A Cherokee young 'un belongs to his ma's clan, so any brother of hers is like the young 'un's pa. More than his real pa, sometimes." Ayen heaved a fallen limb across the cave's opening. "We must've gone to the fort five or six times. Benjamin's ma died the last time we were there. But mostly we just forted up at the Dove & Olive. I was naught but a wee lad when all of that happened."

Rane led the way back across McGuiness Creek and helped Ayen drag Benjamin's canoe deep into the undergrowth behind the springhouse, then paused to survey their surroundings. With the forest behind them, the inn was ahead and to the left. To the right, men ranged along the fork in the trail, near the place where McGuiness Creek ran under a sturdy log bridge before joining Button Creek.

"We'll go to the kitchen first," Rane said, trusting that the king's men would be more likely to enter the larger rooms if they were in search of lodging or plunder. "It will keep us off the main paths a bit longer."

Ayen followed him across the stable yard. Just as they reached the kitchen, a handful of men came out of the great room and thumped down the porch steps. Malcolm Harrod was at their head.

Rane halted behind the corner of the kitchen building, the breath leaving his lungs. *O Lord, arise, help us, and deliver us, for thy Name's sake.*

The officer behind Harrod glanced over. He seemed

familiar, though the distance was too great to be sure. Had Rane seen him before?

The group of Loyalists walked on before Rane found an answer to that. Or to what he would do about Harrod. He checked in all directions and opened the kitchen door.

A mighty grip descended on his shoulder and slammed him into the wall. Reaching for his pistol, he turned to see Benjamin Woodbridge grimacing and holding his bandaged arm against his ribs.

"Armistead." Benjamin stepped back, catching himself on the worktable in the center of the kitchen. His face creased, no doubt from the pain of his ankle failing him. "I didn't know it was you."

Rane straightened his coat over his pistol. A heaping basket of housewares and bedding sat beside the worktable. Benjamin's broken rifle lay across the table's worn surface. "What's happened?"

Kate gave him a too-bright smile. "I asked the good Lord to fill the place up, and I expect that's just what he did."

"I don't reckon the good Lord had anything to do with this," Benjamin muttered.

Kate ignored him. "Ayen, your ma and sister are at Elsie McBraden's place. They stopped here looking for you."

Ayen frowned. "At Miz McBraden's? But why?"

"The Tories must've figured a rebel captain's house would make the best headquarters," Benjamin said bluntly.

"They turned Ma and Susanna *out*?" Ayen doubled his fists. "If'n I'd just been there—"

"Not a precious thing you could do, lad." Kate said it to Ayen, but Rane fancied she was saying it to Benjamin too. "Not a thing any of us could do. At least they were allowed to gather a few of their things."

"What about Uncle Mitchell?" Ayen demanded. "Where'll he stay?"

"He can look out for himself," Benjamin said.

"If Elsie doesn't have room for you, lad, you can come back here," Kate said. "There's room in the stable loft."

Ayen looked fierce. "I ain't takin' care of no Tory horses."

"Come now," Kate said. "We've still a call to be loving our enemies."

Benjamin opened his mouth and shut it again.

"I know how it is, Ayen," Rane said. "But surely the horses can't help it if they're owned by Loyalists."

Ayen looked at him sideways. "Did you ever have to do a thing like that?"

"Yes. And more so."

He felt Benjamin's eyes on him. But he refused to turn and look.

Ayen considered a moment longer, then nodded soberly. "All right. I'll come back tomorrow, Aunt Kate."

He slipped out the door. Benjamin nudged it shut.

"Is this why your friends warned you?" Rane asked.

"They saw men on the mountain. And they've been kicked out of their village for wanting peace." Benjamin sat down and bent over the broken rifle. "I've known them for years. They found me trying to tangle with a bear with an empty gun, and after that Walks-in-Winter started teaching me to hunt and track. No one knew at first if we could trust them; there's been trickery enough on both sides. But they warned us of several raids, and they were right."

"Ayen said you took refuge at Pembrook Station."

"When we had time. Sometimes we didn't. Like now." Benjamin measured a scrap of hickory against the holes he was boring in the rifle stock. "When you and I left camp, Captain Boothe said to send word if there was Indian trouble. Not much hope of that while the Tories are here."

"I saw Harrod as I came back from the woods. I don't think he saw me. But if he's looking for me . . ."

Then Rane had led Harrod here, to these good settlers who had carved out a haven in these hills. If Sunrising was not safe, nowhere in the Carolinas was safe.

"I don't think it's you he's after," Benjamin said. "He asked, sure. But if he has so many men, he planned this long before you came here."

"Still. I should leave."

Elizabeth spun from the hearth, where she had been rattling chestnuts in a skillet as if the familiar action would restore order to her world. "But where would you go?"

"It matters little." He tried to mean it. "What matters more is that I go before I endanger you further."

"You'll do no such thing," Kate said. "You're better off here, with the lot of us to be looking after you."

"But if he finds you've aided me—"

Benjamin turned on him almost savagely. "You think it doesn't matter that you fought for our meetinghouse and hid our horses and saved my life out there on the mountain? You think we wouldn't face Harrod if we had to?"

"You've no idea what you're speaking of."

"Maybe we don't," Kate said gently. "But when Captain Boothe first came, he had the governor's men hard on his heels. Can it be so much worse than that?"

"I'm not fit to be the judge of that, Widow McGuiness."

"Aunt Kate," she reminded. She sat down by the fire and took up her mending, as if the matter were settled.

He could not call her that. Not if he had to walk away. "I cannot tell you whether it's worth the risk."

"Whether what's worth the risk?" she prodded.

"I know, Armistead," Benjamin said. "Harrod told me, that night on the trail."

"Told you what?"

"Told me the thing you're trying to get out of your mouth right now."

"That I was in the Navy."

Benjamin nodded. Rane felt an absurd sense of betrayal, as if Harrod had taken even Rane's secrets from him. But in a way, perhaps, it was a relief.

"The *Navy*?" Elizabeth said, shaking the skillet again.

Rane lowered himself to the bench across from Benjamin and rubbed a hand across his eyes. The scar on his temple was rough under his fingertips. "It was not by choice. There was a press gang . . ."

Ale and seawater on the tavern floor, the thump of boots, the protest that he was not a seaman. Then the betrayal and the ropes and the blow to the head. He could not speak of that.

"I reckoned as much, though how you'd be mistaken for a seaman is beyond me," Benjamin said. "You said you were studying law."

"Law?" Kate tilted her head. "Judge Pembrook would be pleased to speak to you when he gets back from the Indian council. It's precious few lawyers he meets in these parts."

"All the law in the Empire does not avail against a British press gang."

"You poor lad," Kate said. "Do your kinfolk know?"

"I wrote at the first opportunity, though it was a year and more before their reply reached me at my uncle's house. There was little they could do."

"Harrod tried to say you were still serving," Benjamin said. "Ain't no way a Navy man ends up in the Carolina backcountry while he's still on the rolls."

Rane looked at the rifle. Benjamin was shaping hickory pins to join the pieces of broken stock. If only other things could be mended so easily.

"It was the fleet Lord Cornwallis brought to North Carolina four years ago. I served aboard HMS *Solebay*. When we anchored off Cape Fear, I slipped overboard and swam ashore. Harrod was aboard at the time."

Benjamin tested a peg in a hole, shaved off another curl of hickory. The motion was hampered by the way he could not move his right arm above the wrist. "Seems a powerful lot of trouble for Harrod to take over one man."

Trust for trust. Reaching through the neck slit hidden by his cravat, Rane withdrew the oilcloth packet and laid it on the table next to the rifle.

Benjamin cast him a swift glance. Rane nodded.

The paper crackled as Benjamin opened the pouch and pulled out the single sheet. He stiffened. "This is to Patrick Ferguson."

"Yes. Look at the signature."

Benjamin flipped the page over. "Harrod."

"I saw it aboard ship. There were things in it he would not want known. Perhaps you'll say 'twas thievery, but I thought only that it might help me escape."

Kate said softly, "I begin to see what's fretting you."

"Harrod found out you'd taken it?" Benjamin said.

"He must have. I nearly destroyed it when I realized the danger. But he would never know it was gone, and I would lose any power of threatening him."

Elizabeth tipped the roasted chestnuts onto a cloth and wrapped them up to steam in their skins. "What will happen if . . . if he catches you?"

"You know what happens to deserters?" he said quietly.

"Yes," she said in a small voice.

"That is your answer, Miss Woodbridge." The crime was a capital felony, according to Blackstone.

His chest clenched. He should never have spoken. Had the illusion of home so addled him?

If it had, he could not find it in him to be sorry. Only afraid the illusion might vanish like the steam of the chestnuts.

"We'll take it on together," Benjamin said. "Won't be the first hard thing, and I warrant not the last."

Rane nodded toward the letter. "Read it and see."

Benjamin flattened the paper against the table with his left hand and bent over it, his shadow flickering in the light of the hearth. Rane did not read with him. He had no need to; he could repeat the letter by heart. He watched Benjamin's face instead, knowing from its tightening when Benjamin reached the most telling phrases.

No man of the Backwater Clans is to be trusted, no matter his Loyalty. They are a Wretched lot, an inferior Breed, suited only to Strategies that place the regular Troops too much at Risk . . .

All England seems to trust in the notion of partisan Militia— but strongly as I disagree in that Particular, I heartily concur with you that these Rebels are to be tamed only by Fire and Sword . . .

"If this got out, the Tories would hate him as much as we do," Benjamin said.

Kate leaned across the table. "What? Why should they?"

"Because he as much as says the backwater Tories are good only for stopping bullets before they get to the king's real soldiers. If he feels that way about the Tories, you can guess how he feels about us." Benjamin paused with his finger halfway down the page. "This says he first held rank in Ireland. But he was a civilian under Governor Tryon."

"There was an uprising in Ireland that nearly cost him his commission," Rane answered. "You'll see on the second page that he sacrificed the men under him to keep from a court-martial. He went to great trouble to conceal his early career. Most think his appointment as major is his first commission, won by his service to Tryon."

"No wonder he's after you." Benjamin flipped the page over and scanned the rest of the letter. "You could ruin the name he's made for himself."

"And no wonder he didn't take kindly to uprisings on this side of the sea," Kate said.

"In Ireland, he responded with 'excessive force,' to use his words," Rane said. "If the British thought it excessive enough for a court-martial, I shudder to think what he did."

"The same thing he'll do here, given half the chance." Benjamin slid the letter back into the pouch and handed it to Rane. "It's up to us to see that he doesn't."

Twelve

MALCOLM HARROD WALKED AROUND THE charred ruins of the rebel meetinghouse, the cold wind seeping under his cloak. Patrick Ferguson had said the Colonies were to be tamed only by fire and sword. He would approve, Harrod thought.

Behind him, Nolan Taggart cleared his throat. "Begging your pardon, sir, but don't you think we could have quartered a good deal of men here?"

"Hope is a powerful thing, Sergeant. A blow to that is a killing blow indeed."

The new lieutenant stopped beside Taggart, scanning the blackened timbers. "You consider this meetinghouse the hope of the settlement?"

Harrod glanced at the young russet-haired officer. James Arnold Gregory still had a reluctant way about him, but he was the only officer at Harrod's disposal while the two other regimental lieutenants were recruiting volunteers throughout the hill country.

"These are dyed-in-the-wool dissenters," Harrod said. "This meetinghouse was the settlement's heart and soul."

"I expect there's room enough for most of the men at

the ordinary," Taggart said doubtfully. "Do you mean to go on searching for that fellow you thought was on the trail the first time you came here? What was his name—Armistead?"

James Arnold Gregory looked up as if startled. Harrod said, "Is something amiss, Lieutenant?"

"No, sir."

"Sergeant Taggart, that is a private matter. Dismissed."

Taggart saluted and strode away. Lieutenant Gregory moved to follow him.

"Remain, if you please, Lieutenant."

Gregory halted and turned to face Harrod.

"A portion of this wood is salvageable." Harrod pointed to a trio of beams that lay across one another like a child's playthings, the ends darkened by fire. "I require a winch to be made. Sturdy enough to raise a keg of powder."

"A few of the men have worked as carpenters, sir."

"Excellent. Have it ready by tomorrow night."

"Yes, sir." Gregory studied the beams. Was he making plans for construction or pondering the winch's purpose?

The ring of hammer on metal clanged from the nearby smithy. Two recruits were already at work repairing weapons that had been damaged on the march northward—or had been in ill repair to begin with. More men were at the trading post, requisitioning supplies. Others had seized the mill on one of the creeks, far upstream outside the settlement.

Harrod spoke over the hammer blows. "Accompany me to headquarters, Lieutenant."

"Yes, sir."

Gregory fell into step behind Harrod. Snow crunched beneath Harrod's boots. It was a boon that the rivers had not yet frozen. Harrod suspected they ran too fast in these hills.

He stepped into Boothe's erstwhile dwelling and shut the door behind Gregory. "Robert Boothe has a daughter."

"Yes, sir." If Gregory was surprised, he did not show it.

"It is imperative that I know when Boothe intends to

return and how many men he will have with him when he does." It was poetic, Harrod thought, to discuss such things whilst headquartered in the man's own cabin.

Gregory appeared far more uncomfortable than he had at the mention of building a winch. "With all due respect, sir, I find his daughter an unlikely source."

"On the contrary. A comely young woman whose suitors are all playing at war—a very likely source indeed."

"Sir, are you suggesting—"

"I am more than suggesting it, Lieutenant. Have one of your men see to it at once."

"Yes, sir."

Gregory wanted to say something else. It was plain on his face. Harrod gave him a moment to change his mind, then said, "Have you an objection, Lieutenant?"

"No, sir. No objection. I was merely wondering if it might be best for me to see to it myself."

Harrod studied him critically. The man was in his middle twenties, an age Boothe's daughter might find attractive. Lean and agile, he must have cut a fine figure in London ballrooms.

"Very well," Harrod said. "I entrust the task to you."

"Thank you, sir."

"Go find your carpenters."

Gregory saluted and went out. But not before Harrod glimpsed a bead of perspiration sliding down his temple.

Harrod frowned. It was a cold day. Lieutenant James Arnold Gregory would bear watching.

Jem stepped out of Captain Boothe's cabin, the cold air bracing. He turned toward the inn and quickened his pace.

At last he could breathe again. Until he thought of what he had just agreed to do.

You are not Jem Flannery, he told himself sternly. You are Lieutenant James Arnold Gregory. You are accustomed to the intrigues of war.

"Psst. Lieutenant."

Jem whirled, one hand on his sword. "Who's there?"

A grimy-looking man with a grizzled beard stepped out of the pines, favoring one leg. "I'm Jonas. Hank Jonas. I believe we've got a mutual friend, name of Boothe."

Jem checked in both directions and stepped into the shadow of the pines. "Are you—"

"The fellow you was meant to meet six weeks ago and didn't? That'd be about right."

"How did you get here?"

"Came into town with Mitchell Boothe, the preacher. Been doin' it for nigh on to ten years and don't aim on stopping." The man waved Jem deeper into the shelter of the trees. "Never mind how I got here. I seen how *you* did."

"You were watching?"

"Of course I was. That sentry by Harrod's camp came up on you out of nowhere."

"I swear to you, I had no intention of joining his men. It was a case of do or die. You must believe me."

"I seen enough to get the general notion. I had an almighty craving to see what you'd do once you got roped in where you didn't aim to be. And I'm thinking you'll do Captain Boothe the most good right spang where you are."

"You mean be a—" Jem stopped short, as if even saying the word might be enough to hang him.

"The way I see it, it's a spy or a parole breaker, what with the deal you made Captain Boothe."

Jem fidgeted with the haft of his sword. A bit of the sharkskin grip, bound to the haft with a spiral of wire, was loose beneath his fingers. "Woodbridge knows I'm here."

"Get word to him, then, if'n you can. But you'll be seeing me from time to time."

Jem savagely snapped the torn sharkskin free.

"Think of it this way," Hank said. "A month ago you was a Tory, plain and simple. Ain't that much trouble to do it again, now is it?"

Was he a Tory still? Or was he a rebel now? He had no answer for that. "I want your word I'll be free."

"I can't speak for the captain, but if that's the bargain he made you, he'll keep it."

"Very well. But only until I've a chance to get away."

"Seems reasonable. What've you got to tell me?"

Jem told him. Harrod's recruits, the fire at the meeting-house, the search for Captain Boothe. Hank grunted when Jem reached that point. "He's after the captain, you say."

"Harrod speaks little of his plans. I rarely know what's to be done until I'm ordered to do it. Today he ordered me to build a winch that could raise a powder keg. But he gave no explanation."

"A winch for a powder keg." Hank scratched his beard. "I'll pass that along."

"Do you know where Captain Boothe is?"

"Now don't you be askin' me a thing like that. And no, I don't. I just tell the next man in line."

Hank said the words casually enough. But shrewd eyes under bushy brows seemed to take Jem's measure. Jem knew there was little use trying to hide anything.

"Jonas, there's one thing more."

"Out with it," Hank said, scratching behind his ear.

"I've been told to find out when Boothe will return—"

"You done said that already."

"—by getting it out of his daughter."

Hank's eyebrows all but disappeared into his equally bushy hairline. Jem winced. Judging by the sudden rush of warmth through his neck, his face no doubt matched the hue of his coat.

Hank cocked his head and squinted. "If you don't do what you're told, Harrod gives the job to somebody else, ain't that so? Somebody who'll follow his orders and go after Miss Susanna forty ways from Sunday. You just let Harrod think you're doing what he wants of you. Miss Susanna is better off with you than with any of his other men."

That was the very reason Jem had told Harrod he'd see to the task himself, but he had hoped Hank might disagree. "I'm talking to her, and no more. You had best be sure you get that clear before you pass your report along."

"Good. Because if you lay a finger on that girl, you'll know where Captain Boothe will be. Diggin' your grave."

"You have my word."

But he couldn't speak for Harrod or Taggart. And what good, really, was the word of a man like Jem Flannery?

He had hated the English once with all the passion of an Irishman. But working for his passage had shown him the contempt many held for the Irish. It had been easier to start over, to take a new name and new voice and new loyalty.

But each lie came easier than the one before. Until he found himself here, pledged to fight for both sides at once.

The next several days were a misery of waiting for the moment when he could no longer avoid Harrod's orders. Susanna Boothe served at each meal, but Jem had no wish to hasten the reckoning. Nor did he wish to draw the notice of Benjamin Woodbridge, who haunted the great room during every meal. It was a mercy no one considered the injured rebel a genuine threat.

But a week after Hank Jonas had vanished into the woods, as Jem stood watching the men at their evening meal, the great room door opened beside him and Malcolm Harrod stepped inside.

Jem snapped his posture straight. "Attention!"

Forks dropped to plates. Men straightened and froze. Malcolm Harrod said, "As you were."

The clatter of forks resumed. Jem forced himself to relax his stance. "They'll be finished soon, sir. All is in order."

"Very well. I've a courier to meet with tomorrow before dawn, about the hour of four. Keep the sentries away from

Boothe's cabin so we're not overheard."

"Yes, sir."

Harrod's eyes roved the room and came to rest on the back door. Woodbridge leaned against the wall in the corner, his sling white in the shadows.

Harrod did not give Woodbridge a second glance. His focus was on Captain Boothe's daughter, who had just entered with a platter of corn cakes in her hands. Kate McGuiness was at her side.

"And what of Miss Boothe?" Harrod murmured.

"I've had no opportunity as yet, sir."

"I suggest you find opportunity, Lieutenant. Tonight, if possible." Harrod watched Susanna cross the room to the table nearest Jem. "Now, for instance."

"Yes, sir."

Harrod nodded, wheeled, and strode out.

Jem maneuvered around the table and bowed to Susanna. "Good evening, Miss Boothe."

The young woman stiffened and made no answer. Her eyes darted across the room to Widow McGuiness.

Jem took two steps past her and leaned down to a fresh-faced recruit. "Go speak to Widow McGuiness. Do it in front of the rebel Woodbridge."

"Sir?"

"You heard me, Private."

"What shall I say?"

"Whatever you please. Quickly, now."

The recruit looked from Jem to Susanna and back. Then his eyes widened in understanding. For one tense moment, Jem thought the man was going to wink at his superior officer. But the recruit said only, "Yes, sir."

He jumped up from the bench and hurried toward Kate, blocking Benjamin's view. Jem lifted the platter from Susanna's hands. "Allow me to assist you."

"I'm quite finished," she said briskly, turning away.

Jem set the platter down and caught her elbow. She whirled and he braced for a slap, hoping it would not come. For her sake, not his.

But it did. The sting of it made his eyes water. He spun her toward the wall, putting himself between her and the men who might have seen her slap their officer. "Miss Boothe, I advise you to restrain yourself."

"I hope you are aware that men who behave this way toward women in the Blue Ridge do not generally live to change their ways." Susanna eyed him coldly, although she seemed to know it would do her no good to struggle.

"If the fathers of said women have any say, I do not doubt that is true. But your father is not here." He had to warn her despite the scores of watching eyes. "And a great number of my colleagues would dearly love to find him."

"As he would to find them." Fire in her eyes now. "You're hardly the first man who's tried to get to my father through me. A vestryman tried to do it years ago, and I must say you're doing a worse job than he did. Now unhand me."

He dropped her arms but braced his hand against the wall beside her. Captain Boothe's daughter was a beautiful woman. But Jem had seen her catch Benjamin Woodbridge's eye. He wanted no part of a frontier blood feud.

Woodbridge. He would want information as much as Hank Jonas did—any information Jem could give him. And he might find it useful to know Harrod was meeting a courier before dawn with no sentries about.

Jem lowered his voice still further. "Miss Boothe, Major Harrod meets with a courier tomorrow morning at four o'clock. He's gone so far as to order me to keep the sentries away from your family's cabin. I daresay he wants my answer now."

"Tell him he'll have his answer when my father finds him." She looked him in the eye. "And tell him my father is a better man than you and your lot could ever hope to be."

Then she ducked under his arm and was gone with a bang of the door.

Jem wheeled. The men studied their empty dishes, the silence awkward. Jem raked them all with an imperious glance and stalked from the room.

The moment he reached the dogtrot, he shut the door and leaned on the wall. His face still stung. But Susanna's words stung deeper.

Aye, she was far safer saying such things to him than to his men. But was she right? Was there no hope of a man like Jem Flannery ever becoming a man like Robert Boothe?

Something welled in him, fierce. He pushed off the wall and strode down the steps.

He had changed once. He could do it again.

Thirteen

"HE'S GONE." BENJAMIN SHUT THE KITCHEN DOOR and turned to the waiting faces behind him. "Back toward the creek path."

Kate resumed her vigorous sweeping. Rane nudged Ayen and started piling wood in the woodbin again.

"Likely going to report to Harrod." Susanna Boothe splashed a tin plate into her dishwater. She had said only that Lieutenant Gregory had tried to talk to her, but that right there was enough to set Benjamin's blood afire. Never mind that Gregory was supposed to be on their side. Could Benjamin afford to tell Susanna the truth about him?

Or was it the truth? Had Gregory merely deceived him for the sake of a chance at freedom?

Elizabeth took the plate from Susanna and shook it. Ayen yelped and wiped droplets from his forehead.

"I didn't mean to be doing that," Elizabeth said, handing Ayen her towel.

Benjamin took up the hearth shovel and held it for Kate's sweepings, then stepped around Magdalen Boothe to empty the shovel into the fire. "This kitchen is too small for so many people."

"It's not so bad," Kate said. "My Arthur and our lads and I lived in this very room while the inn was a-building."

"That's four of you, Aunt Kate. We've seven of us."

"Kind of you to do the ciphering for me, lad. I'd lost count at six."

He laid aside the shovel, looking at Susanna. "It's you I'm worried for. You women, I mean."

"It's Pa I'm worried for." Susanna plunged another plate violently into the water. "The Tories want to find him. Or at least to know when he's coming back."

He should have known she would not fret for herself. Susanna was a kind and caring woman, but fierce when she feared for those she loved. He ached to take that fear away from her and fling it down the mountain. But he could not say so unless she wanted to hear it, and her rigid stance said she did not.

"How long until Rob's lads get back?" Kate asked.

"I've had no word from the couriers," Benjamin said.

"Nor have I," Magdalen added. "Mitch left this forenoon to preach elsewhere, but he promised he'd be back as soon as he could. Perhaps he'll hear something while he's away."

"I was meaning to speak to him," Elizabeth said, drying the next plate.

"About what?" Benjamin asked.

"About—" Elizabeth hesitated. "Never mind. It doesn't matter now."

Whatever it was, it did matter. He could see that plainly. But he did not press the question.

"If Mitchell can get out of the settlement, surely I could ride out and fetch Captain Boothe," Rane said.

"The couriers don't know you," Benjamin said. "We can't get through to the fort; the Tories are watching for that. And the men at Pembrook Station are gone, same as Captain Boothe." He fingered his kerchief, thinking. "These Tories are staying for a fair spell. Tories don't do that most places.

But we can't leave the horses in the cave much longer, even if there are only three of them since Mitchell left."

"There's room in Saul McBraden's barn shed," Magdalen said. "Elsie's brothers usually keep their mounts there, but they're all with Rob right now."

"That ought to do it if Elsie's willing. So long as we're careful, the Tories won't know anything's changed. Ayen is over there often enough, looking in on you and Susanna."

"Gregory said something else," Susanna said.

Benjamin turned toward her. "What was it?"

"Harrod is meeting a courier tomorrow morning at four. The sentries will be ordered away from the cabin and the creek path while the courier is there."

A courier and no sentries . . .

Was that a warning? An invitation? A trap?

It didn't matter. He would take the risk.

"No," Elizabeth said, as if reading his face. "No, Benjamin, you mustn't."

"We can move the horses while the sentries are away. But Harrod must have something important to say to that courier. If I can find out what, I can get word to Hank Jonas."

"And Hank can get word to Gunning and Gunning can get word to Pa." Ayen brushed wood chips from his palms and snatched a leftover biscuit from the table.

Rane cleared his throat. "Perhaps you had best say 'if *we* can find out what.'"

"We agreed you'd stay out of sight, Armistead."

"I hardly thought you meant to do such a thing *in* sight, Woodbridge. I've had some experience in not being seen."

An Anglican barrister who had a Tory uncle and had served in the Royal Navy and knew how to evade watching eyes. What a motley partner Benjamin had found.

"The Button Creek ravine is close behind the cabin," Benjamin said. "No one would see us down there."

He'd said *us*. Too late now.

"But your arm," Elizabeth said. "And your ankle."

"My arm and my ankle are fine." He'd been removing the sling a little longer each day to strengthen his shoulder and forearm. "Ayen, you've been down that ravine, right?"

"Just last month," Ayen said.

"Why?" Elizabeth asked.

Ayen shrugged. "Because I took the notion." He took a large bite of biscuit and went on with his mouth full. "You can come right up behind the cabin. It's a good place for listenin'. There's a real fine hiding spot under the window by Susanna's end of the loft."

"Ayen John Boothe!" Susanna said. "Do you eavesdrop on Betty and me?"

Ayen made a face. "Why would I want to do that? All you 'uns ever talk about is—"

"Oh, hush," Susanna said.

Ayen shrugged again.

"That's our path to the cabin, then," Benjamin said. "We'll move the horses first, as soon as the sentries are gone. Then we'll make for the ravine."

He glanced at the corner where Old Sandy leaned against the wall. The hickory pins had been driven into the stock, the broken piece fitted tightly into place with the help of a mallet and pine resin. Smoothing the rough places along the crack had been a kind of ritual the last several nights. But he could not climb a ravine and carry a rifle at the same time. Nor could he pull his bowstring with any strength.

"A bit of prayer might serve you well," Kate said.

He pulled his gaze from the rifle. He didn't feel like praying, but he would not say so.

Rane looked wary. "Is it true Baptists pray in strange tongues and bark like dogs and fall down as if slain?"

"I've heard tell of it, but I've surely never done such a thing," Benjamin said. "Is that what you were so nervish of at Sunday meeting?"

"One reason, I suppose."

"Well, I've heard that Anglicans pray in Latin."

"It's papists who do that. I assure you I do not share that belief."

"What *do* you believe?" Ayen asked curiously.

"Ayen," Magdalen said.

"It's all right, Mrs. Boothe." Rane turned toward Ayen. "I'm a member of the Church of England, Ayen. My uncle is a clergyman. But we parted ways after I refused to pray for the king's success against his enemies."

"Your uncle tried to make you pray for that?"

"No. The prayer book did." Rane shook his head. "Any number of men who love liberty remain in the Church of England. General Washington is one. George Whitefield, who preached the awakenings, was another. But I . . ."

"You can't reconcile it with your conscience," Benjamin said quietly.

"My conscience says freedom is a natural right. Even Sir William Blackstone said that the king is subject to the law of the land. But as a member of the king's church, I've given him my religious allegiance. That is what I cannot reconcile."

"Maybe you ought to start by asking whether the king has any right to your religious allegiance."

Rane wore the same expression he'd worn when Benjamin called the Anglican clergy *blaspheming*. Benjamin had a feeling he'd pushed far enough.

"You told me once that you have no hope but the merit of Christ," he said.

"Yes," Rane said cautiously.

"And I can say the same."

Rane nodded and relaxed. Benjamin felt his own tension ease a notch. Their differences could not be simply ignored. But if nothing else, this was common ground.

He motioned to Kate. "Come and pray with us."

Fourteen

THERE WAS NO SIGN OF SENTRIES AS BENJAMIN and Rane led the horses past darkened cabins to Saul and Elsie McBraden's shed, nor as they slipped across the creek path. The sinking moon cast a ghostly glow over the rocks and crags of the ravine. Benjamin eased down the footholds, keeping a left-handed grip on whatever was within reach. His shoulder ached without the sling.

He thumped lightly to the broad shelf of rock below, feeling the shock in his weakened ankle, and looked around as Rane landed beside him. The rocky walls of the ravine rose like the walls of the dogtrot at the Dove & Olive. Button Creek poured into the chasm at its far end, tumbling down in a curtain of water that rarely froze even in dead of winter.

The roof of Captain Boothe's cabin was silhouetted atop the bluff just to the left of the falls. Benjamin picked his way forward along the ledge until he stood almost directly below the cabin, then stopped and turned to face the bluff.

A massive flat rock, twice his height, lay against the wall of the ravine. There was a cave back in there somewhere; he had explored it as a lad only a few years older than Ayen. Benjamin ran his hand lightly over the rock, seeking a foothold.

His sleeve brushed something to the left, hidden in shadow away from the moonlight. Wood thunked dully.

Wood?

He groped in the darkness. A wooden handle, the sort that might turn a crank. A crude frame, the rough fiber of rope. "Now this is interesting."

"What?" Rane leaned over his shoulder.

"A winch. Never seen it before." Benjamin glanced at the ledge beneath him, spotted with red clay. "You should see the mess of clay on the floor in the great room. I'll warrant the Tories have been climbing around in here for days."

"But why?" Rane asked.

Benjamin did not answer. He tilted his hat back and eyed the great flat-faced rock, noting the way it lay against the bluff. A smaller boulder was wedged half behind it, the perfect mounting block to start his path up the bluff.

He did not recall those rocks being in such a position when he had explored the ravine as a boy. But that was years ago now. Things always seemed different in the dark.

The hush of the hours before dawn settled over the ravine, a damp stillness that ached in his shoulder. In the distance, hooves thumped on the McGuiness Creek bridge. The sound came nearer, then stopped.

"That'll be the courier," Benjamin said. "If I don't come back, go to the ordinary."

He clambered atop the small rock wedged behind the flat one and found the next foothold. The muscles of his right shoulder felt strange and weak. He pulled himself to the top with his left hand and peered over the edge.

A horse was tethered to one side, up close to the path. The cabin was dark and silent.

Benjamin hauled himself up and flipped his body over the edge. Snow clung to his back and shoulders. He rose to a knee, waited, kept his eyes on the horse. It made no alarm. He got to his feet and ducked behind the building, pressing his back to the rough bark of the logs.

"His Lordship wishes to confirm that you received the gifts he authorized." The courier's voice was low, barely above a murmur. Benjamin strained to hear.

"The records are here." Papers rustled as Harrod spoke. "All is safely stored until needed. You may deliver this copy to His Lordship; the original will remain in my keeping."

"I am ordered to request your presence in his camp as soon as possible. He has received news of Major Ferguson's misfortune and wishes to reassure himself with regard to the frontier campaigns."

"I cannot leave until after Christmas," Harrod said. "The men are unaccustomed to campaigning and will expect certain festivities. I will leave only if I am confident all is in order. Express my regrets to His Lordship."

"Yes, sir. You'll be apprised of any further orders."

"Of course. Now about my Indian agent."

Both men lowered their voices still further. Benjamin strained to hear but could catch no more than a word or two.

Harrod had an Indian agent. Was that the man who had made such trouble for Selagisqua and Walks-in-Winter?

And what papers were on that table?

The scrape of chair legs punctuated the conversation. Harrod's voice rose to an audible pitch once more. "I'll escort you out of the settlement."

Benjamin held himself perfectly still, willing his body to blend with the shadows. On the other side of the cabin, the door closed. He heard the slipping of the horse's tether, then footsteps on the frozen earth of the creek path.

Those papers. Left unguarded, an answer to an unspoken prayer.

He checked cautiously around the corner and made a dash for it. Slipping inside, he eased the door to a crack.

A table strewn with papers stood near the hearth. The fire's light flickered over the table and across the underside of the sleeping loft above. Benjamin crossed to the table and stood with his back to the firelight, keeping the front door in the edge of his vision.

On top of the stack was a crudely inked map. Sunrising, with Button Creek on the north and McGuiness Creek on the east. A map of the whole ridge was beneath it, the Yadkin Valley dotted with precisely inked crosses.

He shuffled the maps aside and angled the next layer of papers toward the firelight. Letters. One from Cornwallis, in a tight slanting script Benjamin fought to decipher. *You have demonstrated yourself well suited to the Rigours of Backcountry Campaigning. Your Cherokee Agents assure me these Gifts will be satisfactory. I hold every Hope of your final Success . . .*

Another, unsigned and in a different hand. *Further Intelligence will be by Letter. I have maintained Secrecy and pray you to conceal our Relation from your own Men as well as Others.*

He would have time to think on the letters later. He flipped them over, found a lengthy list. A supply order?

Black Powder, 800 Pounds.

Round Shot, 400 Pounds.

Muskets, 40.

Long Rifles, 40.

Horse Pistols, 20.

His fingers tightened on the paper. These were not merely supplies.

Trade Blankets, 40.

Knives, 20.

Hatchets, 20.

He ran his eye swiftly down the rest of the list. These were trade goods. What had Cornwallis's letter said? *Your Cherokee Agents assure me these Gifts will be satisfactory.*

Snow crunched outside the door.

Benjamin lunged around the corner of the table and slipped through the bedroom door beside the hearth. He eased it shut just as the hinge pegs of the front door creaked.

Steps crossed the room, then paused. Papers rustled across the table. Benjamin tensed and reached for his knife.

But Harrod gave no sign of alarm. Benjamin stepped silently to the window and drew his knife. A few quick strokes slit the greased paper from its frame. He sheathed the knife, listened a moment, and wriggled through the opening.

Harrod might notice the missing window paper and wet footprints. Or he might not. At least not until after it mattered. Either way, there would be no one to blame. Benjamin dropped lightly to the ground, the first drops of rain pocking the snow around him. His tracks would be gone by daylight.

He half climbed, half slid down the bluff to the ravine, catching himself just short of sliding through a gap behind the massive flat-faced boulder. When he reached the ledge, Rane said, "Thank heaven."

"Harrod pert-near caught me. But I got a look at his papers." Benjamin nodded to the sea service pistol in Rane's hand. "You didn't plan to use that on me, I hope."

"If you were someone other than yourself, yes." Rane slipped the pistol under his cloak. "What did you find?"

"A couple of maps and some letters. And a supply order for arms and trade goods. I'm not certain, but . . ."

His gaze landed on the dim nook where the winch had been hidden.

Black Powder, 800 Pounds.

He turned his back to the waterfall and squinted down the ledge the other way. The shelf of rock ran far downstream into shadow, but he knew it eventually sloped to meet mud and dark water. Men could come into the ravine that way if they were bold enough to brave the cold river. Button Creek was still mostly free of ice, easily wide enough for a canoe. And this ravine was full of caves.

The sudden certainty of it was as hard and unyielding as the granite beneath him. *Lord Jesus, when I figured to break into Tory headquarters, I didn't half reckon on this.*

"It wasn't a supply order," he said quietly. "It was a list of gifts for the Cherokee. And I'm thinking Harrod's storing it all right here in this ravine."

Rane was silent. The waterfall went on rushing over its course, running on its merry way.

"The winch," Rane said at last.

"Aye." It felt good to clench his right hand. Had Gregory known of all this and not thought it worth telling?

He moved to the towering flat rock and crouched to examine the ledge. The waterfall's spray had frozen on the cold granite. But when he swept his hand over the gritty crust of ice, an arching furrow met his fingers.

"There's a mark here. Somebody moved this boulder."

Rane tipped his head back. "They moved that monstrous rock?"

"Not so monstrous if it's flat and you have the men for it." Rising, Benjamin pointed to the smaller rock he had used as a foothold. "There's a gap there that I all but fell through on my way down. They blocked off that cave for a reason."

He mounted the wet rock again and peered into the gap. Water trickled somewhere deep in the cave. A stocky, barrel-shaped object caught his shadow.

He lowered himself cautiously into the crevice, praying the cavern had a floor and nothing lived back there in the dark. The thud of his landing echoed dully. His hip brushed something cold and hard. Metal clattered on rock.

Moonlight angled through the gap overhead, dimmed by the coming rain, painting the cavity in pale gray light.

The cold of the cavern ran straight up his neck. "It's here. All of it."

Fifteen

THE CAVE WAS FULL OF MUSKETS AND RIFLES
and horse pistols, gunpowder in hogsheads and in smaller
kegs, boxes of lead balls and stacks of blankets and bundles
of tomahawks. The thought of it dogged Benjamin's steps all
the way back to the ordinary. Rane was as silent as he was.

Susanna and Magdalen were already in the kitchen
with Kate and Elizabeth, preparing for breakfast. Kate laid
down her spoon when Benjamin and Rane slipped inside.

"You lads are back safe. Praise be."

The dampness on Benjamin's hunting shirt turned to
steam in the warmth of the fire. "Bad news, Aunt Kate."

"Worse than we've had already?"

"Harrod's men are storing arms and trade goods in a
cave in the ravine."

"Oh, mercy," Kate said. "Whatever for?"

He hated the fear it would cause Elizabeth. But she
would have to know sometime. Better to have it in the open
where they could all face it. "Gifts for the Cherokee."

Kate and Magdalen exchanged glances. The Indians had
been mostly peaceable where Sunrising was concerned, but
Benjamin had heard stories of the settlement where Captain

Boothe had lived right after he wed Magdalen. Cherokee attacks had burned it to the ground.

"Can't Judge Pembrook . . ." Elizabeth began.

"He's trying," Benjamin said. "And he's not here."

"Maybe if Uncle Mitchell were here, he'd know what to do," Susanna said. "He speaks Cherokee well."

"He should be back any day," Benjamin said slowly.

"God willing," Magdalen said. "'Twas only a few meetings he had to preach before he returned."

Benjamin nodded, thinking. The fire snapped under the kettles, its shadows orange and black on the floorboards.

"'When sorrows come, they come not single spies, but in battalions,'" Rane said.

"If that was Shakespeare, he surely hit that nail on the head." Benjamin shook his head. "I wonder how they knew about that cave. And why nobody's warned us."

Rane glanced at him sharply, no doubt thinking of Gregory.

"I don't mean only folks in the settlement," Benjamin said, though he was thinking of Gregory too. "Selagisqua and Walks-in-Winter should have warned us again. Unless they don't know about it." He shook his head. "We'd best part ways for now. I'll join you in the stable, Armistead."

Rane went out. Magdalen touched Kate's shoulder. "We'll be setting tables in the great room."

She and Susanna slipped outside. Kate said, "You'd best put your sling back on and give that shoulder a rest."

"Captain Boothe's own orders couldn't make me put that sling back on," Benjamin said.

Kate gave him a look. This wasn't Captain Boothe's orders; it was Aunt Kate's appeal. "All right, just for a bit."

Elizabeth took Benjamin's sling from the top of the cabinet and brought the ends up behind his neck. Her fingers were ice cold through his collar and kerchief. They shook a little as she fumbled the knot.

He glanced up at her. "All right, Mouse?"

"This awful war," she said, low and angry.

He pulled the strip of fabric out of her hands and stood up and put his arm around her shoulders. She trembled against him, tears welling. "I'm just so tired of it."

He wished he'd burst into the common room of Robert's cabin and faced Harrod once and for all. "We're all tired of it, Mouse."

"Sometimes I don't think you are," she said into his shoulder.

"I'm tired of what it's done to folks I care for." He nodded toward the rifle in the corner. "Every time I look at Old Sandy, I think of Pa. And with that crack in it now . . ."

"Oh, mercy, that reminds me." Kate hurried to a basket in the opposite corner and rummaged for a moment. "I had to clean your scrip after that fall you took, and I plumb forgot to put your Testament back inside." She held up the small book, triumphant. "Here it is. There was a wooden thing too, something you'd been carving. But it was stained bad from that wound in your arm. No point in keeping it."

One more thing the Tories had ruined. The last thing Elizabeth needed was a bloodstained spoon. Benjamin put down the sling, took the New Testament, and flipped open the worn leather cover. The corners of the pages bore a dark stain of their own. "If only we could get Harrod to read this."

"And since he won't, or will and won't believe it, there's a reason we're God's witness to the world, aye?" Kate said.

He snapped the book shut. "If you're telling me to love my enemies, I've had about all of that I can stand."

"Loving them doesn't mean letting them go on and do as they please, lad." Kate checked the skillet of crackling salt pork and motioned for Elizabeth to stir the porridge kettle. "It's doing what's best for them, even if that means keeping them from sinning more than they have already."

"Aye, well, it's more than that I'd like to do. I'd like to

make them pay for the sinning they've already done."

Elizabeth stabbed her long-handled spoon into the thick cornmeal porridge. "Making them pay isn't going to bring Pa back, Benjamin. Nor Ma either."

He blew out a breath. How to explain this festering restlessness that had a hold of him? It felt sometimes as if all the ugliness that overshadowed the backcountry had sunk its talons into him.

"The war calls it back to me, I reckon," he said at last. "And if I don't get it out of me, it's going to hurt somebody. It already has."

"What do you mean?"

He meant the way Susanna Boothe would not look at him, the pain in her face every time she turned away. But he would not mention that. "All the talk I've stirred up, for one thing. How the orphan lad that Aunt Kate was fool enough to take in didn't have the decency to hold his temper in a room full of guests."

Kate flicked one hand. "Folks don't mean a thing by that, lad."

"Aye, they do. And they're right." A bitter laugh slipped out. "I dealt you and this place a royal blow when I went after Nolan Taggart for what he said about Pa. Turned the great room into a brawling house is what I did."

"*You* didn't," Elizabeth said. "Mr. Taggart did."

"No, Mouse. I did. And I'd do it again. I'd kill Nolan Taggart if I had the chance. I should have done it then."

The words shocked him. Not because he did not mean them. But he had not known they were so near the surface.

"Benjamin—"

"Never mind."

Elizabeth wasn't looking at him. She was looking past him. He turned his head.

Susanna stood in the doorway. She did not so much as glance in his direction. But he knew she must have heard.

"The tables are set," she said quietly. "Shall I help with the dishing out?"

For a moment no one said anything. Then Benjamin cleared his throat.

"I'm sorry." He set the New Testament on the mantel, brushed past Susanna, and strode out the door. If they only knew how sorry he was.

The stable was empty. Benjamin glimpsed Rane and Ayen at the well, drawing water for the trough. He took up a pitchfork and went after a dirty stall, finding a bitter refuge in the punishment of his aching shoulder.

Only a few minutes hence, he would stand watch as the women served breakfast. But he dared not walk into a room full of Tories while he was in this frame of mind.

Lord God, you tell us to love our enemies, but you say you're a man of war. What can a man do when he can't do either one?

A familiar voice called across the yard. Rane answered. Benjamin turned toward the door, stowing the anger down deep once again as Mitchell Boothe stepped into the stable.

"You're back." Benjamin offered his hand, and Mitchell gripped it. Ordinarily they would have made a contest of it, though Benjamin's grip was still weak. But today Mitchell seemed to have other things on his mind.

"Saw Hank while I was away," Mitchell said. "He'll be along once he figures it's safe. Everything all right here?"

"Just puzzling out why it's easier to say I believe a thing than to outright do it."

Mitchell didn't seem surprised by that answer. "You're not the only one."

"Any word from Hank?" Maybe he'd seen Selagisqua or Walks-in-Winter. "Or help from the fort?"

"The fort fell to the Tories and a Cherokee war band a fortnight ago. All the men were with the army, and the women and children had gone back to their settlement."

Pembrook Station, occupied by the very men Judge Pembrook had tried to make peace with. Benjamin wanted to be angry again, but he'd done enough of that today. "No bloodshed, then. Thank God for that."

"Aye. None there, at least." Mitchell paused. "Walks-in-Winter is dead, Benjamin."

"What?"

"He was trying to get to Hank. Somebody shot him."

Benjamin rammed his fist into the crossbeam of the stall. The blow jarred his shoulder. Not Walks-in-Winter. Not the patient old warrior who had taught him to read a broken twig as clearly as words in a book.

He tried to say something, anything, but his voice would not let him. He turned away, swiped at his eyes, found blood on his knuckles.

Mitchell clapped a hand on his shoulder, silent.

"What of Selagisqua?" Benjamin said roughly.

"He took up with some other renegades who think the British are playing them for fools." Mitchell shook his head. "The lot of them are all right for now, but they won't last long against warriors with British muskets."

Benjamin wiped his knuckles on his hunting shirt and took a deep breath. There would be time enough to nurse his wounds later. "How many renegades?"

"Twenty, mayhap. Why?"

"The Tories are stockpiling Indian gifts from Cornwallis. We found powder and arms and trade goods hidden in a cave along Button Creek."

Mitchell rocked back on his heels. "No wonder Walks-in-Winter tried to warn us. How much is there?"

Benjamin stabbed the pitchfork into a clump of straw and let it thump against the gate of the stall. "Enough to give Selagisqua and his lads a fighting chance."

Sixteen

THE MEASURED TREAD OF MARCHING FEET
echoed on hard ground. Malcolm Harrod's shouted orders
carried on the damp air. Kate sighed as she crossed the settlement, basket in hand and Elizabeth on her heels. It would be
Christmas soon, and Kate did not fancy the festivities Benjamin
had heard Harrod speak of. 'Twas one thing to tell Benjamin
to love his enemies, and quite another to be doing it herself.

Especially when she was about to borrow a canoe for
the sole purpose of smuggling arms and trade goods out
from under those enemies' noses.

Benjamin had apologized for his outburst. Then he had
set his jaw the way her Arthur used to do and told her the
Tories had killed one of his Cherokee friends. He and Mitchell
and Rane aimed to give the Tories' trade goods to the renegades who were left, if only Kate would ask Elsie McBraden
for her husband's canoe.

Kate had agreed to do it, but with a bargain of her own.
He had to wear his sling again until it was time to go back
into the ravine. He'd given her a crooked grin with no mirth
in it and let her tie the knot behind his neck.

She sighed again. *Be leading him, Lord. 'Tis all I'm asking.*

"All right?" Elizabeth asked from behind her.

"Just thinking on your brother."

"He counted Walks-in-Winter a friend."

"Aye, that he did." Kate hadn't known Walks-in-Winter or Selagisqua well; they'd not set foot in the settlement more than a handful of times. But a friend was a friend. The king's men had torn another hole in the weave of Benjamin's life.

She paused at the trading post with a jar of basswood honey for Deacon Ashe's sister, tucking it into an out-of-the-way corner so as not to draw the notice of the Tories who came for supplies—obtained by neither credit nor hard money. Maybe the gift would raise Miss Ashe's spirits, though it would hardly make up for the damage done to her brother's livelihood. There was not enough basswood honey in the Blue Ridge to make up for the damage the Tories had done.

Pushing such thoughts aside, Kate beckoned Elizabeth toward Saul and Elsie McBraden's cabin and knocked at the door. Saul had been gone with Captain Boothe since September, long enough for Elsie's rounded belly to remove all doubt that she and Saul would see a new bairn come spring.

Elsie peered out, then pulled the door wide. "Come in."

Kate stepped into the cabin. Saul and Elsie's three other young 'uns fairly tumbled over one another in the small space. The oldest, a girl of eight, was carefully turning a spit over the fire, but the youngest ones gamboled hither and yon on the floor. There might have been more room to move about if not for the belongings Magdalen and Susanna Boothe had brought after being ordered away from their home.

Elizabeth went to the younger children right away, joining their game with a winning smile and quick laughter. Kate began unpacking her basket. "How do you fare?"

"Some better." Elsie's comely smile lit up her face, taking away some of the weary look. "Not so tired, and I know your tonic will ease my stomach."

Kate looked down as little hands tugged her skirt. The

two-year-old boy peered up at her, clearly wanting to see what was in her basket. "Nothing here for you, laddie. You and your sisters look hale enough."

Elsie ruffled the boy's blond-red hair. "Only a bit of a cough. The winter's young, but I pray it grows no worse. It's a trial on them to be indoors all the time."

"And a trial on you too?" Kate said in an undertone.

Elsie smiled again. Kate knew it for the smile of a woman who dearly loved her children but craved a mite of peace now and then.

They all craved a mite of peace these days. She should find a way to pack that in her basket too. "I'll bring some ginger for them. And we'll see how the wee one gets on. You'll be in need of some partridgeberry tea before long."

"This one kicks," Elsie said. "Another boy, I'm thinking, and a hearty one. A handful, I expect."

"Takes after his pa, then."

Elsie laughed. "He could do worse."

"Speaking of Saul—I fear I came to ask as well as give."

"Ask what?"

"Saul's canoe."

"Benjamin has one of his own, doesn't he? Is something wrong with it?"

"No. It's safe enough, hidden by the creek. But the lads have need of two canoes, though I can't be telling you why."

"You're welcome to it. But Saul left it in the barn shed. It won't be easy to get it to water without the Tories seeing. You'll have to be mighty careful."

Kate had a notion that her days of being careful were long over. "They're drilling right now. If we're quick, we'll have it moved before they're finished. Come, Betty."

Elizabeth stood, gently detaching the younger girl's grip from her fingers. Elsie gave Kate's arm a quick squeeze. Kate gestured to Elizabeth and slipped outside.

Benjamin's mare nickered when Kate entered the barn

shed. Rane's gelding seemed more wary. Kate fondled her own mare and spoke to the others softly, fearful they would make noise enough to show themselves to the Tories.

The horses quieted, and Kate surveyed the shed. The canoe lay along one wall, the tight-stretched birch bark pale in the dim light. A paddle was wedged snugly under the thwarts.

The craft seemed longer than Kate remembered. She eyed it, doubting herself for a moment. Well, it might be awkward, but they would manage.

Elizabeth lifted one end of the canoe. Kate lifted the other. Together they flipped it over for a better grip, and Kate backed out the door. "Here we go."

"I hope those Tories drill a good long time." Elizabeth sounded breathless. "But not so long they're better fighters."

Kate didn't answer. Walking backward was hard enough. Kate McGuiness, you should know better, she thought. A woman of your years, sneaking a canoe across a settlement!

They were halfway down the creek path when Elizabeth's lips suddenly parted. Kate turned her head. A lone Tory stood at the fork of the rivers, near the bridge across McGuiness Creek. A sentry, peering down the mountain, rifle in hand.

"Brace up, lass," Kate murmured to Elizabeth. "We're not done for yet."

She scanned the ground for a rock to throw. To distract the sentry or to hit him, she wasn't sure which.

But before she could find one, the Tory turned around. Kate gave him a bright smile, as if nothing were out of the ordinary. At least he wasn't Nolan Taggart.

"Widow McGuiness, is it?" He stared. "What in the name of sense are you doing?"

"We're on our way to do a bit of foraging," she told him cheerily. Whatever they had been doing a moment ago, they'd be going foraging now. "There's a fine stand of cattails along Button Creek, and a crabapple tree downriver."

"No one's supposed to be about on the creeks." The

sentry was a man of middling age, with a square, solid face and square, solid shoulders. "The officers won't like it."

"The officers have to eat too," Kate said firmly. "And if we haven't meat enough, then cattail roots it's to be."

He regarded the canoe. "I didn't go to turn folks out of their homes, ma'am. And I'm only to keep a watch along this trail. I can do it just as well if I'm handling that canoe for you." He laid his rifle over his shoulder and took the end of the canoe from Elizabeth.

Oh, mercy. "Really, there's no need. We haven't much to look for."

"No trouble." He hefted the canoe higher, nearly lifting it from Kate's grasp. "It's only fair if we're to eat of what you find. And I'll speak to some of the others about hunting for our keep. No need for you to be out of meat because of us."

"We could use the meat," Kate admitted. "But I don't think Mr. Taggart would like you helping us."

"We don't all think like Taggart, ma'am." He was striding forward now, taking the canoe along with him at such a pace that Kate nearly tripped in trying to keep up. Elizabeth hurried behind, eyes wide. "Lieutenant Gregory's not a bad sort, I reckon. But Major Harrod now—he's a man who won't take to losing. That's why I threw in my lot with him after what those cursed rebels did to Ferguson."

He stopped. "Begging your pardon, ma'am, I forgot you was a Whig. This a good place?"

"I can't thank you enough," Kate said hurriedly. "If you'll go on to the kitchen, I'm sure—"

"Oh no, ma'am. I'm to keep watch." He settled the canoe down in the water. "Step on in."

Lord, preserve us. Kate took the hand he offered and stepped into the canoe. Elizabeth did the same.

"We can manage from here," Kate said desperately.

He didn't even answer that, just propped his rifle beside him and pushed off from the bank with long steady strokes.

Find something to forage, Kate mouthed at Elizabeth when his head was turned.

Elizabeth searched the snow-rimmed edge of the creek and pointed to a patch of tiny green leaves clustered atop the water. "There's still watercress here, see?"

She was scared to death. Kate knew that. But she was bearing up, and that was all that mattered.

The Tory paddled in close to the bank. Kate raked the plant from the frigid water by handfuls and piled it in the bottom of the canoe.

"You say Harrod hasn't a chance of losing." She wondered if she could forage for information as well as food. "I reckon it's a good thing to be having faith in your leader."

"It's more than I'd have in some of your leaders," the Tory said. "Look at your General Gates, now."

"I'd really rather not," Kate said. "I heard he behaved in a ghastly manner, and the militia not much better."

"That's what I mean. Ran clear away and let the rest of 'em get killed. If Harrod did that, I'd go home to my wife."

"And I shouldn't blame you. But Gates isn't our leader, you know. You've likely heard how folks back at the beginning said, 'No king but King Jesus.'"

"Seems to me the good Lord said a body ought to be loyal to the king, ma'am."

"To honor him, leastways. But the king's not the highest there is, now is he? The law's higher, and God is higher yet. Seems to me if the king is breaking the law of the land and the law of God, and if good men stand up to him about it, we're dutybound to switch our loyalty over to them."

Elizabeth was staring at her, as if she couldn't quite believe Kate was arguing politics with the Tory whom they desperately wanted anywhere but here.

The Tory grunted. "That's not in the Good Book."

"We're to obey God rather than man. That, sir, is in the Good Book."

"I don't see it that way."

"Nobody said you had to. And I'd have been just as glad as you if everybody had kept civil to one another, but when folks start taking over my livelihood, keeping civil is a mighty hard thing."

"I can't blame you there, ma'am." He grunted again. "Some rebels burned my cabin."

"'Tis sorry I am to hear it." It wasn't her place to judge if he'd done aught to deserve such a thing. "Up by the bank, if you please. There's more watercress, and some good birch."

But drills would be over soon. She had to find a way to get rid of this Tory, and fast.

A patch of dry, wilting rushes caught her eye. An idea began to form.

"There are the cattails over yonder," she said, pointing at the rustling blades and praying their oarsman didn't notice it was a bit late in the season to be digging cattail roots, even if the creek did keep the mud from freezing.

The Tory obligingly steered closer. When his head was turned, Kate winked at Elizabeth. Then she reached over the gunwale, stretching toward the cattails as far as she could.

The Tory gave a shout of warning. Kate poised an instant for dramatic effect and toppled neatly over the side.

The numbing shock of the water stole her breath. If she'd known it would be so cold, she might have found another way. She floundered in the shallows, sputtering like a helpless ninny until the Tory got out of the canoe to lend her a hand.

"I'm all right," Kate said breathlessly. "I think—if I can only make it back to the ordinary . . ."

"Are you quite sure you can manage the walk?" Elizabeth sounded properly alarmed. "Maybe Mr.—Mr.—"

"Macauley, miss. Aye, I'll help you, ma'am."

"And I'll follow with the watercress," Elizabeth said quickly. "We can come back later for the cattail roots and crabapples, if we've a mind."

Kate took the Tory's arm and straggled up the bank, her wet dress flapping with every step. She made sure to breathe hard and cling to his arm more than she had to. Nolan Taggart, naturally of suspicious temper, might not have been so easily fooled. She nearly wished it were not such a pleasant fellow they had to deceive.

When they hove in sight of the inn, Benjamin came striding out of the stable. He was not wearing his sling. Kate had a feeling they'd all seen the last of that sling.

Benjamin fixed his eyes on the Tory. "What's going on?"

"We were out foraging in the *canoe*, and I fell out of the *canoe* into the creek." She hoped he caught her emphasis. "This gentleman was good enough to help me home."

"I can fetch your canoe over for you," Macauley offered.

"Thank you kindly, but the lass will manage it." Kate patted his arm. "You'd best get back to your post, and don't speak of all this to Mr. Taggart. I wouldn't want you to get into trouble on my account."

He bent his head to her and walked away. A moment later, Elizabeth hurried up, holding a mound of watercress like a sheaf of posies.

"The canoe is in one of the crannies upriver," she said in an undertone. "How you startled me, Aunt Kate. And then I had all I could do to keep from laughing."

"How dare you think of laughing." Kate lifted her chin. "I'm cold and wet and suffering and need help to get home."

Benjamin shook his head. "You beat all, Aunt Kate."

"We got your canoe for you, didn't we?"

"You surely did." He took her elbow and steered her toward the kitchen.

"When do we—you know."

"Christmas night." Benjamin gave her that mirthless grin again. "General Washington surprised the Hessians at Trenton on Christmas. I reckon we can do the same to Harrod."

Seventeen

CHRISTMAS NIGHT BROUGHT A STORM OF THICK, drifting snowflakes. Not that the Tories noticed. They had clearly brought their own goods to celebrate with, for Benjamin had never heard anyone make that much racket on the mild drinks Kate supplied. Her husband had suffered an accident at the hands of a drunken hunter, and Kate vowed she'd be no party to another woman's sorrow. At least the Tories did not seem to notice when the women slipped away.

"Harrod went back to Captain Boothe's cabin already," Kate whispered to Benjamin as they crossed the darkened stable yard and neared the bluffs by the ravine. "Taggart will stand watch there tonight after he finishes his celebrating— but between you and me, I'm doubting he'll be up to it."

"I hope you're right." Snow slanted under the cocked brim of Benjamin's hat and melted on his skin as he helped Kate down onto the ledge above Button Creek. "Watch your step."

"You know this is madness, lad." She shook her head, flinging flakes from the hood of her cloak. "But I wouldn't have it any other way."

Her mischievous smile tugged an answering grin from him. It felt good to smile again, if only for a moment.

"'Though this be madness, yet there is method in 't,'" Rane said from behind Benjamin.

"I'll wager Shakespeare never did what we're about to do." Benjamin gave Magdalen Boothe a hand, then helped Susanna down. She did not look at him when their hands met.

Elizabeth eyed the drop doubtfully but said nothing. She'd seen worse as a lass of twelve, following Benjamin on his hunting trails. He caught her around the waist and lifted her down, his shoulder protesting sharply. She offered a smile, more shaky than Kate's but there all the same.

Kate was right. This was madness, even more so with Harrod just above them. But they would have no better chance.

Rane handed Elizabeth one of the pierced-tin lanterns he held, flinging a pattern of starry pinpricks over the snowy ledge. The falls plunged down to meet the creek, where the two canoes rode the current between ice-rimmed banks. Mitchell Boothe had smuggled both crafts out of their hiding places. He stood on a rock near the bow of the foremost canoe and gave Benjamin a cheerful wave.

At the top of the bluff, Ayen perched behind a stubby pine, ready to whistle at the first sign of trouble. Benjamin edged past the women to the massive flat boulder that leaned against the bluff like an ancient door. Rane had already shoved a smaller rock into place as a mounting block. Benjamin climbed atop the boulder and lowered himself into the cave, reaching back for Elizabeth's lantern. He scanned the dark cavern, his free hand on his knife. "All clear."

He set the lantern carefully to the side where there was no danger of blowing up several hogsheads of Tory gunpowder. Then he helped the women into the cave. The piles of muskets and rifles cast strange shadows in the dim lantern-light. "Beware of the water running along the back."

"Don't drink it, lasses, no matter how thirsty you get," Kate said. "My Arthur drank cave water once and like to died."

Benjamin only wished he knew how the Tories had

found out about this cave and had time enough to fill it. He moved to a stack of rifles and began pulling one weapon after another from the rear of the pile. "We'll take them from the back, where they won't be so soon missed."

"Do we use the winch you found?" Kate asked, nodding toward the cave's mouth.

"Best leave it where it is. We don't want anyone seeing it's been moved and coming in here to find out why."

He found a toehold and launched himself to the top of the boulder in the mouth of the cave. Rane waited on the ledge below. Benjamin knelt atop the snow-slicked granite. "Send 'em up, Mouse."

Elizabeth passed him the first rifle. He leaned down and handed it to Rane. Mitchell reached up, took the rifle from Rane, and nestled it in the canoe.

"Do you know how many Cherokee this would fit out, along with their own bows and tomahawks and whatever guns they've already got?" Mitchell's voice came from just below Rane's boots. "Too many. I don't like that at all."

"Isn't there anybody left to parley with?" Benjamin kept his voice low. The rush of the falls would cover it, but one word too loud might drift straight up out of the ravine to Harrod.

"Pembrook has tried." Mitchell wedged another rifle into the growing stack in the canoe. "But if it's not safe in the council for Selagisqua, there can't be much chance of peace talk just now. Any notion where Rob is?"

"Headed to Hillsborough, last I knew. I was supposed to get word to him of Indian trouble, but there's not been much chance of that either."

The snow had eased, moonlight glimmering between the clouds. Benjamin took the next rifle and thought of the line of Milton he had quoted to Rane in the camp after Kings Mountain. *And all the spangled host keep watch in squadrons bright.*

It was a poem about the Nativity, fitting for tonight. But he could not help thinking of the lines that came later.

No war or battle's sound
Was heard the world around;
The idle spear and shield were high up-hung.

Nothing could be less fitting this Christmas night.

"That's the last one," Susanna said from behind him.

"Room for more?" he called down to Mitchell.

"A few," Mitchell said.

Benjamin pivoted back toward the cave. "Three more."

He waited as Susanna disappeared into the dimness of the cave. Mitchell would paddle one canoe, and Ayen the other. Benjamin's shoulder could not take the strain of paddling, and Rane had likely never paddled a canoe in his life, unless canoes were a craft of choice in the Royal Navy. Susanna was as skilled with a paddle as Benjamin, but he would not ask her to take a canoe full of rifles downriver to the Indians. Even though she doubtless would have done it.

She passed him the first rifle he'd asked for. As Elizabeth passed him the others, a rustle of sliding brush and mud came from the bluff up above. Benjamin peered around the flat boulder in front of the cave.

Ayen thumped onto the ledge and sprinted down it, unheeding of the snow-covered stone. "Gregory and Taggart are coming over from the ordinary. I couldn't whistle without them hearing."

Rane sprang from his crouch. "I'll go up. If they come this way, I'll head them off."

Benjamin leaped down from the rock and passed the last rifle down to Mitchell. "I'll get the women out. Go, go."

"And Godspeed," Mitchell said from below. Ayen faded into the dark where the ledge led down to the sand and mud of the creek a hundred yards downstream.

Rane headed for the footholds they'd come down. Benjamin clambered back atop the boulder and gave Elizabeth a hand up, then Susanna, then Magdalen and Kate. How they managed it so swiftly in skirts, he didn't know.

And not only skirts. Magdalen's apron bulged oddly, and Kate clinked as she walked.

"Aunt Kate?" he began.

"Don't ask, lad," she said, panting.

He didn't ask.

Mitchell steered the first canoe past with a quick salute, Ayen behind him. Magdalen murmured what sounded like a prayer. Kate took Benjamin's elbow as he guided her along the ledge and down the long slope to the creek.

On his other side, Elizabeth gave a little gasp. A pang sharper than the water's bite ran through Benjamin's chest. What kind of brother protected his sister by making her wade through an ice-cold river under the noses of the enemy?

She still had not spoken to Mitchell about whatever it was that was on her mind. But Mitchell would not be back in the settlement until next Lord's day, maybe later.

Kate splashed along resolutely on his other side, her tight grip on his arm the only sign she might be nervous. A shout and the crack of brush tightened her grip even further. "Rane never should have gone up there."

"He can take care of himself." Benjamin tried to say it like he meant it. He pushed a low-hanging branch aside and scanned the incline that led from the river to the path. Feathery snowflakes caught the moonlight. "A mite farther, and we can climb up and take the back way to the ordinary."

Another shout echoed from far upriver. Benjamin thought of Harrod and Taggart on the trail outside Sunrising and the brief moment of stark fear in Rane's eyes when he had heard Harrod was in the settlement.

He glanced down at Kate. "I'll get you to the kitchen. Then I'll go back and look for Armistead."

Eighteen

THE CREEK PATH WAS DESERTED WHEN BENJAMIN slipped away from the kitchen again. Not until he passed Captain Boothe's cabin and paused at the edge of the woods did he hear voices.

"I saw something. I know I did." Taggart's words were slurred at the edges.

"Sergeant, you're hardly fit to stand watch." Gregory, on the other hand, sounded fully sober. Had others in the great room been sober enough to notice Kate's absence? "Perhaps one of the horses is out."

"A horse wouldn't get out in this foul weather."

"Look by the meeting grounds. I'll check the wood."

Taggart's silhouette, weaving slightly, crossed the creek path up ahead. Benjamin wondered if a man so inebriated would know a loose horse if it ran over him.

Gregory's cape was a dim blot against the snow and night as he made for the woods along the creek. Rane was in those woods. Benjamin slipped around the far side of the cabin and broke into a light run.

The moon cast long shadows through the trees and highlighted the tracks Gregory left in the fresh snow. There would be more snow to cover those tracks by morning. Benjamin ducked between two loblolly pines and glimpsed Rane darting through the trees ahead of Gregory.

The lieutenant did not slow or change course. He lunged just as Rane's boot slipped on a snow-crusted root.

The two men went down together in the snow. Gregory said, "Whoever you are, you had best think twice before you creep around in the dark, or—"

Rane rolled over and went rigid. "Jem Flannery?"

Benjamin halted behind a tree. Who was Jem Flannery?

Gregory's free hand came down over Rane's mouth, forcing his head into the snow. Benjamin nearly came away from the tree. He held himself still as Rane twisted away.

"Armistead." Gregory stood, breathing hard. "You—I thought you were in—"

"The Navy? I was." Rane got to his feet. Benjamin had never heard such bitterness from him, not even when Rane spoke of Harrod. "I thought you were still in Cork."

"There was nothing for me there. I worked for my passage to New York." Gregory gripped the hilt of his sword, let go, gripped it again. "I'm James Arnold Gregory now. No one knows—"

"No one knows what?" Rane's voice hardened. "That you're no Londoner at all? That you're nothing but—"

"A wharf rat from the worst rebel city in Ireland?" Gregory's laugh was harsh, empty. A strained edge of Irish crept into his words. "Harrod would hang me if he knew."

"'Tis a fine thing to work for Harrod after you've hated the British all your life."

"I work for myself, Armistead. Always have."

"Even when it means betraying a friend."

"Even then."

"Woodbridge helped you escape in exchange for your loyalty. Are you playing him for a fool as you did me?"

"I never meant to play either of you for fools. A man

does what he must to be free. Surely you know that."

Rane nodded toward the pistol in Gregory's belt. "Then shoot me and go your lying way with nothing to fear."

The two men stared at each other. Wind lashed the branches overhead. Benjamin drew his knife softly from its sheath and flipped it in his hand, ready to throw it if Gregory raised the pistol.

It had seemed right to save Rane from the king's men. It had seemed right to save Gregory from Captain Carr. But tonight Benjamin wished sincerely that he had never let himself in for such complication.

Gregory stepped back. "You've three minutes before I shout and tell Taggart I've found nothing."

"Flannery—"

"He may already know there's nothing by the meeting grounds, drunk though he is." Gregory spun on his heel and spoke over his shoulder. "Armistead. Go."

Benjamin drew back into the shelter of the pine. Gregory strode past, looking neither right nor left. Benjamin let him pass before he stepped out from behind the tree.

Rane wheeled toward him, drawing his own pistol in one swift move. Benjamin sheathed the knife, though he kept his hand near it.

Rane lowered the pistol. "Where are the others?"

"Safe at the ordinary." Benjamin nodded toward the mangled snow on the riverbank. "What was that?"

Rane's scar was pale in the shadows. "A man does what he thinks best at the moment it must be done."

A man does what he must to be free, Gregory had said.

There were dark, hard secrets behind those words. But Benjamin knew the truth of them all too well.

They stood there a moment, measuring each other. The river rushed on through the dark, plunging over the falls to the ravine. The ravine where Rane had just risked his life, same as Benjamin.

"Your three minutes are half gone," Benjamin said at last. "Come on."

He led the way through the deep woods and back to the ordinary, where he knocked softly at the kitchen door. Kate opened it, already in dry clothing and looking as if she'd been roused from sleep instead of just come in from a frolic in a ravine. "Trying to start a scandal, lads? Prowling about in the wee hours?"

"Just wanted to be sure you were safe." Benjamin glanced around the room. Elizabeth stood by the hearth. Susanna was gone. She and Magdalen had no doubt already returned to Elsie McBraden's cabin.

All was in perfect order. Except for the blanket that lay on the floor with several pounds of gunpowder spread out to dry. No wonder Magdalen's apron had bulged.

"Aunt Kate, if any Tories walked in here—"

"First of all, lad, if any Tories walked in here at this time of night, I'd shoot them," Kate said coolly. "And second, I'd fold that blanket up on itself and no one would be the wiser. Maggie's apron got wet in the wading up the creek. But the rest is hid safe away with the shot we brought back."

He was about to ask how they had opened a powder keg and where the shot was hidden, then thought better of it. "Be careful. That's all I'm going to say. Did Mitchell and Ayen get off safely?"

"Aye, so far as we know."

"How long will it be until the Tories notice what's missing?" Elizabeth asked.

"I reckon we'll find out." Benjamin realized suddenly that he ached in every joint. "Either way, we're obliged for the help. To the both of you."

"We'd not have had it any other way." Kate gripped Rane's fingers with one hand and clasped Benjamin's in the other. "'Twas a brave thing you did, putting yourself in harm's way for us." She squinted at Rane. "But mercy, lad, you look as if you've seen a haint."

Rane furrowed his brow. "A what?"

"A haint. You're white enough to be one yourself."

"Oh. A *haunt*."

"That's what I said." Kate squeezed Benjamin's hand and let go. "Get some sleep, lads, and merry Christmas."

Christmas. How could there be Christmas at a time like this? But maybe that was what Christmas was. The Word made flesh amid the muck of a fallen creation. Peace on earth, good will toward men. Benjamin tried to believe that.

He motioned Rane outside and pulled the door quietly shut. He kept his hand on the haft of his knife as they crossed to the stable, but the yard was still and deserted.

Once inside the stable, Rane said quietly, "Will Mitchell Boothe preach again when he and Ayen return?"

"He'd like to, I'm sure." Benjamin let Rane climb the ladder ahead of him, then followed, wondering if Rane was feeling a need for some preaching. "The Tories won't cotton to folks gathering, but Mitchell would find a way."

"Perhaps it would be just as well," Rane said. "Go on as if nothing is different."

"Is anything different, Armistead?"

Rane turned and met him eye to eye. "No."

Benjamin nodded. "Good."

He lay down and rolled his blanket around him. In the dark of the loft, he saw again the thunder on Lieutenant Gregory's face and heard Rane's demand. *Are you playing him for a fool as you did me?*

Was Gregory playing them all for fools?

Benjamin lay staring into the dark, listening to the wind, until the gray dawn of a new day crept through the window.

 Nineteen

KATE FORCED THE HEARTH SHOVEL BETWEEN two floor puncheons and pushed down with all her might. One of the smoothed logs jerked from its place and settled back again, catching her fingers. "Mercy, now that hurt."

"Mind yourself, Aunt Kate," Susanna said from the table, where she was peeling the chestnuts Kate had boiled for flour—as many as were left after Elizabeth had roasted part of the harvest. "If you hurt yourself, what would we tell . . ."

"Benjamin?" Kate shook her pinched fingers. "You can be saying his name, you know. It's not a curse."

"I know."

"Then try to look it." Kate levered the shovel again and heaved the puncheon up until she could push it atop the one beside it. "Why aren't you ever speaking to him, lass?"

"What's there to speak of?" Susanna gave a little laugh.

Kate glanced wryly at Magdalen, who stood on the other side of the table, slicing nuts as Susanna peeled them. "Folks thought there was plenty to speak of once. Those nuts you're peeling—if those were the hickory nuts I've stored away, you know the talk that would be going 'round."

"That I'd be making him a hickory nut cake. Doing all

the work a lass does only for the lad she fancies." Susanna sighed. "But that was before. I don't want him to get any thoughts in his head about me. Not while he's so angry."

"Well, I can be understanding that." The New Testament still lay on the mantel where Benjamin had left it. "I love him like my own, you know, but I wouldn't marry him myself with the frame of mind he's in just now."

Elizabeth passed her an empty meal sack. Kate scooped a shovelful of dirt into it.

"I'm hurting him." Susanna picked at a stubborn bit of brown chestnut skin. "I can tell it in the way he looks."

"And it hurts you to hurt him."

"But I can't see my way clear to do anything else."

She shed no tears, but Kate knew she was shedding them all in her heart. A woman who cared as deeply as Susanna could not do otherwise.

"Hold your peace and pray, lass. 'Twas the best thing I ever did for my Arthur, even after we'd been wed for years." Kate shoveled another load of dirt into the sack, then cocked her head and listened. "Hear you a horse?"

Magdalen opened the door a crack. "Someone's riding into the settlement, but I can't see him yet."

Kate craned to see over Magdalen's shoulder. A burly rider hove into sight on a familiar roan. "Oh dear."

"Oh dear what?" Elizabeth asked anxiously.

"It's Judge Pembrook, back from the council," Kate said. "And he hasn't the least notion there are Tories about."

Magdalen pulled the door open farther. But even as she did, a knot of sentries converged on the bridge. Judge Pembrook said something Kate could not hear and heaved himself from the saddle. The pickets closed around the judge and marched him up the creek path to Captain Boothe's cabin.

"I expect the best thing to do is pray," Kate said grimly.

Magdalen closed the door. Kate went back to the corner and took up her shovel, but she knew by the silence behind her that the other women were doing just as she had said. *Lord, our help's not in the judge; it's in you,* she prayed silently as she dug. *But be looking out for him, won't you?*

When the sack was full of dirt, she decided she'd dug enough. She beckoned to Elizabeth. "Ready."

Elizabeth reached into the bread oven, soon to be heated to dry the chestnuts, and withdrew a burlap bag. Its contents clinked as she carried it across the kitchen. Kate knew its weight well; she had waded Button Creek with that bag bound up in her cloak.

Elizabeth thumped the bag of shot into the hole, and Kate pushed it as far to one end as she could. "Now the powder."

The powder had been dried and poured into an empty keg, stacked innocently with a pair of flour casks. Kate scraped more dirt from the hole and shoveled it into the hearth at the edge of the fire, where it would soon blend with ash and soot. Elizabeth helped her wrestle the keg into the hole and lay the puncheon back in place.

Kate stamped her foot on the puncheon. It rocked a bit, then settled. "That ought to do it. A bit of sweeping, and no one would ever know."

"I'll do it." Elizabeth reached for the broom.

"Good lass. Maggie, have you some nuts I might bring to Elsie McBraden? I told her I'd bring some gingerroot for the bairns, and I warrant they'd fancy some nuts as well."

"I've a neat little pile not sliced yet," Magdalen said.

"I'll take those now, then. Save some of the water from the boiling—Rane's had a bit of a cough, and it might help him. I'll stop at the stable and tell Benjamin the judge is back."

Kate packed the ginger and boiled chestnuts into her basket, donned her cloak, and stepped outside. The air was crisp and cold, thin shafts of sunlight lancing through breaking clouds. Last night's rain had left the ground muddy, and she lifted her hem as she crossed toward the stable.

The door opened when she was only halfway there. Benjamin stepped out into a patch of sun that turned his kerchief to flame, his hair and skin as tan as the beech-leaf dye of his hunting shirt. He was a man made for the outdoors, not this business of hiding in stables and standing watch at meals. His bow and quiver still hung in the great room, waiting for the day when he could hunt with Selagisqua like old times.

"What is it, Aunt Kate?" he asked, coming toward her.

"I'm off to Elsie McBraden with some nutmeats and ginger. I might carry some to Sarah Perry too. But Benjamin, Judge Pembrook is back. The Tories took him up to their headquarters."

"I saw from the stable." He tucked his kerchief inside his collar, and she saw the tension of the cords in his neck. "Maybe Harrod won't dare to trouble the man who could keep the Cherokee away. But everybody knows how Pembrook hates Tories, and Harrod has Indian agents enough of his own." He lowered his voice. "I hope your powder and shot are hid safe. I've seen Taggart about this morning."

"Under the floor, safe and sound. Here's hoping we never need it."

She knew he did not quite agree. He would relish an open fight. It showed in the tightening of his jaw as he turned back toward the stable and said only, "Tell Elsie we'll get the canoe back to her."

"I will."

Hammering rang from the smithy. The Tories were at work again. Kate passed Alec Perry's house and crossed the path toward the McBraden cabin, thoughts awhirl. Benjamin was still grieving for Walks-in-Winter. Kate could see it in the way he stared off at nothing when he didn't think she was watching, then went at his work with double vengeance.

Lord, I'm that glad to see his arm is better. But the anger in him troubles me. He's the only son I've got left.

One lad lost to an Indian skirmish on the far side of the mountains. The other gone in his own way, like the prodigal son in Scripture. Few in Sunrising even remembered the McGuiness boys anymore.

"Good morning, Widow McGuiness."

The voice startled her out of her thoughts. Nolan Taggart fell into step beside her.

Kate sent up another silent prayer. Taggart was one of the few who did remember the McGuiness boys—too well, mayhap. "Good morning, Mr. Taggart."

"Out visiting? Carrying honey to a friend, mayhap?"

He had seen her gift to Amelia Ashe, then. Kate raised her chin, though she wanted to slap him. "It does a body good to get about, now that the weather's cleared some."

"Aye, it was a hard snow these last days."

He hadn't stopped her to speak of the weather. "And what brings you out this morning?"

"I've every right to be neighborly, Kate."

"'Tis a fine time to begin. And don't be calling me Kate."

"Come, now. Let bygones be bygones, aye?"

"You must still be drunk to think it's so simple."

"Kate. And you a good Christian woman."

Kate bit her tongue. She'd been half glad to see Benjamin throw Taggart's trencher of supper at the man's head that fateful summer day. Not that she'd tell Benjamin so, and not that she was proud of thinking such a thing.

"Where's Mitchell Boothe gone?" Taggart asked. "I've not seen his brother's runt either."

"I really couldn't say." She veered to the right, taking the shortcut past Judge Pembrook's house.

Taggart followed her. "Couldn't or won't?"

"Just what I said." The Blue Ridge was a powerful big place for a man and a boy and two canoes. She nodded back toward the creek path. "Was that Judge Pembrook I saw?"

"Back from one of his councils, I'll be bound. The lads took him to Major Harrod."

"What will Harrod do with him?"

"It's no concern of yours. Harrod's business is his own."

"And yours too, mayhap?"

He stopped suddenly and turned, blocking her way. "You're full of questions. Answer a few of mine. Someone's been stirring around in the dark along the creek path, and I've a notion that between you and Woodbridge and Mitchell Boothe, one of you knows who it is and why."

She made to step around him. "Really, Mr. Taggart—"

He caught her arm, pushing her against Pembrook's cabin. "You can answer me, or I'll take it out of them."

He hadn't mentioned Rane. The lad had stayed out of sight, then. "Is this the way you treated your wife, God rest her? I don't wonder your daughter took up with my son, if you're what she was used to. You've taken one lad from me with your scheming ways, and you'll not take another."

Something flashed in his eyes—anger, but for a moment Kate thought it was pain. It was an unfair blow she'd struck.

Snow crunched at the corner of the cabin. A deep voice interrupted Taggart's reply. "Let the lady alone, Sergeant."

Judge Pembrook. So the Tories had let him go.

Taggart drew himself up to his full height, like a banty rooster taking on a fighting cock. "I was just asking her if Mitchell Boothe would be preaching this Sunday."

That was not what he'd asked at all. But Kate didn't see much point in arguing.

"You've no call to trouble a preacher, other than your own wretched temper," Pembrook said. "Begone with you."

"I'll have you arrested."

"Your men already tried. Speak to your Major Harrod about it if you've a mind, but keep yourself clear of me. I've no use for your ilk, and well you know it."

Taggart backed up another step. "We'll see what Harrod says to that."

"Aye. So we will. Now get out of my sight."

Taggart glanced from one to the other and strode away.

"Harrod truly let you go?" Kate asked.

"He hadn't much choice, not when I'm the man who can keep the Cherokee away from him."

"But he has his own Indian agents. Benjamin says so."

"Keep your voice down. And never you mind that. I'll have to be careful, that's all."

A shiver ran through her. All those trade goods, waiting for the Cherokee. But she dared not tell Pembrook what she had helped to do. Not if he already had to be careful.

"Was it being careful to speak so to Mr. Taggart?"

"I don't fret about Taggart, and neither should you." He offered his arm. "Shall we get you home?"

"I was going to McBradens'. But it's just as well if I wait." She laid her hand through his elbow, feeling she had to tilt her own elbow far too high to do it.

Pembrook shortened his stride so she could keep pace. "They burned the meetinghouse, I see."

"Aye. If Mitchell does preach this Lord's day, it'll be in the clearing by the creek, I'm fearing."

"Someone should tell him it's foolhardy to carry on so with these villains about."

"You be telling him, then. You know what he'll say."

Pembrook shrugged. Kate nearly lost her grip of his elbow. "Something about doing the right thing, I'm sure."

"He's right, of course." Her conscience pricked her. She hadn't exactly done the right thing in her speech to Taggart.

"Now, Kate. He'll be making a Baptist of you yet."

"I didn't mean he was right about that. But it'd do you good to listen to him now and again."

"My dealings with the Almighty are my own." He smiled down at her, but she sensed the subject was dismissed. There was a warning in his eyes. "Watch yourself, Kate. And tell Mitchell the same."

Twenty

"BENJAMIN. WAKE UP."

Benjamin opened his eyes. Elizabeth crouched beside his bedroll.

He flung his blanket aside and sat up. "What is it?"

"Harrod's gone. Him and maybe twenty men, sometime last night. Aunt Kate said I should tell you."

Benjamin looked over at Rane, who was sitting up with his blanket still wrapped around his shoulders. "Harrod said he wouldn't leave until he was confident all was in order," Benjamin said grimly.

"He's bound for Cornwallis, then," Rane said.

"Aye. And who knows what after that. At least he never did catch sight of you." Benjamin pulled himself to his feet and folded the blanket. "Are Gregory and Taggart still here?"

"I saw them gathering the men for breakfast," Elizabeth said. "Aunt Kate was hoping to get folks fed quick this morning so we'd have time for meeting."

Lord's day. Benjamin had near about forgotten. And Mitchell was back in the settlement, Ayen with him.

"I'll go out now and see what's afoot," he said.

Elizabeth hurried down the ladder. Benjamin shook his

hair free of straw and tied it at the nape of his neck, then belted his hunting shirt. "Keep out of sight, Armistead, until we're sure Harrod's gone."

When he reached the creek path, there was nothing to see. Nothing but the places where horses' hooves had struck snow and frozen earth. The settlement seemed eerily quiet, holding its breath against Harrod's return.

For he *would* return. Benjamin had no doubt of that.

He stood watch in the great room again while the Tories broke their fast. When the men had gone, Benjamin escorted Kate and Elizabeth toward McGuiness Creek. The sheltered clearing on the creek's far bank had known many a prayer meeting, but always in summer, when there were too many folks to fit into one sweltering room. Never in winter, and never because the king's men had burned the meetinghouse.

"Do you think the Tories will make trouble with Harrod gone?" Elizabeth asked. "Mr. Taggart wanted to know if Brother Mitchell would be preaching today."

"We'll be away out in the woods. No reason they'd come looking, so long as we slip out yonder a few at a time."

"Is Mr. Armistead going to come?"

"He wasn't sure. I half hope he doesn't. Aunt Kate said Taggart still doesn't know Armistead's been helping us."

But Gregory did. Had he known about Walks-in-Winter too? If he had, and if he knew what Harrod was about and had given no warning, then Lieutenant James Arnold Gregory had a powerful lot to answer for.

Benjamin led the way along McGuiness Creek, holding branches aside for Kate and Elizabeth. Farther upriver, Mitchell Boothe strode along the bank. He wheeled quickly, then lifted his hand when he saw them.

Benjamin returned the greeting. "Mouse, you said there was something you'd meant to speak of to Brother Mitchell."

"Oh. That." Elizabeth fidgeted with her cloak.

"What?" He slowed his pace. Elizabeth was never one

for rushing headlong into saying what she thought.

"You remember the stories Preacher Boothe—Captain Boothe—used to tell about Sandy Creek? All the people who got converted there when Elder Stearns was preaching?"

"Aye," he said.

"And the baptisms that went on for hours, with folks wanting other folks to know what had happened?"

"I remember." It had been thirty years since that mighty awakening at Sandy Creek, but Robert's stories had made it seem like last Sunday's meeting.

"Well, that's what I meant to ask Brother Mitchell."

He glanced at Kate. She shrugged.

"You've a chance now, Mouse." He nodded at Mitchell.

"Oh, no. No, I . . . not today."

Benjamin did not press the question. They came alongside Mitchell, and Benjamin asked him, "Any trouble?"

"None as yet," Mitchell said. "Maybe we'd have had no trouble meeting in the open, but the Tories won't look well on any gathering of the settlement folk at a time like this."

"Not when a rebel circuit rider is doing the gathering."

"True enough. You saw Harrod leave?"

"Elizabeth told me. Bound for Cornwallis, most likely."

The edges of the creek were crusted with ice, though the center of the stream ran free. Harrod would have a cold ride down the ridge, and well he deserved it.

Lord God, I know my mind should be on you just now. But you can't hardly blame me for fretting on Harrod.

More settlement folk joined them. Benjamin glanced back just in time to catch Susanna Boothe's eye. He wasn't sure who looked away faster.

Then he turned the other way, and Rane Armistead was there. "What are you doing here?"

"Coming to form my own opinion," Rane said.

"'Opinion in good men is but knowledge in the making.'"

"More like mere curiosity. I wonder what Milton would

have said to that."

It was more than mere curiosity. Rane was always quiet, but he had been far more so ever since the meeting with Gregory in the woods.

"No sign of Harrod?" Rane said in a low voice.

"I saw where they went out. Nothing more. Gregory and Taggart looked to be in command at the ordinary."

Rane nodded, but his face had gone taut at the mention of Gregory. Benjamin hardly blamed him. Gregory was making Benjamin feel mighty tense too.

He noticed Mitchell glancing their way and spoke more lightly. "Best be careful, Armistead. We might pray in strange tongues and bark like dogs and fall down as if slain."

"Indeed, and I might pray in Latin, so we'll be even."

"That's a strange tongue in itself."

"Whisht, lads," Kate said, shaking her head. "Across the creek with the both of you."

It was a small party on the bank of McGuiness Creek. Mitchell prayed and opened his Bible to the story of Philip the evangelist and the Ethiopian man who had read Isaiah without knowing what it meant.

Why couldn't Mitchell have chosen something like David's mighty men or the final judgment? That would be more in keeping with Benjamin's temper.

Harrod had left Gregory in command. And Gregory was hiding something. The thought of it nagged Benjamin's mind.

"Philip 'preached unto him Jesus,'" Mitchell was saying. "That fellow in the chariot, he didn't need to be a better man. He didn't need to be a Jew. He didn't need anything but *Jesus*. And I'm thinking Jesus is what the lot of us need, right here on this riverbank."

Benjamin jerked his attention back to Mitchell, ashamed of himself.

"It's time some of us stopped trying to fix things on our own and looked to Jesus," Mitchell went on. "His life in us.

Why do you think the Ethiopian asked to be baptized? Right there in the next verse—'here is water; what doth hinder me to be baptized?' Because baptism was what he needed? No. Jesus was what he needed. He knew that, better than some folks do now. And he wanted to show his colors."

Elizabeth tugged at Benjamin's elbow. "Benjamin."

"Mm."

"I know I said not today . . ."

"About what?" he whispered.

"Being baptized."

He bent his head. "That's what you were trying to say?"

"Yes. But I do want to. Today."

"Mouse—"

"Here's water, like the Ethiopian said." Her whisper was deadly earnest. "All that's hindered me is my fear."

He'd wondered for years when she would gather up the courage to declare her faith in front of everyone. But *today?* With Tories in the settlement and ice on the riverbank?

"Folks are dying right now for what they believe in," Elizabeth said. "I want to show my colors."

Kate would not agree, but neither would she object. And Benjamin had no more right to stand in his sister's way than the Church of England had to stand in his.

"If God's leading you, do it," he said at last.

She nodded again, her eyes shining with eagerness.

Something yawned open inside, an emptiness where that kind of joy had once been. He'd been twelve when Robert Boothe baptized him in the Haw River. Right before his world—Elizabeth's world—went all to pieces.

"Proud of you, Mouse," he said hoarsely, hoping she wouldn't ask if he was all right, because he wasn't.

Rane bowed his head for Mitchell's prayer, but his thoughts refused to lie in quiet reverence. Benjamin had asked him whether the king had any right to religious allegiance. Rane did not have an answer for that. But what an extraordinary lot he had taken up with. Not least of whom was the circuit rider who wore buckskins and preached on creekbanks after coolly hauling a canoe full of British arms downriver to renegade Indians.

The prayer ended. Elizabeth Woodbridge hurried up to Mitchell and began speaking earnestly in low tones.

Rane slipped his prayer book surreptitiously out of his pocket. The Revered Doctor Ezekiel Warwick had no right to his religious allegiance, however strong their tie as nephew and uncle had once been. But surely the king's authority was not entirely unwarranted. Render unto Caesar the things that are Caesar's.

And to God the things that are God's.

Did religion belong to God or to Caesar?

That seemed simple enough. So simple it jarred him. The very thought of Uncle Warwick's reaction made him feel like an infidel.

Mitchell's voice broke into his thoughts. "Listen up, the lot of you. Elizabeth has asked me to baptize her."

Rane glanced around the gathering. Some ministers of the Church held immersion as the proper biblical mode. But Uncle Warwick had described it as a ritual nearly pagan in its exposure of the human form, blasphemy of the holy Trinity already invoked at christening. Though Rane doubted Elizabeth Woodbridge had ever been christened.

He did not quite believe, as the Thirty-Nine Articles taught, that baptism grafted a soul into the kingdom of God. Even Sir William Blackstone's *Commentaries on the Laws of England* had assumed baptism as the entrance to Christianity, but Rane's own dealings with God had challenged that notion. And yet . . .

He slipped the prayer book back inside his coat, fingering its outline. *From all false doctrine, heresy, and schism; from the hardness of heart, and contempt of thy Word and*

Commandment, Good Lord, deliver us.

"You've asked to be baptized," Mitchell said to Elizabeth, stripping out of his coat as he spoke. "As Philip said, 'If thou believest with all thine heart, thou mayest.'"

Elizabeth handed her cloak to her brother. "As the Ethiopian said, 'I believe that Jesus Christ is the Son of God.'"

"Tell me what the Bible says baptism is," Mitchell said.

"The answer of a good conscience toward God."

"What does it show?"

"That when Christ died, I died with him, and when he rose, I did too."

Setting his boots aside, Mitchell stepped into the water and helped Elizabeth off the bank beside him. "Then I baptize you in the name of the Father, the Son, and the Holy Ghost, buried in the likeness of his death—"

He plunged her under, brought her up. "Raised in the likeness of his resurrection."

Water streamed from Elizabeth's hair. She gasped with the cold. Benjamin helped her up the bank and flung her cloak around her shoulders. She embraced him, wearing the brightest smile Rane had seen from her yet.

Buried in the likeness of his death, raised in the likeness of his resurrection . . .

Mitchell prayed again, shorter this time. "And all God's people said—"

"What's the meaning of this?"

Rane wheeled. Nolan Taggart strode out of the trees, Jem Flannery behind him.

No, not Jem Flannery. Lieutenant James Arnold Gregory. What a cowardly lie.

Benjamin had gone as taut as a ship's halyard in the freezing rains of the North Atlantic. His sister pressed against him, her plaited hair dripping on his Sunday coat.

Rane moved forward a step, catching Benjamin's eye. The man's place was with Kate and his sister. Let Rane intervene, if it came to that. After all, his desire in reading law had been to aid the oppressed. And he was weary of hiding.

Benjamin shook his head. Rane folded his arms.

Mitchell broke the tense silence. "This is a celebration of the Lord's redemption. I'd have invited you lads, had I known you wanted to come."

Jem Flannery's uniform was a stark splash of crimson against the gray landscape as he pivoted slowly to scan the gathering, his face utterly impassive. Another lie. When his eyes landed on Rane, he jerked his gaze away.

Taggart moved toward the river, where Mitchell had stepped onto the bank and pulled on his boots. Rane found himself leaning forward as if coiled to spring.

He might not know what he thought of all this. But he would not let Jem throw someone else to the wolves.

"All I know," Taggart said, "is that we've found Major Harrod's goods missing from his keeping place, and we've seen folks along the creek path of a night. You know anything about that?"

"Even if I did," Mitchell said, "it's no cause for you to interrupt this set-apart time."

"Your set-apart time looks a mighty lot like sedition to me."

Benjamin snorted. "Everything looks like sedition to you."

"I don't preach sedition; I preach Jesus." Mitchell pulled his coat on, never taking his eyes off Taggart. "If you don't like it, you had best talk to him."

Taggart hit him in the mouth. Mitchell spat blood on the ground. Rane sprang forward, nearly colliding with Benjamin. "Let the man alone, Sergeant."

Taggart stepped back. "Not so quiet as you seem, eh?"

"You cannot punish a man for speaking his conscience. He's done you no harm."

His words rang in his own mind, stirring up echoes four years gone. *Let him alone, sir. He's done you no harm.*

"You a Baptist like the rest of this rabble?" Taggart said. "Or a Presbyterian like Kate, mayhap?"

"Neither. I hold to the Church of England."

Was that still true? Either way, it would shock some of the settlers gathered around. Well, it was time they knew.

Taggart spat in the mud. "Let's hear the prayer for the king's success, then."

"Sergeant," Jem began.

"Prayer is not a thing done for sport," Rane said. How had Taggart known to choose the sorest point? That prayer had caused the final break between Rane and his uncle.

"It's better sport than some other things I've heard done," Taggart retorted.

"Let him be, Taggart," Benjamin said sharply.

"You hate Anglicans as much as you hate Tories."

"Aye, when they deserve it. This one doesn't."

Taggart turned back toward Rane, the look in his eyes every bit as vicious as Captain Symonds of HMS *Solebay*. He moved forward, edging Rane toward the river. "You stand with these Baptists? You had best be one of them, then."

Elizabeth screamed. That was all Rane heard before he went under.

Water surged over him, tangled his cloak around him. A hundred nightmares sprang to life. Freedom slipping away. Jem standing by. Pain radiating through his head. And then nothing.

Twenty-One

BENJAMIN LUNGED INTO THE WATER, GRABBED
Taggart by his collar, flung him backward. Taggart landed
with a splash and a curse. Benjamin turned Rane over and
dragged him ashore. Rane's dark hair plastered his face, water
running pink across a gash in his forehead. Mitchell helped
lift him onto the bank.

Behind Benjamin, Taggart started getting up. Benjamin
swung around. *One good fight, Lord. Just one good fight.*

But Elizabeth was watching. Her day had been ruined
enough already.

"Lieutenant Gregory," he said, still keeping his eyes on
Taggart. "Get your sergeant out of here."

Taggart moved in. Benjamin said, "You heard me."

"Enough, Sergeant," Lieutenant Gregory said sharply.

Fine time to be stepping in, Benjamin thought. Taggart
hesitated, then stepped up on the bank to join Gregory.

The lieutenant glanced at Rane, an unreadable expression in his eyes. "Get him indoors," he said, low and hard,
and wheeled and walked away.

"Take Elizabeth to Elsie's place with you and Susanna
and get her dry," Kate murmured to Magdalen.

Benjamin did not look at Mitchell's cut lip as they lifted Rane together. He was angry enough already.

By the time they reached the kitchen at the ordinary, Benjamin's shoulder felt wrenched all over again. Kate made a hasty pallet by the hearth. Benjamin eased Rane down and stepped out of the way.

Kate pushed Rane's hair aside and examined his forehead. The gash wasn't deep, but a bruise had already risen.

"That'll be swole up good by tonight," Benjamin said.

"Not if I can help it." Kate cut an onion from the braided strand beside the hearth and tucked it in the coals to roast. "Get his wet things off."

"His saddlebags are in the loft," Benjamin told Mitchell.

Kate began boiling water as Mitchell went out. Benjamin peeled Rane's sodden cloak, coat, and waistcoat away and undid the linen cravat, then opened Rane's collar and rolled him onto his side. The shirt's neck slit stretched and slid down over Rane's shoulder. "Oh, Lord, have mercy."

The firelight spilled across Rane's upper back. Scores of old scars crisscrossed the skin, angry welts long healed. Benjamin could feel more of them through the wet linen.

Kate turned before he could stop her. Her mouth fell open. She snapped it shut and cleared her throat. "The poor lad. He'd not be wanting us to see . . ." She trailed off. "Well, it's too late now. Go on and hurry before he wakes."

Mitchell came back with the saddlebags. Kate shooed him back out with orders to make sure no Tories came nosing about. Benjamin laid Rane's wet pistol aside with his damp prayer book and the oilcloth pouch that held Harrod's letter to Ferguson. Then he wrestled Rane into dry clothes, his mind churning with questions.

Rane did not stir until Kate started to clean the gash in his forehead. He coughed raggedly and winced.

Kate made mother-hen noises. "There, now, you're all right." She bandaged the onion poultice in place and said to

Benjamin, "Hand me that mug yonder."

Benjamin handed her the mug, eyeing the jagged mark on Rane's right temple. What had been done to him in the Navy? What did Lieutenant Gregory have to do with it all? Rane took the sip Kate coaxed him to, then pushed the mug away, his gaze searching the room. Benjamin pointed to the oilcloth packet. Rane relaxed.

"Now," Kate said. "How long have you been feeling poorly and not telling me? That cough was hounding you before today, and I've a notion you'd have come around a good deal faster just now if you weren't already ailing."

"It's been this way a good while. The cough. Not—" Rane moved one hand weakly. "Whatever else happened."

"Taggart shoved you in the river," Benjamin said. "You hit your head on a rock, looks like."

"How long is a good while?" Kate demanded, pushing the mug on Rane again.

Rane took another careful sip, not quite hiding a grimace. "Four or five years, perhaps. It's no matter."

Since the Navy, if Benjamin's guess was right. "Looks as if you'll get a new scar to match that old one there."

Rane plucked the dry shirt away from his skin, his eyes on Benjamin's. "You saw the rest."

It was not a question. Benjamin nodded.

"Captain Symonds mishandled the cabin boy. I spoke out and paid the price." Faint bitterness edged his words. "I ought to have known today would be no different."

"It was a brave thing you did, standing up for Brother Mitchell," Kate said.

"A lot of good it did." Rane coughed again.

Kate tsked. "If everybody was after doing as you did, this world would be a better place, it would."

"Did Gregory have aught to do with . . ." Benjamin paused. It was no concern of his.

"Gregory's not what he seems, Woodbridge."

"Don't I know it."

"In any case, I've drawn Taggart's notice now." Rane closed his eyes. "No doubt he'll come here to investigate as soon as he has opportunity."

"Let him," Kate said. "This is my home, what's left of it, and I'll not be letting the likes of Nolan Taggart be scaring me out of it. Nor the likes of James Arnold Gregory either."

"Aunt Kate—" Benjamin began.

"And I'll not be letting the likes of you talk me out of my own mind." Kate swept onion skins off the table and fed them to the flames on the hearth. "For all we know, we're borrowing trouble. He may not come 'round at all."

Rane opened his eyes again, focusing on Benjamin. "You told Taggart you hate Anglicans only when they deserve it. I suppose I ought to thank you for deciding I don't deserve it."

"That might have been a poor choice of words."

"You said once that my uncle was everything you hate about Anglicans."

Benjamin was in no frame of mind to argue religion with Rane. Not today. "Let's just say he preached loud and clear that backwater folk were the scum of the earth and it was heresy for a man to have personal dealings with God."

Rane winced. "I heard him say the same."

"Did you agree?"

"I regret to say I avoided thinking about it."

"This war has got us all thinking about things we'd rather avoid." Benjamin got to his feet. "I'm going to see whether Elizabeth's ready to come home."

He strode outside. Elizabeth was just walking into the stable yard, Susanna beside her.

"All right, Mouse?" he said to Elizabeth.

"Dry, at least," she said with a little grimace.

"Rane's faring better; go on in."

Elizabeth slipped past him. Susanna turned to go.

"Susanna. Wait."

She stopped and turned back. For the briefest moment he saw something in her eyes, a caring so deep and open that he felt all the more wretched.

"You barely speak to me," he said. "I thought we—"

She sighed. "Everyone did."

"Didn't you?" he said, low.

"I see this anger in you, Benjamin. I'm frightened of it."

"You needn't be. It's not you I'm angry with."

"I know. But anger is like poison. It makes men do things they never thought they'd do. That's what frightens me."

"Sometimes a man has a right to be angry."

"I'm sorry about Walks-in-Winter. Truly I am." She lifted one hand as if to reach for him, then drew it back and laced her fingers together. Hardworking hands that had helped many a settler, and had likely helped him when he was lying on a table too insensible to know.

"He was a good man," Benjamin said. "There have been too many good men . . ."

"Like your pa."

Straight to the heart of the matter, that was Susanna. "You don't think I've a right to be angry about that?"

"Of course I don't think—" She stopped herself, and he half wished she would go on so he could argue. "It's not mine to say what you've a right to be angry about. That belongs to the Lord. Take it to him, Benjamin. He knows what it is to grieve."

"I've had enough of grieving." He could feel the low fire building in him, would not let her see it and think she was right. "Don't fret, Susanna. You've naught to fear."

She started to speak, then simply nodded. "I'm praying. I never stopped praying."

"Maybe yours will get answered," he said, and turned and walked into the kitchen.

Twenty-Two

THE DAY PASSED SLOWLY. STANDING GUARD during the Tories' meals only fanned the flame of Benjamin's anger. He quelled it tightly, hoping Kate and Elizabeth could not see the wrath in him. They had enough to fret over already.

After the evening meal, Benjamin went out to the stable to help Ayen with the horses. Rane was in no state to do the chores, and Mitchell had slipped out of the settlement in search of Hank.

Mitchell was right to go; maybe Hank would know why Harrod had left. But Benjamin could not help feeling that one more support had been kicked out from under him.

He emptied a pail of water into the trough, his right shoulder aching. Droplets spattered the hunting shirt and leggings he'd thrown on after the baptism. *A baptism, Lord. You could have at least kept the Tories away from a thing like that.*

Lieutenant Gregory's dun-colored gelding whickered softly and nudged Benjamin's good shoulder. He straightened and rubbed the gelding's handsome muzzle. "Reckon it's not your fault if Gregory owns you, aye?"

The man had had one opportunity after another to intervene or give warning of Harrod's intentions. But good men were dead and good women suffered, and Gregory had done nothing to stop it.

I don't care for my own sake, Lord. Benjamin hoped the Almighty believed him. *But Elizabeth? And Armistead? What have they ever done?*

Walks-in-Winter hadn't done anything either. And look where that had gotten him.

Ayen clattered into the stable, water slopping over the rim of his bucket. "Benjamin! Lieutenant Gregory just went into the kitchen!"

Benjamin swung around. "What?"

"He came down the path at a powerful pace and just knocked on the door and Aunt Kate let him in."

Gregory had had his chance. Benjamin should have left him in the prisoner camp. He flung his empty bucket aside. "Stay out here."

He pushed past Ayen, strode out the door, and doubled his pace across the yard. His rifle was in the loft, hidden from Tories who might happen into the stable, but there was no time to fetch it. And he didn't need a rifle for this.

He slammed the kitchen door open. Gregory's back was to him. Kate stood at the table, calmly chopping vegetables. Beside her, Elizabeth clutched a ladle in a white-knuckled fist. Rane leaned on the wall, his arms folded, looking like he needed to lie down.

Gregory turned at the sound of the door. Benjamin shut it hard. "What do you want, Gregory?"

"Taggart is on his way here."

"Because you sent him, aye?"

Gregory flinched as if Benjamin had struck him. Benjamin wanted nothing more than to do just that.

"No," Gregory said. "No, I let him come, but I—"

His eyes darted toward the door, and he pushed past Benjamin. "I must go."

Benjamin caught him by his epauletted right shoulder

and spun him around, shoving him back a step. "After all Captain Boothe did for you?"

Gregory spoke through clenched teeth. "Has it not occurred to you, Woodbridge, that a spy must act as one?"

Kate gasped. Benjamin stepped closer. "Is that your reason for breaking up my sister's baptism today?"

"Benjamin, please," Elizabeth said in a small voice. "That was Mr. Taggart's doing."

"Gregory's responsible for Taggart. Harrod left him in command." Benjamin kept his stare fixed on Gregory, on the scarlet coat, felt the rage rise in him like a living thing. "What about when you accosted Susanna Boothe? When you arrested Judge Pembrook? When you let Taggart question Aunt Kate?"

"I didn't—" Gregory began.

Benjamin grabbed the lapel of Gregory's coat. The olive-green facing tore in his grasp. "And when your men killed Walks-in-Winter?"

Gregory looked confused. Salt in the wound. "I've no idea what you're speaking of. Taggart mentioned an old savage, but there's nothing I—"

Benjamin's vicious right to his jaw sent him crashing against the wall. Pain jarred through Benjamin's knuckles and up to his shoulder.

He gripped the torn coat and jerked Gregory upright, wishing it were Taggart or Harrod he had in his grasp. "That *old savage* was a better man than you'll ever be."

Kate and Elizabeth and Rane were saying words he did not hear through the rush of blood in his ears. He pulled Gregory away from the wall and flung him backward.

Gregory landed hard against the table. Kate's vegetables went flying. Elizabeth jumped out of the way, past the edge of Benjamin's vision.

The door opened. Gregory forced himself to his feet. Benjamin moved in, crowding him against the table, willing Gregory to strike back and give him the fight he wanted.

But Gregory shouted over Benjamin's shoulder. "Taggart! Arrest this imbecile."

Taggart's name was flint on steel. Benjamin swung around, fist arcing in a fierce backhanded swing.

The back of his hand met soft flesh and braided hair.

Elizabeth. No.

His sister uttered a quiet cry and folded against the wall. Rane caught her and eased her down. Benjamin took a step toward her, feeling as dazed as if he'd taken the blow himself. Straight to the heart.

Taggart's grip on his wrist stopped him. He twisted away and drove a left to Taggart's face.

A brutal right hook came straight at his chin. Lights burst in his head like priming sparks. He staggered, trying not to fall on top of Elizabeth.

Taggart slammed him against the wall. Benjamin threw him off, fighting the haze that clouded the room. Taggart came in again, wrenched his shoulder back, twisted his arm high behind him.

The world turned gray. Benjamin doubled over and fell to his knees. Right where he belonged.

Behind him, Elizabeth whimpered softly.

Oh God. What have I done?

Twenty-Three

"IF I WERE GREGORY, I'D HAVE PUT YOU OUT OF your misery." Taggart opened the door of Captain Boothe's cabin and pushed Benjamin inside. The strip of whang leather binding Benjamin's wrists burned at the tug on his elbow.

"Lucky for me you're not Gregory." The room was dim, lit only by the dull glow of the hearth. Taggart marshaled him across the room to the same bedchamber where Benjamin had hidden on the night of the first foray into the ravine. Taggart shoved him through the doorway and slammed the door.

Cold air washed over Benjamin, setting his bruised jaw to throbbing. The window must still be uncovered, though Taggart might not have seen it in the dim light. Could Benjamin slip through with his hands bound behind him?

Not likely. And not much use if Taggart lurked nearby.

Benjamin leaned against the wall, his head pounding. Did Elizabeth have the same pulsing headache? A bruise by her brother's own hand?

He tried to ignore the pain that stabbed his shoulder. That pain was easier to ignore than the ache somewhere under his ribcage. The ache that said, *This is all your fault.*

It wasn't his fault. He'd been trying to protect Kate and

Elizabeth, that was all.

But Gregory hadn't hurt them. Hadn't even tried to hurt them. Benjamin had done that just fine on his own.

Taggart is on his way here, Gregory had said. A warning. Gregory had taken a risk to deliver that warning. A risk Benjamin had more than doubled. A prudent man would have asked more questions before reacting. The Book of Proverbs said it was folly and shame to a man if he answered a matter before he heard it.

Benjamin blew out a breath and rested his head against the wall. This wasn't about Gregory at all. It wasn't even about Harrod or Taggart.

This was about him, Benjamin Woodbridge. And the anger he had nurtured until it was a living, breathing part of him.

God, I don't know how to fix this.

The front door slammed, a welcome interruption to his thoughts. Two pairs of boots thudded across the floor, a not-so-welcome reminder that Benjamin was at the mercy of the man he'd accused of treachery and thrown into a table.

"Go to the inn and ensure that the men are retiring in good order," Gregory said. "Return here for further orders."

"Yes, sir." The front door opened and shut.

Footsteps approached Benjamin's door. He straightened away from the wall and braced himself.

The door opened and Gregory stepped inside, a gleam of steel in his hand. Benjamin's hunting knife.

Benjamin clenched his bound hands behind his back. He didn't know how to stop being angry. But he could at least try to do the right thing. "Gregory, I was wrong."

Gregory's step hitched, as if Benjamin had surprised him. That was enough for a new wash of shame.

"We've no time for that." Gregory motioned with the knife. Benjamin turned, keeping Gregory in the corner of his vision. The coolness of the blade brushed his forearm. The whang leather pulled tight, then fell away.

He flexed his shoulder, glad to find the pain had eased. "Gregory, whose side are you on?"

"My own." Gregory sheathed the knife. "Though I've done my best to do right by you and the captain."

"Even though you had me arrested."

"Taggart had his finger on the trigger. You would be dead otherwise. And I had a need to speak with you. Goods are missing from a cave where Harrod stored gifts for the Cherokee. That's why Taggart interrupted your meeting at the river and why he came to the kitchen just now. I assume you know where those goods have gone."

At least Benjamin's arrest had distracted Taggart from his purpose. "How did you know where we were meeting?"

"Taggart told me. How he found out, I don't know. There's a good deal I don't know."

The dim light from the window fell across the dark bruise already mottling Gregory's jaw. Benjamin knew he had one of his own to match.

"Did you know about Walks-in-Winter?" he asked quietly.

"No. I swear to you."

"Tell me what you do know."

"Harrod has two hundred Cherokees at his beck and call, but he's still recruiting. I don't know who his agents are. Some of the Indians are holding the stockade at Pembrook Station. Harrod has Loyalists there as well. His lieutenants in the valley are rallying more. We're a full-fledged regiment now, like the American Volunteers."

There was no mistaking the bitterness in his voice. Benjamin turned toward the window, thinking. "The Volunteers came from up north, I heard."

"Aye, from New York. Edmund Fanning mustered the provincials and called them—us—the Associated Refugees."

"Edmund Fanning." Benjamin wheeled swiftly. "He was in Governor Tryon's inner circle, same as Harrod. Now Harrod's doing the same thing Fanning did. You're called the Second Associated, aren't you?"

"Yes, but . . ."

But with a grim twist, if Rane's stolen letter was to be believed. "Harrod thinks the backcountry partisans are worthless, Gregory. He's using you for his own ends, though I don't know how."

He had not thought Gregory could look any more haunted. But Gregory did.

"I wouldn't blame you if you wanted to get out while you can," Benjamin said.

"I've enough on my conscience as it is." Gregory shook his head. "Cornwallis wants to overpower the American army and cut supply lines to the backcountry. Harrod is joining Cornwallis now. But he'll return. Eight weeks, he told me. He'll call in his men from Pembrook Station, and this settlement will go up in flames. He's using Sunrising to prove to Cornwallis what he can do."

"I'm not surprised he has it in for Sunrising. Captain Boothe knocked Harrod unconscious and killed his henchman almost ten years ago."

"I daresay Sunrising now represents all the backwater men who caused Ferguson's demise." Gregory paused. "Harrod and Ferguson were friends, it's said."

"I've heard the same." He wouldn't say where he'd heard it; that would mean betraying Rane's letter. But what bitter irony that Benjamin wanted revenge on Harrod and Harrod wanted revenge on Benjamin.

"I've not seen the captain's courier in weeks," Gregory said. "Someone must warn Boothe before it's too late."

"Gregory, I can't up and leave at a time like this."

"It's your neck Taggart's after. You're not safe here. I'll protect your sister and Widow McGuiness, but somebody's got to be warning the captain before it's too late."

There it was again, the rough edge of brogue Benjamin had heard in the woods. If only he could see behind the man's flat, shadowed expression. He could sense the tension Gregory carried, a desperation that was not feigned.

"What's in it for you?" Benjamin asked.

"A chance to get away from all this," Gregory said. "And perhaps to atone a bit for my part in it."

Eight weeks. This settlement will go up in flames.

Selagisqua and his renegades could not last long against British-armed warriors and Tory partisans. The Dove & Olive would end in ashes just as the meetinghouse had. He did not want to think what could happen to Kate and Elizabeth.

"Taggart will return at any moment." Gregory handed him the sheathed knife. "You'll have to escape while he's here, or he'll blame me for letting you slip away."

Benjamin secured the sheath to his belt and held out his hand. "You do wrong by your end of the bargain, I'll find you."

"I've no doubt of it." Gregory's thin smile did not reach his eyes. His grip was firm, but his palm was clammy against Benjamin's. "Best of luck, Woodbridge. You'll need it."

He stepped back into the common room. The front door opened and shut. Taggart said, "The men are in order, sir."

"Excellent. Our prisoner is as well."

Benjamin hooked his toe under a stool and hurled it at the door. That ought to prove he was still under lock and key.

"Sergeant, where is the rebel's knife?" Gregory asked.

"I had it right here in my belt, sir . . ." Taggart trailed off. "I must have dropped it on the way here, sir."

Benjamin laid his hand over the hilt of that very object. Now Gregory was a pickpocket too?

"No doubt you'll find it tomorrow," Gregory said. "All quiet in the settlement?"

"Yes, sir."

Benjamin took that as his cue. He crossed the room and wriggled through the window. There was no rain to hide his tracks, but he would be far and away by the time anyone knew.

But first he had an apology to make.

The settlement was silent. Benjamin crept through the last shades of twilight until he was safe in the trees along McGuiness Creek. The baptism seemed an eternity ago.

Slipping out of the cover of the woods, he crossed to the stable. He let himself in silently and climbed the ladder, mindful of the two rungs that creaked.

"Woodbridge?"

Rane's voice was barely a whisper. It still made Benjamin jump. "Aye." He stepped into the loft and felt along the wall until his fingers found his rifle. "All right?"

"Well enough. Did they release you?"

"Yes. And no." Benjamin groped for his saddlebags. "Harrod's coming back in eight weeks with more Tories and the Cherokee. In the meantime, he's ravaging the valleys and riding to join Cornwallis. Leastways that's what Gregory said."

"You believe him?"

"I don't know, Armistead. You'd have believed him, I think, if you'd seen him say it. But either way, I can't take the chance. I'm riding to warn Captain Boothe." He paused in his rapid packing. "Is Elizabeth all right?"

"In body, yes. Aside from a bruise."

Benjamin winced, glad of the dark. "I made a fool of myself."

"You could not have known Gregory came to warn us that Taggart was on his way."

"Aye, but I could have found out if I'd stopped to listen."

Rane did not disagree. "Is there aught to be done in your absence?"

"Pray. And keep that pistol of yours handy."

"Have no fear for that," Rane said grimly.

"Look, Armistead, I know what it means for you if Harrod comes back—"

"We both know it. There's no use in discussing it." Straw rustled as Rane stood. "The women are still awake, I warrant. I saw the light go out just as you came in."

Benjamin nodded, though Rane likely couldn't see him do it. "Godspeed, Armistead."

"And you, Woodbridge."

They shook hands. Benjamin put on his hat and slung the saddlebags over his shoulder, took Old Sandy in one hand, and made his way down the ladder.

Kate opened the kitchen door at his first tap, so quickly he knew she had been waiting for news. He slipped inside and shut the door as she gripped his arm. "You're safe, lad?"

"For now." He leaned past her until he spotted Elizabeth, sitting on her pallet with her knees drawn up tight to her chest.

Something tore wide open inside of him. What a boor he'd been. And now he had to leave, and he hated himself for that too. Elizabeth's whole life had been scarred by the leaving of the people she loved.

He detached himself from Kate's grasp and crossed the room to crouch beside Elizabeth. "Mouse, I'm so sorry."

"You didn't mean to hit me," she said, her voice muffled by her skirt.

"I'm not sorry just for that, though glory knows that would be enough. I'm sorry for all of it. I let my anger grow and grow until it took any target it could find."

She sniffled. "If I hadn't asked for baptism . . ."

He could have kicked himself. "Don't ever regret following your conscience. Taggart's got to answer for his own actions, and so do I for mine."

"I forgive you," she said in a small voice.

Benjamin stood and turned toward Kate. "Aunt Kate, I don't know what to do. Somebody's got to warn Captain Boothe of what's happening here. Harrod's coming back in eight weeks, and he'll have more men and the Cherokee with him. Now's our only chance, while Harrod's gone."

Kate drew a long breath. He saw the familiar set of her shoulders, the strengthening in her gaze as she nodded. "Then you'd best go, lad."

"Oh, Benjamin," Elizabeth said, getting up. "Must you?"

"It's the only way, Mouse."

"How long will you be gone?"

"Until I find a courier or bring the captain home myself."

And until this restlessness was taken out of him.

Kate's hand brushed his shoulder. "You're going for the right reasons?"

"I think so, Aunt Kate. I hope so."

"Then go with God, and come back as soon as you can."

"I will." He pulled Elizabeth in for a quick, one-armed clasp. "Be strong. Let the Almighty be strong for you."

He felt a fearsome hypocrite. But the words were true, whether he deserved to speak them or not.

She rolled her shoulders back and nodded.

"If Taggart asks, tell him the last you saw of me I was headed down the mountain. And—I can't tell you if you should trust Gregory, but you might have to."

"Is it true what he said?" Kate asked, barely above a whisper. "About being a spy?"

"True enough. He's supposed to report to Captain Boothe. Whether he's done it—well, I reckon we'll find out."

"We'll be praying," Kate said.

"I'll need it. Goodbye, Mouse."

He shouldered his saddlebags and turned toward the door. At the threshold, he paused and crossed to the mantel and squinted at the dim shapes stacked there.

"What is it?" Kate said.

"Never mind. Found what I was looking for."

He scooped up the New Testament from beside the volumes of Milton and slipped it into a saddlebag. Then he embraced Kate and Elizabeth one last time and slipped out the door and walked into the night.

PART II

VICTORY

January 1–March 31, 1781

But thanks be to God, which giveth us the victory through our Lord Jesus Christ.
1 Corinthians 15:57

Twenty-Four

THE FOOTHILLS WERE THICK WITH SNOW IN THE
low places the sun did not touch. Benjamin rode slowly down
the slopes, scanning the crusted snow. Plenty of game sign.
Moccasin prints once, maybe Cherokee. Maybe even Selagisqua, searching for the same man Benjamin was searching for.

He didn't know where Captain Boothe was, whatever
Lieutenant Gregory thought. But he knew whom to ask.

After riding all night and most of the day, he was well
away from the ridge and as tired as his horse. He found a
sheltered place and made camp, taking the risk of building
a small fire to keep away varmints.

But when he rolled himself in his bedroll next to the fire,
sleep would not come.

He knew he had to warn Captain Boothe's men, even if
he had to go clear to the front lines to do it. But there was a
lot more he didn't know. Such as how to fix the mess he'd
made of things, both in Sunrising and in his own heart.

A man ought to forgive his enemies and trust the Lord
for the rest. Benjamin would have said he believed that. He
had heard such things from the pulpit many a time. But could
he say he believed it if he had not lived it?

A man may be a heretic in the truth; and if he believe things only because his pastor says so, or the Assembly so determines, without knowing other reason, though his belief be true, yet the very truth he holds becomes his heresy.

He wanted to curse his memory for Milton. But that would not fix things either.

The New Testament poked him in the chest as he rolled over. He sat up and pulled the book out of his hunting shirt and flipped it open.

If he couldn't argue with Milton, there was no way he could argue with Scripture. But maybe it was time he stopped arguing and tried to change.

The words of the Watts hymn they had sung the day of the fire at the meetinghouse were scripted across the flyleaf. Mitchell Boothe had preached from the book of Colossians that day. Was that the last time Benjamin had read his Bible?

No. It had been even longer than that; he'd left his New Testament in his saddlebags after his return from Kings Mountain. Little wonder he'd gone wrong.

He turned the thin pages to Colossians and leaned toward the fire until he could make out the fine print.

Paul, an apostle of Jesus Christ by the will of God . . .

Two chapters later, he threw another stick on the fire and went back to reading.

But now ye also put off all these; anger, wrath, malice . . .

He closed the book and tossed another length of pine into the flames. *All right, Lord. I'm done being angry.*

Sparks snapped from the wood. Benjamin slid the New Testament back inside his hunting shirt and lay down.

He would read every day until he had put himself to rights. He had gotten himself into this mess; surely he could get himself out of it.

The next morning, he started early and rode until he ran across a campsite. Abandoned, though not too long before.

Light snow ringed the cookfire, but the ashes had melted through. Though anybody could have made camp there, chances were good it had been a courier, and Benjamin just happened to be looking for a courier.

He picked up a fresh trail from the campsite and followed it, now losing it, now finding it again, until he reached the South Fork of the Yadkin River.

Gunning had been a courier for Captain Boothe ever since the war came to the Blue Ridge. Before that, he'd kept an ear to the ground for the Regulators in Piedmont country. And he knew how to hide. Sometimes in plain sight.

He was also a good hand with a canoe, so Benjamin scouted the bank of the river in search of Gunning's favorite haunts. He passed a group of burned-out cabins on the way. No one was there, so he rode on, wondering if the destruction had been Harrod's doing.

Night was coming on when his eye caught a line that seemed out of place in the landscape. A dim shape, no more.

Benjamin halted Sassafras and studied the riverbank. Sure enough. A canoe lay overturned in the snowy brush.

He swung out of the saddle and eased forward, leading Sassafras. The canoe hadn't been there long. But there was no sign of—

The hair on his neck stood up. He swung around.

No one was there.

Which meant Gunning probably was. Benjamin crouched beside the canoe, his rifle across his knees. "Show yourself."

"Why should I? I can see you fine from right here."

"Aye, well, I can't see you. As you know right well."

Gunning's deep chuckle rolled from the shadows. He stepped out of the trees, his dark skin blending with the twilight. The laughter swiftly died. "Were you followed?"

"No. I was careful."

"Good. Careful's one thing you can't be too much of these days. What are you doing here?"

"I was going to ask you that. You weren't in the valley. I saw your campsite."

"Tories found me, and I had to run. Didn't have time to cover my tracks like I wanted."

Nobody ever found Gunning unless he wanted them to. When it suited him, he let folks think he was a settler's slave. Which he had been, back before Captain Boothe gave him his freedom. There weren't many places Gunning could be as free as he was out here in the backcountry. "How'd they find you in the first place?"

"I purely don't know. I've pondered it and pondered it. But then I reckon you found me without too much trouble."

"Only because I knew where to look."

"Well, maybe they did too. Though who would have told them, I don't know. But I answered your question. How about you answer mine."

"I need to know where Captain Boothe is."

"You and the Tories both."

"Gunning, Harrod's men are holding Sunrising."

"Hank told me. Mitchell told him." Gunning shook his head. "I saw a troop of Tories ride through a few days ago. Torched some cabins that belonged to Whig settlers."

"That was likely Harrod. He left a detachment in Sunrising and is on his way to join Cornwallis. He'd give Captain Boothe a hard time if he found him."

Gunning's dark eyes narrowed. "I was going to leave out and tell the captain about Harrod being in Sunrising, but since those Tories got on to me, I dassn't go for fear of leading them right to him. They're one step behind me."

"Then I'll go. Harrod's working with the Cherokee, and we've got less than eight weeks to stop him. Tell me where to find the captain."

"He was with Daniel Morgan's men last I knew."

"Not with Colonel Shelby in Hillsborough?"

"He was. But when he got there, a new commander had

taken over for General Gates. Nathanael Greene, a good man. General Morgan took a command west from Greene, and the captain went with him. They've gone hunting for Banastre Tarleton. You know about Tarleton?"

"I've heard the stories." The British cavalry commander and his ruthless British Legion had terrorized civilians all over South Carolina and were moving northward. Kate had whispered reports she'd overheard in the great room. "Sounds about like what Harrod's trying to do."

"Then you know you'd best be careful wandering around looking for Morgan and the captain. Things are shaping up for a big fight down there."

"Good." The mood Benjamin was in, he was ready for a big fight. "Down where?"

"Morgan was at Charlotte a while. Then headed southwest. Camped at Grindal's Shoals, but that was days ago. You've got as good a chance of finding him now as I have. Poke around long enough, and if you don't find the captain, his boys will find you."

"And what of you?"

"I'll go north, lead the Tories on a merry chase for a few days while you make it to the captain. Then I'll hunker down till they're off the scent and I can clear out back to the hill country." Gunning turned toward the woods. "Bide the night. We'll know by morning if anybody followed you."

It was not until daybreak that Benjamin realized he had forgotten to read his New Testament.

Twenty-Five

KATE SCRAPED THE LAST BIT OF SAUSAGE FROM the crock Rane had brought in from the springhouse, then laid down her spoon with a sigh. Some days it was powerful hard to feed the very folks who had done a body wrong.

"All right?" Elizabeth asked from across the table, elbow deep in dough for tomorrow's baking.

"We've only a few crocks of sausage left." Cold air swirled her petticoats as Rane came in with an armload of kindling. "I know 'tis a sin to be fretting, but Mr. Taggart's run hither and yon all day, and it's wearing on my nerves."

"The wicked flee when no man pursueth." Rane dumped the kindling beside the hearth and knelt to stack it.

"Meaning me with my fretting or Taggart with his dashing about?"

"I consider you bold as a lion, which answers to the description of the righteous."

"Go on with you." Kate swatted at him. "I know we're to love our enemies and all, but he tests me on it every time."

"And when he tests you on it—what does one do then?"

"Forgive him with the good Lord's help, I suppose. Though some days it's beyond my ken."

Rane stared into the fire, the kindling lying all in a heap.

Kate wondered if they were still talking about Taggart.

"The Lord is the one who said to love our enemies, aye?" she said. "So faith is taking hold of that and doing it."

"'Tis not so simple."

He wasn't talking about Taggart at all. Kate could feel that in her bones. "Hard as the day is long, but it's simple enough. Forgiveness isn't the sort of thing a body has to feel; it's the sort of thing a body does because the Master says to."

Rane nodded, his shoulder still turned away from her.

Kate set the skillet of sausage over the coals to fry for supper. "Rane, lad, you've been forgiven?"

"By the Almighty? Yes."

"Tell me of it."

"I was told as a lad that the Church was the kingdom of God, and my baptism was a sign of regeneration that grafted me into it. But after the Navy—when I came to the end of myself, that was no longer enough. I'd had no consent in it, and I knew Scripture spoke of calling on the name of the Lord."

He stood and turned to face her. "You said faith is taking hold of what God said and doing it. Well, that's what I did."

"Called on his name?"

"Yes. He promises his forgiveness. But I can't tell you how adrift I've felt since then. Uncle Warwick put little stock in the notion of personal faith, but he was my strongest link to the Church. When we parted ways . . ." He shook his head. A dark curl fell over his forehead, not quite hiding the bandage there. "Sunday was the first time I began to question how wrong he might have been."

"Questioning is good, lad. So long as it takes you back to Scripture."

"Woodbridge told me the king has no right to religious allegiance. Uncle Warwick would have suffered a fit."

"Benjamin and I don't always agree, but if you'll pardon my saying it, maybe a fit would have done your uncle good.

And you ought to put an onion on that bruise again."

"It's no matter." He turned away and coughed raggedly. The harsh sound of it made Kate wince.

She frowned. "You ought to—"

"Put an onion on that too. I know." Rane half smiled.

A rapid knock cut off her reply. "Who's there?"

"Let me in," a hurried voice answered.

Hank Jonas. Kate opened the door.

The courier limped inside, his bad ankle clearly feeling the weather. Snow blew in with him.

"Come in and set a spell." Kate shut the door. "When did you get into the settlement?"

"Crack of day. Reckoned it was time I seen for myself what's happenin' in these parts." He ignored the chair Kate nudged toward him. "That scoundrel Taggart is headed this way again. Says he'll search the place but good."

"It'd do him good to pester somebody else, though I'd pity anyone who got him. When's he coming?"

"Any minute, looks to me like." Hank rubbed his beard. "Kate, he knows there's a passel of stuff missing from the ravine. Ain't no way we'll be talkin' him out'n it."

Rane stopped beside her. "Has he men with him?"

"Don't know. I was lookin' to get near to headquarters, and here he comes bustin' out the door, goin' on about findin' the truth once and for all. I ain't seen Lieutenant Gregory yet, but I don't reckon he knows or he'd have stopped him right quick. Leastways I surely do hope so."

Elizabeth stopped kneading. Kate felt a qualm. She wasn't afraid of Taggart, but she wasn't the only one at risk.

"We're obliged, Hank," she said. "You'd best go before he sees you."

But as she said it, she heard the shout outside. Hank jerked toward the sound. Kate pushed him behind the door.

Rane stole a quick glance toward the puncheon floorboard by the wall. "Kate, is everything—"

"All safe. All but us." She clasped his hand. "Pray, lad."

A mighty pounding rattled the door. Kate swept it open, pressing Hank tight against the wall behind it. "What is it now, Mr. Taggart?"

He pushed past her. "I've a notion you know right well. The king's property is going missing right and left, and I swear if you're hiding it here, I'll find it."

"Then you'll waste your time. At least you won't be galling some other poor soul in the meanwhile." She leaned against the door, feeling it stop against Hank's sturdy frame.

Three men followed Taggart inside. Rane took an easy step backward, planting himself on the guilty floorboard.

One man pushed Elizabeth aside and overturned the table, strewing dough and flour across the floor. Another crouched to tap the puncheons. The third started rifling the cabinet. Kate saw him slip a bottle inside his hunting shirt. Her good whiskey, the kind she brewed for her tonics.

Taggart turned on Rane. "You again. I've a notion about you too. Harrod's been after a man with a scar such as yours. You know anything about that?"

Rane held his peace. The silver of his eyes had gone to steel.

"Speak up, rebel."

Rane still did not speak. Kate took a wee bit of pleasure in the contrast of that with Taggart's reddening face. Rane's right hand moved ever so slightly toward his hip.

Taggart turned away and started toward Elizabeth. "Maybe the wench will tell me your name."

Brass and steel flashed in the light of the hearth. Rane clamped his left arm around Taggart's neck and pressed the pistol into his ribs. "Tell your men to place their weapons against the wall."

The door behind Kate quivered. Hank wanted to burst into the open. Kate curled her fingers around the edge of the door until Hank nudged her knuckles with the barrel of his rifle. She grasped the rifle and pulled it from behind the door as if it had been leaning there the whole time.

Taggart's eyes flicked to her, then to his men. The three Tories had frozen, as if a single breath out of line might cause either Kate or Rane to pull the trigger.

Rane cocked the pistol. "One wrong move, Sergeant."

"Do as he says," Taggart said hoarsely to his men.

They hurried to lean their long guns against the wall across from Kate. What would they do if they knew Taggart stood over the very thing they were looking for?

"Now," Rane said, "you will right the furniture which you have overturned. Miss Woodbridge will remove the flints from your weapons."

With a startled glance at him, Elizabeth brushed the flour from her hands and crossed to the wall where the guns leaned.

"You will then continue your search like gentlemen," Rane went on. "There will be no further involvement of the ladies and no further rifling of spaces too small to conceal that which you seek."

"And give back that bottle of whiskey," Kate said.

Two of the men turned the table right side up. The third put the whiskey bottle back in the cabinet. Then all three of them angled toward Rane and hesitated.

"Go on," Rane said. "You've come to search; now search."

They looked at one another. One peered gingerly into an open flour cask. The others turned about halfheartedly, one finally poking through the woodbin and the other rapping an upturned kettle. He shook his hand, knuckles red.

Taggart grunted against Rane's grip. "They aren't half trying."

Rane abruptly let go, nearly sending Taggart sprawling. Kate saw him slip Taggart's hunting knife free. "You had best help them, then."

Taggart stepped warily away from him. He led his men around the room, keeping well clear of Rane. And the floor beneath Rane's feet. Taggart looked in the flour cask. Poked through the woodbin. Eyed the upturned kettle. Looked at Rane again, glanced around, and started for the door.

"Mind your manners, sir. Acknowledge your hostess."

Taggart shot Rane a malevolent look. But he bowed to Kate and mumbled something she couldn't quite make out, though she wasn't sure she wanted to.

"In future, you will refrain from violating the privacy of these women," Rane said.

"Wait until Lieutenant Gregory—" Taggart began.

Rane's hold on the pistol tightened. Kate saw it from across the room. Taggart must have as well, for he broke off and motioned his men outside, barely pausing for them to collect their weapons. Kate resisted the urge to trip them as they passed. She shut the door firmly after them.

Hank Jonas came away from the wall and sucked air. "You tryin' to squeeze the breath clean out of me, Kate?"

"I could feel you wanting to show yourself." She barred the door and hurried to turn her cakes of sausage before they burned. "Rane, lad, you were a wonder. I'd never have known it was in you."

"Shakespeare said, 'Beware of entrance to a quarrel; but being in, bear 't that the opposed may beware of thee.' I've found it good advice." Rane uncocked the pistol and covered it with his coat. He looked tired. "I've known a few of Taggart's ilk. Too many."

"Won't he come back?" Elizabeth asked.

"He might, Miss Woodbridge. But not too readily, I warrant. He thought he had finished with me when he pushed me into the river, and he's shaken now."

"Maybe we shouldn't have . . ." Kate trailed off. Would they be in any less danger if they had not stolen Tory goods and hidden them under the floor?

"Carry on, Aunt Kate," Rane said quietly.

She looked at him in the firelight, with his handsome,

scarred face and the fine way he held himself. She thought of all the other scars he carried.

He was in far greater danger than she. If he could be strong, she had no right to waver.

But the next morning, Nolan Taggart was back. This time he knocked politely and stood with his hat in his hands when Kate opened the door a crack.

"You're wanted in the sleeping cabin," he said.

"And why would that be?"

"Some of the men are ailing." Taggart's focus strayed past her. Rane had been breaking his fast, though he was likely on his feet now. "Lieutenant Gregory sent me."

"He did, did he?" Gregory could not have known Kate was a healer. Which meant Taggart had told him, and Gregory had made him come and ask. Likely because of all the trouble Taggart had caused. "Well, let's see what's ailing them."

Rane spoke at her shoulder. "I'll come with you."

"Bar the door and keep the fowler handy," Kate told Elizabeth, and followed Taggart out. She wasn't afraid of him, but she wasn't sorry for Rane's protection either.

Taggart led the way to the dogtrot between the cabins. She kept pace with him, spine straight, telling herself she hadn't yet agreed to help.

But she knew she would. The Lord had commanded it. It was hard to argue with that.

As Taggart opened the door that led into the dogtrot, a man rushed out of the sleeping cabin and bolted down the rear steps to the privy. Kate raised her brows as he disappeared inside. "I take it that's one of them."

"Aye." Taggart sounded irritated. "Six in all. Don't know what's got into them."

The putrid stench of illness wafted out of the sleeping cabin, a harsh contrast to the fragrance of the fresh dough Elizabeth had been shaping into loaves. Kate glanced at

Rane, but he showed no signs of quailing. Doubtless he'd smelled worse in the Navy. She'd heard those big wooden ships had no air at all below decks.

She stepped inside the cabin. Five men lay on pallets on the floor. Some held their stomachs. One, pale and sweating, was curled on his side. Another got to his feet and dashed past her out the door.

Kate pursed her lips and crossed to the nearest man. "Are you in pain?" she asked, though it seemed plain that he was.

The man managed a nod. Kate felt of his forehead. No fever. "How long have they been like this?"

"Come on sudden last night," Taggart said.

"Have they been eating anything they ought not?"

"Just the six of 'em? Don't reckon so."

Kate asked her usual questions for stomach complaints. One or two of the men might have been embarrassed to answer, but she'd seen and heard worse. The symptoms seemed familiar, as if she'd treated the like before. But then, she'd treated just about everything in these hills.

The cabin was kept clean; she saw to that herself. There should be no dysentery, though it was a plague of soldiering folk. She could ease them for the time being, at least. Make the illness, whatever it was, easier to bear.

It was a hard thing to be thinking of. But it was the right thing, if she was to love her enemies as the Good Book said.

"Can they take water?" she asked Taggart.

"A bit, mayhap."

"I'll make a tea of sweet fern and colicroot. We'll try alumroot if that doesn't help."

She turned toward the door, feeling the force of Rane's silent presence beside her. He'd asked her how one went about forgiving a man like Taggart.

Perhaps this was a beginning.

THICKETTY CREEK,
SOUTH CAROLINA

 Twenty-Six

*IF YOU DON'T FIND THE CAPTAIN, HIS BOYS WILL
find you.*

Gunning's words drifted back as Benjamin led Sassafras
under low-hanging limbs draped with Spanish moss. The
world was still, caught in the pale gray mist of yet another
morning on the edge of swamp country. He'd gone first to
Grindal's Shoals as Gunning had told him, but Daniel Morgan's army was long gone. Precious days had been spent
following the trail farther south.

"Halt! Who goes there?"

Benjamin breathed a sigh of relief and shook his head
at the familiar voice coming from a curtain of Spanish moss.
"You know right well who goes here, Alec."

The swath of moss parted, revealing Alec Perry and his
rifle. Alec surveyed Benjamin from hat to moccasins and
back again. "I should have known. How do you do it?"

"Do what?"

"This." Alec jerked his head for Benjamin to follow.
"Show up just as there's a ruction on the horizon."

Benjamin switched the mare's lead to his right hand
and the rifle to his left. "I can smell it, I reckon."

"If the Tories can't sniff us out, there's no way you can."

"Gunning told me where to look."

"You talked Gunning into—"

"Malcolm Harrod's Tories are in Sunrising, and they're treating with the Cherokee."

A muscle worked in Alec's jaw. "So that's why he told you. Why didn't he come down here himself?"

"The Tories were after him. He led them away from me, but knowing Gunning, he's back in the hill country by now."

"Never thought anybody'd get on to Gunning."

"Still don't know how they did."

"And everybody back home? They're all right?"

"For now. But the Tories burned the meetinghouse to the ground and took over the ordinary and Captain Boothe's cabin. A lot of other things besides. Harrod's come east to help Cornwallis lick the American army, and then they'll cut the supply lines and Harrod will level Sunrising."

Alec shook his head. The wordless anger radiating from him matched anything Benjamin had ever felt. At last he said, "We're all under orders. Captain Boothe gave his word that he'll stick with the army, and he always keeps his word. He broke out of jail to keep his word once, remember."

"That's it, then?" Benjamin's own anger flared, with a new target now. "We stay here and let Harrod do as he likes?"

Alec halted and swung around, his eyes dark as gunmetal. "You think the captain's family isn't there? You think my family isn't there? Reckon we don't care? Is that what you're saying?"

"Alec, I—"

"Because if it is, you can go find yourself a swamp and stay in it until your head clears."

Hadn't Benjamin just told God he was done being angry? "Look, Alec, I didn't mean that. I know you hate the Tories as much as I do."

"Is that what I just said?"

"You said—"

"I said my family's there." Alec shot him a rock-hard look. "The best fights, Woodbridge, are for what a man loves. Not what he hates."

He pushed past a wall of drooping cypress limbs and into a clearing that bustled with the sounds of camp. "Now you stay here and think on that while I go find the captain."

Benjamin waited with Sassafras at the edge of a bivouac much like the camps before and after Kings Mountain. Saul McBraden, one of Benjamin's longtime friends, raised a hand in greeting, his red-blond hair catching the morning light.

Before either of them could speak, Alec came back with Captain Boothe. Robert looked weary, his face leaner than the last time Benjamin had seen him. "Woodbridge. Wish I could say it's good to see you."

"Same here, Captain."

"Tell him what you told me," Alec said.

Benjamin did, and then some. Robert didn't get angry out loud. But he got so quiet and still that Benjamin knew he was as angry as Benjamin and Alec put together.

"Somebody's let things slip," Robert said. "They can't have known about Gunning otherwise. But I'd stake my command on the loyalty of anyone else in Sunrising."

Alec snorted. "So would I. Once."

There was heat in the words, but sorrow too. Benjamin felt the weight of it down deep. "Only six weeks left."

"It'll have to be enough." The thunder of hooves interrupted Robert. A mud-spattered rider leaped from the saddle and dashed toward a cluster of tents. Robert added, "Gunning told you about Morgan and Tarleton?"

"Not much. But I got the general notion."

"Tarleton's Legion is crossing the Pacolet River, coming this way." Robert rubbed the nape of his neck. His hair had grown, clubbed into a short queue instead of cut to his collar as usual. "Right now he's worse than the Tories and Indians together. Worse than Ferguson, back at Kings Mountain."

Alec nodded toward the tent where the rider had disappeared. "I'll warrant that's our courier. Which means Tarleton's crossed the river."

Benjamin glanced at the tent. "And you'd be deserters if you left now. I understand." He wished he didn't, but he did. Too many militiamen went home whenever it suited them.

"Aye," Robert said. "But you're not under orders. You're a courier. Morgan wouldn't stop you if you went home."

"I told Mouse I wouldn't come home without you." He looked around at the camp. Men he had ridden with and marched with, fought beside and scouted for. Most of them were Robert's own scouts, Benjamin's friends and brothers in the faith. He could not save Sunrising without them. "Let's get this fight over with."

As the last light faded behind heavy clouds, Benjamin slid out of the saddle and stretched weary legs. Long shadows spread across a familiar meadow. Hannah's Cowpens, the last rendezvous on the way to fight Ferguson, back in October.

He'd thought that fight would be the last one he needed to settle his spirit. He'd been wrong. As long as the British were in the Carolinas, there would always be another fight.

He slung his saddlebags down. Campfires had already begun to spring up across the pasture. In the distance, the Broad River rushed through the deepening twilight.

"Sure wish that river was between us and Tarleton," Benjamin muttered to Alec.

"It's too high. Tarleton catches us in the middle of the crossing, our hides are in the loft." Alec paused, his arms full of deadwood for the cookfire he was building. "Might be just as well that we're on this side of it. The militia can't run."

Benjamin snorted. "You reckon some of 'em would?"

"Some of *us*," Alec corrected. "I don't just reckon it. I know it." He nodded toward the middle of camp, where General Morgan was deep in conference with his officers.

"And Morgan knows it too."

Benjamin thought of the Tory bayonets at Kings Mountain. "Tarleton's as bad as folks say, then."

Alec started laying the fire. "Likely worse. His men go over the field after a fight and bayonet the wounded."

"That's savagery."

"Sure it is. That don't stop Tarleton. But Morgan's not stopping either. Folks call Tarleton a lot of names. Bloody Ban, for one. But Morgan, he just calls him Benny." Alec stood. "Here, get this fire going while I see to the horses."

Benjamin took the tinder box Alec handed him and snapped a spark from Old Sandy's flint into the bits of tow and dried leaves. He blew gently on the small flame, watching the thin wisp of smoke curl upward.

Last night, he had read his New Testament in the glow of his small fire until his vision blurred, trying to make up for the nights when he'd forgotten. He had read the third chapter of Colossians over again and found a matching theme in the fourth chapter of Ephesians. *Be ye angry, and sin not . . . Let all bitterness, and wrath, and anger, and clamour, and evil speaking, be put away from you, with all malice . . .*

How could he be angry and sin not? All his anger had ever done was lead to sin.

A pair of muddy black boots stopped on the other side of the flame. "Find dry wood enough?"

The booming voice wasn't Alec's. Benjamin glanced up, then sprang to his feet. "General Morgan. Sir."

Daniel Morgan was built like an ox, shoulders straining his uniform, with a raw power that his easy expression did nothing to hide. Captain Boothe stood with him. Though solidly built, Robert looked small beside the general.

"You didn't answer my question, son."

"Yessir. The wood's dry enough, sir."

"Good. Going to be a cold night." The strengthening firelight caught a puckered scar on Morgan's neck and another on his cheek. Benjamin tried not to stare. He'd heard how Morgan had been shot through the jaw by Indians years ago. The general's aide stepped up beside him, but Morgan kept his eyes on Benjamin. "You from Carolina, son?"

"Yessir. The Blue Ridge."

"Mighty pretty country up there."

"Yessir."

"Got you a sweetheart back yonder?"

Susanna Boothe's blue eyes flashed across his mind. Just like they'd flashed away from him when he'd seen her before the preaching meeting. "Maybe."

Morgan's eyes twinkled under shaggy brows. "You want a little advice, boy, when you get home, you turn that maybe into a yessir."

A smattering of laughter sounded behind Benjamin. He didn't have to look to know Alec and Saul and a handful of other scouts had gathered. His neck warmed. "Yessir."

Morgan nodded to his rifle. "Ready for tomorrow?"

"What I wouldn't give to get first crack at Tarleton, sir."

The general's grin showed a gap on the lower left where the Indian bullet had knocked out several teeth. "Careful what you wish for, son."

Alec spoke from behind Benjamin. "Reckon a lot of us feel the same as Woodbridge here, sir."

They all knew by now about the Tories in Sunrising. Benjamin had seen the shock and outrage and resignation as the news spread among Robert's scouts. Now they all wanted to get this fight over with, same as Benjamin did.

"I'm glad to hear it," Morgan said. "Gather 'round, boys, I've something to tell you."

The men clustered on either side of Benjamin. Morgan eased himself down on a fallen log.

"See those knolls over yonder?" He motioned at the middle of the meadow. The campfires danced, throwing long shadows over gently rolling swales. "Howard's Continentals will be on that first rise. A hundred fifty yards in front of them will be Pickens's Georgia militia. And in front of *them*, I want a hundred twenty of the Georgians and you Carolina boys."

The general's easy expression did not change. But Benjamin thought he might have seen a wink. They'd get first crack at Tarleton, all right.

"All I want from you boys is two volleys," Morgan said. "Then drop back into Pickens's line, nice and easy. Three fires there, and draw back behind the Continentals. The British will think you're running, and they'll follow you up over that first hill. And that'll be the last mistake the lot of them will ever make."

Benjamin stared out over the darkened meadow and tried to imagine the picture Morgan had described. Part of him wished he hadn't imagined it as well as he did.

"Let me tell you lads a tale." Morgan shrugged out of his coat and waistcoat and handed them to the aide, the brass buttons flashing in the firelight. "I was a wagoner back when the English were fighting the French and Indians. Lot of you here are too young to remember that. But some of you do."

Robert nodded. Benjamin knew his stories of scouting for an English general back in his early days as a circuit rider.

"Those British officers were an arrogant lot, same as they are now," Morgan went on, untucking his shirt. "I argued with one of 'em. Knocked me down with the flat of his sword, and I got up and sent him down like a parcel of musket lead. When he woke up, he didn't have the gumption to fight me himself. So he called down the wrath of the army."

He got up from the log, turned around, and pulled up his shirt. A murmur ran through the men around Benjamin.

Rane Armistead had not carried half so many scars, but there was no mistaking the same marks of the lash.

"Four hundred ninety-nine." Morgan dropped his shirt-tail and turned to face the men. "Should have been five hundred, but the drummer miscounted and I didn't bother to tell him so. The British have owed me one lash ever since. And when you're out there on that skirmish line, you lads remember what I've told you. A man can take anything he's got to take for the right to speak his mind."

A cheer rose around Benjamin. But Benjamin only nodded, those scars still fresh in his mind.

Morgan nodded back, seeming to understand. "Ready twenty-four rounds per man. We'll have nothing but downright fighting tomorrow, but the old wagoner will crack his whip over ol' Ben Tarleton, sure as you live."

He saluted the men, motioned to his aide, and walked stiffly away. Benjamin said, "Four hundred ninety-nine . . ."

"Enough to kill most men," Captain Boothe said. "He swears he never lost consciousness. Get some rest, lads. Busy day tomorrow."

Benjamin prepared his twenty-four rounds and wrapped himself in his bedroll, his saddle under his head. He could hear Morgan going throughout the camp, joking with the men, explaining his strategy, sharing his scars. Yet another man the British had done wrong.

He thought of Lieutenant Gregory then, and his vow to protect Kate and Elizabeth while Benjamin was gone. The women would be asleep already, Kate's ancient fowling piece close beside her pallet. Elizabeth had carried it once or twice when Benjamin let her join him on his hunts, but she had never had to fire on more than small game.

Six weeks.

Would he be home after this fight with Bloody Ban? Would there be more fighting yet before they were free to return to Sunrising? Or would none of them return at all?

The questions chased themselves around his dreams until the general's voice thundered through the gray-blue hour before dawn.

"Boys, get up, Benny's coming!"

JANUARY 17, 1781
HANNAH'S COWPENS,
SOUTH CAROLINA

Twenty-Seven

THE BREATH OF A HUNDRED AND TWENTY skirmishers formed clouds in the frosty morning air. Benjamin stood between Alec Perry and Saul McBraden and looked over his shoulder at the road that split the meadow in two. The rolling swell of the pasture behind him hid the second line of militia and the neat ranks of battle-hardened Continentals commanded by Colonel John Eager Howard from Maryland.

General Morgan was back there somewhere, watching beside William Washington's cavalry. But out here on the skirmish line, spread out on either side of the road, there was no cover save for the dry grass and a smattering of trees. Farther ahead, the road disappeared into thicker forest that would have been more to Benjamin's liking. But Banastre Tarleton's men were somewhere deep in that forest.

Birds twittered in the stillness. Benjamin tucked his kerchief inside his shirt where the bright red would not be a target, then ran a hand over the mended place in his rifle stock and wondered if it would hold through a hard fight.

At the verge of forest and road, shadows began to move. "Here they come," Saul McBraden muttered.

Benjamin leveled Old Sandy and bent his thumb over the hammer. The skirmish line was silent. Waiting.

The best fights are for what a man loves.

He would stop Tarleton or die trying if it meant keeping the British away from the American army and Patriot supply lines. He'd go clear across Carolina if it meant saving Sunrising. Maybe that was a step on the right path.

Tarleton's infantry paused at the edge of the woods, facing the skirmish line. Even the birds were silent now.

Then the first shot shattered the stillness. An officer in the center of the British line stopped and fell where he stood.

It had begun.

Benjamin sighted down his rifle, his pulse roaring in his head. But when he pulled the trigger, his mind cleared.

There would be regret later. He knew that. But for now he had work to do.

Shots popped and thumped around him. He measured powder down the barrel, took a ball from his pouch and a patch from the patchbox, rammed down the ball and patch. Then a rumble of hooves drew his eyes upward.

The British Legion thundered forward, sabers drawn.

"Steady," Alec said on Benjamin's other side.

Benjamin primed the pan and cocked the hammer and watched down the barrel. He focused on the horses, then the plumed helmets, looking everywhere but at the sabers and the faces of the dragoons. There had been no cavalry at Kings Mountain.

Robert shouted, "Fire!"

Benjamin squeezed the trigger. Smoke billowed along the skirmish line. When it lifted, empty saddles dotted the band of retreating cavalry.

"One blow struck for the Old Wagoner," Alec muttered.

"Aye. But only one."

The great red mass of infantry began moving and shifting, pouring out of the forest, wheeling and closing up into perfect ranks. The first rays of morning sun glanced off the line of bayonets, turning the steel bloodred.

A tingle crawled up Benjamin's spine. He shook it off and reloaded. Too cold out here, that was all.

Drums rolled and fifes shrilled. Tarleton's field guns roared. The British line went on forming. Benjamin had never seen the like. Not at Kings Mountain, sure, where the rough terrain had allowed for ragged ranks at best.

"Steady," he muttered to himself, since Alec didn't.

Then the redcoats were moving forward, coming on at a trot, with a mighty shout rising above the artillery.

General Morgan shouted louder. "They give us the British halloo, boys—give them the Indian halloo!"

The general's oath was lost in the war cries that erupted from the skirmishers around Benjamin. He added his own war cry, thinking of Walks-in-Winter and Selagisqua, and thumbed the hammer back.

"Don't fire, don't fire," Robert called, and Benjamin steeled every nerve, waited, thought, Come on, Bloody Ban, take what's coming to you . . .

"Fire!"

Gaps opened in the British line. Benjamin reloaded swiftly as he dropped back with Alec toward the second line of militia as Morgan had ordered. The other skirmishers gave way in twos and threes, pausing to fire as they went.

The British infantry surged after them, over the long rise in the pasture. Behind that rise was Colonel Andrew Pickens and a lot of Georgia militia. Benjamin found his place in the line and wheeled to face the oncoming infantry.

"Good work," Robert said. "Get ready, here they come."

The captain moved away down the line. A militiaman's rifle spoke. Then another and another.

Then the British line stopped and leveled muskets.

The wall of fire and smoke was a thing of awful beauty. The mighty roar of it rolled up and over the meadow. Lead hissed overhead.

"Redcoats never could aim," Alec said, raising his rifle.

Benjamin rammed another charge home. The long line of British muskets flashed out and down into one solid row of bayonets.

Slowly, as one, the line drove forward.

Benjamin slammed the ramrod back into place, primed the pan, and leveled the rifle.

"Let 'em think we're running scared," Robert said.

Benjamin fired one more shot into the drifting smoke. He did not have to try hard at playing scared as he dropped back beside Alec again, reloading on the run, his eyes fixed on the lethal line of shining steel.

The British field guns screamed grapeshot and fury. Colonel Howard's line opened up to let the militia pass. Beyond the red and blue of the Virginia Continentals, William Washington's cavalry waited in reserve.

The field guns roared again. Dirt spurted up between the Continentals and the cavalry.

Alec grunted and lurched against Benjamin.

Benjamin fell to a knee. Alec sprawled beside him. Blood poured from a ragged hole in his hunting shirt, staining his side crimson.

Lord, not Alec.

"I'm all right," Alec said through gritted teeth.

"No, you're not." Benjamin ripped back the bloodied buckskin and homespun. The piece of canister shot had gone clean through just above the hip.

The noise of battle died to a faint roar. Off to the right, hooves thundered and steel clashed on steel in a mad tangle of cavalry and militia. To the left were the lowlands. Behind him, the Continentals. Straight ahead, the river.

Alec said, "Leave me and go."

But there was nowhere left to go.

His men go over the field after a fight and bayonet the wounded.

Benjamin shoved Old Sandy into Alec's hands. Alec gripped the barrel as if holding on to life itself. Sweat sheened his face as Benjamin dragged him behind the nearest oak. What had Aunt Kate done for wounds?

Lord, help me.

The ground was soft where it began its slope down to the marsh. Benjamin raked aside the fallen leaves and acorns at the base of the tree and found what he was looking for.

Moss. God be thanked.

He rinsed Alec's side with water from his canteen, then tore up a handful of the dry moss and packed the wound as swiftly as he could. Blood darkened the spongy fibers. He loosened Alec's neckerchief, wadded it over the wound, tied his hunting belt tight against the wadding, and prayed.

Alec breathed hard through his teeth.

Then a new sound raised the hair on Benjamin's neck. The keening wail of bagpipes, wild as a Cherokee war cry, blending lament and challenge in the ancient refrain of war.

Tarleton had called in his Highlanders.

Benjamin dragged Alec farther behind their meager shelter and pried his rifle from Alec's clammy hands.

The Virginians poured past the tree, parting around it like a Red Sea of retreating soldiers. Benjamin's heart thundered. If the Continentals were running—

He cocked his rifle, said without thinking, "Stay down."

"Sure," Alec said without opening his eyes.

The Highlanders charged after the Virginians, more British infantry pressing close alongside. Smoke drifted in heaving gray clouds over the long lines of men.

Benjamin picked out a target and fired into the rush of charging infantry. The earth trembled with the pounding of feet. He turned back to the shelter of the tree to reload.

A burly Highlander appeared out of the smoke beside Alec, bloodied bayonet in hand. Benjamin dropped his powder horn to dangle from its strap across his chest.

The steel flashed up and back, poised for Alec's heart. Benjamin screamed a war cry he barely heard and blocked the blade with his half-loaded rifle.

The Highlander shouted back, a deep, full-throated brogue. His tartan war bonnet was stained darker red on one side. Benjamin gripped the man's musket above the bayonet and drove the butt of it backward into the Scot's ruddy face. The Highlander reeled and fell.

Benjamin primed his rifle's charge, his hands steady now. Through the gaps in the smoke, he saw General Morgan riding along the line of retreating Continentals. The British infantry rushed on as if mad with the scent of blood.

Morgan's voice boomed over the clamor. "Face about, boys! Give 'em one good fire and the victory is ours!"

The Continentals stopped and wheeled and leveled their muskets.

Benjamin flung himself in front of Alec.

The American line blazed fire and smoke into the riot of infantry. A musket ball thudded into the trunk of the oak. The British ranks staggered and buckled. Another Highlander fell across the man who had tried to kill Alec.

"Charge bayonets!" Colonel Howard shouted.

Benjamin got to his feet as the Continentals surged forward, their bayonets thin slashes of light through the smoke. Alec said through his teeth, "What's—happening?"

"The British are throwing down their arms and asking quarter." One redcoat hurled his musket to the dry grass barely a yard from Benjamin, so close Benjamin could see the fringe of the epaulet on the man's right shoulder. Same as Lieutenant James Arnold Gregory.

Shouts rose from the American ranks. "Tarleton's quarter! Give 'em Tarleton's quarter!"

Alec groaned.

Benjamin's hands fisted around Old Sandy. He would have joined that cry for revenge once. He still wanted to.

"No!" Morgan bellowed at the shouting men. "Give 'em quarter, boys. Give 'em quarter."

Benjamin turned back to Alec. And saw the Highlanders still coming. So close he could make out the stripes of the tartan and the basket-woven hilts of the massive broadswords.

A Scotsman charged him, the broadsword swinging, and Benjamin blocked it, clubbed him with his rifle, the range too close for firing. The man kept coming, and Benjamin reached for the tomahawk in his belt, found it was not there.

Then a rifle shot cracked behind Benjamin, and the Highlander stopped short and sprawled beside Alec, blood blossoming across his sword arm. A familiar war cry pierced Benjamin's eardrums.

Saul McBraden.

Captain Boothe shouted from his other side. He and Benjamin fired as one.

The Highlanders faltered. Behind them, their colors fell. The field guns went silent.

Benjamin dragged in a hard breath. Sweat streamed into his eyes. He swiped it away, and the moisture that gathered with it, and saw his knife and tomahawk lying where they had fallen after he'd used his belt to help Alec.

Robert was already kneeling next to Alec, one hand on Alec's shoulder to keep him from sitting up. Beside them, Saul handed his canteen to the wounded Highlander.

"All right?" Robert said, looking up.

Benjamin nodded. "Now that the lot of you are here."

Hooves thundered in the distance. Benjamin squinted across the smoke-hazed field just in time to see the British Legion cavalry, the scourge of the Carolinas, wheel their horses and gallop out of sight.

Benjamin picked up his tomahawk and knife and did not let himself wonder what he might have done if General Morgan had not kept the men from revenge.

Twenty-Eight

EVENING SETTLED OVER THE BROAD RIVER AND its banks like ointment over a wound. The sun dropped low behind bare trees, mingling stripes of golden light with the glow of cookfires. It hardly seemed real that only five miles and as many hours had passed since the clash in the pasture and the grim work of tending the dead and wounded.

Not that Benjamin was done tending the wounded. Most had been left on the field with army doctors and a flag of truce, but Alec was too stubborn to be left behind, and Captain Boothe was too stubborn to leave him. Benjamin peeled the makeshift dressing away from Alec's side, pleased to find the bleeding had stopped. "Hold still."

Alec drew his breath sharply as Benjamin probed. "I've already been shot once in my time. Wasn't once enough?"

"The Almighty thought otherwise." Benjamin took the flask Robert handed him. "This is going to hurt."

"Can't be worse than the five miles from the battlefield to here." Alec arched his back as Benjamin rinsed the wound and wiped the rum away.

"Looks like you'll live for the next five miles too." Benjamin lightened his tone to hide the knot in his throat.

"I reckon I ought to be grateful, but at the moment, I don't want to think about going anywhere." Alec fidgeted with the edge of his torn shirt. A scar still marked his left shoulder where Charles Drake's pistol ball had struck him ten years earlier.

Benjamin knotted the strip of homespun that served for a fresh bandage. He'd wash his belt in the river later; his hand kept looking for his knife and not finding it. "Be grateful I didn't forget everything Aunt Kate taught me."

"Not everything, eh?"

"Nothing that's going to kill you, leastways."

"Good to know," Alec said sarcastically.

Benjamin wiped his hands on his leggings. "You don't like my work, I can fetch the surgeon."

"You let that old sawbones touch me, you'll be needing him next."

"You'll have to catch me first." Benjamin gave him a slug of the rum, then handed the flask back to Robert. "How long do we camp here on the river?"

"Not long," Robert said. "Morgan wants to join up with General Greene before Lord Cornwallis comes after us to try retaking the prisoners."

"At least we took prisoners," Benjamin said bitterly.

"Aye. Though not everybody wanted to."

Benjamin didn't answer. Robert said, "Did you?"

"Did I what?"

"Want to take prisoners."

"There's a time when a man ought to be angry. Same as you were when you heard about Sunrising."

"That's so. And we'd all best keep as close to the Lord as we can so we know when those times come."

Benjamin stared out over the Broad. Crossing that river had put a measure of safety between Morgan and any British pursuers. But it had been a challenge too. Seemed like life was one crossing after another.

"Alec told me the best fights are for what a man loves, not what he hates."

"So you were listening," Alec said.

"Aye, but it's hard. Hard to reckon out which one you're doing, when you're spang in the middle of it."

"Out there at the Cowpens," Robert said. "Were you thinking how many Highlanders you could take down?"

Benjamin knew he'd see those Highlanders in his dreams.

"I was mostly looking to keep 'em away from Alec."

"And that's what Alec was speaking of. Right, Alec?"

"I took a piece of British canister just so's to show him what I meant," Alec said.

"I can't help but think of Sunrising, Captain."

"You're not under orders, Woodbridge."

"I'll stay until we join up with Greene. If we can't leave by then, I'm going."

"I can't blame you for that." Robert shook his head. "At least Harrod's out here and not in the mountains."

"I wonder how he knows what's going on back in the Blue Ridge," Benjamin said. "He knew the routes in and out, even before his men came. And he knew about the ravine. He must have hidden the trade goods first thing."

"Is Nolan Taggart still stirring up trouble?" Alec asked.

"He's a sergeant in Harrod's militia," Benjamin said. "But he couldn't have known about Gunning or Walks-in-Winter or our meeting place by McGuiness Creek. And there ain't no way he would have found that cave; he'd draw someone's notice if he so much as hunted along there."

"What are you thinking?" Robert asked.

"I don't know yet. But I'm starting to think Alec was right when he said he'd trust the loyalty of any man in Sunrising—*once*."

"I hope you're wrong," Robert said grimly.

"I hope so too."

Twenty-Nine

KATE HELD THE KITCHEN DOOR AS ELIZABETH staggered in with a tub of wet linens. Susanna Boothe carried the other side of the tub. Snowflakes swirled through the door and melted into the mound of wet fabric. The girls set the tub down out of the way, near where Magdalen Boothe strung up a line for drying.

Rane came in with more water, and Kate stirred up the fire under the big copper kettle. Glad she would be indeed when spring came and she could do the washing outside. The kitchen had stunk of chamber lye all Lord's day while the slop wash soaked.

"'Tis quiet out there this forenoon," Magdalen said.

"Some of the Tories are feeling poorly again." Kate went to the cupboard and took out the balls of ash she'd made from burnt nettle and thistle, the way she'd done ever since her girlhood in the old country. She added the ash to the kettle of water and let the water come back up to a boil.

Elizabeth pulled linens from the tub and dropped them into the kettle. Kate took up her laundry beatle and began working the mass of cloth back and forth. Sweat gathered under her cap. At least when it was spring and time for the great wash, there might be a breeze to be had out of doors. A knock on the door interrupted her thoughts. "If that's Mr. Taggart, tell him I'm in no frame of mind to be talking to him at the same time I'm washing his dirty linens."

Rane went to the door, one hand mighty close to that brass-trimmed pistol he kept under his coat. He opened the door a crack. "Sergeant Taggart. How may I be of service?"

"I want to see Kate."

"Widow McGuiness is otherwise engaged. In the sartorial ablutions to which your men have compelled her."

"My men haven't done anything of the kind." Taggart sounded as if he were growing red in the face.

Kate tossed down her laundry beatle. "Never mind. I'll speak to him."

Rane pulled the door fully open. Taggart stepped inside.

Kate dried her hands on her apron. "What is it this time, Mr. Taggart? Are your men ailing again?"

"You know very well that they're ailing again."

"Well, I must say I'm not surprised."

He pointed a finger in her face. "I knew you had a hand in this."

"I haven't the least notion what you're speaking of."

"Then how did you know they're ailing again?"

"A bit hard to ignore the mad dashes for the privy every time I look outside."

Taggart grunted. Kate sighed. Loving her enemies hadn't gotten any easier. "I'll make some more tonic."

"Lieutenant Gregory wants to speak with you."

"And whose idea was that? Very well, lead on."

"Kate," Rane began.

"I'll be fine, lad." Kate shut the door before he could object—and before she could slip and say his name. Taggart did not need to know that Rane was indeed the man Harrod had sought. "Let's not keep the good lieutenant waiting."

At Captain Boothe's cabin—Kate refused to think of it

as Tory headquarters—Taggart held the door, though not with a very gentlemanly manner. "Widow McGuiness, sir."

Lieutenant Gregory rose from his seat at the table. "Please be seated, madam."

Kate took the chair he offered and was glad when he resumed his own seat. This was awkward enough without his towering over her. "What's this all about, Lieutenant?"

"My sergeant believes you have poisoned his men."

A laugh burst from her before she could stop it. "That surely does sound like something he would come up with."

"All I know is that you dosed them with that potion of yours and they were fine for a week," Taggart said. "Even went back to work. Now they're down harder than before."

"Mr. Taggart, if I wanted to poison your men, I'd have picked something that didn't take a week to do it."

"Aye, or maybe that's what you wanted us to think."

"Mind your tongue, Sergeant," Gregory said dryly. "I daresay if it's come to such straits as that, we're in need of her now more than ever."

Taggart looked at him askance.

"If she knows the poison, she must know the antidote," Gregory said bitingly. "You are dismissed, Sergeant."

"But sir—"

"Sergeant."

"Yes, sir."

Taggart shot her a dark look and went out. Gregory shook his head. "It sounds foolish, but I had to ask."

"I don't blame you for taking your sergeant's word over mine, but I never heard something so clot-headed. What *is* wrong with your men, Lieutenant?"

"A return of the same symptoms as before. Only the same six men."

"Most sicknesses are catching. Odd that no one else has taken ill. Might I visit them again?"

Gregory appeared surprised. "Do you wish to?"

"Why wouldn't I?"

"Madam, I was under the distinct impression that you are a Whig of the most ardent variety."

"So I am." She leaned forward. "I'm under the distinct impression that you're a Whig of the most secretive variety." His gaze darted to the door. "Widow McGuiness, please."

"As you will. Either way, I'm a Christian first and foremost, and the good Lord says I'm to be loving my enemies. Not poisoning them, whatever Mr. Taggart thinks."

Gregory opened his mouth, then closed it again. He stood and strode to the door. "Come along, then."

She was hard put to keep up with his long-legged stride and was a wee bit out of breath by the time they reached the sleeping cabin, but drawing a deep lungful meant taking in all the odors of a sickroom, so she settled for small breaths through her mouth. "I've asked it before, but I'll ask it again—have they eaten anything the others haven't?"

Gregory shook his head. "Not to my knowledge."

"Nor to mine. Is there aught else they've done of late?"

Gregory hesitated. "They've been working in rather close quarters together."

"What sort of close quarters?"

"Really, Widow McGuiness, I don't see how that can possibly matter."

Which meant it did matter, at least to Gregory. Perhaps he was afraid Taggart lingered outside and would hear him.

Kate crossed her arms and worried her lower lip. Something seemed so familiar about this sickness. It might be any number of things, but the way no one else had come down with it—that was what seemed familiar.

Her Arthur. She remembered him like this once, not long after they'd wed and left the old country. He'd been exploring this grand new wilderness . . .

A shiver ran down her spine. She held herself erect to hide it. If this was what she thought it was, then the Tories had men working in the ravine again.

"Can you do anything more for them?" Gregory asked. He looked weary. And guarded. Kate laid her hand on his arm, not surprised when he flinched away. "I can make more tonic. But they'll be fine, Lieutenant."

"Are you certain?"

"Certain as I can be." She gave him her best smile. "As long as you tell them to stop drinking cave water."

Rane considered it a wonder that he ever got any work done in the stable. First Kate came to tell him that the Tories were at work in the cave again. Then Mitchell Boothe and Hank Jonas appeared with plans for another foray into the ravine. Rane did not ask when or how they had gotten back into the settlement. After Mitchell and Hank left, Ayen came rushing in to do his chores so he could scout for his uncle as soon as the evening was dark enough.

"You know what I'd really like to do?" Ayen said.

"What?"

"Let the Tories take care of their own horses for once."

Rane pushed his pitchfork into a pile of straw. "Does the name of Colonel Ethan Allen signify anything to you?"

Ayen wrinkled his nose. "I don't think so. Who's he?"

"He took Fort Ticonderoga from the British in New York during the early part of the war. I met him after he was captured by the British in Quebec."

"Where's that?"

"Canada. Far to the north."

"I ain't never heard of it."

"It exists nonetheless."

"And he got captured there?"

"Yes. I met him whilst he was in captivity."

"When you were in the Royal Navy?"

"How do you know I . . . Never mind." Rane did not want to know where Ayen got his information. Nor did he want to explain that Ethan Allen had been a prisoner aboard the very ship where Rane had served. "Colonel Allen was not like your father, Ayen. He was a hard man. Wrong in many ways, particularly about the Almighty."

"Was he Anglican?" Ayen asked with interest.

"No." Rane found himself half smiling. "He wasn't much of anything at all. But for all that, he taught me something of value. In times of injustice, good men are not content to do nothing. Never content. But they are patient."

Ayen twisted his face. "You're telling me to be patient."

"I'm telling you Colonel Allen told me to be patient."

"That's how you got out of the Navy? Being patient?"

"In a manner of speaking."

"Sounds like something Pa would say." Ayen twirled his pitchfork. "Why is doing the right thing so hard?"

"What would your father say to that?"

"Probably that the spirit is willing, but the flesh is weak." Ayen fell silent, the only sound the rustle of straw.

Patience was one thing. But Rane was weary of fleeing. From Harrod, from the nightmares, from forgiving Jem Flannery. Even though he had already told God that he did.

Weeks had passed since Mitchell's sermon by the creek. Rane might admit that no earthly monarch could claim headship of Christ's church, nor claim the right to dictate another man's beliefs. But if Christ was the only head—then nothing else could stand between a man's conscience and his God. Not a king, not a prayer book, not a well-meaning uncle. Not even Rane's own failure to do what he knew he ought.

The thought brought a strange kind of relief, a return of the liberation he had felt when he had first cast himself on the mercy of Christ, his only mediator. Kate had asked if he had been forgiven. Perhaps from that forgiveness, he too could forgive.

"You reckon it's dark enough to scout?" Ayen said.

Rane laid his thoughts away for later and checked the

window. "I would think so."

Ayen put down his pitchfork and went out. Rane brushed himself off and climbed to the loft. He donned cloak and riding gloves, checked pistol and letter. Then he went down the ladder and across the yard to the kitchen.

Mitchell Boothe was waiting inside. Hank Jonas was with him, muffled up like a bear. Mitchell greeted Rane with, "More snow coming."

"It will cover your tracks, aye?" Kate said.

"Any word from Woodbridge?" Rane asked Hank.

"I heard from Gunning, our courier," Hank said. "Our boys licked the British at some place called Goatpens or some such. Likely that's what's kept 'em so long."

"Then perhaps they'll return soon." Rane leaned against the wall, weariness pulling at him like a tide. He smothered a cough with his cloak, but not before Kate frowned at him.

"I didn't half think, lad. You ought not be out in the cold."

He gathered in a careful lungful of air and held up a hand. "I'm all right, Aunt Kate. No cause for alarm."

She didn't believe him. He could see that plainly. But she knew well enough that he would not be swayed.

Three taps on the door. Rane straightened, reaching again for the pistol. Then a pause and three more taps, and he relaxed. Kate put down her paring knife and let Ayen in.

"There's a guard, all right." Ayen blew on his red fingers. "Close by the top of the path you took last time. And another one farther along, behind the cabin."

"I'll take care of 'em right enough." Hank looked at Kate. "I won't let 'em freeze out there, if'n that's what you're thinkin'. I might shoot a Tory dead if he comes at me, but it ain't my way to make one freeze to death." He nodded toward the hearth, where a block of maple snapped cheerily. "Wait here till that log burns down. That'll be time enough."

Rane offered his gloved hand. "Go with God, Jonas."

Hank returned the grip, strong and sure. What unexpected

company Rane had taken up.

The log seemed like the burning bush of Moses's time, aflame yet not consumed. But at last it was no more than embers. Mitchell waved Rane to follow and slipped outside.

There was no moon. Rane was both glad of that and unnerved by it when they reached the long ledge above Button Creek. He placed his left hand on the rocky bluff and felt his way forward, thankful for his riding gloves. Mitchell carried a shielded lantern, but he would not uncover it until its light would be hidden by the rocks.

Six men working for no less than two or three weeks, Kate had said. Long enough and hard enough to develop a thirst. Something was happening.

"I hope whatever we find down here is worth the trouble," Mitchell said under his breath.

"It will be, if only to set Kate's mind at ease." Kate likely would have investigated for herself if she'd had to. "Though I admit I'm as anxious as she to know what that handful of Tories has been doing down here."

The cough rose, and Rane forced it down. There could hardly be good news to hope for if the Loyalists had been working in the cave again. But at least the Whigs of Sunrising would know what they were up against.

His gloved fingers met the great flat rock that guarded the cave's entrance. The rock had been moved. He knew that at once. He maneuvered carefully around it and found a narrow gap where there had been only rocks before.

Slipping a hand to his pistol, he stepped inside.

Mitchell's lantern threw spangles of light over Rane's shoulder. Several stacks of muskets were gone.

"They're getting in motion," Mitchell said grimly.

Rane did not reply. What answer was there for a band of Tories bribing Indians against a settlement whose fighting men were gone?

A throb of pain stabbed his temples. He coughed in the

damp air. The sound resounded through the cave and died away, leaving a familiar ache in his chest. When he could speak, he said, "Have you any news of Woodbridge's friend Selagisqua?"

"Nothing. Which I take to mean he's gone into hiding."

"Is there any way he can help?" Rane wondered what Uncle Warwick would have thought of the notion that a savage could be of help. Uncle Warwick had been wrong in more ways than one. Perhaps in more ways than he'd been right, but Rane did not have time to think on that tonight.

"He might could help, if'n we could find him," Mitchell said. "But he'd be mighty outnumbered. We need Rob and his lads. It's been near a month, and no sign of Woodbridge. Maybe Gunning—he's Rob's courier—knows something."

Water dripped in the silence, somewhere in the deep recesses of the cave. The same water, according to Kate, that six Loyalists had ignorantly imbibed during their exertions. "We've another month yet, according to what Woodbridge told me before he departed."

Mitchell turned toward the mouth of the cave, his lantern's light splashing across the dark rocks. "It's time we told Judge Pembrook about all this, even if he still has to stay shy of Harrod. Maybe he can find out where the British are meeting their Indian allies. Then I'll ride out to see if I can find Gunning and maybe Selagisqua."

Another month. Then Harrod would return, and he would find Rane and—

No. Rane took a deep breath, coughed again, forced the fear away. "Is there aught I can do in the meanwhile?"

"Hold the fort." Mitchell led the way outside. "And pray Woodbridge gets here with Rob before it's too late."

Thirty

MALCOLM HARROD RODE ACROSS CLARK CREEK,
the current running high, cold rain pelting his shoulders. It
had been a long ride from the Blue Ridge, longer yet to rally
more men and educate the scattered settlements on the folly
of Whig sentiment.

A bitter stench seeped through the rain. He turned his
attention forward.

Smoke. Thick and black, tendrils of it creeping through
the trees ahead.

Brigadier General Charles, Earl Cornwallis, was camped
on the other side of those trees. Or so the scouts had said.

Harrod motioned to the stocky man riding abreast of
him. "Collins, stay with the men whilst I reconnoiter."

"The smoke, sir. It may be a skirmish. There was a bad
fight here last year, I'm told."

"We would hear the weaponry if it were a skirmish. I'll
signal you when I wish you to follow."

He rode ahead, the stallion gaining the bank with ease.
Collins would obey; the man had served him well as a regimental lieutenant rallying men in the valleys.

James Arnold Gregory, alone in command of Sunrising,

was another matter. Nolan Taggart would watch him narrowly, loyal as any king's man could wish. Harrod's Indian agent was in the settlement too, though tasked with strict secrecy. If Gregory rose to the test, well. If not, Harrod would return soon enough.

The smoke grew thicker as he rode, a haze that the rain did not clear. But it was not the foul smoke of gunpowder.

Ahead of him, the forest opened. In the clearing stood Derick Ramsour's mill, as the scouts had said. But no sign of the British army. Only a vast heap of smoldering rubble.

The stallion snorted at the stench. Harrod took no notice and guided the beast nearer the pyre. Here a charred wagon wheel, there a half-burned chest, bindings burst by heat. Blackened dishes spilled from it. Another wheel, more chests, the glimmer of molten silver.

A piece of a cask lay well away from the heap, near a torn mass of tent canvas. Harrod dismounted and picked up the splintered wood. Liquid lingered in a crack, smelling of molasses. Rum.

Harrod tossed the fragment into the midst of the heap and watched the liquor flare up amid the hiss of raindrops. This was no mere rubbish heap, and no mere burning of rebel goods. He knew of only one place in these wilds where wagons and chests, china and silver, rum and tents might all be found together.

Cornwallis's baggage train.

There were no signs of a skirmish, nor any evidence of rebel thievery. His Lordship had burned his own wagons. Harrod had never known a general in this war to destroy soldiers' supplies and officers' possessions alike. Only an urgent need for haste could compel such a decision.

Harrod remounted and rode back through the woods and waved for Lieutenant Collins to join him with the men. His band had grown by forty since leaving the Blue Ridge. Some had come for the lure of destroying rebel property.

Some were confident in king and country. Others were frightened of the rebels. It made little difference to Harrod.

But when Collins met him at the edge of the woods, another man was with the band. A settler, by the look of him, his wide-brimmed hat spotted with rain. Harrod said, "What's this?"

"One of the locals, sir," Collins said. "He appears to have some knowledge of what's happened."

"What's happened is clear enough." Harrod motioned toward the clearing. "His Lordship has burned his baggage train, no doubt to speed his travel."

"Right you are, sir," the settler said. "He was after the prisoners Morgan took at the Cowpens, I reckon. And he wants General Greene something fierce. He left here two days ago at a good clip, bound for the Catawba."

"I see." Harrod could esteem a man who would break with tradition to reach a goal. The rebel general Nathanael Greene commanded the entire southern army, a much larger force than Daniel Morgan's at Cowpens. If Cornwallis could overtake Greene, he would scatter the rebel troops and cut the supply lines to the frontier. The backcountry rebels would not last long.

"It's proud I was to have His Lordship so near my own land, of course," the settler added quickly.

"Of course." Harrod allowed himself an edge of sarcasm. "Why did you not go with him so as to be nearer yet?"

"I've my own goods to look after, sir. The rebels might take over my property if I were gone."

"Of course," Harrod said again. "In that case, my good man, you will no doubt be equally proud to play host to a band of His Lordship's friends. We'll dine at your board before we ride on."

The man cast a startled glance around at the sixty men. Harrod offered him a thin smile.

Resignedly the man led them through the driving rain

downriver to a small farm. Harrod doubted the rebels would gain much if they did seize it. What a travesty to think such folk could govern themselves.

The food was spartan, the man and his wife sullen but afraid to show it. Harrod finished his draught of despicable spirits, brewed of persimmon or something equally wretched, and sent Collins for his writing materials.

He drafted a swift missive to Cornwallis and handed it to one of the better riders of his band. "Find His Lordship and deliver this with my compliments. We'll follow straight-way, though you'll have greater chances than we if the rebel army is between us and His Lordship."

The courier saluted him and went out. A moment later, his horse galloped off.

Harrod rose and issued brief orders to Collins for the gathering of the men. Then he bowed to the woman of the house. "Your hospitality will doubtless be rewarded when the king crushes this rebellion, madam."

"You with your fine promises," her husband burst out. "And what's to come of it, I ask you?"

"Reward enough if you hold with the Crown," Harrod said. "And a just punishment if you do not. A good day to you both."

He went out and mounted. "Collins. Leave a man to see the goodman of the house doesn't run to the rebels with this little adventure. If he does, or complains to his friends of his treatment, burn the property. Cornwallis is not the only man who can destroy what no longer serves him."

"Yes, sir."

Harrod spurred the stallion and turned northeast to follow Lord Cornwallis.

Thirty-One

"YOU SAID YOU'D STAY TILL WE JOINED GREENE.
This is where we part ways, then." Captain Boothe offered
his hand to Benjamin. "Godspeed, lad. Give my love to
Maggie and the rest."

"Yessir." Benjamin mounted Sassafras, keeping her a
safe distance from the swollen Yadkin River. Whitewater
churned over rocks and fallen branches, already higher than
when Nathanael Greene had joined General Morgan a few
hours before and ferried the troops across.

A knot of wagons sat on the bank like a covey of grouse,
exposed to any predators that happened along. Cornwallis
would not be pleased when he found that Greene had crossed
the river ahead of him and taken all the boats save a few
canoes for the militiamen who lingered by the wagons, waiting to fire a volley or two at the approaching enemy. The
British vanguard was somewhere to the west and closing in.

And Benjamin was headed for Sunrising.

He saluted his captain and wheeled Sassafras. A light
misting rain spattered his face as he rode along the river.
Alec was already on the other side, ferried over to join the
army while his wound went on healing. Benjamin wished

they'd had more chance to say goodbye.

Several days' ride lay ahead of him. But at least he was on his way. No matter how long the ride, it would be worth it to stand with Kate and Elizabeth against whatever came next.

Dull hoofbeats thudded along the wet clay on the other side of a stand of moss-covered trees. Benjamin reined Sassafras behind a tangle of branches.

A lone rider came into view between two trees, his horse lathered. A courier, if Benjamin had his guess, and one who'd been riding hard. But for whom? He was not bound toward the river as a Patriot courier would be.

The man was riding west. Toward Cornwallis's distant army, and a British vanguard that was not so distant.

Well, Captain Boothe's men would stop him soon enough. Benjamin had lost enough time already.

Putting his heels gently to Sassafras's sides, he watched the courier ride on. The man paused as if to get his bearings, then angled farther west.

The rider would slip right past Robert's men on that course. But the British army was already on the move; what harm could one more courier do?

Benjamin started to turn Sassafras, then stopped, hearing Alec's voice in his head. Any scout knew better than to leave an enemy courier alone. That courier might have news that could alter the campaign. Even if he didn't, the possibility of it would dog Benjamin's trail all the way to Sunrising.

He guided Sassafras forward and swung wide to circle around the stand of trees. The least he could do was stop the courier and turn him over to the captain. After that, he could ride for Sunrising with a clear conscience.

Glimpses of the rider's movement flashed between the trees. At the last moment, Benjamin pushed Sassafras to a hard run and burst into the open ahead of the courier.

The rider halted, lather flying from his mount's flanks. Benjamin leveled his rifle. "Off the horse. Nice and easy."

"No cause for alarm, lad. I'm a friend to government."

"Pity for you I'm not. Leastways not the government you're speaking of. Looking for a king's man this side of the river?"

The courier's hand went to a flat lump under his coat. He jerked his fingers away as if burned. "I thought—"

"I don't know what you thought, but you'd have been better off thinking otherwise." Benjamin motioned with Old Sandy. "Now get off the horse."

The courier dropped from the saddle and stared at him defiantly.

"Weapons on the ground."

The man tossed down a pistol and a belt ax. Benjamin said, "What, a wilderness rider like you and no knife?"

Sullenly the courier unsheathed a scalping knife from a scabbard around his neck and flipped it blade first into the soft red clay.

Benjamin dismounted, rifle at the ready. "Let's make this quick. I've places to be. Where were you bound?"

"It's no business of yours."

"No. Nor is the packet you've got under your coat. But I aim to have a look at it all the same. Hand it over."

The courier's gaze darted from side to side, seeking aid that was not there. Benjamin stepped forward, close enough to nudge him with the rifle. "Don't keep me waiting."

The courier pulled out an oilcloth packet and handed it over. Benjamin tucked it inside his own hunting shirt. "Take off your crossbelt."

With a glance at the rifle, the courier obeyed.

"Hands behind you."

"Now see here—"

"Unless you'd rather I put it 'round your neck. No? Didn't think so." Benjamin rested Old Sandy against a tree within easy reach, bound the courier's hands with the crossbelt, and collected the weapons from the ground, sliding them into his own belt. Then he picked up the rifle again and took the oilcloth packet back out of his hunting shirt and opened it. "Have no fear. If I'm mistaken and this dispatch turns out to be of a peaceable sort, you'll be on your way none the worse."

He held the packet against the barrel of his rifle, pulled out the paper it held, and split the seal with his thumb. A fine script covered the sheet, the strokes firm and precise in a patch of gray light that filtered between the trees.

To Gen. Charles, Earl Cornwallis.

My Lord—
Having been apprised of the unfortunate Loss of the Light Troops under Col. Tarleton, I am convinced it is of greater Necessity now than ever to press my Designs upon the Western Quarter. I shall venture to meet with you at the Trading Ford of the Yadkin R. with such Partisans as I have at my Disposal—however I think you will find that I have all I need to compel the Backwater Men to the utmost Extremity in Light of your Orders that such as are caught should be hanged as a Reward of their Perfidy.
I await your Correspondence and am eager to join your Pursuit of Greene—my Agents are standing by and within four Weeks the pestilent Fellows of the Backcountry will cease to trouble you— so much the more when we have captured Greene.

Your obedient Servant, &c.
Maj. Malcolm Harrod.

The old familiar heat gathered under Benjamin's skin. *Four weeks.* Aye, they'd let Harrod see just how pestilent they could be. "Harrod is here?"

"Coming on to join Cornwallis any minute. Serve you right if he ran across you on his way."

Benjamin nearly crumpled the letter in his fist. Sunrising would have to wait yet again. For a moment he half wished

Harrod *would* run across him so they could settle this and Benjamin could go home once and for all.

He folded the dispatch and tucked it inside his hunting shirt. "Start walking. And mind, I've got my rifle at your back."

He gathered the reins of the courier's horse in his left hand with Sassafras's reins and led the horses back the way he had come, marching the courier ahead of him. On the other side of the trees, just as the river came in sight, he spotted Captain Boothe. "Captain!"

Robert turned his gray charger, the other men behind him. "What, back already?"

"I've got a prisoner for you."

The courier slowed. Benjamin nudged him with Old Sandy's barrel. "If it weren't for you, I'd be on my way home. Don't try me."

The captain met them halfway. "What's this?"

"Courier bound from Harrod to Cornwallis." Benjamin let the horses stand and fished the letter from his hunting shirt. "Take a look at this."

The rest of the scouts crowded around as Robert skimmed the letter. He looked up and moved closer to the prisoner. "What of these agents who are standing by?"

"Don't know. Maybe a couple of couriers in the mountain country. His Indian agent, for sure."

"Where'd he come by an Indian agent?" Benjamin demanded.

"How do I know? Sometimes he sends a man in. Sometimes he turns an agent who's already there. He doesn't ask my leave."

Benjamin knew the moment the thought entered Robert's head, because it entered his too, and he saw the tight reining of the captain's face.

There was only one man in Sunrising who was an Indian agent and knew where Gunning was and where Mitchell held prayer meetings and whose side Walks-in-Winter had been on. The same man who'd had a fort named after him. A fort that the Tories were holding.

I hope you're wrong, Robert had said in the camp by the Broad River.

I hope so too, Benjamin had answered.

He nodded at the courier. "What'll we do with him?"

Robert slid the letter inside his own hunting shirt, his face unreadable. He motioned for Saul McBraden to help the courier mount his horse. "We'll take him to General Greene. You're free to go, Woodbridge."

Benjamin started to answer. Before the first word was formed, a band of horsemen broke through the trees to the north, headed straight for the scouts.

"That's Major Harrod," the courier said, maneuvering a leg over his saddle. "You'll get your dues now."

Robert was already wheeling his horse. "Come on, lads. We'll run upriver. And fight 'em on the way if we have to."

Benjamin swung into the saddle and joined Robert, pushing away the fleeting urge to break away and ride for the Blue Ridge. His place was here, at least for today.

Up ahead, the open ground ended in a blockade of fallen trees and river boulders. Harrod's men disappeared behind a spinney of pines, then came back into the open, this time giving chase.

A pistol shot cracked behind Benjamin. The ball hissed overhead. Answering shots exploded from rocks and trees where the other scouts had taken cover. He wheeled Sassafras behind a mass of uprooted trees.

The westering light outlined a brown-black charger and a familiar profile. Malcolm Harrod.

Benjamin raised his rifle.

The courier wrenched free of his bonds, fell from the saddle, and dashed toward the British pursuers. "Major! It's Captain Boothe!"

No way to shoot a moving target among so many other

men. Benjamin leaped from his saddle and lunged. The courier went down hard under him. Hooves pounded past, narrowly missing them both.

"Give him up, Boothe!" Harrod shouted.

Captain Boothe's silver-barreled pistol answered. Harrod cursed.

Benjamin slammed the courier's head against the ground and picked up his rifle. The rush of the swollen river swallowed the courier's groan. Across the river and a hundred yards downstream, boats danced on the tide under the bluffs where the American army had moored them. Out of reach of the British. And Benjamin.

A low tramp of feet reached his ears through the sounds of the skirmish. He turned and saw a dark mass of men cresting the distant hill.

Cornwallis's vanguard, bound for the ford.

If Robert's men couldn't get across the river, it wouldn't take long for Harrod to come back with help.

Benjamin caught Sassafras's lead and tied her to a branch, then dragged the courier to the tree where Saul McBraden was reloading. Benjamin handed over the weapons he'd taken from his prisoner and said, "Keep an eye on him."

"Where are you going?"

"To get a boat."

Chips of bark showered Benjamin. He tugged off his hat and outer hunting shirt, laid his tomahawk and rifle beside them, and shucked out of his moccasins and stockings and the heavy buckskin leggings that covered his knee breeches. Then he thrust his knife into his waistband and ran down the bank.

The water was icy cold. It pulled against him as if it too were on Harrod's side. Benjamin pushed on, up to his waist, breathing through the shock of it, and plunged in and swam.

Why hadn't the British sent somebody across already?

A few strokes farther, and he knew why. The current

wrenched at him, taking him downstream toward the bluffs.

He should have gone on to Sunrising when he had the chance.

His shoulder ached with each thrust, then went numb. He gasped in a breath and angled his body toward the boats.

A musket ball sent up a spurt of spray beside his head. He breathed again and went under. Stroke after stroke, lungs bursting, shoulder coming alive again and screaming.

Lord Jesus.

It was all the prayer he could manage. A fallen tree bit at his ankle. He kicked away, fought to the surface, breathed.

The nearest boat bobbed just out of reach.

He thrust himself forward with a final desperate kick and caught the gunwale.

Another shot thumped across the river. Finding his footing on the river bottom, he drew his knife, slashed the mooring line, and lashed the boat to the next one in line, then clambered aboard the second boat and cut that one loose too.

The oars were wedged under the rowing thwart, barely visible in the twilight. He wrestled them out and into the oarlocks, shaking the water from his eyes.

I thank you, Lord. Now get me back across.

The river fought him every bit of the crossing. So did his shoulder. He pushed the pain out of his mind and focused on the hard rhythm of each pull, expecting a British musket ball at any moment.

Rane Armistead is a Navy man, he thought with a twist of irony. *He ought to be rowing boats instead of me.*

But Rane had his own battles to face. And he'd have more if Benjamin didn't get these boats to the captain and they didn't keep Harrod out of Sunrising.

He hauled on the oars again, feeling that his shoulder would fly from the socket. But he was so close. One more pull. Almost to shore.

Saul waded out and dragged the boat to the bank.

Benjamin leaned on the oars, heaving for air. If Harrod's men saw the boats, there'd be a fight for them. But Benjamin would sink the craft before he'd let Harrod seize them and ferry British troops to Greene's side of the river.

"Where's the courier?" he asked.

"Dead." Saul towed the boat up onto solid ground. The second boat trailed behind, bumping the stern of the first. "We drove Harrod back, but he shot his courier as he left."

"His own courier."

"Aye. So he couldn't tell us any more than he already did, I reckon."

Benjamin looked up at the bank, where two of the captain's men were digging a hasty grave. "I know he was the enemy, but that doesn't sit right with me."

"Nor with the rest of us," Robert said as he came down the bank. "McBraden, you take as many of the lads as will fit. Come back for the rest of us if you can. Otherwise we'll shift for ourselves."

"You first, Captain." Benjamin pulled himself out of the boat. "We can't afford to lose you."

"I'm staying here till the rest of you lads are safe." Robert's collar was open, his hat missing, silver-barreled pistol still in hand. "You'll have trouble enough swimming the horses across."

They all wanted to argue. But no one did. There wasn't time. Saul cut the boats apart, and the scouts piled in. Benjamin shook his head when they motioned him to join them. He'd stay with Captain Boothe.

"Going across after all?" Robert said.

"Someone will have to tell General Greene about that courier."

He didn't want to. He still wanted to ride for home, to be there for Kate and Elizabeth. But as long as Harrod was here, he was not in Sunrising. That was some small consolation.

The pair of boats shoved off with the horses fighting the

current behind them, the whites of their eyes showing in the dusk. Benjamin gathered his rifle and tomahawk and shoved damp feet into his stockings and moccasins.

Robert ran the pistol through his belt, turned to Benjamin, and offered his hand. His grip was warm and strong against Benjamin's cold, wet skin. "We're all obliged to you, son."

Benjamin shrugged. His shoulder ached. "Somebody had to do it. The Almighty got me there and back. Couldn't have done it otherwise."

Robert clapped him on his good shoulder and went back to watching the boats. Benjamin retied his leggings and pulled his hunting shirt on over his wet clothes, then worked the knot out of his kerchief and wrung the water out of the worn silk. "Captain, what that courier said about Harrod's Indian agent—"

"I know what you're thinking. I thought it too." Robert's voice was hard. "And thinking's all we're going to do until we're sure."

"Yessir." Benjamin knotted his kerchief again and rested his back against a tree, his legs threatening to buckle. He did not look at the men who were still digging. "What kind of man shoots his own courier?"

"One who thinks his men are naught but tools to be used."

A shiver ran across Benjamin's flesh. Not just from cold wind on wet clothes. "Wish we could have stopped Harrod for good and all."

"Come morning, we'll tell Greene and Morgan what's happened. Then you can light out for home. But there's something I don't like about tonight." Robert straightened as the first boat touched the far bank, almost out of sight in the dusk. "Harrod's seen us fight. Next time he'll be ready for us."

Thirty-Two

MORNING FOUND A PAIR OF BEDRAGGLED SCOUTS following an aide to General Greene's headquarters. Benjamin had dried out as best he could, but his skin still felt clammy.

A rumble like thunder reverberated up the Yadkin. The earth shuddered beneath Benjamin's feet. Royal artillery roared from the bluffs across the river, where Lord Cornwallis and his men were camped on the ground the British vanguard had held through the night. "Does Cornwallis think he's doing us real harm, or is he just riled that Greene made it across and he didn't?"

"Riled, I reckon," Captain Boothe answered. "He's not hitting much, though he's making a powerful lot of racket."

The aide saluted the sentry, who opened the door and announced them, speaking loudly over the crash of an iron ball bounding off nearby rock. The aide waved Benjamin and Robert inside and shut the door.

Nathanael Greene and Daniel Morgan stood at a small writing table. Benjamin came to attention beside his captain.

"At ease, gentlemen," Greene said.

Morgan pointed a thick finger at Benjamin. "I know you. You're the Carolina boy with the maybe sweetheart."

Benjamin's neck burned under the damp kerchief. He didn't look at Robert, his maybe-sweetheart's father. "Yessir. Benjamin Woodbridge, sir."

Morgan nodded to General Greene. "This boy's all right, Nat. I saw him take on a wad of Highlanders singlehanded at the Cowpens."

Benjamin cleared his throat. "Not singlehanded, sir."

"Don't naysay your officers, son." Morgan turned toward Robert, his face creasing with pain. The Old Wagoner was in agony, his rheumatism inflamed by weeks of cold and wet. "Glad to see you made it, Captain. Checked downriver last night and didn't see you come in."

"Woodbridge found us a couple of boats." To Benjamin's relief, Robert did not delve into details. "He also found us a courier. Going to Cornwallis from Major Malcolm Harrod."

Greene leaned forward. "Go on."

Robert nodded to Benjamin. Benjamin described the courier's message and untimely end.

He didn't speak of Sunrising. Greene and Morgan knew he and Robert hailed from the Blue Ridge and any strike on the western frontier would be mighty close to home.

"Is Harrod with Cornwallis now?" Greene asked when Benjamin finished.

"So far as we know, sir."

The two generals were from opposite backgrounds—Morgan a hardfisted brawler from the backside of Virginia, Greene a Quaker-born businessman from the coast of Rhode Island. But in this moment, both showed the same single-minded intensity.

Greene said at last, "General Morgan leaves today for Guilford. We will join him there after continuing our withdrawal. Retreat is disagreeable, perhaps, but not disgraceful."

Morgan huffed a quick laugh. "I'm as keen on a fight as the next man, but there's something to be said for what old Nat here has done to the British. Cornwallis has burned his supplies, he's running his men ragged, he's foraging from land we've already picked over."

A thunderous boom rattled the cabin, splintering shingles overhead. Benjamin said, "And he's plenty mad about it. Sir."

Greene ignored the noise. "I had intended, Captain, for your men to accompany General Morgan. But I believe you would be of greater service as intelligence against Cornwallis. The ford is still rising. He's likely to seek another crossing. When he does, and Major Harrod with him, I wish to know as soon as possible."

"All of us, sir?"

"As many as you need. Be prepared to split into two parties. You'll lead one, Woodbridge the other."

"Sir, I—"

Benjamin stopped. How many hundreds of men in this camp wanted to ride for home just as badly as he did? How many stories had Greene already heard?

"Yes, Woodbridge?"

"Never mind, sir. It's an honor." And it was, though one he could do without.

"We'll get in position at once, sir," Robert said.

"Thank you, Captain. Dismissed."

Robert saluted. Benjamin did likewise and followed the captain out.

Neither of them spoke until they were well away from headquarters. Even then, Benjamin found he had nothing to say that he had not said already.

"We'll find the lads and give them our orders," Robert said at last. "And try to keep Alec from coming with us."

Benjamin mustered up a shadow of his usual grin. "Facing Harrod would be easier than that, I reckon."

Robert chuckled. "You may be right."

On the opposite bank of the Yadkin, Malcolm Harrod stood atop Gowrie Heights with Charles, Earl Cornwallis, and looked across to the rebel camp. Under his left sleeve, the linen bandage was tight around his forearm where Boothe's pistol shot had grazed him.

Cornwallis had his spyglass in hand, a grave expression on his face. "You can see why I am reluctant to risk any of the troops on another venture in the western front."

"I regret my delay in answering your summons, sir, but the time has not been wasted. My men are in position."

"My stipulation stands, Major." Cornwallis raised the spyglass and shook his head. "The roof of that cabin is too low for accurate visibility."

Harrod bit back a caustic retort. What was a cannon range when he could unleash havoc on the entire frontier if Cornwallis would only take the risk?

"I heard of the skirmish last night," Cornwallis added.

He did not say what he had heard. Harrod said evenly, "It was unfortunate. One of my couriers was killed in the melee. The backwater men are unscrupulous fighters."

"And if you display your skill with this settlement of yours, I will gladly supply the men with which to subdue the rest of the frontier."

The army was Cornwallis's life, and so much the more after his wife's shattering death. He lived a soldier and would likely die a soldier. Harrod respected the devotion Cornwallis had earned from his men. But he still could not look at the earl without seeing the stolid officers who would have court-martialed Harrod for treating the Irish rebels as they deserved to be treated.

"You shall see what I can do, my lord," he said coldly.

"I know I can rely on you, Major." Cornwallis lowered the glass. "In the meantime, we have only to catch Greene and sever the rebel supply lines, which will in turn contribute greatly to your eventual success."

"You would have me remain with you?"

"If you wish. Many of our officers share your indifference to militia. I doubt they will take much account of your men, whether present or absent."

Harrod's feeling went far past indifference. But there was little to be gained by saying so. He knew how Cornwallis disapproved of Banastre Tarleton's rumored cruelty and the wanton destruction caused by his own army—men who loved Cornwallis enough to follow him blindly into battle but not enough to obey his orders to stop looting and burning. Cornwallis would hardly approve of Harrod's plans, though he might approve of their result.

A rapid tattoo of hooves joined the artillery's rumble in the earth beneath Harrod's feet. A courier was entering camp.

"Some message from the patrols, I presume," Cornwallis said, closing the spyglass. "I had best return to headquarters."

Harrod fell into step beside him. When they neared the officers' tents, the courier met them on foot. He saluted Cornwallis but said, "Message for Major Harrod, sir."

Harrod took the dispatch and opened it, conscious of Cornwallis's eyes on him. He checked the signature first. From his Indian agent.

The letter was brief, but enough to make him swear silently to himself. The rebels of Sunrising had discovered his store of gifts for the Cherokee and were plundering the supply to arm their own allies.

He would have to ride west at once. It would take days to contact his agents and gather his forces for an assault on the ridge.

"It appears you must carry on without me, my lord," he said to Cornwallis. "My presence on the frontier is required with all haste."

Thirty-Three

THE HORSES PLODDED ALONG THE RIVERBANK,
mud sucking at their hooves. Benjamin shook the tension from
his upper back and flexed his right shoulder. Ever since his
swim across the flooded Yadkin, the joint had felt weak again.

On the far side of the river, the bank rose to meet thick
forest that rolled away and away to the west. Somewhere
over there was Sunrising, and likely a traitor.

Somewhere else over there, much closer, was the British
army. And Malcolm Harrod.

After five days of the scouting mission Greene had
ordered, Benjamin had led his command to rejoin Captain
Boothe's. Cornwallis had given up waiting for Trading Ford
to go down and was hunting another crossing. Now and
then Benjamin glimpsed the column of men snaking slowly
along the opposite bank. A British patrol had fired across the
river once, but no one had been hit.

Captain Boothe suddenly slowed. Benjamin brought
Sassafras alongside. The terrain up ahead was gray and still.
A cluster of ramshackle cabins, weathered to their own dull
shade of gray, stood like tired sentries on the bank above the
flat expanse of the river. No smoke rose from their chimneys.

"Shallow Ford," Robert said without turning.

Benjamin ran his gaze down the broad swath of water. "A good place for a crossing."

Robert seemed not to hear him at first. Then he shook his head as if to clear it and said, "As good as any."

"Reckon those cabins are friend or foe?"

"Empty, some of them. The settlers fled when Governor Tryon was marching across North Carolina."

"Shallow Ford. Isn't that where—"

"Harrod and Drake. Aye."

Benjamin studied the landscape, envisioning the stories he'd heard. Captain Boothe, arrested for treason, crossing Shallow Ford with Colonel Charles Drake. Malcolm Harrod, waiting for them. Then Mitchell and Saul and the rest of Sunrising's menfolk, disguised as Cherokees to demand the captain's release. And the final struggle that ended with Drake dead and Harrod unconscious.

Robert's focus had sharpened again. "It'll be dry, at least. A bit of cover while we wait for Cornwallis."

The riders gathered around the nearest cabin. Judging by Saul McBraden's unusual gravity, he remembered this place too. A few feet from the door, a lone arrow stuck point first in the clay chinking, its bare shaft quivering in the wind.

"Hank Jonas did that." Robert nodded at the arrow. "You lads take a few minutes out of the wet."

No one asked where he was going. If it had been Benjamin, he would have wanted to be alone too.

He tethered Sassafras at the rear of the tumbledown building and walked around to the front, suddenly wondering what struggle Robert had endured these last weeks behind his quiet ways. Benjamin had thought of little beyond his own troubles, but surely the captain yearned to be home as much as Benjamin did.

The air in the cabin was dank and musty. More so when a dozen damp and unwashed scouts crowded inside. Benjamin leaned his rifle against the wall and looked around the small common room, seeing not his friends and fellow scouts but Harrod and Drake and all the arrogance and tyranny that had turned a deaf ear to men like Captain Boothe.

And men like his father.

Captain Boothe had escaped the governor's men alive. John Woodbridge had not.

The pain of it seized him like a raw and visceral ache, down deep beneath the wet and the weariness. The air was too close, too heavy. He gripped Old Sandy's barrel, trying to stave off the flood of memories.

His vision blurred. He picked up the rifle and moved blindly for the door.

A scout needed a clear head. He had to put this to rest, at least for now. Same as Captain Boothe was likely doing.

No one stopped him. He stepped outside into a cool spattering rain that drifted beneath the brim of his hat. The drops clung to his lashes, blurring his vision even more. He swiped the dampness away, strode along the riverbank, dragged in a tight breath.

A pile of stones and rotting timbers lay high on the riverbank. He wondered if that was Colonel Drake's grave.

He knew Robert had not wanted to kill Charles Drake. But Drake had made his choices.

Same as Harrod. Same as Benjamin. And heaven knew Benjamin's choices hadn't always been the right ones.

He kicked a stone from the edge of the pile, watched it skitter across the clay and splash into the river.

"God, I don't know what to do with this anger." The tightness in his throat was fierce. He was twelve again, Captain Boothe telling him his pa would not come back from what should have been just another meeting. "I don't know why you let good men die. I don't know why Pa let himself get killed in a losing fight. Maybe this is a losing fight too. And when I think what Harrod did then, and what he's doing now, it tears me to pieces."

His shoulder throbbed. He could make an uneasy peace with Lieutenant James Arnold Gregory. But he could not for the life of him sort out what to do about Harrod.

Because he knew with every breath in him that Malcolm Harrod had to be stopped.

And could Benjamin be the one to stop him? Stop him for the right reasons and not look back in another ten years and see how wrong his own choices had been?

He scrubbed the heel of his hand across his eyes and saw Robert standing away downriver, his face tilted toward the leaden sky. Praying, mostly likely. Benjamin would wager the captain's prayer sounded better than his own.

But then, what did that matter? Wasn't the whole point supposed to be that he could go boldly to the throne of grace, not when his prayers sounded good, but when he wanted grace to help in time of need?

The kerchief felt damp around his neck. He worked the knot loose. Maybe it was better not to carry the reminder around with him.

No. He needed the memory of the good man Pa had been. A good man Benjamin was trying to be, and failing.

He tugged the knot tight and picked up another stone and flung it as far as he could, so far he could not see it arc down to meet the river, only the white spurt of water where it landed.

Then he saw them. Redcoats, dozens of them, now hundreds, pressing out of the forest on the opposite bank.

There would be time for doubts and questions later. He wheeled and sprinted along the bank. Robert met him halfway. They ran for the cabin together.

Benjamin reached it first and slammed the door open. "Cornwallis is crossing. Let's go."

Thirty-Four

GENERAL GREENE GOT THE ARMY IN MOTION AS soon as the scouts reported Cornwallis's crossing. Benjamin rode alone on patrol, night after night, as seven hundred light troops shielded the withdrawal and led the British on a merry chase.

Frost crackled on the leaf litter under Sassafras's hooves. The chill night air raised gooseflesh on Benjamin's neck. But at least it kept him awake. Six hours of sleep every other day was wearing mighty thin, and Cornwallis had given no sign of stopping for the night.

For three long days, they had kept Cornwallis guessing while Greene's army made for the Dan River and friendly territory in Virginia. But now the game was up. Cornwallis knew Greene was bound northeast to the lower fords. The light troops' only task now was to hold the British off long enough for Greene to get there.

The fatigue pressed in on Benjamin like fog. He was still shaken by the weakness he had felt at Shallow Ford, his utter lack of ability to set himself to rights. Now, as he rode alone in the dark, the opening lines of Isaac Watts's hymn played through his mind like a condemnation.

Shall we go on to sin
Because thy grace abounds,
Or crucify the Lord again
And open all his wounds?

He did not want to go on to sin. But he could not seem to stop himself.

He pressed his fingertips against his eyelids, felt the gritty sting of too little sleep and too many hours straining to see in the dark. Suddenly he missed Susanna. Not as she had been these last several months, but as she had been when everyone spoke as if they were betrothed in all but word. She would have nudged him straight to Jesus, with no condemnation but no excuses either.

She had tried to do it as he grieved for Walks-in-Winter. But he had pushed her away. Had pushed his Lord away. Little wonder the divide had grown so great.

Light flickered dimly in front of him. He blinked and shook his head.

The light remained. Narrow glimmers of it, flickering with a faint orange hue.

Not fatigue. Campfires.

His hands tightened on the reins. Sassafras halted at once, but his grip stayed clenched. The only men ahead of them were Greene's troops. The troops that the covering force had to protect at all costs.

Musket fire popped sharply in the distance behind him. Sassafras perked her ears.

Benjamin's pulse quickened. The British vanguard was within firing range of the American rearguard again.

He wheeled Sassafras toward Captain Boothe's post a hundred yards away. The captain was already moving when Benjamin reached him. "Saw the fires?" Benjamin said.

"Aye. Nobody can get close enough to see who it is. But if it's Greene—"

He stopped. The covering force's sole duty was to shield Greene's men from the British. If those were Greene's campfires ahead of them, and Cornwallis was within musket range behind them, the covering force was done for.

And so was Sunrising.

Benjamin pushed Sassafras to a run, her hooves pounding to the rhythm of the song still hammering in his head. These had been Morgan's troops. But the Old Wagoner had gone home to Virginia, racked by brutal rheumatic pain. Colonel Otho Holland Williams led the light troops now, and he'd have a hard choice ahead of him.

When Benjamin and Robert reached the column of light troops, the alarm was already spreading, borne on the uneasy voices of men preparing to sacrifice themselves. Colonel Williams rifled through a stack of Greene's dispatches, a map at his elbow, his face grim with the task of protecting his own men as well as the entire southern department.

Williams held up one of the messages. "The night before last, Greene sent the baggage and stores ahead to the ford and ordered General Lillington to file off to Cross Creek." He stared at the dispatch, then at the map, clearly plotting Greene's route in his mind. At last he gave a quick breath of relief. "He's well ahead of us by now. If those fires were his, they're long abandoned. Spread the word—we press on."

The march dragged on into the night. They passed through the deserted camp, savoring the fleeting warmth from the abandoned fires.

Long after dark, the cavalry in the rear sent word up to Williams. Cornwallis had halted.

Benjamin found a sheltered spot and thumped his saddle down and dropped his hat beside it. The song came back as if to haunt him. *Shall we go on to sin?*

Surely he had disappointed the Almighty. But what else was there to do?

Susanna would point him back to Scripture. Yet hard as

he'd tried, it didn't seem to do much good.

Put off all these; anger, wrath, malice . . .

The desperation he had felt at Shallow Ford seized him again. *Lord, I need you. I can't do this.*

He shook his head and pulled out the New Testament. He needed sleep, but the Word of God suddenly seemed a lifeline, his only hope.

The hum of camp rose and fell around him. He shifted closer to the fire and ran his eye over the opening lines of the third chapter of Colossians, words so familiar now that he barely saw them.

If ye then be risen with Christ . . .

Wait.

He was tired. He knew that. But something there had caught him.

The message didn't start with putting off anger. It started with an *if*. Since. Because of this.

Seek those things which are above, where Christ sitteth on the right hand of God. Set your affection on things above, not on things on the earth.

For ye are dead, and your life is hid with Christ in God.

He closed the book, feeling shaken in a different way. He'd heard those words all his life. But could it be true that he was dead to his anger and alive to God? That he was hidden in Christ, and the Almighty saw him as perfect and righteous no matter how much he had failed?

Lord God, it feels blasphemous to think it. I know what I am. And yet—if it's true—

He swiped at his eyes, not caring who saw him. *Show me.*

The fire had burned low. He wrapped his blanket around himself and laid his head on the saddle and fell asleep praying.

The rest was brief. But the hours of sleep had helped. Benjamin relieved Saul McBraden on patrol until the troops stopped again, this time for a quick meal of bacon and corn cakes.

The smell of it set Benjamin's mouth to watering, though it was the same as they'd eaten for the last four days. He wondered what Kate and Elizabeth had made for breakfast at the ordinary. It would be something good, even if Tories were the only folks there to appreciate it.

"How far off do you think we are?" he asked as he and Captain Boothe saddled up again.

"Thirty miles." Robert swung into the saddle, the tired lines by his eyes a little fainter than before. "Maybe less."

If Benjamin figured right, Captain Boothe's enlistment was up, and the same for the rest of the scouts. But no one spoke of it. Not when General Greene was so close to safety.

There was no musket fire in the rear today. Either the cavalry was out of the British vanguard's range, or they had made an uneasy truce to avoid a pointless skirmish.

Benjamin turned Sassafras northeastward and spurred her to a trot. The road was broken and rutted, churned by the passage of Greene's army a day or two before. Each cycle of day and night had turned the roads to thick, pasty mud, then to shards of ice, then to mud again. Benjamin had seen the bloody footprints and felt guilty for being on horseback.

His thoughts drifted toward Sunrising again. Captain Boothe's must have done the same, for he said, "Any more thought as to what's afoot back home?"

"Not unless Armistead or Gregory knows something. I told you of Harrod's letter. What would a man do with a passel of men he figured were worthless for anything but baiting traps and keeping bullets away from his regulars?"

A mud-spattered courier hove into sight, coming on at a gallop. Benjamin moved Sassafras aside to let him pass. The rider sped by.

"Well, he wouldn't much care how many came out alive." Robert shook his head. "Baiting traps. I half think that's what Cornwallis has in mind for this river crossing. If he'd caught us last night, we'd have been trapped like rats."

Alec rode up beside them, his posture still hunched slightly to the left in protection of his wound. "This waiting," he said. "Never have been fond of it."

"'They also serve who only stand and wait,'" Benjamin said.

"You and your everlasting Milton. Look me in the eye and tell me *you* like waiting."

"I hate it," Benjamin admitted.

He rode on between the two men who had stood in the gap for him time and again. Milton was well and good. But Scripture had poured through his mind all morning, verses he had always known, but verses that somehow seemed new.

I am crucified with Christ: nevertheless I live; yet not I, but Christ liveth in me . . .

Reckon ye also yourselves to be dead indeed unto sin, but alive unto God through Jesus Christ our Lord . . .

Therefore if any man be in Christ, he is a new creature: old things are passed away; behold, all things are become new.

"Captain."

"Aye."

"Do you recollect that hymn by Isaac Watts? 'Shall We Go on to Sin?'"

"Yes, I recollect it, and no, we shan't."

Alec snorted. Benjamin shook his head. "How does the second stanza run? I've had no time this morning to look in my New Testament."

"'Forbid it, mighty God, nor let it e'er be said, that we whose sins are crucified—'"

"'Should raise them from the dead.'" He remembered now. *We whose sins are crucified.* "It's been running through my head, that's all."

"You could have worse things running through your head," Alec said.

"That's the truth. Look, Saul's coming yonder."

Saul McBraden thundered up on his roan, man and horse

both grimed with mud. "Greene's supply wagons went over last night," he said breathlessly. "The troops are crossing now."

"God be thanked," Robert said. "Cornwallis can't hope to catch Greene now."

Three o'clock. Fourteen miles from the river. Another courier galloped through the lines to Colonel Williams, his message spreading fast.

All our Troops are over, and the Stage is clear . . . I am ready to receive you and give you a hearty Welcome.

The shout that went up must have been heard for miles. All that was left was for the light troops to save themselves. But for Benjamin, and the rest of Captain Boothe's men, the crossing of the light troops would be only the beginning.

Just as dusk started to fall, Benjamin heard something above the tramp of feet. Alec said, "Is that—"

"Water," Benjamin said. "A lot of it."

He crested the hill beside Alec, and there it was, wide and shimmering in the blue twilight.

The Dan River. And waiting on the bank, General Greene.

Benjamin reined Sassafras on the hill where he could watch in both directions. *Lord, we're so close.*

At last a band of riders galloped through the dusk, voices raised in a cheer of their own. Benjamin waved his hat, ignoring the pain in his shoulder. "Here comes the cavalry!"

The final shades of twilight were long gone when the last man of Lee's American Legion stepped onto the opposite bank. But they were in time. General Greene had outfoxed Cornwallis once again.

Captain Boothe led his scouts in three lusty cheers. Then he turned to Benjamin and said, "Now for Sunrising."

Thirty-Five

JEM FLANNERY STEPPED INTO THE COOL DIMNESS
of the stable, its quietness a balm. Drilling a band of militia
was hard enough, it was, to say nothing of playing the loyal
officer while secretly wreaking havoc with British policy.

He often thought he saw Nolan Taggart watching him.
Did Taggart suspect? Or perhaps it only seemed that way.

The stable boy was nowhere to be seen. Mayhap he was
stealing a few winks in the loft. Jem had done that a time or
two as a hand in George Armistead's stables, working his
only honest job after years of thieving cargo on the wharves.

He leaned over the gate of his gelding's stall and shook
his head at the thought. Let it wait for the wee hours, then,
when all the other memories came back to haunt him.

A throat cleared behind him. Jem swung about.

Hank Jonas, beard matted and buckskins filthy, leaned
against the timber of the opposite stall.

"How long have you been standing there?" Jem hissed.

"Since you come in," Hank said laconically.

Jem hoped fervently that his face had not betrayed his
inmost thoughts. "What do you want?"

"Go on with what you was doin'." Hank relaxed against

the timber and folded his arms.

Jem turned back to his gelding. "Now will you tell me what you want?"

"What I want is anything you got."

Jem tightened his fingers on the stall gate, feeling the roughness of the wood against his palm. "We drilled today. Harrod will return in two weeks. Possibly longer if he stops for more recruits. We've begun to transport powder and arms from the ravine to our allies among the Indians. There will be some signal to them; Harrod's not told us what."

He hated saying *we* and *our* and *us*. But he was as responsible as the rest.

Straw rustled as Hank shifted his position, likely easing the weight on his game ankle. "Who are your Indian allies?"

"I don't know. Six of our men move the goods to the fort at Pembrook Station; a detachment is holding the stockade there. Harrod's Indian agent arranges the rest. I've never been told the man's name."

"Seems a mite odd, that."

"Not if you know Harrod."

Hank grunted. "Anything else?"

A sudden rush of footsteps outside put a quick halt to any answer. Jem wheeled, hoping Hank could see the warning on his face. But Hank appeared unmoved.

Nolan Taggart burst into the stable and stabbed a finger at Hank. "There he is. I saw him headed this way." He held out a slip of paper to Jem. "This was found at headquarters, sir."

Jem unfolded the paper, stained with the grimy imprint of Taggart's thumb.

Hank Jonas is a rebel spy.

Jem's mouth went dry. He crumpled the paper in one hand and thrust it into his pocket. "This fellow is Hank Jonas?"

"It's him right enough, sir. A pestilent rebel, by all accounts. Works with Mitchell Boothe, the dissenter."

Was it Jem's fancy, or was Taggart watching him too

closely? He could not afford to rouse suspicion.

Jonas, I hope you're a good liar, he thought. "What have you to say for yourself, rebel?"

"Well, of course I'm a spy." Hank hooked his thumbs in his hunting belt.

Jem plunged his hand into his pocket and gripped the slip of paper. "I beg your pardon?"

"I said I'm a spy." Hank shrugged. "You asked what I had to say for myself. Sure, I'm a spy. Why else would I be here in broad daylight in a settlement full o' folks who know me by name?"

"This is no time for mockery," Taggart said sharply.

"What do you want me to do, say I ain't a spy so you 'uns can try to prove that I am?" Hank sounded plaintive now. "That sounds like a waste of time. For ever'body."

Jem's gelding moved restlessly in the stall, as if sensing the tension in the stable. Taggart said, "And what's to say you aren't telling us you're a spy so as to make us believe you aren't a spy when by all rights you *are* a spy?"

Hank looked at him blankly. "If that ain't the beatin'est mouthful of words I ever did hear."

Taggart reddened and started forward. Jem pushed him back, caught Hank's hunting shirt, and thrust him against the timber of the stall. "Don't lie to us, rebel."

Please, lie to us, he thought.

Hank folded his arms. "You keep your dirty paws off'n me," he said mildly.

Taggart moved forward again. Jem stopped him with one upraised hand. "You heard me, Jonas."

"Sure I heard you. If I'm lyin' to you, then I ain't a spy. Can't get no clearer than that."

"Sergeant, this is absurd," Jem said to Taggart. "The man may have a vexing sense of humor, but he's done no more than stand in a public stable."

"But sir, if he's working for the rebels—"

"Then we will arrest him when the evidence warrants."

"Do it now and save yourself the trouble," Hank said, unmoved.

"Don't tempt me, Jonas. You're not safe yet."

Hank shrugged again.

Jem turned back to Taggart and was struck by the unease he saw in the man. Taggart was not safe yet either. No one was safe until this contest was decided, until either Sunrising or Malcolm Harrod emerged the victor. "I'll escort him out of the settlement, Sergeant. That ought to put the fear of the king into him. Send a man if I don't return."

"Yes, sir." Taggart looked between them, uncertainty creasing his face. He saluted Jem and strode from the stable.

Jem dared to breathe. "Let's go, rebel."

Hank let himself be marched out the door and down the path out of Sunrising. When they had crossed the bridge, Hank said from the side of his mouth, "Who turned me in?"

"The note was in a man's hand. Who might have known your reasons for being in the settlement?"

"Other than you?"

"I had nothing to do with it. I swear to you."

"You do your stuff like an old hand, that's all."

"I am an old hand, Jonas."

"I know it. And you were keeping Taggart off me. I'm obliged to you for that. But you throw me around like that again, I'll lam you one you won't forget."

"Sure, and be getting yourself in a right lot of trouble, you would." Heaven help him, the Irish was slipping out again. You are James Arnold Gregory, he told himself.

Drawing a deep breath, he went on more carefully. "It will be impossible for you to return for the duration of our campaign. I'll endeavor to communicate through Mitchell Boothe if necessary."

"He's done left the settlement," Hank said. "And you can give up the British bit when you're talkin' to me."

Jem stopped short. "What?"

"My mam was from Cork. I know the signs."

"Jonas, if you breathe that to a soul, I'll give you to Taggart myself."

"Trust me, Lieutenant." Hank gave him a cockeyed grin. "I know how to keep a secret."

Jem watched Hank vanish into the forest, feeling a cold stab of fear. A settlement in the backmost mountains of Carolina, and the past haunted him even here. His own voice betrayed him. He would never be anyone but Jem Flannery, Cork Harbor wharf rat. He was a fool to think otherwise.

And Jem Flannery had always run from trouble.

A deep voice hailed him as he came abreast of Boothe's cabin. Simon Pembrook crossed the path toward him.

Jem halted, his palms damp. He had known the big Tory-hater would search him out sooner or later. Just as Patrick Carr had after Kings Mountain.

Pembrook stopped in front of him. Jem felt that the judge could see straight through him, through all the lies and deception that made up Lieutenant James Arnold Gregory. He took a step backward and found himself against the wall of Boothe's cabin.

Pembrook pinned him there with a piercing scrutiny. "I've been meaning to speak with you, Gregory."

If only Jem were a praying man. But the Almighty did not trifle with the likes of Jem Flannery.

The clatter of spoons barely slowed as Kate hauled another kettle of stew through the great room door. Magdalen Boothe hurried past with an empty platter and whispered, "You'd think it was their last meal."

"If only," Kate muttered.

A tin cup banged on one of the long trestle tables. "More stew, Widow McGuiness."

"Bide your time, sir. I'm a-coming."

Elizabeth held the kettle while Kate ladled the stew into waiting trenchers. Nolan Taggart sat at the head of one table, watching the room in silence. Lieutenant Gregory was nowhere to be seen. Maybe he could take his meals in peace and quiet, being a lieutenant and all.

"It's all real good, ma'am." This from the square-faced, square-shouldered Tory who had carried the canoe. A pair of his messmates murmured agreement.

"Thank you kindly, Mr. Macauley." Kate motioned Elizabeth to go on down the table. Susanna came in with a pitcher and refilled mugs and tin cups, then hurried out.

The front door opened. Lieutenant Gregory stood in the doorway, his lean frame silhouetted against the dim light from the dogtrot. The men snapped to attention.

Something was amiss. Kate sensed it in the shift of the room's air, as if Gregory's coming were a rising cloud. He did not even acknowledge the salute of his men.

"Widow McGuiness, I wish to speak to you privately."

She set her ladle down. Elizabeth put the kettle down next to Mr. Macauley and followed Kate to the door.

If Gregory even noticed Elizabeth, he gave no sign. He held the door open, and Kate stepped out into the crisp fresh air of the dogtrot, Elizabeth at her heels.

Gregory shut the door. Now that they were outside, desperation tautened his features. "Which way would Hank Jonas have taken down the mountain?"

"Last I knew, he told me he wanted the stable to himself a wee minute. I didn't know he'd gone."

A plank of the porch creaked. Rane Armistead moved into the dogtrot on Gregory's other side.

The lieutenant did not look at him. "Jonas left half an hour ago. I must know which path he took."

"There are several he might have used," Kate said.

"What of Mitchell Boothe? Is he in the settlement?"

"He left some time ago."

Gregory swore and wheeled toward the porch steps.

"Mind your tongue before the women," Rane said sharply.

"I've just been told Harrod may return early. He knows you've discovered the stores in the ravine; a courier reached him." Gregory's hands crushed the folded brim of his hat. "I thought perhaps—but what's the use."

"The captain's lads are on their way home," Kate said. "We got word last week."

"It's a matter of days," Gregory said. "Perhaps hours. The men holding Pembrook Station are already on the march. And I—"

He broke off, shook his head, and brushed past Rane. On the porch steps he paused and turned back, a hunted, haunted look strong in his eyes.

"Don't trust Simon Pembrook," he said, and then he was gone.

Kate stared after him. "I wonder what he meant by that. The judge already knows about Rob's lads coming home."

"I hope it's not as it sounds," Rane said grimly.

"Rane, you don't think Judge Pembrook—"

"I don't know what to think." He coughed, gripping the porch rail. When he could breathe, he said hoarsely, "But in the meantime I'd do as J—as Gregory said and not trust him."

"Your cough, lad." There was a touch of flush in his face now, worse for the pallor around his lips. "You ought not be out in this cold air."

Rane smiled thinly. "It's better than inside with the Tories."

"What are we going to do?" Elizabeth asked softly.

"I'm thinking we'd best be prepared for anything," Kate said. "Rane, lad, tell Ayen what's happened. Benjamin and Rob and the rest of the lads must be across the Yadkin by now. If only we had a way to warn them."

Elizabeth opened her mouth, then closed it again. Rane hurried down the porch steps, coughing on his way.

Kate waved Elizabeth back inside and went back to serving as if nothing had happened. When Magdalen passed with an armload of empty dishes, Kate murmured, "First chance you get, spread the word to be ready to fort up if Harrod gets here early. Take Susanna with you."

Magdalen hurried past, but Kate knew she had heard. At the door, Magdalen paused and discreetly beckoned Susanna.

The men finished their meal and went out, some loud and boorish, others more polite. Kate thought of Macauley and how he'd said he would put up his gun and go home if Harrod ever abandoned his men as General Gates had done to the Patriots at Camden. If only it could be so simple.

She took up her own armful of empty dishes and went out, expecting Elizabeth to follow. But when she reached the kitchen and turned around, Elizabeth was not there. Kate frowned and started back toward the great room.

Just as she reached the door, Elizabeth rushed out, a stack of trenchers in one arm and a bundle of cloth under the other. Kate said, "What—"

"Not now." Elizabeth hurried ahead of her and nudged the kitchen door open.

Rane was inside. He sprang up from the bench where he had been waiting and put a hand on the table as if to steady himself. "Ayen says Lieutenant Gregory came for his gelding and rode out of the settlement."

He paused to cough. Elizabeth set her stack of trenchers down and slipped behind a pile of sacks in one corner.

"Might he know where Captain Boothe is?" Kate asked.

"Perhaps. Perhaps not." Rane's voice hardened. "We're on our own now, Kate."

"Well, I'll not have folks forting up in a room full of dirty dishes." Kate plunged her hands into her dishwater.

Rane buttoned his coat. "I had best hide our horses outside the settlement again before Harrod arrives."

"Don't hide all of them," Elizabeth said.

Kate and Rane both turned. Elizabeth had come out from behind the sacks. Her petticoat was tucked up as it would be if she were wearing her Sunday gown with its flounced underskirt. But instead of the underskirt were soft doeskin leggings, like the Indian women wore. The cape over her shoulders was the same material.

"Betty, lass," Kate began.

"I sneaked my riding things out of the loft after the Tories went out." Elizabeth fastened the cape's ties. "You said Benjamin and Captain Boothe should be warned. They must be nearly to Hunting River Gap by now if they've crossed the Yadkin. I can take your riding mare and—"

"If anyone goes, it ought to be me," Rane said.

"You can't," Elizabeth said simply. "You or Ayen would be missed straightway, and besides, you don't know the shortcuts as I do. I guess if Benjamin can be brave enough to fight the Tories, I can be brave enough to warn him they're coming. Only seems fair, seeing as he's the one who let me go with him on the trails when he was hunting."

Rane leaned on the table as another fit of coughing seized him. Kate's heart clenched. *Lord, be our helper.*

He straightened and drew a careful breath. "Then take Macy. He's strong, and faster than the mare."

"I'll be careful of him," Elizabeth promised.

Kate dried her hands and wrapped together some jerked meat and leftover frycakes. Rane reached into the pocket of his coat and pulled out a leather pouch and a small powder horn.

"You know the workings of a pistol?" he asked quietly.

Elizabeth gave a small nod.

"Take this." He drew the brass-trimmed pistol from under his coat and handed it to her with the shot pouch and powder horn. "And Godspeed, Miss Woodbridge."

Thirty-Six

HUNTING RIVER GAP STILL GLISTENED WITH snow and ice. Benjamin, leading Sassafras over the steepest point, paused to catch his breath. Below him, the West Yadkin sparkled in the afternoon sun, a few fractured masses of ice still drifting with the current. On the far side of the river, the Blue Ridge seemed to float amid clouds of mist.

"That's a sight for sore eyes," Alec Perry said.

"Aye, it is that." Benjamin glanced over. Alec was leading his chestnut gelding, looking tired but bearing up well.

Alec stopped. "Is that Mitchell Boothe I see coming? And Hank Jonas. Over yonder, aside of that rock."

Benjamin followed Alec's gesture. Sure enough, a lean, darkheaded figure waved his hat and hallooed a greeting. Hank Jonas stood beside him.

"Wonder how they knew we were coming." Captain Boothe turned to Alec. "You and Saul McBraden take a dozen men and cover the rest of us. We're wide open while we're crossing the ford."

"Yessir." Alec saluted with a lift of his rifle and began choosing men.

Benjamin followed Robert down the slope. Sassafras's

hooves crunched through the crust of snow, her breath forming short puffs in the clear air.

Robert embraced his brother and slapped him on the back. "What brings you here?"

"Had a hankering to see if you were still in one piece." Mitchell grinned, but it didn't reach his eyes. "Gunning told me you were headed this way."

"How'd he know?" Benjamin asked.

"Saw you come through the valley. Though knowing Gunning, you likely didn't see him see you." Mitchell's smile fell away. "No, Rob, I came to tell you Selagisqua's lads are coming in to help defend Sunrising against Harrod. Hank found me on my way and has a report of his own."

"Finally got back into the settlement," Hank said. "Took me long enough. But Gregory says they've been drilling and expect Harrod back in a fortnight. A mite less now."

"That ought to give us time to prepare," Robert said.

"Harrod's got men at Pembrook Station," Hank said. "And he's got some signal rigged up to his Indian allies, but Gregory didn't know what it would be."

"What of Armistead?" Benjamin asked sharply.

"Still in Sunrising, but feeling poorly last I knew."

Benjamin shook his head. "I shouldn't have left."

"Well, nobody asked me," Hank said, "but from what I seen, there ain't nothing you could have done. Not with Nolan Taggart after your hide."

Benjamin grimaced. "Thanks for reminding me."

"Most of the arms and trade goods have been moved out of the ravine," Mitchell added. "But no one seems to know who their Indian agent might be."

"We've a fear about that," Robert said.

"And somebody turned me in," Hank said. "Slipped a note to Taggart, said I was a spy. No harm came of it, thanks to Gregory's playacting. But he didn't know who told on me."

"We've a fear about that too." Benjamin thought of the

unsigned letter he'd seen on the table in Tory headquarters, back when he and Rane had first ventured into the ravine. *I have maintained Secrecy and pray you to conceal our Relation from your own Men as well as Others.*

Benjamin did not know Judge Pembrook's handwriting well enough to recognize it, but he would dare to wager it was the same handwriting as the note that had betrayed Hank.

He started to speak of it, then glimpsed movement beyond Captain Boothe. A black horse picked its way down the bank, bearing a caped figure. A dark skirt blew in the wind.

"That's Elizabeth. On Armistead's horse." Benjamin ran forward, throwing up a hand at the covering party on the rocks above and behind. "Don't fire."

The gelding was halfway across the river now. Benjamin waded into the swollen current, took Macy's bridle, and led the horse to the bank, then gave Elizabeth a hand out of the saddle. "Mouse, what in the name of sense are you doing here?"

She threw back her hood. "I came to warn you about Harrod."

Benjamin led Macy away from the river, motioning Elizabeth to join him. "Mitchell and Hank said he's coming back in a fortnight."

"No." Elizabeth shook her head. Wisps of hair blew into her face. "Lieutenant Gregory found out after Hank left. Harrod's coming back early. Maybe even today."

Mitchell exchanged glances with Hank. *"Today?"*

"Gregory said it might be days, might be hours. Harrod's men are on the move from the fort. And he said not to trust Judge Pembrook."

"Sounds as if we were right, Woodbridge," Robert said grimly. "But if they're coming from the fort . . ."

At the edge of Benjamin's vision, sun flashed on the river.

Not only on the river.

Sun on steel.

"Get down!"

He lunged for Elizabeth. Gunfire exploded on all sides. The day shattered into fragments of fire and smoke.

"Get her behind the rocks," Robert shouted, his silver-barreled pistol in his hand. "I'll cover you."

Benjamin pulled Elizabeth to her feet, shielding her with his body. Mitchell followed with Macy, lashed the reins to a scrub pine near the gap, and dashed back to his brother's side.

"Did they follow me?" Elizabeth's voice shook.

"Don't reckon so. They were already here. Stay down." He pushed her down behind a boulder and crouched beside her, rifle balanced atop the rock. A muzzle flash exploded across the river, and he fired back at it. The recoil set his shoulder to aching again. He ignored the pain and reloaded.

The covering party opened fire. Acrid black smoke billowed, making a mockery of the crisp clear sunlight. Crystals of snow spurted up in front of Benjamin. He shook the pellets from his eyes and fired another shot. Had it found a mark? He thought the man staggered, but he couldn't be sure.

They had been so close to Sunrising. So close.

Mitchell stumbled and fell to a knee. Elizabeth gasped. Robert shouted his brother's name.

"Just a scratch," Mitchell shouted back. He got to his feet, grimacing, and took aim into the smoke.

Shadows moved along the shelter of the bluff. The Tories were on the near side of the river now too. Benjamin muttered a prayer. He could not reload fast enough.

"Here." Elizabeth pushed something at him. A steel-barreled pistol. Belt hook. Brass fittings. "It's primed."

It was also Rane Armistead's, but there was no time to ask. Benjamin passed her the rifle and angled his body in front of her, taking a two-handed grip of the pistol.

"Load quick, Mouse," he said over his shoulder. "And try not to see what happens."

Rane's pistol thundered in his hands, knocking a Tory to the ground. Chips of rock stung Benjamin's face as a ball struck the boulder in front of him. There was blood on the snow. A friend's, an enemy's, his own—he didn't know. He prayed Elizabeth saw nothing but the rifle she was loading.

He reached left, and she handed him Old Sandy and took the pistol. He fired into the smoke again, missed. When he reached left again, she had the pistol waiting.

Benjamin risked a glance. Elizabeth's cheek was smudged where a tear had mixed with black powder. But her lips were set as she took the rifle and started loading.

Then her eyes darted past his shoulder and went wide. "Benjamin! Behind you!"

He whirled, raised the pistol, fired. The ball took the Tory high in the shoulder, dropping both him and the tomahawk he carried.

Lord Jesus, have mercy on us.

"Fall back!" Captain Boothe shouted.

The words seemed strange and distant through the foul blanket of smoke. Benjamin grabbed the shot pouch and loaded the pistol himself. He thrust it through his belt and took Old Sandy from Elizabeth. "When I shout, get up behind those scrub pines."

She nodded and rose to a crouch, poised to spring.

He pivoted, sweeping the space with the rifle. "Go, go!"

Elizabeth sprang up and dashed behind the pines. Benjamin leaped over the rocks, loosing Macy's reins on his way, and got the horse to the cover of the pines just as Robert caught up, Mitchell and Hank beside him.

"Back through the gap." The captain was breathing hard. "We'll cover you again. Mitch, take the horse."

Benjamin nodded to Elizabeth. She scrambled for the opening. He followed a step behind and to the left, ready to trip her and fall atop her if the enemy fired on them.

At the steep part of the gap, Alec Perry sighted over a fallen tree, his face streaked with soot and powder. He motioned them past. As Benjamin escorted Elizabeth into the gap, the covering party fired a final volley and followed them. The enemy fire formed an erratic drumbeat, slowly fading to sporadic bursts.

"Everyone here?" Robert asked, tucking his own pistol through his belt.

Nods all around. Benjamin's muscles eased a notch.

"If they've driven us back, they'll be off their guard," Robert said. "We'll rest a minute, talk out what to do. Woodbridge, see to your sister."

Benjamin took Elizabeth's elbow and led her to the shelter of an uprooted scrub oak, its massive roots a natural breastwork. "All right?"

She looked up at him, her eyes filling. He tugged her farther back against the web of roots and soil, putting himself between her and the rest of the world.

She rushed him then and clung as fiercely as she had when she was eleven and he had nearly lost a tangle with an angry bear. He put his free arm around her shaking shoulders, a fierceness of his own welling up within him.

This, then, was what Alec meant when he said the best fights were for what a man loved and not what he hated. Because Benjamin would fight a thousand Harrods and Fergusons, even a thousand Greenes and Morgans, to protect Elizabeth. The thought alone filled him with a simmering rage. As it should be, mayhap, and yet so easy to misuse.

Lord, I can't do this alone.

"All right?" he asked again, quietly.

"I thought you were going to get killed like Pa," she said, her voice muffled by his shirt.

"Maybe Pa was fighting to save you too," he said gently. "You bore up well back there. I was proud of you."

Elizabeth drew a shuddering breath and straightened. "Not so proud of me now, going all to pieces."

"Plenty of folks do, after the danger's over. I've seen brave men get sick all over themselves as soon as the white flag goes up."

She wrinkled her face at him. He shrugged.

"I'm sorry I didn't get here sooner," she said. "Maybe if I had—"

"If you had, they'd have bottled us up in the gap instead of down where we could fight them off." He offered the tail of his kerchief, and she blotted her eyes with it.

"You should wash that," she said, wrinkling her nose again.

"I swam a river with it. That count?"

"No. It doesn't."

He laughed. It felt good to laugh, and yet he felt guilty for it after all that had just happened. If this was Judge Pembrook's doing . . .

What a man loves, not what he hates.

"I don't think I should call you Mouse anymore," he said.

"I think I might miss it." She pinched her thumb and forefinger together. "A little."

"Woodbridge," Robert said from behind them.

Benjamin turned. "Yessir."

"Get your sister home. Mitch and Hank will go with you. I want somebody to report back if Harrod has more men bound for Sunrising."

"Yessir." Benjamin straightened his hunting shirt, the pistol's weight unfamiliar against his hip. If Harrod had more men bound for Sunrising, this battle was far from over.

"Leave the horses with us," Robert said. "You'll do better on foot."

Mitchell came over, Hank Jonas on his trail. Benjamin eyed the bloodstains on Mitchell's leggings.

"Like I told Rob," Mitchell said. "Just a scratch."

Benjamin offered Elizabeth his arm, putting his hand just a few inches from the pistol in his belt. "Then let's go."

Thirty-Seven

BENJAMIN LED THE WAY ACROSS THE WEST YADKIN at the most sheltered point he could find. Mitchell and Hank followed him silently, Elizabeth between them, up the long slope of valley turning to foothills. Benjamin found it an honor that Mitchell, a man with decades of experience in the ways of the backcountry, let him take the lead.

The foothills rolled up and away ahead of them, studded with bare trees that slanted shadows downhill in the late afternoon light. Smoke still hung in the air, staining the light a pale gray. But no tracks marred the patchy snow.

Elizabeth said in a hushed voice, "Where did they all go?"

"Back to the holes they crawled out of." Old Sandy was heavy in the crook of his right arm. He moved the rifle to his left, easing the ache in his shoulder.

No one had come this way from the valley. Maybe Sunrising would be safe awhile yet, and Captain Boothe could lead his men into the settlement without fear . . .

But there was the other trail, the path that led up through the ledges where Taggart had had his revenge on Benjamin. Harrod knew of that path, had been on it that day and likely other days since. If he had taken that path again, the enemy was already ahead of them.

Mitchell's breathing turned labored. Benjamin shot him a sharp glance. Mitchell didn't meet his eye.

Benjamin started to ask if he was all right. But there was no point in making Elizabeth fret. And there was no going back now. He looked up at the rising terrain. They would reach Sunrising by dusk.

"Tell me where things stood when you left Sunrising, Mouse," Benjamin said. He winked as he said the nickname.

She shook her head at him. "There were maybe forty men left in the settlement, mostly at the ordinary. Aunt Kate still has our powder and shot hidden in the kitchen."

"Forty men in Sunrising, and Harrod coming back with more," Benjamin mused. "How many, we don't know, but we met up with some of them just now, I'll be bound."

"And the Cherokee at his beck and call," Hank said. "Don't be forgettin' that."

"Trust me. I'm not forgetting it."

"Captain Boothe has more than forty men with him," Elizabeth said.

"Aye. And they'd be fighting on their own ground once in the settlement."

"Harrod's no fool," Mitchell said. "He'll get his new recruits and his Cherokees into Sunrising ahead of Rob. He's got to. Leaving those forty men there alone would be . . ."

"Murder?" Benjamin finished. "Or bait in a trap?"

"Lord, have mercy," Hank said.

The wind freshened, plastering Benjamin's wet leggings to the stockings beneath. A cloud passed before the sun.

Mitchell stumbled.

Benjamin reached to give him a hand. Then he saw the blood on the snow.

Mitchell pulled himself to his feet. "I'm fine."

"That's not just a scratch."

Mitchell gave him a game grin. "Want to wager on that?"

"You're a preacher," Hank said. "You can't wager."

Mitchell limped forward. "I'll still wager I make it to Sunrising before the lot of you."

"You know what Aunt Kate would tell you," Benjamin said.

"Sure. To shut up and stop being stubborn. But I hate to tell you, Woodbridge—you aren't Aunt Kate."

Benjamin motioned Hank in beside Mitchell, not liking the pale cast of Mitchell's skin or the dark stain spreading around his knee. "I can be as stubborn as you can."

"Care to wager on that too?"

"I wouldn't if'n I was you," Hank said to Benjamin.

Mitchell was talking through his teeth now. But he didn't slow his pace. Elizabeth hovered behind him, worry pinching her forehead. Benjamin hoped his own worry didn't show. He forced himself to focus on the trail and keep moving.

"There's one thing we don't know," Hank said. "If Harrod's using those Tories as bait, is he leaving 'em *in* Sunrising so the captain will take 'em on and Harrod can come in from behind, or is he sending 'em *out* of Sunrising to draw the captain out there while Harrod comes in and takes the whole place over?"

"Wish I had an answer," Benjamin said. "Either way, they'll likely turn out to join Harrod and be out of Aunt Kate's way for once—"

He stopped. Hank said, "Now what?"

"Nothing."

But it was not nothing. When the Tories turned out to join Harrod, the British would have no more need of the ordinary. And the British burned what they had no more need of.

Mitchell swayed. Benjamin grabbed his arm and sat him down against a tree. "Hold still."

"Woodbridge, I'm—"

"You heard me." Benjamin tugged at the torn buckskin along Mitchell's left leg. A bloodied furrow creased the side of his knee. "How on earth did you make it this far? And how long till you were going to mention it?"

"Till we got to Sunrising, most likely." Mitchell winced, then tried to cover it with a smile. "I can keep going."

"You keep going like this, you'll fall out in the trail on me."

"Your boot's full of blood," Hank said. "No wonder you're feeling dizzy-headed."

"I'm not feeling—"

"Shut up and stop being stubborn," Benjamin said.

Mitchell huffed a pained laugh. "Respect your elders."

"That's what I'm doing. Give me your kerchief."

Mitchell unknotted the square of fabric and handed it over. Benjamin tied it firmly around the wound. Mitchell grimaced. "You're right, you are as stubborn as I am."

"And don't you forget it." Benjamin braced his shoulder beneath Mitchell's arm and helped him to his feet. "Take it slow."

Mitchell raised his head. "What's that?"

Benjamin listened. Far away, twisted by the ridges and hollows, the sound of men and horses drifted down the mountain. Elizabeth moved closer to Benjamin.

"On second thought," Benjamin said, "take it as fast as you can."

Thirty-Eight

FOR EVERY ROCK AND TREE HE PASSED, JEM
Flannery wondered how many Indian allies Simon Pembrook
and Malcolm Harrod might have in these hills. Jem could
hear Pembrook's rumbling whisper even now.

The judge had not minced words. He had heard that the
Whigs were stealing British trade goods and knew of Harrod's
ties to the Cherokee. He had heard that Captain Boothe was
on his way home. He had sent a courier to Harrod with the
news and been told Harrod was on his way and to get the
men at the fort in motion.

After that Pembrook had heard nothing, long enough
that he had abandoned his orders to maintain the masquerade
and had told Jem what he knew.

Surely you'll know what to do, he had said.

Aye, and Jem had known what to do. Saddle up and get
out of the Blue Ridge. He might have stayed if Hank Jonas
hadn't already vanished, but he had no way to warn Boothe
now. Not until it was too late and Boothe and Woodbridge
blamed Jem for an attack that came two weeks early.

The westering sun lanced between budding branches of
redbud, lighting an unfamiliar trail. The shortest path from

Sunrising would be too easy to follow, so Jem had taken a southerly route through winding defiles and over rocky balds, trusting that it did indeed lead to the Yadkin River Valley as he had heard that it did.

So far he had wandered in circles at least twice that he knew of. It had given him plenty of time to think. Was he looking for Captain Boothe or fleeing to save his own skin?

He had not answered that yet. Perhaps he would not know until he reached the valley.

Up ahead, the trail narrowed and snaked around a granite outcropping ringed by towering pines. Reining the gelding, Jem walked the horse carefully around the sharp bend. The rocks on the left dropped sheer away to the ledges below. The view was breathtaking, the height stomach turning. Jem focused on the trail and breathed easier as soon as the trail broadened between bare trees again.

His sigh of relief died as quickly as it had begun. A clatter of hooves rolled up the trail from beyond the trees.

He knew echoes could carry for miles along the hills and hollows. Maybe the riders were not really on this trail. Maybe they were miles away, or across the ridge, or—

A flicker of scarlet flashed between the trees up ahead. Then another and another.

Jem wheeled the gelding. If he could get through that narrow place before they saw him, he would have plenty of time to find a hiding place or another path. A large riding party would need a fair deal of time to get past that ledge.

But even as he spurred his horse, he heard the shout. "You there! Hold hard!"

He tightened his hold on the reins. Which was worse: to face them and try to explain or to let them wonder why a man in their own uniform was running the other way?

Panic won out. He planted his heels in the gelding's flanks and pounded up the trail toward the rocks.

"Halt in the name of the king!"

Harrod's voice now, and closer. Jem did not halt in the name of the king.

The trail narrowed ahead of him. Only a little farther. The cold rush of wind stung his face. He leaped a rotting log and sent a rain of rock fragments rattling down the trail.

A pistol shot cracked behind him, and the gelding reared and came down hard. Reins and mane and pommel slid past Jem's grasp.

Every bone jarred against snow-covered earth. The air left his lungs.

"Lieutenant Gregory." Harrod dismounted. If he was surprised, he hid it well. "What is the meaning of this?"

Jem hauled in a breath and got to his feet. Snow clung to his coat. "I beg your pardon, sir. I thought you were rebels."

"In these uniforms? I ordered you to halt in the name of the king. What of that could you mistake for a rebel?"

"I didn't hear you, sir."

"Indeed." Harrod studied him, one hand on the pistol in his sash. "Is it possible that you were fleeing your post?"

"Sir, what reason would I have for that?"

"Perhaps you should answer that yourself, Lieutenant." Harrod looked up at the mounted men behind him. "Continue up the ridge. I will join you outside the settlement." He nodded to three men Jem did not recognize. "Remain."

The riders filed up the trail. Harrod said, "I've a bargain to strike with you, Lieutenant."

Jem laughed shortly. "I've had enough of bargains."

"You may find this one attractive. I'll overlook this breach of conduct if you lead tonight's charge against Robert Boothe. Consider it your opportunity to clear yourself of suspicion."

"Why me?"

"You are a competent officer, Lieutenant. Or were, as the case may be. We shall find that out tonight."

"I'm no such thing, Major, and we both know it. If I lead that charge, it will be death for me inside the first volley."

Harrod did not answer. A hot, angry fear kindled in Jem's gut. "And that's what you're banking on, aye? The rebels will save you the trouble of a court-martial. And what of the men I'm to lead, then?"

"You'll draw Boothe away from the settlement," Harrod said. "That is all that is required of you."

"Away from the settlement?" The anger was growing in him, the same way it had the last time he defied his grandfather. "The lot of us out in Boothe's own wilderness, fighting him for his very hearth and home? That's suicide, Major."

"It is necessary," Harrod said evenly.

The gifts in the ravine, the Cherokee, the way Harrod never discussed his plans—it was one grand scheme now, fitting together like bricks and mortar. Harrod would sacrifice forty men to draw the Patriots out while his Indian allies and the rest of his troops claimed the victory.

Jem looked at the men behind Harrod. "You want to wager your lives that I'm lying, lads?"

Uncertainty flickered in their eyes. Then it vanished. Jem should have known. No one would challenge Harrod on the word of a deserter. Jem wished he dared push Harrod off the ledge, or jump off himself. Maybe this was justice for what he'd done to Rane Armistead.

But it was not justice Jem was wanting. It was mercy.

"We're wasting time," Harrod said. "Refusing to lead the charge will accomplish nothing. Someone will lead it."

"Sure, and it won't be me."

"You'll watch it, then. I'll not have you running to warn Boothe. As you were attempting to do, I warrant." Harrod pivoted on his heel and motioned to the three men. "Bind his hands. Then we make haste for Sunrising."

Thirty-Nine

KATE FORCED HERSELF TO SWEEP THE GREAT
room after supper as usual, to keep her hands busy and try
not to think of Elizabeth out there on the mountain. Surely
by now she had found Benjamin. But if she hadn't—

Lord, set a watch on my thoughts. You're out on the moun-
tain same as you are here.

The great room was too quiet, even though Elizabeth
was rarely one for much talking. It was growing late, and the
Tories had not come in to bed down as they usually did.
Something was happening.

Magdalen hung the hearth shovel and tongs in their
places, their metallic clinks loud in the quiet. Susanna washed
tables in silence. Ayen fetched water, equally silent. That
alone meant something was amiss.

Rane was in the stable. And Elizabeth—

There I go again, Lord.

Susanna lifted her head. "Did you hear something?"

Kate listened. A thump, over by the kitchen.

"I'll see what it is." She set the broom in the corner, not
minding the idea of leaving all this peace and quiet for a bit.

"Maybe I'd best go with you," Magdalen said.

"There's no need." Kate stepped around Ayen and slipped out the back door.

Light glowed from the kitchen door, bright against the snow. Someone was inside. Kate hesitated. Mayhap Magdalen had been right.

But Kate was not one to quail. She lifted her chin, as centuries of her Gaelic forebears must have done, and slipped closer, doing her best to walk the way Benjamin did when he was tracking game—or trying to startle Elizabeth.

Shuffles and thumps emanated from the open door. Kate pressed herself to the outside wall and peered through a gap in the chink.

Nolan Taggart. With her floorboard pried up and the powder and shot on the floor beside him.

Kate spun away from the wall and marched to the door. "Nolan Taggart, you should be ashamed."

He stood, lifting the bag of shot with one arm and the powder keg with the other. "No, Kate. 'Tis you who should be ashamed."

"You'd steal a woman's home and her defense too?"

"I had a notion this was here somewhere. And you'll get your dues for it soon enough." He pushed past her, and she saw his men clustered near the creek path.

Kate dashed into the kitchen and snatched up the fowling piece from the corner. When she gained the door again, he was nearly in among his men.

She longed to send a good dose of birdshot screaming through the air over his head. But lead was too precious to waste, especially now that her secret supply was gone. It was his conscience; he'd have to answer for it.

Oh Lord, I'm to be loving my enemies. And vengeance is yours, you said. I'm holding you to that.

The night was cool but clear. She lingered on the kitchen step a moment, mastering herself before going back to tell the others of the loss.

Light steps rustled in the shadows by McGuiness Creek. Kate trained the fowler in that direction, mindful of Nolan Taggart still within earshot. "Who's there?"

"It's me." Elizabeth's voice, slightly breathless. "And Hank. Benjamin's coming, but he sent us on ahead when we got close to Sunrising."

"Come in, quick." Kate stepped aside and waved them through the door. "You're afoot, lass. Where—"

"I left Macy with Captain Boothe." Elizabeth stared at the gaping hole in the corner. "Aunt Kate, what's happened?"

Kate shut the door, eyeing its crooked hinges. "Nolan Taggart, that's what's happened."

"He's spoilin' for a fight," Hank said. "I'll go after him."

"It'd do no good. He's with his men now. Betty, lass, you found the captain, then?"

"Aye. But the Tories found us too, and there was a fight. Harrod's men, Benjamin thinks."

"Then they're nearly here." Kate studied Elizabeth in the firelight and saw the smudges on her face, not dirt but powder. "God help us."

"Captain Boothe is on his way, but he sent me and Benjamin on ahead with Hank and Brother Mitchell."

"Mitch is hurt," Hank said. "Nasty crease along his knee. Woodbridge wanted you to be ready."

Elizabeth shuddered. Kate set the fowler down and put a steadying hand on her arm. "You've been brave, lass. Be brave a mite longer."

"You want I should get Armistead?" Hank asked.

"Not now. Let him rest. We'll need him enough later."

A quick tapping came at the door. From outside, Magdalen's voice said, "Kate?"

"Let them in," Kate told Hank.

He opened the door. Magdalen hurried in, Susanna and Ayen flanking her. "Someone's coming up the trail."

Kate craned to look over Hank's shoulder. Torches

swarmed along the trail like angry fireflies. Hooves rang against frozen earth and thudded over the logs of the bridge. She heard Susanna ask what had happened to the floor, and she heard herself answer. But she did not move from the door, standing with Hank, watching the torches come closer until their light plainly showed the band of riders and the cloaked man at their head.

Harrod was back, then. Kate gripped the doorpost, nails biting wood.

"Be brave a mite longer, Kate," Hank said. "Same as you told Miss Elizabeth."

The band halted as Nolan Taggart approached Harrod and spoke. The rider behind Harrod wore a coat with an epaulet that looked reddish in the torchlight. But he did not sit his saddle like a proud officer. Shoulders bent, profile downturned, as if he were ill or weary or—

A prisoner. He dismounted at a word from Harrod, and Kate saw the pale hemp binding his wrists in front of him.

James Arnold Gregory. *Lord, help him. Help us all.*

Taggart and another man led him to Captain Boothe's cabin. Gregory's own headquarters, only a few hours past.

"Rob had better get here soon," Hank said grimly.

Kate turned from the door. "Ayen, you'd best fetch Rane and help him with the horses, what with all these Tories coming and going."

Ayen darted out the door.

"What are we going to do?" Elizabeth said softly.

Kate turned and took her hands firmly. "We are going to get ready to help Mitchell. And we are going to pray as hard as we know how and keep that fowler handy."

As soon as Rane looked out the loft window and saw the men and horses streaming along the creek path, he knew Malcolm Harrod was back. Knew it even before he saw the long sweep of Harrod's cloak and the dark sheen of his charger, black as night in the light of the torches. Even before he watched Taggart speak to Harrod and escort Jem away.

Rane turned from the window. *Lord God, be my strength.*

He buttoned his waistcoat and picked up the coat he'd laid aside only minutes before. The letter crackled through the broadcloth of the coat, where he had kept it since Elizabeth's baptism. He reached for the place his pistol should be, the empty spot making a mockery of his ritual. Dropping his hand, he started for the ladder.

The south door opened. "Mr. Armistead?"

"Ayen?"

"Aunt Kate sent me. Harrod's coming with more men."

Rane lowered himself from the ladder and turned to face Ayen. The stable spun, then righted itself. His temples throbbed as he lit the lantern in the center of the aisle. The flickering light swayed, tightening the headache.

Ayen said, "You don't look too good."

And he likely felt worse than he looked. Hiding his cough and fatigue from Kate had become a daily battle, and a losing one. "We haven't time for that. These stalls are not ready if Harrod wants them."

"I can help." Ayen grabbed a pitchfork from its place against the wall and headed for one of the stalls.

This was the last place Ayen should be if Harrod came looking for Rane. "Finish as swiftly as you can, then go help Aunt Kate. She'll need it more."

"If you say so," Ayen said, vigorously forking dirty straw.

Rane himself ought to be the one helping Kate. Yet he dared not. Leading Harrod to the kitchen would be worse than facing him in front of Ayen.

But when both doors opened at the same time, he knew it was already too late.

The draft set the lantern to swinging again. Malcolm Harrod stepped into the dancing circle of light.

Four men were behind him. Two more shut the opposite

door. The scene was a strange blend of hazy and crystal clear. But perhaps that was only the fever.

"Do you require assistance with your horses, gentlemen?" Rane said quietly, meeting Harrod's gaze.

"I require a great deal of assistance, Armistead." Harrod's voice held the same faintly caustic edge Rane had heard in his nightmares. "Though not with the horses. Sergeant Taggart told me I would find a man of your description here."

Ayen said uncertainly, "Mr. Armistead?"

"Go to the kitchen." Rane caught himself short of saying Ayen's name. If Harrod knew who the lad was, Ayen would be his next target.

"Not so fast." Harrod motioned with one gloved hand.

The pair of men by the far door caught Ayen by either arm. Rane started toward them.

"Not another step, or he suffers," Harrod said sharply.

Ayen stared at Rane wide eyed, shaking his head. Not fear, but defiance. Rane reached for his hip, forgetting the pistol was not there.

Two men lunged at him, wrestled him down. Ayen shouted angrily, then yelped.

Rane rolled onto his back, his clasp knife open in his hand. The faces blurred above him. A boot struck his arm, sending the knife into the straw. Rough hands flipped him over and slammed him to the floor.

Dust and straw filled his vision, filled his lungs. He choked, coughed, felt the pain of it sear through his chest and head. Rope cinched tight around his wrists, the familiar burn of it stinging far deeper than skin.

The men dragged him to his feet and shoved past Ayen and led Rane out into a night that spread over the settlement and the forest beyond, dark as the waters of Cape Fear.

In the hour of death, and in the day of judgment, Good Lord, deliver me.

Forty

BENJAMIN HALTED ON THE SLOPE THAT LED TO McGuiness Creek, twenty yards behind the Dove & Olive. Men with torches thronged the northeastern edge of Sunrising. "Stay here."

"Somebody'll have to tell Rob." Mitchell hadn't complained once, though he'd been leaning on Benjamin almost since Hank and Elizabeth had gone on ahead.

"Aye. But not you."

Benjamin moved forward in a crouch, scanning the darkness for any sign that they'd been spotted. He doubted anyone was watching. All the commotion seemed to be on the outskirts of the settlement, near the bridge and the main trace up the mountain. The fork of the path was filled with men and horses.

And somewhere, Malcolm Harrod.

Benjamin turned back toward Mitchell. "Let's get you to Aunt Kate."

He slid his arm under Mitchell's again and helped him forward. Mitchell gritted his teeth as they waded the creek.

Sparks of light shone through the chinking of the kitchen. Benjamin should have fixed that before he left. Should have fixed a lot of things before he left.

He wondered briefly what Kate would say to him. But there was no time to think of that.

When they reached the kitchen door, Mitchell leaned against the wall while Benjamin knocked. Kate opened the door almost at once. "Come in, quick."

Benjamin helped Mitchell inside. His quick survey of the room told him Hank and Elizabeth were already here. The welcoming scents of hearth and home cloaked him in a warmth he wished he had time to enjoy.

He pulled his hat off and eased Mitchell onto a bench. "What's happened?"

Kate shut the door, blocking out the hubbub of militia on the march. "They started coming up the ridge not a half hour ago. Taggart had the rest of the men out to meet them before they came so far as the bridge." She nodded toward the corner, lips tight. "And he found our powder and shot."

Another defense gone. "I didn't see Gregory out there."

Kate pulled the bloodsoaked wrapping away from Mitchell's knee and shook her head. Whether at Benjamin's question or Mitchell's wound, he couldn't tell. "He told us Harrod was coming back early. Then he left the settlement, but Harrod brought him back a prisoner."

The feel of a big fight, a hard fight, was thick in the air. Benjamin could sense it like coming rain. "Where are Harrod's men now?"

"All around the ravine," Hank said. "Spreadin' out from there."

"Waiting for the Cherokee from Pembrook Station, no doubt." Benjamin heard Elizabeth's sharp intake of breath. "Courage, Mouse. We're not licked yet. Where's Armistead?"

"In the stable." Kate motioned for Mitchell to stretch out on the bench. "I sent Ayen to help him. He's not been well, though he's tried to hide it."

"I'll speak to him," Benjamin said. "Hank, don't shoot

me when I come back."

The door crashed open. Benjamin whirled, lifting his rifle. Ayen stumbled inside, all but falling over his own feet, tears and grime streaking his face. Rane's clasp knife was in his hand.

"Ayen!" Kate said. "What on earth—"

"They got Mr. Armistead." Ayen's narrow chest heaved. "Harrod came in and Mr. Armistead told me to go but Harrod's men grabbed me, and he tried to fight back but then they tied him up and took him away."

"Oh, Lord, have mercy," Kate said.

"Which way did they take him?" Benjamin demanded.

"I don't know. They dragged him out the north door. But they were gone when Harrod's men let me go."

First Gregory. Now Armistead. "Somebody will have to report to Captain Boothe while I go after them."

Mitchell struggled to sit up. "I can—"

"You'll fall out of the saddle. Hank, tell the captain the Tories are in Sunrising and took Gregory and Armistead prisoner. The way up the ridge is clear for the time being, but he ought to be on his guard."

"On my way." Hank slipped out into the dusk. He'd find a horse somewhere, Benjamin had no doubt of that.

"I'll pray," Elizabeth said, her hazel eyes large in her pale face.

"Pray hard, Mouse." Benjamin drew her in for a brief, fierce embrace, ignoring the ache in his shoulder. He handed her Rane's pistol and shot pouch and powder horn, then reached for Mitchell's rifle and propped it against the table within reach of Mitchell's right hand. "Mitch, if any Tories try to come in here while I'm gone—"

"I can shoot lying down," Mitchell said.

"And I can shoot standing up." Kate clasped Benjamin's hands briefly. "Godspeed, Benjamin."

Old Sandy rested heavy against his shoulder as he

stepped outside, his knife and tomahawk heavy on his hip. The sharp tang of smoke lingered in the air, a portent of destruction to come.

He strode toward the stable, noting there were almost no Tories in the paths between cabins. But then, why should there be? The only danger to the Tories would come from without, not from within. Rane had been the only threat left in the settlement.

Rane had been dragged out through the north door, Ayen had said. Benjamin scouted the ground there, grateful for moon enough to make out the scuff marks in the snow where a bevy of men had left the stable.

The marks led north, toward the creek path and the ravine beyond. Lights flickered there, bright angry flashes that splashed off the rocks along the creek. The store of arms was down there, or what was left of it. Doubtless Harrod's men were down there with it.

Would Harrod be so bold as to hold a prisoner in the very place where that prisoner had helped to defy him?

If Benjamin knew his man, Harrod would be so bold as to do nothing else.

He saw Elizabeth's face, the smudges of powder and tears. He would fight for her a hundred times over. And for Kate. Even for Susanna, even if she never looked his way again. And for the quiet Anglican rebel who had run out of rope.

At the edge of the stable yard, an idea wormed its way into his consciousness. A bold thought, bold as Harrod himself, mayhap. And yet—

He turned and made for Simon Pembrook's dwelling.

The cabin was dark. But Pembrook could not have failed to hear the rising wave of Tories. If he was in the settlement, he was awake. Benjamin knocked swiftly.

Pembrook opened the door, fully dressed. "Woodbridge! Is Kate safe? Have you need of—"

"The Tories have Armistead." Benjamin did not have to

feign the tension in his voice. "I'm thinking they've got him down by Button Creek. There's a way down by Captain Boothe's cabin, next to the falls—over the bluff, not hard for a man with the will for it. But if I don't come back—"

"Of course. Kate and your sister will never want a protector. But are you certain you can—"

"I've no time to argue it, Judge." And if he stayed longer, he'd yield to temptation and ask Pembrook some hard questions. Questions that would be answered soon enough, if God willed.

He spun from the door and moved across the open ground, softly like an Indian, and made his way through the thick shadows along the path, letting Pembrook think he was bound for the bluff.

His heart thundered with the venturesome thing he had just set in motion. And he prayed it was not already too late.

Forty-One

RANE SAT WITH HIS BACK AGAINST A POWDER KEG, all the fear of his darkest nights staring him in the face. It was not so much the blackness of the cavern, or the glare of the torches outside on the ledge, or even the rope that trapped his wrists behind him. It was the sense of utter defeat.

He had spent four years looking over his shoulder, waiting for the day of reckoning. At last it had come.

But Harrod would not get the letter. Rane had bent his head as far as he could and pulled the packet from his coat with his teeth. It was behind the keg now, in a seam of the rock where his fast-numbing fingers had found a dry crevice. He had finished moments before Harrod's men came back to search him.

The great flat rock had been moved aside, the way open for the arming of the Cherokee or whatever other purpose the three remaining kegs might have. Rane knew all too well the audacity that would make Harrod force Rane to witness the very deed his stolen letter could have thwarted.

A shadow blocked the mouth of the cave. Rane pulled himself to his feet, squared his shoulders, fought down the cough. Harrod would not see him waver.

Harrod stood between Rane and the light, casting his own face in deep shadow. "My men tell me they have found nothing."

The cold wind stung Rane's skin where Harrod's men had torn open cravat and collar and shirt in their search for the letter. But Rane did not feel cold. He knew it was fever, but for a moment it felt like courage. "Did you expect that they would find otherwise?"

"Theft from an officer of the king is no small matter."

"Is it theft to seize evidence from one's captors?"

"I see your insubordination has not changed." Harrod's tone carried the sting of the lash. He had watched as Rane paid the price for defending Captain Symonds's cabin boy.

He gestured sharply toward the ledge outside. Nolan Taggart and another officer dragged a bound man into the mouth of the cave. Torchlight glinted on tangled chestnut hair and a lean, bruised face.

Jem Flannery.

Rane's lungs clenched tighter still. *Oh God, what more do you ask of me?*

"Sergeant Taggart heard you speak to each other in the passage at the inn," Harrod said. "It appears that you and my erstwhile lieutenant are better acquainted than strangers on opposite sides ought to be."

"Sir, I—" Jem began.

Harrod backhanded him swiftly. Jem staggered and would have fallen if Taggart had not held him up.

Rane stepped forward, forgetting his hands were bound, forgetting the breath was leaving him. "Harrod, 'tis no way to treat a fellow man."

Harrod tugged his riding gloves tighter, as if the blow had loosened them. "When men rebel, it is the right of their betters to correct them. And when one man stoops to share another's rebellion, he shares in the punishment as well. You, I believe, have had that experience."

Jem's gaze flicked to the darkness behind Rane, to the kegs beside him, everywhere but Rane's face. He had never been aboard HMS *Solebay*, had not seen the wrath of the Navy. But surely he could guess.

"What do you want, Harrod?" Rane said quietly.

"I want you to know that a significant measure of your respective fates rests on your willingness to reveal what you know of each other."

"And if not?" Rane did not look at Jem.

"Then my signal to the Cherokee will be your demise as well as the settlement's." Harrod nodded toward the powder kegs. "I give you fifteen minutes."

He motioned to Taggart and strode back out along the ledge. Taggart shoved Jem into the cave and followed Harrod.

Far back in the grotto, water trickled in the silence.

Rane had been forgiven. Christ alone was his mediator, his salvation, his refuge. He would cling to that, would let that forgiveness flow through him to the man he had never thought he would see again.

O Lamb of God: that takest away the sins of the world; grant us thy peace.

"Tell Harrod what you wish about my movements here," he said at last. "It makes little difference now."

"'Tis I who should be saying that." Jem huffed a flat, acrid laugh, his back to Rane. "He caught me fleeing to the valley. He'll be killing me either way. He can do no worse if he knows the truth of it. Sure, what's a Cork Harbor wharf rat to him?"

"Harrod hates the Irish."

"Harrod hates everyone. Why should the Irish be otherwise?"

"The rebels in Cork nearly cost him his career." Rane coughed against the hoarseness seizing his throat.

"You'll do well to tell him what I am, then. It's the chance you've wanted." Jem turned toward him suddenly, as if driven to it. "But you ought to know—I never forgot, Armistead. God knows I've tried, but I never did."

Jem's betrayal was the reason Rane had been forced to serve in the Navy. There could be no plainer truth than that. And yet—was it the truth? Or did a greater power than Jem have a purpose even in that?

Rane lowered himself to the floor and leaned against the keg that shielded the letter, feeling the tug of old scars.

There is one mediator between God and men, the man Christ Jesus.

He took as deep a breath as he could manage and said the words. "God knows I've forgiven you, Jem."

"Don't call me that."

"You cannot change yourself so easily as you wish." The strength was leaving him, ebbing like a tide. "But I give you my word I won't betray you to Harrod."

"Don't trouble yourself." That bitter laugh again. There was something of a sob in it. "Forgiveness is a lie men hide behind while they're after their revenge."

"God forgives."

Even the two small words cost him. The cough shook him with a force he could not fight. This time the shaking lingered.

"God may forgive." The heel of Jem's boot ground against damp rock as he turned away. "Harrod does not."

Forty-Two

BUTTON CREEK RAN SWIFT AND COLD. BENJAMIN'S first step was shock, then numbness. His shoulder throbbed with the memory of his swim across the Yadkin, or mayhap only with the cold and the weight of his rifle. He held the gun above the water's reach, moccasins finding careful purchase on the stony bed of the river.

Far ahead, garish torchlight danced on the black water. He waded toward it, slow and silent, his eyes on the long slope of bank that led up to the ledge.

In the woods a bird called. Another answered.

He knew that sound. Selagisqua, signaling his mates. Benjamin plunged forward, quickening his pace.

How had Elizabeth been baptized in water so cold?

He saw again the joy on her face. He knew what baptism was—the demonstration of death and burial and new life with Christ. He could have argued that with Rane Armistead until kingdom come.

But he had only now begun to live it.

Mud squelched under his feet as he climbed onto the sloping bank. A step or two had him on solid rock, sheltered by brush and fallen stones, the broad ledge open before him.

The flat boulder had been moved, opening a narrow gap behind it. Five men ranged along the ledge as if waiting for something. That was a double edge—they would be easily distracted, but easily alerted as well.

He moved forward slowly, picking his way over twigs and rocks, the thin soles of his moccasins warning him of anything that might make a noise and betray him. The river's sibilant hush hid the soft sound of his feet.

One man turned half toward him. A dark cloak brushed the rocks, a flash of torchlight shadowing a narrow face and crooked jaw. Benjamin shoved his kerchief inside his collar and crouched behind a boulder, his fingers tense on the rifle.

Harrod wheeled suddenly the other way. The shadows along the ledge shifted. A massively built man appeared over the bluff, his movements unsure, like a man who made no habit of climbing down ravines.

Simon Pembrook. Benjamin's muscles tightened with the urge to pull the trigger.

He could not shoot Pembrook without sacrificing Rane. For an instant he was back at Cowpens, fearing what revenge he might take if nothing was there to stop him.

Lord, I'm not strong enough for this. Do it through me.

Pembrook spoke to Harrod, and the two men moved down the ledge together. Harrod turned back and called over his shoulder. The others followed him toward the falls.

Benjamin eased to his feet. The bird's call came again. Was Captain Boothe out there now, joining Selagisqua?

He could not linger to find out.

He sidled along the ledge, keeping his weight low. The rock's jagged shadow loomed in front of him. He slid into the gap behind it and pressed himself to the bluff until he could see past the boulder's edge.

Harrod and Pembrook stood near the falls, gesturing along with their words. Benjamin imagined the ambush they must be planning for him and how surprised they would be if they knew he was only a dozen paces behind them.

He listened hard, the way he would on a hunt when there was nothing to see. Water dripped from the big rock.

In the cave, someone coughed. A deep, racking, familiar cough.

Benjamin darted a last glance at Harrod and stepped into the cave.

Sheer blackness greeted him. The hoarse cough echoed against the rocks. A clipped whisper said, "Who's there?"

"Gregory?"

"Woodbridge?"

"Aye. And Armistead?"

"I'm here." Rane's whisper was weak. Another cough followed it.

The blackness dissolved into dim shapes as Benjamin's eyes grew used to the dark. Rane leaned against a trio of kegs, his shirt torn half open, the white linen pale in the dim glow of the torches outside. Benjamin crouched and rested the rifle beside him.

"Down behind this keg," Rane whispered.

"What?"

"The letter. A crack—in the floor—"

Benjamin dived his free hand behind the keg and pulled the packet free. He thrust it into his hunting shirt next to the New Testament, then drew his knife.

"Flannery too," Rane said on a labored breath.

"He means me." Gregory's whisper sounded tight and hard. "Never mind. I deserve what I get."

Benjamin sliced the knot in the rope that lashed Rane's wrists, then turned toward Gregory. Rane coughed again and spat. "When Harrod comes—he's going to—"

More coughing. Benjamin said, "Going to what?"

"He'll ignite this powder." Gregory held out his bound hands for Benjamin to free. A stroke of the knife, and the rope fell to the floor. "The explosion will alert the Cherokee.

And the rest of his men, coming from the fort. They'll take Sunrising while Captain Boothe is fighting outside."

Benjamin jammed the knife into its sheath. "What of the Dove & Olive?"

"It hasn't a chance. Even before he left Sunrising, Harrod spoke of destroying it. He knew what it meant to the settlement. Nearly as much as the meetinghouse."

For once, Benjamin had not wanted to be right. "We've got to warn Captain Boothe before Harrod comes back. The men are looking the other way. We'll sneak behind that big flat rock outside and down the bank to the river. Then I'll get you to the captain, and you'll tell him what you told me."

"There's no way—" Gregory began.

"Then stay." Benjamin helped Rane to his feet and guided him toward the mouth of the cave. Gregory's boots scuffed softly behind him.

Rane's shoulders shook under Benjamin's hand as he battled another cough. But he slid behind the big rock as Benjamin motioned him to do. Gregory followed. Benjamin slid in after them.

Over by the falls, Harrod gave a shout. Gregory cursed softly. Benjamin pressed his back against the bluff and peered down the ledge.

Harrod wasn't looking at them. He was looking up at the top of the opposite bluff. A shadow flitted through the trees, orange light on painted skin.

Selagisqua. Harrod was distracted. Benjamin nudged Rane and Gregory through the gap. The shadows of the bluff crowded in thick, offering a moment's shelter.

Far above, in the deeps of the forest, a shot cracked.

"Fire away, lads! The battle is the Lord's!"

Captain Boothe's battle cry. Benjamin gripped Old Sandy tighter. Robert did not know how many Tories and Indians were only awaiting their signal. A signal that would cave in half the ravine and likely take Robert's cabin with it.

"Head for the brush," he said. "It'll be close, but—"

"I'll slow you." Rane stumbled against the bluff, tremors racking his body. "Take Jem and go."

"I'm taking both of you." Benjamin shrugged out of his hunting shirt, shoving his New Testament and Rane's letter inside his lighter shirt. He flung the heavy linen around Rane and fitted his shoulder under Rane's arm. Gregory— or Flannery or Jem—did the same on the other side.

Muzzle flashes pierced the dark on the far side of the ravine. Powder smoke hazed the torches. Robert might be able to hold Sunrising for now, but what would happen when the Cherokee attacked? When Tories for miles around rallied to Harrod's flag?

A losing fight. Just like Alamance. Good men getting themselves killed, and for what? For men like Malcolm Harrod and Nolan Taggart.

As if in answer to his thoughts, Taggart's wiry figure separated from the bluff ahead of them.

Benjamin let go of Rane and brought the rifle up, his finger on the trigger.

Taggart lunged forward and knocked the barrel away. The shot blasted over the river, ringing through the ravine like the roar of cannon fire. Benjamin clubbed at Taggart with the butt of the rifle. Taggart caught the rifle, grappled for footing on the wet rocks.

Benjamin wrestled the rifle away, or tried to, fighting Taggart's desperate grip. Taggart twisted the rifle over and down, all his weight behind it.

Blinding pain exploded in Benjamin's shoulder. He landed hard, arched his body, kicked straight up. Taggart staggered back and over the brink of the ledge. The splash of his fall seemed to come from a great distance.

Benjamin struggled to sit up, felt hands probing his shoulder. It was out of joint again, he knew that dimly, and knew also that Harrod was shouting from far up the ravine.

"Don't move," Gregory said, gripping Benjamin's arm. A mighty agony wrenched his shoulder. Then the pain died to a dull, hammering ache. Gregory's face came into focus above him. "Harrod's moving his men out. Getting ready." Benjamin pulled himself to his feet, feeling a bit light-headed. His shoulder throbbed. "What of Taggart?"

"I don't know. He fell over the edge."

Benjamin glanced up the ledge. Harrod and Pembrook were moving toward the cave. A torch was in Harrod's hand.

Rane leaned against the bluff, Benjamin's hunting shirt still around his shoulders, sweat sheening his face. Benjamin looked at him and looked back at Harrod. And he knew why good men sometimes let themselves get killed.

"Get this to the captain and tell him what's afoot." He pulled out the letter and handed it to Rane, then unstrapped his knife and tomahawk. "And take these in case you meet trouble. I'll stop Harrod until you can warn the captain."

"Your family," Rane said, and coughed again.

"They'll be the first to suffer if Harrod has his way. Tell them what you'd want somebody to tell yours." The last word caught in his throat. He nodded to Gregory. "Go."

Gregory slid the knife and tomahawk into his belt and helped Rane down the ledge. He did not look back.

Benjamin flexed his right arm carefully. Shafts of pain darted through the joint, quick and sharp as Cherokee arrows. If Harrod knew he had a bad shoulder, he was dead.

God help me.

He took Old Sandy in his left hand. Then he turned and strode up the ledge to stop Harrod.

Forty-Three

SIMON PEMBROOK MET BENJAMIN OUTSIDE the cave. The judge was breathing heavily. Benjamin offered him a canted grin. "Not used to climbing up and down ravines, eh, Judge?"

"Where is Armistead?" Pembrook asked. "I came to help you find him."

The torch Harrod had carried was stuck into a crevice in the face of the bluff, throwing its light across the mouth of the cave. A shadow shifted in the orange glow. "Do you think I don't see Harrod lurking back yonder listening?"

"What? Is he?" Pembrook turned as if to look. "Then you're wise to—"

"Give it up, Judge. I know you've been lying."

"Lying? Woodbridge, you—"

"Even lying to Aunt Kate. You know what they'll do to her ordinary." Saying the words lit a desperation in him. The best fights were for what a man loved, and the people he loved most in the world would be the first to face destruction. "How could you?"

"I made an offer he could not refuse." Harrod stepped into the open. His cloak stirred with the wind, exposing the pistol and sword in his officer's sash. He held a length of stiff and blackened cord. Match cord, ready to be lit.

Benjamin looked from Harrod to Pembrook and back. "And all he had to do was turn on Sunrising, is that it?"

"I never meant to turn on Sunrising," Pembrook said. "My task was merely to treat with the Cherokee on the king's behalf."

"You rat," Benjamin said. "All that talk about how you hated Tories."

"I did." Pembrook glanced at Harrod. "Once."

"Enough," Harrod said sharply. "Go find Sergeant Taggart and tell him to clear the men from the ravine."

Good luck with that, Benjamin thought. "Judge, does Harrod here know you got in Taggart's way once already?"

"He overstepped his bounds," Pembrook said angrily. "Accosting Kate that way—"

"Kate would tell you to get on your knees and get right with God." Benjamin looked Pembrook in the eye, suddenly more sorrowful than angry. The judge wasn't the only one in need of repentance. "She'd be right."

"The rebel cause is hopeless, lad. The far greater reward lies with the king's friends. Any man with any sense of business would do as I've done."

"No man with any sense of decency would do as you've done."

"Pembrook," Harrod said crisply. "The sergeant."

The judge wheeled and made his way along the ledge.

"And you." Harrod turned toward Benjamin. "Get out of my way."

Benjamin moved farther into the mouth of the cave, blocking the way to the powder kegs, gambling that Harrod might think the rifle was loaded. "Or what? You'll kill me as your men killed my father?"

"I have not the least idea who your father was," Harrod said. "But if he was half the rebel you are, the world is well rid of him."

"If you were half the man he was," Benjamin said in a low voice, "the world would be a better place all around."

Harrod jerked the pistol from his sash. Benjamin ducked. The blast thundered off the rocks, a deafening, dizzying wave of sound. Benjamin lunged blindly through the shock, hoping to shove Harrod out of the cave and off the ledge into the river.

Harrod whipped the pistol at his head. Benjamin blocked the blow with the empty rifle. The pistol flipped away and landed with a splash far below. Harrod's sword hissed from its scabbard.

Benjamin blocked again, keeping his right arm as close to his body as he could. The blade keened off the steel of Old Sandy's barrel.

Harrod feinted back and struck. Fire sliced Benjamin's cheekbone. He sucked a breath between his teeth, danced back a step, blocked another thrust that forced him deeper into the cave.

The clash of metal on metal echoed through the cavern. Harrod thrust again. Benjamin parried. But his shoulder would not obey.

He knocked the blade away, saw Harrod's face in the glow of the torch, and knew.

Harrod knew he had an empty gun and a bad shoulder.

Benjamin swung the butt of the rifle at Harrod's head. Harrod caught the rifle by its barrel and drove the butt into Benjamin's right shoulder.

Flesh and bone screamed in agony. Harrod hit him again. Benjamin fell to a knee, saw Harrod's boot come at him, could not dodge the blow.

His head snapped back and he landed hard over the powder kegs. The torchlight and shadows swirled around him like some nightmare of the underworld.

"This is for Ferguson," Harrod said.

The sword flashed. Benjamin rolled away. White-hot pain lanced across his ribs.

He clamped his arm to his side and kicked up at Harrod's right arm. The sword clanged to the rocky floor. Benjamin fell off the powder kegs and landed beside them.

Harrod thrust the rifle downward at the place Benjamin had been. The blow smashed through the staves of the nearest keg, spilling powder over the tangled ropes that had bound Armistead and Gregory.

The acrid stench of saltpeter stung Benjamin's nostrils. He grabbed the stock of the rifle and shoved the gun upward. The motion spun Harrod half around.

Enough for Benjamin to get to his feet.

"This is for Sunrising," he said.

His hard left caught Harrod under the jaw. Old Sandy clattered on the rocks. Harrod staggered and grabbed for Benjamin's right shoulder. His weight took them both into the wall. Benjamin struggled for a left-handed grip. Harrod grappled with him, threw him off, reached for the sword where it lay by the powder kegs.

Benjamin lunged into the opening. He landed hard, Harrod's sword arm pinned beneath him. Something snapped.

Harrod cursed. Benjamin threw his left arm around Harrod's shoulders, forced his way up to one knee, twisted his upper body, and hurled Harrod into the wall.

Harrod crumpled beside the kegs and lay still.

Benjamin grabbed the sword and got to his feet. The cave swayed around him.

But Harrod did not rise. His shallow breathing was his only movement.

Benjamin gripped the ivory of the sword's haft, his own breaths coming hard and ragged. He swiped blood from his cheek with the back of the hand that held the sword and stepped forward softly, warily.

Outside, Captain Boothe's voice echoed up the ravine.

Boots thumped on the rocks. Benjamin looked down at Harrod's unconscious form, then at the slender blade in his hand.

It would be so easy. No one would know.

This is for Pa, he thought. And Walks-in-Winter. And all the other good men.

But the old Benjamin Woodbridge who wanted revenge was dead. And a man who was alive in Christ could not rob justice from the hands of his God.

Lord Jesus. Help me.

He ran the sword through his belt and picked up the rope that had bound Rane. He rolled Harrod onto his face and put a knee in his back and lashed his hands. The voices of Robert's men carried from outside.

Benjamin stood and took up his battered rifle and walked to the mouth of the cave. Then he glanced back and spoke to the man whose lust for vengeance he knew all too well. "This is for Christ."

Forty-Four

"THANK GOD YOU'RE ALL RIGHT." CAPTAIN Boothe clasped Benjamin's good shoulder. "Where's Harrod?"

Benjamin jerked his head toward the cave. The ravine seemed to tilt under him. "Tied up in there. Unconscious."

Alec Perry moved forward as Robert stepped into the cave. "Then you didn't—"

"No. I didn't." Benjamin's voice came out rough. He turned away from the cave. "Anybody else would have been right to kill him. But I wouldn't."

"Then you did the right thing," Alec said quietly.

"The Tories?" His cheek stung like fire when he spoke.

"Think we got 'em licked. And the captain has Armistead's letter. The things Harrod wrote ought to make any Tory in his right mind see what the British have in store for the folks they recruit."

If the Tories would accept it. "Armistead got to you, then."

"Gregory near about had to carry him. We sent him to Kate as soon as the way was clear." Alec studied him, his face half in shadow. "Selagisqua's boys shot Pembrook."

Benjamin huffed something too grim to be a laugh. "With Tory powder and arms."

"They don't stand for treachery."

Benjamin shook his head. "How does a man fall so far?"

"By telling himself a lie and believing it. One day at a time."

Benjamin glanced again at the cave. He had told himself lies enough these last ten years. Only God's truth had saved him. Same as it would have for Pembrook and Harrod, if only they had believed it. *And still revolt when truth would set them free*, Milton had said.

"I saw myself in there," he said, low.

"It's a hard thing to see," Alec said quietly. "But good, sometimes."

The captain's sharp voice rang out inside the cave. Benjamin gazed down the ledge, dimly remembering the brief fight that had dislocated his shoulder. He stepped past Alec. "I've something to see to. I'll be back."

Alec did not stop him. Benjamin walked down the ledge, his right arm pressed to his side. His ribs and shoulder throbbed in unison. The ledge seemed long, far longer than before.

He stopped where the bluff started to curve to meet the river and peered over the edge.

Nolan Taggart lay half in the river, half on a rock. A faint puff of silver clouded the air with each breath.

Benjamin leaned Old Sandy against the bluff, picked his way down over the rocks, and gripped Taggart's shirt with his left hand. Taggart's eyelids twitched as Benjamin dragged him to the sand beneath the ledge. Blood streamed from his hairline, staining the sand.

Benjamin looked around for something to bind the gash with. But there was nothing except Taggart's mud-soaked clothes and Benjamin's own bloody shirt.

Nothing except . . .

He took a deep breath, unknotted Pa's kerchief, and tied it clumsily over the gash on Taggart's temple. The red of the silk looked black in the moonlight.

This is for you too, Lord.

Taggart half opened his eyes, tried to lift his head, let it drop. His eyes fell closed again. Benjamin looked up at the ledge. There was no way he could haul Taggart up there.

He gave Taggart's still figure a last look and made his way back up over the rocks, Harrod's sword clattering against them as he climbed. The rifle seemed unbearably heavy when at last he gained the top and picked it up.

What had Armistead suffered, dragging himself down this endless ledge? What was he suffering still?

Alec met Benjamin near the cave. Robert and Hank Jonas held Harrod between them, his right arm at an odd angle. His gaze met Benjamin's with such venom that Benjamin's hand tightened reflexively on the barrel of the rifle.

This fight wasn't over. There were more Tories just waiting for the signal.

"Everything all right over yonder?" Alec asked, nodding downstream.

"Taggart's down on the bank under the ledge. Banged up some. I couldn't—"

He broke off. The torchlight wavered and faded. The ledge beneath him whirled.

Alec caught him. "Your shirt's soaked clean through, lad."

Benjamin fought to right himself. "I'm all right. But Harrod's got more men—waiting to come into the settlement, and—"

"I'll tell the captain."

"And Taggart—"

Alec jerked his head, beckoning two of the younger scouts. "Edward and Owen will go fetch him. Let's get you to Kate. It's time for somebody else to do the work awhile."

The way to the kitchen seemed long and dizzy. Benjamin was vaguely aware of warmth and firelight and voices, sharp flashes of pain and the sound of the door. The buzz of sound told him nothing.

When at last he came fully to himself, he was lying by the hearth, his ribs bandaged beneath a clean shirt. His rifle and Harrod's sword leaned against a bench by the table. Across the room, someone coughed hard and long.

Benjamin tried to lift his head. "Armistead?"

"He's here," Kate said. "You're here. And you'll both be just fine, God willing. Now lie down and keep still."

He lay down and kept still. Kate probed his shoulder gently. Elizabeth hovered behind her.

He tried to wink. Elizabeth tried to smile.

"What's going on?" he asked.

"The settlement folk forted up in the great room as soon as the Tories left to join Harrod. But Rob's lads have driven back the last of the scoundrels, I'm thinking." Kate patted his shoulder. "We'll put that arm in a sling again, but it'll be all right for now so long as you don't move it."

"I don't much want to move anything."

"I'm not surprised." Kate raised her hand as if to touch his cheek. He winced just thinking of it. "Your poor bonny face, lad."

"'Twasn't so bonny to begin with," he said.

"That's the truth if I ever did hear it," Mitchell Boothe said from the other side of the room.

Benjamin turned his head. Mitchell sat on a bench, his bandaged leg stretched out in front of him. Rane lay on a pallet nearby, eyes closed and face flushed with fever.

"Good to see you," Mitchell said. "But what is this, a kitchen or an infirmary?"

"You hush," Kate said. "Betty, lass, I'll need more of that poultice."

Elizabeth flitted to the table and poured a stream of dried herbs into Kate's mortar. Rane started coughing again, deep and racking.

Kate gathered up an onion plaster from the edge of the

hearth and hurried to Rane's pallet. Elizabeth set the mortar and pestle down beside Benjamin's head and began gingerly dabbing at his cheek with a wet rag.

He yelped. "Easy, Mouse. You're worse than Aunt Kate."

From the pallet, Rane murmured, "'Though she be but little, she is fierce.'"

Shakespeare, if Benjamin had his guess. That was a good sign. He turned his head again, disregarding Elizabeth's huff of frustration. "Armistead. You made it."

"I'm told that I did." Rane did not open his eyes. His voice was papery. "I'm not yet certain of it myself."

"Lieutenant Gregory carried him in," Elizabeth whispered. "Didn't that give us a turn, though."

Where was Gregory now, Benjamin wondered. "We stopped Harrod, Armistead."

"God be thanked," Rane said huskily, and coughed again.

"No more talking," Kate told Rane firmly.

"Yes, ma'am," he whispered.

Susanna Boothe let herself into the kitchen and shrugged out of her cape, setting her basket on the table beside Mitchell. He poked at the covering. "Come to visit your poor uncle, niece of mine?"

"I saw folks limping over here and thought Aunt Kate might need help." Susanna came over to the fire. "Getting on all right, Betty?"

"No." Elizabeth made a face. "But the Lord is helping me all the same."

Susanna leaned over Elizabeth's shoulder and squinted at Benjamin's cheek. "Oh, Benjamin."

He knew she meant *You must be in pain* rather than *I'm so glad to see you*. But it was good for a moment to think that she cared, even if it was only as a woman might care for anyone in need of her aid.

"That might want sewing." She examined the gash with gentle hands, avoiding his eyes so hard he knew she desperately wanted to look at him. He hated that he'd let Harrod and Taggart and his own fool stubbornness get in the way of what might have been.

"If it'll make you feel better, you can stick me with the needle as hard as you want," he said.

That made her look at him. "It won't, thank you very much. What happened?"

"Harrod got in a few licks before I got in mine."

He saw the quick shuttering of her gaze. She didn't want to know the rest of that story. Or maybe she did, and didn't want him to see it.

Elizabeth measured out a length of thread and snipped it, the snick of Kate's shears loud in the silence. He braced himself for the searing pinch and tug of needle and thread.

"I'm glad you're all right," Susanna said quietly.

A spate of rifle fire burst in the distance. Instantly the kitchen went still. Mitchell reached past his bandaged knee for his own rifle.

"That was by the bridge," Benjamin said at last, trying not to move his cheek.

"Is that the Cherokee?" Elizabeth asked.

"No," Mitchell said. "We'd hear the war cries if it were the Cherokee."

Susanna took her final stitch and tied off the thread. Elizabeth handed her the shears, watched her cut the thread, and said, "Shall I put his arm in a sling now, Aunt Kate?"

Kate knelt by Rane's pallet, helping him with a steaming mug. "Finished with the poultice too?"

"Mostly. It's just his face."

"Just my face," Benjamin said. "Thanks, Mouse."

Elizabeth rummaged in Susanna's basket and brought out a strip of linen. Susanna daubed poultice carefully over the line of stitches in Benjamin's cheek. He ignored the sting, thinking of the rifle fire and taking a mental tally of anyone who might still be near the bridge.

Robert and his men would be there, Alec with them. Selagisqua might be there or might still be in the woods on the far side of the ravine. Ayen Boothe would be wherever the captain told him to be. Pembrook was dead.

Someone would have to tell Kate about that. Benjamin did not relish the thought.

The door opened. Benjamin looked past Susanna as she wiped her hands and slid the sling into place.

Alec Perry stepped inside and shut the door. Selagisqua was with him, still dressed for war, the lower half of his face smeared with black paint.

"Welcome to hospital quarters," Mitchell said.

Alec eyed Mitchell's bandaged knee. "You just didn't want to pull your weight with the rest of us."

"Come over here where I can reach you and say that again," Mitchell said.

"It's not worth the trouble." Alec moved farther into Benjamin's line of vision. "We chased off the last of the Tories."

"What of Taggart?" Benjamin asked.

"Gone. The lads found his tracks, but he'd up and left. There's not much of a trail to be had along the creek there, though I surely did look. Reckon he'll not be back. You did the right thing, pulling him out of the river."

Susanna's gaze flitted to Benjamin and away. Was she so surprised by that? Had she thought he'd leave Taggart there to fend for himself?

If she had, she might have been right not long ago. The knowledge of that shamed him.

He shifted to better see Selagisqua. "I'm sorry about your uncle, oginalii."

"He died with honor," Selagisqua said quietly. "More honor than the men who killed him."

Alec glanced at Susanna and Elizabeth before he spoke again. "Harrod is dead, Woodbridge."

Benjamin pushed himself upright. He knew for a fact

he'd seen Harrod walk out of the cave. "Dead?"

"Down by the bridge. He tried to make a break for it. Same as Ferguson tried to do." Alec shook his head. "No way to know which of our shots was the end of him. Maybe it's better that way."

"But I thought—" Susanna said, and stopped.

"That I killed him?" Benjamin said.

"You wanted to," she said. "Didn't you?"

"Aye," he said quietly. "Once."

That shamed him too. Not the desire for justice, but the hatred that had come of taking justice for himself. But there was no condemnation to those who were in Christ Jesus.

He wished Harrod had known that, or believed it. It startled him to think of that, as if such a thought had come from outside himself. Perhaps it had.

Selagisqua moved farther into the kitchen, and Susanna turned away from Benjamin and busied herself with her basket. But not before he saw a spark of something, a kind of hope that kindled an answering hope in himself.

"My friends thank you for the rifles," Selagisqua said.

"You got here in time," Benjamin said. "That's thanks enough."

"The war chiefs will not fight without a leader. You need not fear another attack, at least for a time."

"And the captain has Armistead's letter to spread around to the Tories," Alec added.

"It'll be a job of work to get 'em to believe it."

"Did you capture a man named Macauley?" Kate asked.

"The lads are holding quite a few prisoners," Alec said. "What's he look like?"

"Square and strong, with a ruddy face and fair hair and a beard."

"Might have seen him. What of it?"

"He told me once that if Harrod ever deserted his men as General Gates did his, he'd put up his gun and go home.

And he meant it too."

"Then we'll start there. One riled Tory might be all it takes to start a mutiny."

"Where's Gregory?" Benjamin asked.

"With Hank Jonas." Alec gave a half smile. "I haven't figured out yet if Captain Boothe is protecting him or holding him prisoner." He nodded across the room. "I got the notion he and Armistead knew each other."

"It's a long story," Rane said, his eyes still closed.

"And I won't have him telling it," Kate said sternly.

"Well, either way." Alec looked down at Benjamin. Powder stains smudged his face. "It was a brave thing the lot of you did tonight."

"My uncle would say the same," Selagisqua said quietly.

Benjamin tried to answer and found he could not. Selagisqua nodded and followed Alec outside.

Forty-Five

THE LAST SUNDAY OF MARCH DAWNED CLEAR
and soft, its sunlight welcome after storms that had blanketed
the rooftops of Sunrising with snow as deep as a new straw
tick. When Benjamin backed out of the dogtrot, balancing
one end of Kate's trestle tabletop in a left-handed grip, he felt
he'd been loosed from prison.

Rane must feel the same, out of doors for the first time
in weeks. Benjamin doubted Kate would have let Rane out
in the cool spring air for anything less than the celebration
of the work that would soon begin on the new meetinghouse.

Benjamin risked a glance over his right shoulder, past
the knot that held his sling, and sidestepped down the porch
steps. The corner of the board thumped the railing.

"A bit to the left." At the other end of the long board,
Rane spoke through layers of wool muffler, courtesy of Kate.

Shifting to the left, Benjamin held his end of the board
steady, the muscles of his left arm burning with the weight,
as Rane navigated the other end down the steps. "Does Aunt
Kate know you're helping with this?"

Rane took one hand from the table long enough to slide
the muffler down. "Surely Milton said something regarding

the value of silence."

James Arnold Gregory came out of the dogtrot with an X-shaped trestle over each shoulder. Benjamin said, "Gregory, you're sworn to secrecy."

"I've had enough of bargains," Gregory said shortly.

"Who said anything about a bargain?" Benjamin stole another glimpse over his shoulder, measuring the distance. Lively flames billowed from a pile of brush and rubble that had been cleared to make way for the new and larger meeting-house. Not long hence, the open ground would be abustle with settlement folk gathering to eat and sing and pray over the work that would start tomorrow.

"Kate said there's some good come of all this." Rane sounded only barely out of breath, and he did not cough when he spoke. "She said she'd never have known otherwise what truly plagued me."

"Swamp fever from when you fled the Navy, Mouse told me."

"Aye, and a lung complaint with it. It may never leave me, but Kate's boneset and bloodroot have eased it considerably."

"Someday I'm going to ask how you got taken for a seaman."

Gregory's step faltered.

Rane quieted a moment. "Some things are best forgotten."

Benjamin knew that all too well. The events of the past month were best forgotten too. Alec and Saul still prowled the settlement, watching for Tories or Indians who might not have heard—or believed—Harrod was dead.

Near the bonfire, Gregory set the trestles in place. Benjamin said, "Reckon you didn't figure on this when Captain Boothe offered you shelter."

Gregory shrugged. The fringe of the hunting shirt Kate had sewn for him stirred in the light breeze. "A man must have something to do."

"I was wrong in the way I doubted you." Benjamin

helped Rane lift the tabletop and lay it over the trestles.

"No. You weren't." Gregory did not look at him. "I was running when I left the settlement. Perhaps I meant to find Captain Boothe and warn him. But I doubt my nerve would have held." He turned away. "And you may as well be calling me Flannery. I know it's galled your mind ever since Armistead said it."

"Jem Flannery." Benjamin turned the name over. "That'll take some getting used to."

Jem picked away a splinter where the board had struck the porch railing. "Armistead told me a man can't change himself so easily as he might wish."

"Don't I know it."

Jem wheeled, snapping the splinter between his fingers. He flung the bits of wood into the bonfire. "But you changed. Folks said—I heard Widow McGuiness speak of it—you hated Harrod and Taggart for years."

"Aye. Shames me to say it." He found, to his surprise and relief, that it did shame him to say it.

"And that's what I'm speaking of. It didn't shame you once." Jem shook his head. "I thought I could change myself. A fool I was to think it. You don't know how hard I've tried."

"Hard enough to change your name and manner of speaking."

"And a slew of other things too. It's never enough."

"It never will be enough, Flannery."

"You think I don't know it?" Jem said bitterly.

"The only thing that changed me is the power of Christ. That's the only thing that'll change you."

"I could never do enough for that either."

"How much can a dead man do to come alive again?"

"I've no patience for riddles."

"'Tis no riddle," Rane said. "Christ's life for ours. As Miss Woodbridge's baptism was meant to show, I daresay."

Benjamin glanced at him sharply. Rane gave him a half

smile and a shrug.

"It can't be so simple," Jem said.

"The hardest thing on earth for a man's pride," Rane said quietly. "But simple enough."

Jem picked another splinter from the edge of the table. "When a man does wrong, he has to pay. You're a lawyer, Armistead, you know that. Even I know that."

"We all know it." Benjamin leaned across the table. "And justice was satisfied when the Almighty himself took your place. Same as if you'd been condemned, and another man took what you had coming."

Jem's head jerked up. "Who told you of that?"

The look in his eyes made Benjamin's neck prickle. "Told me of what?"

"The Navy. And Armistead." Jem's every muscle was taut now, as if he wanted to bolt and couldn't.

"I know Rane was in the Navy, aye," Benjamin said slowly. "But what has that to do with you?"

Rane said, "Woodbridge—"

"No," Jem said sharply. "It's time I owned it."

"Owned what?" Benjamin demanded.

"That press gang was after me." Jem's voice was rough. "My grandfather was English and a Navy man, always saying how the Navy would do me good. He was my mother's father, and not much of one at that. His name was James Arnold Gregory."

"You shaped yourself—"

"After the man I hated." Jem nodded. "'Twas a game to me once, mocking his manner of speaking. My da was an Irish sailor. Died at sea. I lived on the wharves, thieving from ships' cargo, until Armistead found me a place in his father's stables. My grandfather never lifted a finger to help my mam. But he always had designs on me, wanted me to follow him as a Navy man. After my mam died, we argued. I went to an alehouse by the harbor, and Armistead came looking for me.

When the press gang came in, I knew they'd been sent for me. And I—" He pressed a fist to his lips. "I told them Rane was the one they were looking for."

Benjamin looked at Rane. Rane watched Jem silently, the sunlight playing over his scar.

"They'd been paid," Jem said. "He looked like the grandson of an Englishman. That was all they cared."

"Yet you came to America yourself."

"My mam was dead. I worked for my passage, but the people I met had no love for the Irish. When I landed in New York, I decided to make myself over." Jem made a sound that was not quite a laugh. "It didn't work then either."

"I didn't know a thing about all that," Benjamin said.

"But it's what you meant. One man taking what another man deserved."

"No," Rane said swiftly. "I'm no picture of Christ. He did it freely. I'd have killed you right then, had I been able."

"I wish you had," Jem said bitterly.

"No, you don't. Nor do I."

"You said you forgave me," Jem said. "I didn't believe you. I thought if I could only start again—"

"That's what Christ did for me, Flannery." Benjamin prayed hard as he knew how that he could get the words right. "Took my sin on himself and put his righteousness on me. The same for you if you'll only own up to what you are and rely on him instead of yourself."

"I've no right . . ." Jem said slowly.

"He said we're saved by grace through faith. And he said he wouldn't cast out anybody who came to him."

Jem started to speak, then stopped and shook his head. A thought struck Benjamin, one he was fairly certain hadn't come from himself. He fumbled the New Testament out of his Sunday coat and held it out. "This might help."

He would miss it, as a treasure newly found. But he still had Aunt Kate's family Bible, and Jem did not.

Jem looked from the book to Benjamin's face and back again. He took the New Testament and turned it over.

"Faith," he said. "That's all?"

"That's all."

Jem nodded and stared past the bonfire. Suddenly he said, "Captain Boothe is coming."

Benjamin straightened. Robert Boothe crossed the creek path, rounded the pile of trimmed logs, and set a brass kettle next to the fire. "Glad to see you lads. I've something to mention to you."

Benjamin turned his head. Jem Flannery was walking away. "We could have used you a minute ago."

"How's that?"

"Trying to explain to Gregory—Flannery—how to make his peace with God. What'll happen to him, Captain?"

"He'll stay here until the backcountry is safe for a man who double-crossed the king's friends. After that he can do as he likes. We won't be going back to the army, though. Too much risk of Indian trouble over the ridge."

Robert lifted the kettle's lid, releasing a curl of fragrant steam. Rabbit and dumplings, Magdalen's traditional offering at church gatherings. "Maggie said to stir this. Forgot to bring a spoon."

Benjamin unsheathed his hunting knife, wiped it on his Sunday breeches, and handed it to Robert, haft first. Robert held the blade in the fire for a moment, then poked it into the kettle and said, "Don't tell Maggie."

"Any news of Greene?"

"He lost a fight at the courthouse in Guilford. The Carolina boys didn't do us proud. But Gunning says another loss like that could win the war. The British took the ground but lost too much to make it worthwhile." Robert handed the knife back to Benjamin. "But I didn't come here to talk about Greene. Or about Gregory or Flannery or whatever he's calling himself. I came to talk about Simon Pembrook."

Benjamin wiped the knife on a block of firewood and sheathed the blade. "What of him?"

"He left a void. A big one. The settlers have taken Pembrook Station back. Wouldn't be surprised if it's renamed. But we've no one at the peace talks now. There's a treaty coming, and if it ends as I think it will, someone will have to tell the Cherokee. Someone who has friends there."

"Captain, if you're asking what I think you're asking—"

"I'm not asking a thing but for you to pray about it." Robert turned to Rane. "And you, Armistead, I know you're not here by choice."

"I wasn't once," Rane said slowly. "Now—I wonder."

"Kate told me you'd been reading law. Pembrook left a library of fair size. Blackstone and Coke and all the rest. You would know better than I. But we've need of a good man who knows the law. It's what will tame this wilderness when the war is over."

"It's been years since I've laid eyes on Blackstone," Rane said, a sort of awe in his voice as if he'd found a friend he had never thought to see again.

"As I told Benjamin. Pray on it." Robert pulled an oil-cloth pouch from inside his coat and handed it to Rane. "Hank brought this back. The Tory Macauley did his part to help our couriers, and backcountry gossip will do the rest. We've got Tories on the run all over the Blue Ridge."

Rane opened the pouch and pulled the letter out. "You've no more need of it, then."

"It's yours to do with as you please."

Wordlessly Rane tossed the letter into the flames. The paper curled and blackened.

Benjamin clapped him on the shoulder. Rane let out a long breath.

Robert nodded and started to turn away. He pivoted back and lowered his voice. "Benjamin. You might like to know that Susanna is carrying foodstuffs over from the ordinary. I reckon she could use a hand."

Benjamin's focus strayed that way before he could stop it. "I don't want to shove in where I'm unwelcome, Captain."

"We've had some long talks these last days, she and I. And I wouldn't say you're unwelcome, son." Robert nudged him. "Go on."

Benjamin walked toward the fork in the path, praying with each step that he would not ruin this as he had so many other things. Susanna was in the dogtrot, her basket in hand. Benjamin climbed the porch steps and said, "May I?"

Wordlessly she handed him the basket. At the top of the steps, she stopped and turned to him. "Benjamin, I don't know yet what I think."

"I didn't think you would."

"But I'm proud of what you did," she said abruptly. "Not killing Harrod, I mean."

"I would have if I'd had to, Susanna."

"I know. And if you'd had to—I'd be proud for that too. But differently. Because you *had* to instead of *wanting* to. Does that make sense?"

"I think so." He hesitated. "Susanna, I'm sorry. For everything."

She straightened the cloth over the basket he held, though it looked secure enough already. "Words are easy, Benjamin."

Not this kind, he thought. Not for me. "I've said a lot of words, haven't I. I wish I could take some of them back."

"I shouldn't have avoided you the way I did. I didn't know what else . . ."

"Some days I wanted to avoid myself too."

She laughed a little, then sobered again. "Do you suppose Taggart knows you helped him?"

"I don't know." He eyed the basket, then his sling. "Not sure I have an arm left to offer you."

She settled the question by tucking her hand gently into the crook of his right elbow, fingertips brushing the sling.

His shoulder suddenly felt good as new.

"Benjamin!"

He turned. Elizabeth sprinted around the corner of the kitchen at full tilt. Kate followed at a slightly slower pace, carrying baskets of her own.

"This was by the kitchen door." Elizabeth held out a folded square of cheerful red silk.

His kerchief. Washed and neatly folded, soft against his fingers when he set the basket down and reached for it.

"Had a haunch of venison next to it," Kate said. "Some footprints going northeast, but they stopped at the creek."

Benjamin unfolded the kerchief and tucked it around his neck and knotted the ends. "Aye," he said quietly to Susanna. "Taggart knows."

Kate raised a brow at the two of them and beckoned to Elizabeth. "Come along, lass. 'Tis near time for the singing."

"I think I'll walk with Benjamin," Eizabeth said smugly.

"Go on with you," Kate said.

Elizabeth gave Benjamin a mischievous smile and followed Kate.

Susanna cleared her throat. "The pie will get cold."

"What kind of pie?" he asked, leading the way down the steps.

"Dried apple." She glanced at him, suddenly shy. "Maybe next week a hickory nut cake. Aunt Kate still has some nuts laid by."

"You said you didn't know yet what to think."

"I don't. But it's becoming clearer all the time."

The sound of singing suddenly swelled from the meeting grounds. Susanna said, "That's the Watts hymn. I asked—"

She stopped, blushing.

"You asked what?"

"Well, I knew it was one of your favorites. You have it in your New Testament and all. So I asked Pa if it could be one of the songs we sang today."

"Susanna—"

"I know, it was forward of me. But it's only right, being as it was the last song we sang in the old meetinghouse."

"Susanna, I was going to thank you."

"Oh."

"You can say 'you're welcome.'"

She squeezed his arm lightly instead. "Come on, we're missing it."

He quickened his pace, careful to not outstride her. There was hope in the air somehow, hope that smelled like spring in the Blue Ridge and Kate's best cooking and the good clean smoke of the brush that had been cleared. Tomorrow the walls would go up.

One more day, and they would have the meetinghouse they were waiting for.

Kate and Elizabeth made room for them in the circle near the bonfire. Kate leaned over and whispered to Rane, who gave her a longsuffering smile and tugged his muffler higher. Mitchell was leading the song, on his feet but still wincing a little when he put weight on his injured knee.

Footsteps shifted the melting snow. Benjamin saw Jem Flannery stop hesitantly beside Rane, the New Testament still in his hand. He had it open to the flyleaf, following the words of the hymn. The haunted look was gone.

Susanna's soft alto found a harmony in the glad triumph of the third verse. Benjamin set her basket on the table and joined his voice to hers.

> We will be slaves no more
> Since Christ has made us free,
> Has nailed our tyrants to his cross
> And bought our liberty.

About This Book and Everything In It

FACT AND FICTION
Characters and places

Benjamin Woodbridge, Rane Armistead, Jem Flannery, Kate McGuiness, Malcolm Harrod, Simon Pembrook, Nolan Taggart, and their friends and family are all fictional characters.

The settlement of Sunrising and the fort called Pembrook Station are fictional, as is Ayen Ford. Hunting River Gap is my own name for the crossing through the Brushy Mountains, but other place names are historical. Because Sunrising is fictional, any British plots or story events centered there are also fictional.

I have no evidence for hickory nut cakes being tokens of affection in the 1700s, but the idea was inspired by a reference in *Wild Summer and Fall Plant Foods* (Foxfire Americana Library), suggesting that such a tradition is at least possible.

The uprising that killed Benjamin's father was known as the Regulator Uprising. This event and the battle of Alamance are detailed in *Preacher on the Run*, the first novel in this series.

Patrick Ferguson, the American Volunteers, and Kings Mountain

In September of 1780, the British army occupied Charlotte, North Carolina, harassed by Colonel Davie's Patriot militia not far away. At the same time, Patriot volunteers pursued Major Patrick Ferguson, who threatened to march over the mountains and "lay the land waste with fire and sword." Shortly before the battle of Kings Mountain, he said, "I am on Kings Mountain, I am king of this mountain, and God Almighty could not drive me from it." Ferguson did attend military academy, served in Germany, and advocated total destruction in the Colonies by burning rebel property in the east and equipping Indian allies in the west. His friendship with Malcolm Harrod is fictional.

A detachment of the American Volunteers, also called the King's American Regiment, was under Ferguson's command. These Loyalists were recruited in New York as the Associated Refugees under Edmund Fanning, once a henchman of Governor William Tryon of Regulator infamy. Jem Flannery is fictional, but Lieutenant Anthony Allaire is not. An officer of the American Volunteers, he boasted in his diary that twenty men such as the Volunteers could defy all of Washington's army.

Allaire's diary notes "the disagreeable necessity of detaining a lady of the town, on suspicion of her being a spy." He also recorded a settlement at Pleasant Garden Ford, "composed of the most violent Rebels I ever saw, particularly the young ladies." What those young ladies did is not clear, but Patriot women found many ways to make trouble for the enemy. Several accounts exist of women riding to warn their husbands or brothers of Tory plans, hence Elizabeth's warning to Benjamin.

The battle of Kings Mountain is historically accurate, including the death of Major William "Billy" Chronicle, the attempts at surrender, Ferguson's death, and Patriot officers' struggle to stop the firing. Some writers allege that Patriots desecrated Ferguson's corpse, but this claim has no historical basis, although most of Ferguson's clothing and personal effects were taken as souvenirs or spoils of war.

King's Mountain (with an apostrophe) and *Kings Mountain* (without an apostrophe) both appear in period documents, but the latter is used by Kings Mountain National Military Park and is what I chose for this book.

The aftermath

After the battle, thirty-six Loyalists were convicted of treason and other crimes. Historians disagree as to their guilt; the trial may have been equal parts backcountry justice and a warning to Cornwallis to stop executing Patriots. Nine of the condemned were hanged. Colonel Isaac Shelby intervened to pardon the rest. Shelby later rode to Hillsborough to report to General Horatio

Gates, who had suffered an inglorious defeat at Camden.

Captain Patrick "Paddy" Carr of Georgia pointed at the oak used as a gallows and said, "Would to God every tree in the wilderness bore such fruit as that!" His brutality and coldblooded murder of prisoners led to his own alleged murder at the hands of Tory descendants and this eulogy from a fellow soldier: "Though a honey of a patriot," he left a name "mixed with few virtues and a thousand crimes."

Carr's fictional mistreatment of Jem Flannery was based on a Patriot officer who threatened to hang a Tory officer for refusing to train Patriots. However, other Patriots were known to intervene on the behalf of prisoners and prevent angry militiamen from taking revenge, hence my portrayal of Benjamin and Robert intervening on Jem's behalf.

Charles Cornwallis, Ireland, and HMS *Solebay*

Brigadier General Charles, Earl Cornwallis, commanded the British campaign in the American South despite his original opposition to the use of force in the Colonies. Cornwallis first sailed from England in early 1776 with a stop at Cork, Ireland. Irish rebellions had threatened British landlords in Cork and surrounding areas several years earlier; this is when a young (and fictional) Malcolm Harrod would have evaded court-martial for using excessive force against the Irish rebels.

Cornwallis's fleet included HMS *Solebay*, Captain Symonds commanding. The surgeon of the ship was named North, and Colonel Ethan Allen, victor at Fort Ticonderoga, was a prisoner aboard this ship. Details of Symonds's arbitrary temper and North's kindness are drawn from Allen's account of his captivity. Anchoring off Cape Fear, North Carolina, British officers intended to meet Loyalist troops, who were instead routed by Patriots on their way to the coast.

The fleet moved down the coast and engaged in battles to the south, but not before Rane Armistead's fictional escape from service. His sea service pistol would have been a 1716 model with brass hardware and twelve-inch steel barrel (overall length 19.5 inches). His "swamp fever" would have been malaria. Boneset, the herb Kate treats him with, contains natural quinine, and bloodroot was an early remedy for many lung conditions.

British militia and Cherokee allies

Cornwallis's strategy involved running the American army to earth and cutting Patriot supply lines to the backcountry in hopes that Indian threats and lack of support would keep the deadly frontier fighters too busy to harass his army. Both friendly and unfriendly Cherokee Indians were present on both sides of the Blue Ridge, and British agents such as Alexander Cameron attempted to ensure their alliance by supplying gifts and encouraging attacks against Patriot settlements.

Nanyehi, a Cherokee Beloved Woman known in English as Nancy Ward, sent a message to warn Watauga River settlements of coming attacks in the Cherokee War of 1776. Her actions gave me the basis for Benjamin's friendship with Selagisqua and Walks-in-Winter and their warnings to the settlement.

Although Harrod's schemes are fictional, British officers often held Tory militia in contempt. During the delay at Cape Fear, the British discussed a plan to send men deep into the backcountry to join forces with Indian allies, but this never came to pass.

Nathanael Greene and Daniel Morgan

What Cornwallis was to the British, Major General Nathanael Greene was to the American southern department. One of his right-hand men was Brigadier General Daniel Morgan, "The Old Wagoner," commander of Greene's light troops.

Greene was a former Quaker and businessman from Rhode Island, while Morgan was a backwoods Indian fighter known for brawling and grit. During his service as a wagoner for the British army in the French and Indian War, Morgan received a sentence of five hundred lashes for striking an officer and afterward claimed he never lost consciousness and heard the drummer miss one count. A favorite of backcountry militia, Morgan was plagued by devastating sciatic pain. He later became an elder in his Presbyterian church. Greene's and Morgan's movements are historically accurate to the best of my knowledge.

Banastre Tarleton and Cowpens

One of Morgan's military nemeses was Colonel Banastre Tarleton, known as "Bloody Ban." His hated British Legion was infamous for savagery both on the field and off. After Tarleton crossed the Pacolet River, it's little wonder that Morgan walked among the men to bolster their spirits, sharing his strategy and his experiences in the French and Indian War. His promise to "crack his whip over ol' Ben Tarleton" is a direct quote, as is his wakeup call the next morning: "Boys, get up, Benny's coming!"

Like Kings Mountain, the battle of Cowpens is as accurate as I could make it, including Colonel John Eager Howard's Continentals, Colonel William Washington's cavalry, and Tarleton's Highlanders (Fraser's 71st Regiment of Foot). Where possible, I've used Morgan's direct quotes: "They give us the British halloo . . ." and "Face about, boys! One good fire and the victory is ours!" Tarleton's reputation for withholding quarter from Patriots provoked a desire to give surrendering redcoats "Tarleton's quarter," but Morgan's orders quickly stopped the cry for revenge.

Cornwallis's pursuit and the race to the Dan River

After the destruction of Tarleton's light troops, Cornwallis doubled down on his pursuit of General Greene and the main American army. This included burning his own baggage train at Ramsour's Mill to speed his pursuit.

Greene managed to cross the Yadkin River ahead of Cornwallis, taking the boats with him and leaving a group of militia as a rearguard near some abandoned civilian wagons. The militia fired on the approaching British once or twice as ordered, then escaped downriver. Cornwallis camped on the Gowrie Heights bluffs across the Yadkin, where his artillery cannonaded Greene's camp without doing much damage. From their camp on the east side of the Yadkin, Greene and Morgan sent scouts to report on British movements prior to Cornwallis's eventual crossing at Shallow Ford.

Once across the Yadkin, Cornwallis continued to pursue Greene. The two armies began a race to the Dan River. Travel conditions were poor, and Colonel Otho Holland Williams replaced Morgan in command of the light troops, which acted as a screen to hide Greene's movements from Cornwallis. The false alarm of campfires in the distance nearly caused the light troops to prepare to sacrifice themselves. Direct quotes from Greene's letters are historical.

The end of the Southern Campaign

A month after the crossing of the Dan River, Greene lost a battle at Guilford Courthouse. This battle is not described in the story, although Robert reports it to Benjamin and Rane. What North Carolina militia was present performed poorly, but the British victory came at great expense to Cornwallis, leading many historians to call the battle a Patriot win rather than a loss. As the British campaign turned toward Virginia and Yorktown, attention on the frontier turned toward new treaties with the Cherokee.

My goal with this book was to portray a variety of personalities and motivations, though we have unfortunately few examples of sterling character on the British side—Cornwallis was one of the most humane of the British officers but regularly failed to influence the men under him, just as Patriot officers sometimes failed to control their militia.

War is a complicated business, and it was even more complicated on the southern front, where formal armies functioned in a limited sphere and much of the fight was a civil war between brothers and neighbors. I've attempted to find the truth in the middle and show as accurately as possible what people truly believed in this era. As British novelist L. P. Hartley put it, "The past is a foreign country: they do things differently there."

POETRY AND POLITICS
Milton, Watts, and Aitken

My characters quote or reference a number of seventeenth- and eighteenth-century influences. The first of these is the poet John Milton, best known today for his epic poems *Paradise Lost* and *Paradise Regained*. He is less famous for his other writings, including *Areopagitica*, his defense against censorship of the press. Milton's quotes in this story are taken primarily from *Areopagitica*, the Christmas poem "On the Morning of Christ's Nativity," and his eighteenth and nineteenth sonnets. Milton was popular in both religious and political contexts in early America, and I enjoyed adding this dimension to Benjamin Woodbridge's life.

Benjamin's favorite hymn, "Shall We Go On to Sin?" by Isaac Watts, is found in Watts's 1709 hymnal. Watts had his own brushes with persecution: His father was imprisoned as a Nonconformist minister in England during Isaac's infancy. The eighteenth-century tune "Aylesbury" may have been used with these lyrics, but congregations at this time typically sang hymn lyrics to familiar melodies, so the tune is not certain.

The New Testament in which Benjamin wrote the hymn would have been one of the first English Bibles printed in America. Robert Aitken of Philadelphia risked a charge of treason to print God's Word, which was held under the Crown's royal patent (and still is in the United Kingdom).

Blackstone, Shakespeare, and the Book of Common Prayer

Rane Armistead has an affinity for Sir William Blackstone, William Shakespeare, and the Book of Common Prayer. Blackstone's *Commentaries on the Laws of England*, along with Sir Edward Coke's *Institutes of the Laws of England*, formed the basis for legal study during the eighteenth century and onward. And though plays were frowned upon in many religious circles, Shakespeare was esteemed as a classic English writer by the mid 1700s.

The edition of the Book of Common Prayer quoted in this story is the 1662 edition as printed in 1762. It was printed in a size that could be easily carried and included the Thirty-Nine Articles, the creed to which all Anglican clergy had to subscribe. The prayers for the king, specifically for his success against his enemies, became a sore point with faithful Anglican Patriots.

DIALECT AND DOCTRINE
Accents and idioms

Dialogue would have sounded different in the eighteenth century. North Carolina's linguistic map was diverse, with heavy Scots-Irish influence leading to what we now consider Appalachian or Southern regional dialect. Some researchers believe colonial American speech patterns were similar to Appalachian speech patterns, though a combination of Irish, Scots-Irish, German, Native American, and regional British accents would have been distinctly heard.

Although I've tried to avoid blatant anachronisms, some idioms may not be completely true to the era, such as traditional Southern expressions used for atmosphere or character. In the same way, today's "British accent" was not formed until the 1800s, so British characters would have spoken with regional English accents (as many British subjects still do).

Ethan Allen, Jem Flannery, and Deism

Religion in the backcountry was nearly as complicated as war. There were those who belonged to the Church of England, those who dissented from the Church of England, and those who held their own conglomerate of beliefs or no beliefs at all.

An example of this last group is Colonel Ethan Allen, whom Rane Armistead mentions to Ayen Boothe. Famous for seizing Fort Ticonderoga "in the name of the great Jehovah and the Continental Congress," Allen later expressed his disdain for core Christian doctrines. His writings suggest he embraced a Deistic idea of an impersonal Supreme Being and the importance of self-merit. This is the most likely position Jem Flannery might have taken if pressed—at least at the start of the story.

Charles Woodmason, Rane Armistead, and Anglicanism
Many of the Anglican views Rane Armistead learned from his uncle are based on Charles Woodmason, an Anglican itinerant to the South Carolina backcountry. Woodmason's journals showcase the animosity between the Church of England and backcountry dissenters, especially those who claimed some form of dissenting religion but did not live in a Christian manner.

Woodmason grudgingly praised Baptists or Presbyterians whom he saw as more moderate (though still misguided), but he made no apology for his beliefs that the backcountry settlers were ill bred and the scum of the earth, nor for his belief that personal dealings with God were blasphemous and that baptism by immersion was both heretical and heathenish.

At the same time, many influential figures in the struggle for liberty were lifelong members of the Church of England, as were famous preachers (such as George Whitefield) who were rejected by the Anglican system but never formally left the Church of England. Rane Armistead represents the tension many of these men must have felt.

Kate McGuiness, Benjamin Woodbridge, and Nonconformity
Dissenters from the Church of England fell into several camps, chief of which were Baptist, Presbyterian, and Moravian. (Methodists also influenced the backcountry, but for most of the eighteenth century, Methodism was not formally separated from the Church of England.) The Moravians were German Christians, largely pacifistic, who had their own settlements in the North Carolina Piedmont and had little direct effect on the war, though their settlement of Bethabara was a frequent stopping point for men on both sides.

Presbyterians, on the other hand, were so vehemently anti-Anglican and anti-king that many British officials lumped all dissenters under the name Presbyterian and even went so far as to consider the Revolution a Presbyterian war. This was partly because Scottish Covenanters had their own national church and were violently opposed to the king's established church, causing a political clash between competing forms of church-state alliance. Kate McGuiness and "her Arthur" represent this Scots-Irish Presbyterian element, though perhaps not very loudly.

Baptists were the greatest dissenters from the Church of England in both doctrinal views and political views. Unlike the Scottish Covenanters, Baptists believed the church had no business interfering with the state, nor the state with the church. Their belief in total freedom of conscience put them at odds with most other ideologies, and their belief that each person was fully and personally answerable to God made them a dangerous threat to Britain's religious and political hierarchy, which taught that the Church must intervene between God and man, just as the elite must intervene between the law and the common people.

Benjamin Woodbridge and Robert and Mitchell Boothe represent this desire for liberty on a religious as well as political front, though open persecution was less evident during the turmoil of war. Malcolm Harrod represents the views of those who believed in the divine right of kings and the inability of common folk to govern themselves. His Indian agent and Nolan Taggart represent those who, like many people then and now, believed most of all in their own ends.

CONCLUSION

This story's characters and their exploits exist only in my imagination, but the setting is very real—an era in our country when we fought not only for political freedom but also for freedom to believe and act according to our convictions. I hope you've enjoyed learning a bit about this less familiar aspect of the American Revolution and how it might have affected ordinary people like us.

Selected and Annotated Bibliography

FOR THOSE WHO WANT TO KNOW

Allaire, Anthony. *Diary of Lieut. Anthony Allaire, of Ferguson's Corps: A Memorandum of Occurrences During the Campaign of 1780.* This journal of a Loyalist officer is an excellent (and interesting) primary source, detailing militia life and Patrick Ferguson's campaign.

Allen, Ethan. *A Narrative of Colonel Ethan Allen's Captivity.* This short book (with a subtitle too long to include here) was first published in 1779. After casually picking it up, I was thrilled to discover that it described the fleet where Rane would have served.

Buchanan, John. *The Road to Guilford Courthouse: The American Revolution in the Carolinas.* This engaging, comprehensive military history was my main resource for the Southern Campaign overall.

Draper, Lyman C. *King's Mountain and Its Heroes.* Originally printed in 1881, this book tends to overglorify Patriot exploits but details the sociopolitical climate along with short biographies of major players. It includes Allaire's diary as an appendix.

Foxfire Americana Library. *Folk Remedies* and *Wild Summer and Fall Plant Foods.* The Foxfire series preserves traditional Appalachian knowledge and gave valuable data for Kate's foraging and remedies.

Greene, Nathanael (ed. Showman, Richard K.). *The Papers of General Nathanael Greene, vol. 7.* This is another good primary source for Greene's campaign, with helpful notes and transcriptions.

O'Donnell, James H., III. *Southern Indians in the American Revolution.* This small volume acknowledges the faults of both sides, while avoiding wholesale blaming of either settlers or natives.

Woodmason, Charles. *The Carolina Backcountry on the Eve of the Revolution.* This journal of an Anglican itinerant plainly shows the animosity between backcountry dissenters and Anglican clergy and provided a basis for Rane's qualms and his uncle's beliefs.

Acknowledgments

Words cannot express all I have in Christ, the true hero of this story. I thank him for being my victory, my mediator, my strength. "Without me ye can do nothing" (John 15:5).

It is true that this book would never have been written without him. But it is equally true that it would not have been written without the people who show his love to me in so many ways. I am privileged to thank a few of them here.

Special thanks to

- Mom, for always listening and cheering me on.

- Dad, for never doubting I could do it (and always wanting my villains to get their dues).

- Katelyn, Bethany, and Maralee, for helping me brainstorm and being my first line of critique.

- Pastor Keith Hoover, for all the doctrinal and historical discussions, the trip to Kings Mountain, and the phone call in chapter 2 when I was doubting myself.

- Dr. Ben Townsend, for encouraging my faith and love of language.

- Megan Emery and Isabel Hoover, for sharing my excitement and asking how the book was going.

- Dr. Rob Siedenburg, whose editorial eye for detail is matched only by his encouraging spirit.

- And always, Emma Anderson.

A big thank-you to my beta readers, my launch team members, and all my other cheerleaders:

- Mattea Bricker, Nina Ruth Bruno, Pastor Mike Hoover, Barbara Keigher, and Tona May, who waited oh-so-patiently for book two and never failed to tell me how much they were looking forward to it.

- Eva Cedarland, Katelyn Douglas, Andrea Fell, Elizabeth Gaiser, Bailey Logic, and M. L. Milligan, who reminded me what I love about this book—and about my readers.

- Leona Griesbach, Gwendolyn Harmon, Patricia Haupt, Virginia Henderson, Kati Mills, Rick Schneider, and KyLee Woodley, who made room in their already-busy schedules to invest in this book's success.

- Laura Frantz, Shannon McNear, Lynne Basham Tagawa, D. J. Speckhals, and Patricia Iacuzzi, fellow authors and history enthusiasts whose support means the world.

- Alena Mentink, Faith Blum, Angela Gold, and Marline Williams, authors who survived "Firehose Academy" alongside me and cheered this book's launch every step of the way.

- Thomas Umstattd Jr., James L. Rubart, Sandy Cooper, and Mary Kathryn Tiller, who gave me confidence to go forward in the book business in ways that really matter.

To all these and many more—I'm so honored that you invested such time and attention in this book's success, whether you realized it or not. I hope and pray this story has blessed you as much as you have all blessed me.

Discussion Questions for
Patriot at the River

1. Did you know about the Southern Campaign of the American Revolution before reading this book? What stood out to you about this part of the war?

2. Benjamin Woodbridge and his sister, Elizabeth, both experienced the same losses before the start of the story. How did they handle those losses differently from each other? How did those losses affect their relationship with each other and with people around them (Kate, Alec, the Boothe family, etc.)?

3. Rane Armistead comes from a religious background that has caused some confusion in his life. What are some ways you've had to examine or rethink beliefs you grew up with?

4. Jem Flannery attempts to "make himself over," first as a Loyalist officer, then as a Patriot agent. Later, Benjamin determines to "put himself to rights" by reading more Scripture. To what extent do you think people are capable of changing themselves?

5. Kate says loving our enemies "doesn't mean letting them go on and do as they please. It's doing what's best for them, even if that means keeping them from sinning more than they have already." Do you agree? Why or why not?

6. Benjamin considers Walks-in-Winter and Selagisqua his friends, even though many people might not have trusted them. What are some ways they might have shown friendship to one another despite their different cultures?

7. Rane's past makes him cautious of trusting others. Why do you think he decided to trust Benjamin? Was it easier for him to trust some people in Sunrising than others?

8. After her step of courage in baptism, Elizabeth seems more prepared to face her fears and attempt other brave things. Have you experienced a time when taking one step of faith enabled you to overcome later challenges?

9. Families in Sunrising manage businesses and chores while their men are away at war. How do you think these challenges—and the challenge of living under occupation—would affect daily life?

10. Kate says that "if the king is breaking the law of the land and the law of God, and if good men stand up to him about it, we're dutybound to switch our loyalty over to them." Do you agree? How do you think this belief made the American Revolution different from other rebellions (such as the French Revolution or Bolshevik Rebellion)?

11. What do you think are the main themes of the story? How well are those themes explored or displayed?

12. Who is your favorite character in *Patriot at the River*? Why?

Free short story!

Join Jayna Baas's email list for a free short story, author updates, book recommendations, and more. You'll also be first to know when the next book is released! Sign up at **booksbyjayna.com** or scan the QR code below.

https://booksbyjayna.com/newsletter

Did you enjoy this book?

Share the joy by posting your honest review on Amazon, Goodreads, or BookBub. Reviews help other readers find new books and can also help authors hone their craft. A sentence or two is all it takes, and your time and thoughtfulness are highly appreciated.

BOOKSBYJAYNA.COM

JAYNA BAAS (pronounced as in "baa, baa, black sheep") is the author of *Preacher on the Run* and director of The Christian PEN: Proofreaders and Editors Network.  She writes and edits from beautiful northern Michigan, where she strives to give readers faith-filled adventures bursting with relatable characters and biblical truth.

When she's not writing her own books or editing other people's books, Jayna seeks out new adventures on the screen, on the page, and in the kitchen. She also loves to spend time with her great family of real people and the family of pretend people who live in her head. (Yes, she does know her characters are not real. No, she does not want you to tell them she said so.)

Although her love of words extends to multiple genres, Jayna's favorite story is this: "For God so loved the world, that he gave his only begotten Son, that whosoever believeth in him should not perish, but have everlasting life" (John 3:16).

Learn more and sign up for Jayna's updates, plus book recommendations and a free story, at booksbyjayna.com.

Books by Jayna Baas

booksbyjayna.com

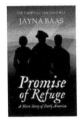

Promise of Refuge: A Short Story of Early America
(For Liberty & Conscience #0.5)

Young circuit rider Robert Boothe and his incorrigible younger brother, Mitchell, cross North Carolina to find their father's old friend. But one courageous young woman doesn't want the old preacher found.

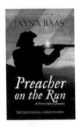

Preacher on the Run: A Novel of Early America
(For Liberty & Conscience #1)

All Robert Boothe wants is a safe place for his family and church to worship God. When the governor's new agent comes to town, Robert refuses to back down. How far will he go to protect his family and flock?

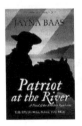

Patriot at the River: A Novel of the American Revolution
(For Liberty & Conscience #2)

With the help of some unlikely allies, Patriot scout Benjamin Woodbridge must fight for what he loves before his settlement goes up in flames—but only if he can fight himself first.

Made in the USA
Columbia, SC
03 October 2024